Dear Reader,

It was several years ago when I became fascinated by the Knights Templar. They were both warriors and mystics, and the legends that grew around them are still alive today. I wanted to write a book that tapped those legends and developed a few of my own. It was to be a simple historical romance but it didn't turn out that way. I dove into the time period and became captivated by the color and pageantry of the era. I suddenly had not only a hero and heroine but an entire cast of secondary characters that meant just as much to me as they did.

I had great fun with *Lion's Bride* as I developed the passion and mystery and friendships that made the fabric of Ware's life. The book seemed to write itself and I didn't want to let it go. I *loved* those characters. Many of you must have agreed with me because to this day every week I still receive letters asking me to write another historical novel that tells the story of Kadar and Selene, who I introduced in *Lion's Bride*.

Next month my first new historical in over ten years will be in bookstores. *The Treasure* continues the story of Kadar and Selene and revisits some of the other characters from *Lion's Bride*. It was wonderful returning to that world.

I had to write that book. What can I say? I had to know what happened to Kadar and Selene too!

en

hansen

PRAISE FOR IRIS JOHANSEN

"Iris Johansen knows how to win instant fans."
—Associated Press

"Iris Johansen is a powerful writer."
—*Atlanta Journal-Constitution*

"[Iris Johansen is] one of the romance genre's finest treasures." —*Romantic Times*

"A master among master storytellers." —*Affaire de Coeur*

"Johansen serves up a diverting romance and plot twists worthy of a mystery novel." —*Publishers Weekly*

"[Iris] Johansen has . . . a magical quality."
—*Library Journal*

"[Johansen is] a consummate artist who wields her pen with extraordinary power and grace." —*Rave Reviews*

"Iris Johansen is a bestselling author for the best reason—she's a wonderful storyteller." —Catherine Coulter

"Iris Johansen is incomparable." —Tami Hoag

BOOKS BY IRIS JOHANSEN

And the Desert Blooms
The Treasure
Touch the Horizon
Golden Valkyrie
Capture the Rainbow
A Summer Smile
Stormy Vows/Tempest at Sea
Stalemate
An Unexpected Song
Killer Dreams
On the Run
Countdown
Blind Alley
Firestorm
Fatal Tide
Dead Aim
No One to Trust
Body of Lies
Final Target
The Search
The Killing Game
The Face of Deception
And Then You Die
Long After Midnight
The Ugly Duckling
Lion's Bride
Dark Rider
Midnight Warrior
The Beloved Scoundrel
The Magnificent Rogue
The Tiger Prince
Last Bridge Home
The Golden Barbarian
Reap the Wind
Storm Winds
The Wind Dancer

Lion's Bride

IRIS JOHANSEN

BANTAM BOOKS

LION'S BRIDE
A Bantam Book

PUBLISHING HISTORY
Bantam mass market published February 1996
Bantam reissue / September 2008

Published by
Bantam Dell
A Division of Random House, Inc.
New York, New York

Cover design by Yook Louie

ISBN: 978-0-553-56990-2

Printed in the United States of America
Published simultaneously in Canada

www.bantamdell.com

OPM 33 32 31 30 29 28 27 26

To L.H.—
thanks for the memories.

Lion's Bride

Prologue

DECEMBER 3, 1188
GATES OF CONSTANTINOPLE

"I HAVE IT!"

Thea whirled to see Selene running through the city gates toward her. The child's red hair had come loose from her braid and was flowing wildly down her back, and her narrow chest was lifting and falling as she tried to catch her breath. She must have run all the way from the House of Nicholas.

Selene thrust the large straw basket at Thea. "I told you they wouldn't see me do it." She glanced at the long line of camels and wagons that had already begun moving down the road. "I couldn't get away earlier. I think Maya was watching me."

"You shouldn't have taken the risk." Thea set the basket on the ground and knelt to hug Selene. "I would have found a way to do without it."

"But it will be easier now." Selene's thin arms tightened

around Thea's neck. "You're taking so many risks. I had to do something."

Thea's throat was tight with emotion. "You must get back. Go through the garden. Selim doesn't tour back there every hour."

Selene nodded and stepped back. Her green eyes were glittering, but Thea knew she wouldn't cry. Selene never cried as other children did. But, then, Selene had never been permitted to be a child.

"Don't worry about me," she said. "You know I'll be safe."

"I know." If she hadn't thought Selene would be safe, she would never have embarked on this wild venture. Though Selene had value, she was only ten; it would be years before she faced the same danger as Thea. "But you must take care of yourself. You must eat well and walk and jump and run in the garden as I taught you."

Selene nodded. "I have to go." She started to turn away and then whirled around. She said gruffly, "I want you to know—it's all right if you can't come back for me. I don't need you. I know you'll try, but if you can't—I'll understand."

"Well, I won't understand." Thea tried to steady her shaking voice. "We'll be together, I promise. As soon as it's safe, I'll come for you. Nothing will stop me." She smiled tremulously. "Just as nothing stopped you when you brought me the basket."

Selene stared at her a moment longer and then ran toward the city gates.

Thea had a wild impulse to go after her, to gather her up and take her safely away. Selene might believe she could care for herself, but so many things could happen to children. What if she became ill?

But her chances of becoming ill were far greater on the caravan. Thea's food supplies were scant, and the journey to Damascus dangerous. Caravans were often attacked by Saracen bandits or renegade knights who had come to the Holy Land only to plunder. Once she reached Damascus, the situation might be even more hazardous. After years of sporadic battles Jerusalem was once more at risk, and the great Turkish sultan Saladin had sworn to reclaim all that had been lost to his people in the previous Crusades. That Damascus was war ravaged would make it easier for Thea to lose herself in it, but Selene was safer here until she could provide a safe haven.

Selene turned at the gate and waved at her.

Thea lifted her hand in farewell. "I'll be back," she whispered. "I promise you. I'll come back for you, Selene."

Selene had disappeared through the gates, and only God knew how long it would be before Thea would see her again.

She must not rely on God. God seldom helped those who sat and waited for His aid. She would work hard. She would never surrender. She would be clever and find a way for herself and Selene.

She bent down, lifted the basket, and slung the attached straps over her shoulders. She hesitated as she looked at the caravan slowly moving away from everything familiar to her. The caravan itself was like a strange serpent, hissing and creaking. Only the soft jingle of the camel bells seemed without threat.

And then there was this terrible dust. She was accustomed to surroundings of absolute cleanliness, and the stinging waves of dust striking her face were terribly distasteful.

Well, there was no turning back. She would become accustomed to all of it, she told herself. She would learn and adapt to every trial.

She adjusted the basket straps on her back and started down the road in the hot, dusty wake of the caravan.

APRIL 21, 1189
SYRIAN DESERT

THE MOONLIT SILVER SANDS shimmered hazily before her eyes.

The mountains on the horizon seemed an eternity away.

Thea staggered, fell to her knees, then struggled again to her feet.

She must keep going....

She must not waste the night. The darkness was less cruel than the burning light of day. Barely.

She tried to swallow.

Panic seared through her. Dear God, her throat was too dry; she would strangle.

She drew a deep breath, trying to calm the wild pounding of her heart. Fear was as much her enemy as this burning desert. She would not be frightened into taking the last few swallows from her water bag.

Tomorrow she might reach an oasis.

Or even Damascus.

She had been traveling so long, surely Damascus was a possibility.

She would not give up. She had not escaped those savages just to succumb to the desert.

She stopped and concentrated. See, she could still swallow. She had not reached the point of total desperation. She started jerkily forward again.

Think of coolness, smoothness, glowing threads of gold on fine brocade. Think of beauty. . . . The world was not this desert.

Yet it seemed to be the world. She could not remember anything but glaring sand by day and shifting sinister shadows by night.

But tonight the shadows seemed more alive, less evanescent and more purposeful. Coming toward her.

Pounding toward her.

Not shadows. Horsemen. Dozens of horsemen. Armor gleaming in the moonlight.

The savages again.

Hide.

Where? No shrubs in this barren place.

Run.

No strength.

There was always strength. Call on it.

She was running. The water skin and the basket on her back weighed her down, slowing her.

She could not drop either one. The water skin was life. The basket was freedom.

The pounding of hooves was closer. A shout . . .

A sharp stitch in her side. Ignore it. Keep running.

Her breath was coming in painful gasps.

The horses were streaming around her, in front of her, surrounding her. . . .

"Stop!"

Arabic. Saracens. Savages like those others.

She darted blindly forward, seeking a way through the ring of horses.

She ran into a wall of iron.

No, not a wall. A broad chest garbed in iron mail. Huge gauntlet-clad hands grabbed her shoulders.

She struggled wildly, her fists pounding at the mail.

Stupid. Hit flesh, not armor. She struck his cheek with all her strength.

He flinched and muttered a curse, his hands tightening with bruising force on her shoulders.

She cried out as pain shot through her.

"Be still." His light eyes blazed down at her from beneath the steel visor. "I won't hurt you, if you don't fight me."

Lies.

She had seen the blood and rapine and the killing. . . .

She struck his cheek again. And again.

Her shoulders went numb as his grip tightened again.

Her body arched with agony. She slowly lifted her fist to strike him again.

"Christ!" He released her shoulders, and his hand swept out and connected with her chin.

Darkness.

"Very good, Ware. You vanquished a helpless woman with one blow." Kadar nudged his horse forward to look down at the figure on the ground. "Perhaps soon you will progress to brutalizing children."

"Be quiet and give me your water skin," Ware growled. "I had no choice. It was either break her shoulders or this. She wouldn't do as I told her."

"A sin, to be sure." Kadar got down from his horse and handed Ware his water skin. "You didn't consider patience and turning the other cheek?"

"I did not." He pushed back the cloth covering the woman's head. "I leave courtesy and gallantry to you. I believe in expedience."

"She appears very young, no more than ten and five. And with fair hair . . ." Kadar paused musingly. "Frank?"

"Possibly. Or Greek." He lifted the woman's head and poured a few drops of water into her mouth, waited until she swallowed before giving her a few drops more. "Whatever she is, she's thirsty."

"You think she may have escaped the caravan from Constantinople that Hassan ibn Narif attacked last week?"

"It seems reasonable. One doesn't find women wandering the desert alone." He called over his shoulder, "Bring the torch closer, Abdul."

Abdul rode forward and Kadar gazed down at the woman with interest. "She's comely."

"How can you tell? She's burned and dry as an overripe date." Ware wrinkled his nose. "And she smells."

"I can tell beauty when I see it."

Ware supposed the woman's features were pleasing enough; wide-set eyes, a small nose, well-shaped mouth. Though the line of her jaw and chin were a bit too firm.

"Once she's clean, she'll be very comely," Kadar said. "I have an instinct about these things."

"You have an instinct about everything," Ware said dryly. "It serves to take the place of thinking."

"Cruel." As he continued to look down at the woman, he added absently, "But I forgive you because I know of your fondness for me."

Ware forced another few drops of water between the woman's lips. "Then you know more than I do."

Kadar beamed. "Oh, yes, infinitely more. How kind of you to admit it."

Ware frowned. "I didn't hit her that hard. She should be awake."

"You underestimate your strength. You have a fist like a mace."

"I never underestimate myself. It was only a tap." Yet she was lying too still. He bent forward and saw the faint movement of her chest. "She must be in a faint."

"Concern?"

"An observation," Ware said flatly. "I feel neither guilt nor pity toward this woman. Why should I? I didn't attack the caravan and leave her in the desert to die. She means nothing to me one way or the other." Though, as Kadar knew, he did admire strength and determination, and the woman had displayed an abundance of both. "I merely wish to determine whether to bury her or take her to the nearest village to heal."

"Burying her would be a little premature, don't you think?" Kadar bent forward. "She's clearly suffering from heat and thirst, but I see no wounds. Though I doubt if Hassan let her escape unscathed. He likes pale women."

"She's not pale now." It was a wonder she had survived ten days in the desert after Hassan had finished with her. He felt a surge of rage that surprised him. He had thought he had grown so hard that he had lost the ability to feel pity or rage for the innocent.

"Well, since you're not going to bury her, shall we take her with us to Dundragon? The nearest village is over forty miles north, and she needs care."

Ware frowned with impatience. "You know we take no one to Dundragon."

"I fear we must make an exception. Unless you intend to leave her here to die." Kadar shook his head. "And that would not be appropriate. It would defy a law of nature. After all, you've saved her life. Now she belongs to you."

Ware grunted scornfully.

Kadar shook his head and sighed. "I've tried to explain this to you before. You don't understand. It's a law of—"

"Nature," Ware finished. "I think it's more Kadar's law."

"Well, it's true I'm often far wiser than nature, and also more interesting, but I can't claim to be as all-powerful." He added, "Yet. But I'm only ten and nine. There's still time."

"We don't take her to Dundragon," Ware said flatly.

"Then I suppose I'll have to stay here and protect her." He sat down beside the woman and crossed his legs. "Go on. I ask only that you leave a skin of water and a few grains of food."

Ware glared at him.

"Of course, Hassan may come upon us. I'll be outnumbered, and you know I have no skill with weapons. There's also the possibility that Guy de Lusanne may pass this way on his glorious journey to Jerusalem. It's rumored his troops are no more godly than Hassan's." Kadar smiled guilelessly. "But you must not worry about me. Forget that I saved your life in that den of assassins."

"I will." Ware stood up and mounted his horse. "I didn't ask for your help then nor your company now." He wheeled, lifted his hand, and motioned the riders forward.

Someone was holding her, gently rocking back and forth.

Mother?

Yes, it must be her mother. She was back in the House of Nicholas, and soon she would open her eyes and see that sad, gentle face. Her mother was always gentle, and her meekness filled Thea with wild frustration.

Not for me. I'll not let them break me. Not you, either. Let me help you and together we can leave this place. You're afraid? Then let me be strong enough for both of us.

But Thea hadn't been strong enough, and her mother would be even more unhappy when she learned how Thea had failed her.

A sharp pang of regret surged through her.

I tried to keep my promise to save Selene. I won't give up. Soon I'll be stronger and try again. Forgive me, Mother. You'll see that Selene—

But her mother would see nothing ever again, she remembered suddenly. She had died long ago. . . .

But if this was not her mother, who was holding her with such tenderness?

She slowly opened her lids.

"Ah, you're awake. Good."

She was being held by a handsome young man with great dark eyes, a sweet smile—A turban!

Savage.

She started to struggle.

"No. No." He held her immobile with surprising

strength for one so slim. "I mean you no harm. I'm Kadar ben Arnaud."

Her eyes blazed up at him. "Saracen."

"Armenian, but my father was a Frank. In truth, my mother's people have proved more civilized than my father's." He gazed soberly down at her. "And I'm not of the band who attacked you. You were with the caravan from Constantinople?"

"Let me go."

He released her at once.

She rolled away from him and scrambled to her knees.

"You see, I don't hold you captive. I wish only the best for you."

She could not trust him.

Yet there was nothing but gentleness in his expression.

But there had been that other man who was neither gentle nor merciful.

She glanced around but saw no one else in sight, only a single horse a dozen yards away.

"They've gone away." He set the water skin before her. "More water? I don't think Ware gave you enough."

She looked at the container as if it were a scorpion about to sting her.

"It's not poisoned." He smiled. "You drank for Ware, now drink for me."

His smile was the most irresistible she had ever seen, and his tone was like dark velvet. She felt a little of her fear subside. "I don't know this . . . Ware."

"Lord Ware of Dundragon. You struck him several times. I'd think some memory would linger."

Cold blue eyes, gleaming mail and helmet, bruising pain in her shoulders. "He hurt me."

"He meant no harm."

Hard, ruthless face, eyes without mercy. "He meant to hurt me."

"He has a great anger in him and he's not a gentle man. I admit he often takes the most direct path to reach his destination. Unfortunately, it's sometimes also the roughest. What is your name?"

She hesitated.

He smiled and pushed the water skin toward her. "Drink."

She picked up the water skin and drank deep. The water was warm but flowed like mead down her parched throat.

"Not too much," Kadar warned. "It may have to last us awhile. Ware and I had a small disagreement regarding your disposition, and he can be very stubborn."

She lowered the water skin. "I... thank you." She searched her memory for his name. "Kadar."

"It was my pleasure..." He looked at her inquiringly.

"Thea. I am Thea of Dimas." Panic rushed through her as she suddenly realized her basket was no longer on her back. "You took my basket," she accused fiercely. "Where is it?"

"On the ground in back of you. I don't steal from women, Thea of Dimas."

The relief flowing through her was immediately followed by shame when she met his reproachful gaze. How foolish to feel shame for doubting a stranger.

He tossed another leather pouch to her. "Dates and a little mutton. How long have you been without food?"

"I ran out yesterday." But she had limited herself to only a few bites a day since she had escaped the attack. She opened the pouch and tried not to snatch at a piece of meat. It was dried and tough, but she chewed blissfully. "You don't wear armor. The others wore armor."

"Because I'm not a soldier. I regard those who battle with lance and sword as barbaric. I prefer my wits."

"You call this Lord Ware barbaric?"

"On occasion. But he has known nothing but battle since he was a child, so he must be forgiven."

She had no intention of forgiving him when her jaw still ached from his blow. Those light-blue eyes and aura of power were imprinted on her memory as vividly as the bruise he'd inflicted.

"He's a Frankish knight?"

He shook his head. "Ware is a Scot."

"Scot?" She had never heard that term. "From where?"

"Scotland is a country far more barbarous than this one. It's north of England."

She knew of England. In Constantinople it, too, was considered a barbarous country.

"And was he going to battle when you came upon me?"

"No, we'd just come from helping Conrad of Monferrai fight off Saladin's siege of Tyre. We were on our way back to Dundragon."

She took another piece of meat. "Then the war is over?"

He chuckled. "The battle is over. I doubt if this war will ever be over."

"Then why do you go home?"

"Ware's contract with Conrad ended with the siege, and Conrad didn't wish to part with any more funds."

"Lord Ware battles for gold?"

"And property." He smiled. "He's the strongest knight in the land, and it's made him a very wealthy man."

Which was not uncommon, Thea thought. Everyone

knew that many knights who had supposedly come on the great Crusades to fight a holy war had stayed to plunder and win vast properties for themselves.

"As for myself, I'll choose a far less dangerous way to riches." He changed the subject. "Thea. You're Greek?"

She nodded.

"And you were traveling with the caravan to Damascus?"

She nodded again.

"You're very fortunate. We had heard no one escaped from Hassan's attack. He brought over a hundred captives to the slave market at Acre and bragged he'd killed another hundred."

Her eyes widened. "You know him?"

"One does not know a reptile. Ware and I are acquainted with him. There's a difference." He dampened a cloth and handed it to her. "Bathe your poor face. Your skin must be very sore."

She took the cloth and then stopped. "You said I shouldn't waste water."

"I've changed my mind and decided to trust in my instincts. Take it."

The wet cloth was heavenly moist on her burned cheeks and forehead. "You're very kind."

"Yes." He gave her another sweet smile. "Very. It sometimes makes my life difficult." He paused. "Were your parents among the slaves Hassan brought to Damascus?"

"No."

"Your husband?"

"No, I was alone."

His brows raised. "Odd. You're very young."

She had blurted the truth without thinking. "I'm ten

and seven. Many women have wed and borne children by my age." But women did not travel without escort. It would be safer for her if everyone believed she had been orphaned during the attack. "I mean . . . my father was killed by that man . . . Hassan."

"Oh, is that what you mean." He smiled. "How?"

He did not believe her. His tone was faintly chiding.

"I don't want to talk about it."

"How cruel of me. Of course you don't."

She quickly changed the subject. "And what of you? You said your father was a Frank. Have you lived here long?"

"All my life. I grew up on the streets of Damascus. Have a little more water. Slowly."

She sipped from the water skin. "Yet you serve this Scot."

"I serve myself. We travel together." He smiled. "He belongs to me. It's rather like owning a tiger, but it has interesting moments."

She frowned in bewilderment. "Belongs to—"

"Shh." He suddenly tilted his head, listening. "Ah, do you hear? He's coming."

She stiffened. She didn't hear the hoofbeats, but she could feel them vibrating on the ground. "Who's coming?"

"Ware." He chuckled. "I warn you, he'll be very annoyed. He doesn't like being thwarted." His smile faded as he saw her expression. "You're frightened."

"I'm not frightened." She was lying. She could still see that looming giant before her. Cold. Fierce. Brutal.

"He won't hurt you," Kadar said gently. "He's only half

beast. The other half is very human. Why else would he be coming back for us?"

"I have no idea." Shivering, she rose shakily to her feet. She did not want to confront this Ware, whom Kadar claimed was half human. She had seen too many beasts of late. "And I don't want to stay here." She slung the straps of her basket over her shoulders. "Will you give me water for my journey?"

"It's forty miles to the nearest village. You're exhausted and weak. You would not survive."

The horses were coming nearer. The man on the first horse loomed large and menacing. "Give me the water skin and I'll survive."

"I cannot do that."

"Then I'll survive without it." She had eaten and drunk deeply and still had a few swallows of water in her water skin. She had traveled far more than forty miles since the caravan had been attacked, and she could go another forty. She whirled and started to walk away.

"No," he said with great gentleness. He was suddenly beside her, grasping her arm. "I cannot let you go. I would worry about you."

She tried to shake off his grasp but couldn't. Desperate, she began to pull at his fingers. "You have no right—"

The riders were suddenly upon them, and she froze.

Kadar stroked her arm as if she were a nervous puppy. "All is well. No one will harm you."

She barely heard him, her gaze fixed on the man who had reined in before them.

"He is only half beast."

Mounted on the huge horse, looking like a centaur, dark and forbidding, he cast a giant shadow on the ground before him . . . and on her. She had the panicky feeling that if she did not move out of that shadow, she would be held captive forever.

He did not look at her, but at Kadar. "Bring her." His tone was crisp and stinging as the lash of a whip. "And if you don't want me to turn your horse loose and make you walk, you'll wipe that smile from your face."

"It's a welcoming smile. I'm always glad to see you." He released Thea and moved toward his horse. "Dundragon?"

"Bring her, damn you."

He was angry. Kadar had said he was filled with anger; nothing could be clearer or more intimidating in this moment.

Kadar did not seem to be affected as he mounted his horse. "My horse will not bear her weight. You will have to take her."

She could feel the displeasure Lord Ware emitted as if it were a tidal wave. "Kadar."

"Well, she's a trifle unwilling. I'm not sure I could subdue her if she struggled."

Ware's icy glance shifted back to Thea. "She does not appear unwilling. I've never seen a more spiritless or bedraggled maid."

She stared at him in disbelief. Spiritless. Bedraggled. What did he expect, with all the suffering and horror she had undergone. This condemnation was the spark that exploded her rage. "I'm sure you prefer women without spirit, as do all cowards."

His gaze narrowed on her face. "Coward?"

She ignored the menace in his tone. "Coward. Isn't it cowardly to hit a woman who cannot defend herself?"

"I have bruises on my face to prove you wrong."

"Good. You should expect nothing better. You ride up and let me think you're one of those savages who killed—"

"You gave me no chance to speak before you struck out at me." He got down from his horse and moved toward her. "Just as you're striking at me now with your words." He should have looked less dangerous off the steed, but he did not. He towered over her, and she had the same sensation of power and boundless authority as at their first meeting. He glared down at her. "Be silent. I'm weary unto death, and Kadar has made sure my temper is raw."

She glared back at him. "Are you going to hit me again?"

"Tempting," he murmured. "By the saints, it's tempting."

Kadar interjected quickly, "He doesn't mean it. Come, Ware, we must get her to Dundragon. She's weak and exhausted."

"Weak?" His gaze raked her defiant stance. "I think she's stronger than you claim."

"I'm not going to this Dundragon." She shifted her basket and stepped to one side to go around him. "So you need not argue as to who is to take me."

"And where are you going?"

"Kadar said there was a village."

"Too far."

She didn't answer as she started away from them.

"Ware," Kadar said.

"I know. I know." His hand fell on her shoulder, and he spun her around to face him. "You go to Dundragon. I don't want you there, and if I had my way, I'd let you walk to Hades, but I've no choice. By God, I'll not have you making more trouble for me."

"I do have a choice. I go nowhere with you."

He studied her defiant expression. "You're a very stubborn woman." He drew his dagger.

She stiffened as her pulse leaped with fear. Was he going to cut her throat?

He smiled with tigerish satisfaction. "You think I might wish to rid myself of a troublesome wench. You're right, I do." The dagger arced downward, piercing and ripping her water skin, then slicing through the leather cord. She stared in horror as the pouch fell to the ground and the last of her precious water spurted out onto the sand. "No!"

He sheathed the dagger. "Now you have no choice either." He turned away. "Throw aside that basket you're carrying. It will be too cumbersome."

She stared at him in helpless fury. With one stroke he had destroyed her chance of reaching safety without him. She wanted to shout, to pound him as she had done before.

He mounted the horse and sat waiting for her.

He expected her to come meekly and do his bidding.

"Throw the basket away," he repeated.

"Or you'll stick your dagger in it too?" She strode forward. "I'll go, but my basket goes also."

"I'll take the basket." Kadar quickly slipped from the saddle. "It will be my pleasure."

"Throw it away," Ware said, meeting her gaze.

He did not care if she took the basket; he just wanted to have his way. Well, he had won enough battles. "I won't give it up."

"It contains such a treasure?"

"Not what you would consider treasure. Nothing that is worth your thievery."

His expression changed, tightened, as if she had struck him. She heard Kadar's inhaled breath beside her.

"Thievery?" Ware said softly.

A little of her anger ebbed, banished by caution. She had stirred something dark and potentially lethal. Yet she could not back down. "Kadar said Hassan was an old acquaintance. Like to like."

"Like to like." His eyes half closed as he savored the words. "Yes, we do have certain similarities and interests."

Kadar jerked the basket from her back. "It's growing late. We must set out, or we won't reach Dundragon before dawn." He grasped her arm. "I've reconsidered. I believe my horse will hold your weight after all."

"Nonsense." Lord Ware brushed his hand aside. "We mustn't risk doing damage to such a fine animal. I'll take her." He remounted his horse, leaned down, and lifted Thea before him onto the saddle. "I've grown accustomed to the idea now."

Kadar started, "I truly think that—"

Ware touched spurs to the stallion, which lunged forward into a gallop. The other horsemen followed, and Kadar had no choice but to do the same.

The links of chain mail were hard against Thea's back. She felt as if she were suffocating, enclosed, bound in iron. He wanted her to feel like this, she realized angrily. She had said something that had struck deep, and he wanted to punish her. She could not give him the satisfaction of letting him know he had succeeded.

Instead of holding herself upright, she deliberately sank back against him.

He stiffened warily.

Let him be uneasy. She didn't have the strength to fight him now with anything but words. "How far is it to Dundragon?"

"Not far." He nodded at the mountains. "There."

Those mountains had seemed terribly far to her only a short time before. "I will not stay at that place."

"I don't want you to stay. As soon as Kadar decides you're well enough, you'll be sent on your way."

"I'm not ill. I could go now." Strange . . . the armor no longer felt uncomfortable, but smooth and sleek against her back. "And Kadar makes no decisions for me."

"Kadar makes decisions for everyone," he said dryly. "As I'm sure you've already noted."

"Not for me." She yawned. "Why should he? You're both strangers and I know nothing about you."

"And we know nothing about you."

Thank the saints, that was true. Kadar might suspect her words about her father's death were untrue, but surely he would not seek to disprove her story. As for Lord Ware, he wanted only to be rid of her and would not ask uncomfortable questions. "I'm Thea of Dimas."

She yawned again. It was odd how the pretense of comfort and confidence had become reality. He did not seem nearly as intimidating now that she could no longer see him. She was aware only of that rock-sturdy strength behind her that could keep her safe from all harm. "That's enough for you to know."

"Is it?"

She nodded drowsily. "Of course. You have . . . no desire to . . ." She trailed off as sleep claimed her.

* * *

"There's nothing as charming as a sleeping child."

Ware glanced over his shoulder to see Kadar riding behind him. He looked down at the slumbering Thea. He doubted if the thunder of Saladin's army could awaken her from that exhausted sleep. "This particular child is dirty, odorous, and overbold," he said.

Kadar nodded. "But brave and determined. The brave deserve to live." He smiled. "And they also deserve kindness."

"Then you may give it to her."

"But you saved her. You were the first one to see her and decide to ride to her rescue. It's your duty to—"

"I have no duty. Nor shall I assume any. I'm content as I am."

"No, you aren't." Kadar nudged closer and even with him. "But I'll persevere until you've reached that state. I know my duty, even if you don't." He looked down at Thea. "She's only ten and seven. Did I tell you that?"

Ware made no response.

"And things go hard for women in this world. Particularly fair, comely women."

Ware did not answer.

"What if she's with child by one of Hassan's men? She's only a child herself. It's enough to touch the heart."

"Your heart."

Kadar sighed. "I'm growing discouraged."

"At last."

"But not defeated." He let his horse drop back to follow Ware up the narrow mountain path.

The woman felt soft and warm and helpless in Ware's arms. He would not look down at her. He would not feel the pity Kadar wanted of him. He would not feel anything but the emotions he chose for himself. It was a mistake taking her to Dundragon, and he would not compound it by allowing himself to soften toward her. Kadar didn't realize how dangerous such an emotion as pity could be. Pity could make one vulnerable.

Pity could kill them all.

The fortress of Dundragon blazed with light. Even from a distance Thea was dazzled. Torches burned everywhere, illuminating every battlement of the grim fortress and, she discovered when they rode through the gates, the entire courtyard. Any chatelaine would have been horrified at the waste of such a display in the dead of night.

"Too much . . . ," she said drowsily.

He looked down at her.

"Too many torches. Waste . . ."

"I like light." He smiled grimly. "I don't regard it as waste, and I'm rich enough to indulge my fancies." He dismounted and lifted her from the stallion. "Kadar," he called, "come and take her."

"I can walk." She took a step back. Her legs buckled.

He muttered a curse and caught her. "Kadar!"

"Stiff," she murmured. "I'll be able to walk in a moment."

His arms tightened around her. "We cannot stay here all night on that premise. Kadar will carry you to your chamber."

"My basket," she murmured. "I can't go anywhere without my basket."

"I have your basket." Kadar appeared at her side. "But you'll have to carry her, Ware."

Ware gave him a cold glance, then lifted her in his arms and strode across the courtyard and into the castle.

Torches everywhere. Servants scurrying about before them. Silk. Stone. Flame. It was too much to absorb when she could barely hold open her eyes. She solved the problem by the simple action of closing them.

Softness beneath her. Suddenly Ware's arms were gone.

Loneliness. As intense as it was unexplainable.

She opened her eyes. He was standing over her, his gaze on her face. His expression was just as hard and impassive, but his eyes . . .

She couldn't look away. There was something there. . . .

He tore his gaze away and turned on his heel. But he whirled back and said haltingly, "You needn't be afraid. You'll be safe here." Then, as if regretting the moment of softness, he said harshly to Kadar, "For God's sake, get her clean clothes and a bath."

"As soon as she wakes. I'll not trouble her now." Kadar smiled down at Thea. "You must forgive him. He has a violent dislike of odor. I think it must be a reminder of those sheepskin drawers."

Sheepskin drawers? She didn't understand and was too weary to question him. "Put my basket by the bed."

He put it down. "It's very light. You must not have much in it."

Her whole world. Selene's freedom and her own. She put her hand protectively on the lid.

"You needn't sleep with it by your side," Lord Ware said roughly from the door. "You may believe me a thief, but I don't steal from guests under my roof."

How strange that her condemnation had hurt him. She would not have thought anything could pierce that hard exterior. She should not care. He was a brutal man, probably little better than those savages who had attacked the caravan.

"But I admit to curiosity." Kadar coaxed, "I don't suppose you'd care to trust us enough to tell us what precious trove is in your basket."

Lord Ware was still at the door, watching her. He may not have brought her there willingly, but he had given her safety, she thought. He might even have saved her life. It was difficult for her to trust anyone, but perhaps it would not hurt to lower her guard a little. She took her hand from the lid of the basket.

"Worms." She rolled over and turned her back to them. She drowsily closed her eyes again. "Hundreds and hundreds of worms . . ."

Chapter Two

THE BASKET WAS STILL in the same place by her bed when she opened her eyes the next afternoon.

"You wish your bath now? It's very late."

Thea glanced at the corner from where the question, spoken in Arabic, had come.

A middle-aged dark-haired woman gowned in flowing blue cotton rose to her feet from a low cushion. "My name is Jasmine. I serve you while you're here." She bustled forward. "I will give you fruit to break your fast, then Lord Ware says you must have a bath. He demands everyone in the household bathe once a day."

Sheepskin drawers. Kadar's sly comment popped into her head, then was gone as Jasmine drew back the gauze cover. "Come. Do you need my help? Shall I bring the food to you?"

"No," she answered in Arabic. She was not ready to be

confronted by this new challenge of a servant for her. The idea was ridiculous. She sat up slowly, carefully. By the saints, she was stiff and sore. "I've no need of a servant. I'll serve myself."

Jasmine shook her head. "Lord Ware says I'm to serve you." She glided across the room and stood behind a chair at a table. "Fruit."

At least the woman was not groveling, Thea thought with relief. On the contrary, her manner was brusque and close to rude. She swung her legs to the floor, then had to stop a moment. The night's rest should have strengthened her, but it appeared to have done the opposite.

"Ask for help and I will give it," Jasmine said without expression.

Definitely not groveling. The woman would probably let her fall to the floor and crawl to the table. A flare of irritation rushed through her. She did not want service, but it would not harm the woman to display kindness. She stood up and then swayed as dizziness washed over her.

Jasmine impassively stood watching her.

The dizziness was gone in a few minutes, and she started across the room. Every muscle in her body was sore; she could manage only a pained shuffle. The journey to the table seemed as long as her trip through the desert. She sank into the chair with a sigh of relief.

"Eat." Jasmine pushed a pewter plate toward her.

After looking down at the slices of pomegranates, oranges, and dates, Thea leaned back in the chair. "Presently. I'm not hungry right now."

"The water for your bath will be coming. I ordered it heated when I saw you stirring."

She met Jasmine's eyes. "Then they will have to heat it again."

Jasmine studied her for a moment and then shrugged. "Yes, they will."

A victory, but it had taken its toll on Thea's meager strength. "I believe I'm hungry after all." She reached for a slice of pomegranate. "You are slave to Lord Ware?"

"I'm a free woman. There are no slaves here."

Thea's eye widened in surprise. Slavery was as common here in the East as it was in Constantinople, and she had a vague memory of a multitude of retainers when they had entered the gates of Dundragon. "None?"

"None." Jasmine moved across the room to the high chest. When she returned, she was carrying an ivory-backed brush. "Your hair is tangled. I must brush it before you bathe."

"I'll do it."

"Eat." The command was brusque, but the pull of the brush through Thea's hair was gentle. "Your hair is very pale. Men enjoy fair-haired women, and you are of an age for coupling. Did Lord Ware bring you to use in his bed?"

Thea stiffened in shock and she felt the heat flood her cheeks. "No, I will never do that."

"You will if he chooses." The brush moved smoothly through her hair. "He is master here. You should be proud if he summons you to his bed. The women of this household come eagerly when he sends for them." Jasmine worked at a tangle at the back of Thea's neck. "He is not always gentle, but he has a great appetite for pleasure."

He is only half beast, Kadar had said. Which side did he show those women who came to his bed? She shivered as she realized she had not even considered this threat. He had been so cold and fierce....

But she should have considered it. Men were always beset by lust, and they considered all women prey. No one should know that fact better than she did, she thought bitterly. "I care nothing for his appetite. As soon as I'm stronger, I'll leave Dundragon."

"That is best. He has no need of another woman," Jasmine said. "But sometimes men think that the fruit they have not tasted is more succulent. Though, in truth, I don't see how you could please him. The skin of your face is red and not at all comely. I will put a salve on it after you bathe." She stepped back. "I heard Omar outside with the tub. Have you finished your fruit?"

"Enough." She had eaten only half the fruit, but she felt sated. Her appetite must have shrunk during those days in the desert. "I would not keep you waiting."

Jasmine ignored the irony in her tone. "It's of no moment. I only serve." She moved toward the door. "We all serve here at Dundragon."

And they all served Lord Ware, master of this vast fortress.

She was probably being foolish to let Jasmine's words disturb her. Lord Ware had been most reluctant to bring her here and was eager for her to leave. According to Jasmine, he had far more comely women to use. Yet for some reason the woman was antagonistic toward her and had attacked her appearance.

No matter. She had other things to worry about. She must leave here and find a place for herself. She could do this by herself, but it would be difficult.

Kadar. He was a strange, quicksilver man, but he had

been kind and appeared to wield some power over Lord Ware. Perhaps he could be persuaded to help her when she gained enough strength to leave Dundragon. "I'd like to speak to Kadar ben Arnaud," she called to Jasmine as the servant opened the door. "Will you tell him to come to me?"

Jasmine stepped aside to make way for a small man in a djellaba and turban who bore a half tub. She smiled at Thea. "Certainly. As I said, I'm here only to serve."

Kadar stopped short, his gaze fixed on her naked breasts and widening in shock. "Dear God, I didn't mean—I'm sorry. Jasmine told me to go right in."

Thea quickly covered her breasts with her arms and scrunched down as far as she could in the half tub. Every inch of her body felt on fire with embarrassment.

Jasmine came forward and said without expression, "You said you wanted to see him."

"Not now." Her voice was strangled. "You know I didn't mean—" She stopped as anger banished shame. Of course Jasmine had known what she had meant, but she had wanted to make Thea uncomfortable. "Turn your back, Kadar."

Kadar quickly presented her with his back.

Thea glared at Jasmine. "And you get me something to cover myself."

"I've not put the balm on your face yet."

She spaced her next words with precision. "Get me a cover!"

Jasmine shrugged, then jerked the gauze cover from the bed and moved to stand beside the tub. She silently draped it around Thea, who stepped out of the tub. Thank heaven, the cloth was not oversheer and large enough to completely envelop her from feet to shoulders, past which hung freshly washed hair.

"Now leave us," she said to Jasmine.

Jasmine shook her head. "It is not proper. He is a man."

"Not just any man," Kadar murmured. "Kadar, the wise, the honorable, the magnificent."

Jasmine ignored him. "Lord Ware brought you here; therefore, you are his property. I'll not have him shamed by leaving you without a woman present."

"Leave us!" Thea could not believe her. Jasmine had deliberately brought Kadar to her when she was naked, and now Jasmine was giving her this outrageous argument?

For a moment Thea thought the servant would hold her ground. Then Jasmine turned and glided toward the door. "I warn you, I must inform Lord Ware of this trespass."

"Any trespass was yours. Get out!"

Jasmine gave her another cool glance before she left the chamber.

"You can turn around," Thea told Kadar as the door closed behind the older woman.

Kadar sighed when he saw the blanket wrapped around her. "It's a hot day and you look very warm. Are you sure you don't wish to shed that cumbersome wrapping?" Then as he saw color flood Thea's cheeks, he said gently, "I was but joking. You are very lovely, but I am no threat to you. What did you do to so irritate Jasmine?"

"Nothing." Thea's hand nervously opened and closed on the edge of the cover. "She doesn't like me."

"Jasmine has had a difficult life and likes few people. But she doesn't try to hurt them as she did you."

"I did *nothing.*" The embarrassment and rage had taken their toll. Her knees were trembling, and she sank down on the stool beside the tub. "She's just a cruel woman. It makes no sense."

Kadar studied her and then said slowly, "Perhaps it does make sense."

She shook her head, then drew a deep breath. She had not asked him there to rail against Jasmine. "You were very kind to me last night. The reason I asked Jasmine to—"

"It was Ware who saw you and made the decision to go help you." His gaze went to the basket beside the bed. "Worms? Were you joking?"

She impatiently shook her head. "I will tell you of that later. As I said, I wished to ask you to help me a little more. I must leave this place and go to Damascus."

"You're not well yet."

"In a few days I will be. I'm very strong."

"When that time comes, we will talk to Ware about it. No one enters or leaves Dundragon without his permission."

Her eyes widened in surprise. "Not even you?"

"It's the law of Dundragon. Ware has reason. He's a great warrior, and warriors have many enemies. Dundragon must remain secure."

"My leaving will not cause this fortress to fall. He does not want me here."

"Where is this balm Jasmine spoke about?"

"What?" The discussion was not going as she had planned. He was being both evasive and distracted. Thea gestured to the small pottery jar on the table. "I'll not ask much of you, but I'm a stranger in this land and I—What are you doing?" He had opened the jar and stood before her with a small portion of a clear salve on his fingers.

"It appears obvious." He carefully spread the salve over her nose and cheeks. "You're not as burned as I thought. The skin may not even peel. A few days should bring about healing."

"I kept my mantle drawn forward over my forehead to protect me." The salve felt cool and tingly. "I learned a harsh lesson the first week after the caravan left Constantinople. I was not accustomed to being outdoors and I burned very badly."

"Did no one warn you of the dangers of the sun?" He dipped his fingers again in the jar. "Your father, perhaps?"

She went still. "I'm willful at times and I did not listen."

He tilted her head and spread a little of the salve on her neck. "I can believe you are willful. I cannot believe you would not listen to warning. I judge you to be very sensible."

She moistened her lips. "I was different before my father died. Sorrow brings wisdom."

"True." He pushed aside the blanket. "Your shoulder blades are burned. The straps of the basket must have pulled the gown from your shoulders." He gently rubbed the salve into her shoulder. "How did you escape from the caravan?"

"I was at the very end of the caravan when Hassan surprised us. I grabbed my basket, water, and some food and hid beneath a wagon. When I saw my chance, I slipped away."

"You were not—" He hesitated.

She gazed at him, puzzled. Then she realized what he meant and shook her head. "They did not see me." She smiled bitterly. "And they were far too busy with the other women to seek me out."

"You were very fortunate. Except for your father, of course. You said he was a merchant?"

"No."

"Perhaps a pilgrim on his journey to the Holy Land? Or a soldier on his way to join the knights who defend this land from—"

"For God's sake, Kadar, what are you about?"

They both turned around to see Ware standing, scowling, in the doorway, his gaze on Kadar's hand on Thea's bare shoulder.

Ware entered the chamber and slammed the door. "If you must couple with the woman, take her to your quarters. I won't have my servants running screaming to me of—"

"I'm certain Jasmine would not scream. It would do damage to her dignity." Kadar leisurely drew the gauze cover back over Thea's shoulders. "I was merely tending to our guest's burn."

"Are you finished?"

Kadar nodded.

"Then wait for me in the hall. I would have a word with her."

Kadar hesitated, then said to Thea, "We will have our talk later."

She did not want him to leave. His dangerous probing had made her uneasy, but not as uneasy as Ware did. He was wearing a simple dark-blue tunic instead of armor, but he still looked like the warrior he was, with broad shoulders and the thick, corded muscles of his arms. His hair was so dark, it appeared almost black and was bound back from a face whose bone structure was clean and bold as the edge of a sword. His glance had the same sharp edge as he stared down into her eyes.

And she felt entirely too small and helpless sitting on the stool. She stood up, facing him as the door closed behind Kadar.

He attacked with no preliminaries. "I'll not have you practicing your wiles on Kadar. You will not display your body or couple with him. You'll not try to use him in any way. Do you understand?"

She stared at him in disbelief. "I did not display—"

"You sent for him while you were naked."

"It was a mistake. I didn't mean—I was in my bath and I—"

"Like Bathsheba on her rooftop."

"No, it wasn't like that at all."

"What was it like?" He drew nearer, his gaze boring down at her. "You're a woman alone and you need protection and sustenance. You chose to inveigle yourself into Kadar's bed to obtain them. Seduction is a woman's way."

She was weary of being battered by his words. She glared up at him. "It's not my way."

"Then why did you send for him?"

"It's true I needed his help, but I—"

He strode toward the door. "If Kadar wishes to couple with you, refuse him. Or you will deal with me."

He had dismissed her as if she were a hound yapping at his heels, she realized in fury. She would not let him leave her like this.

She strode past him and blocked the door.

"Get out of my way."

"You're neither fair nor kind." She was shaking with

anger. "You tell Kadar to take me to his quarters and then order me to refuse him because you fear his displeasure."

"Get out of my way."

"It's true. You fear to lose him because he's the only one who is foolish enough to accept such a brutal, rude, selfish man as a companion. I do not say 'friend' because you could not be friend. You are too guarded and demanding and—"

"Be quiet!"

"And let you abuse me in silence? It's the way of bullies and pompous louts who—"

He tore the blanket from her body.

She stared at him in shock.

His chest was rising and falling with the harshness of his breathing as his gaze raked her from her blazing face to her naked feet, lingering longest at the thatch of hair that covered her womanhood. "You're right, I can be demanding and I will be obeyed in this. Kadar chooses not to bed my women. He regards it as a discourtesy." His hands closed on her waist. "Refuse him, or I'll make certain he refuses you."

She could not speak. She could scarcely breathe. She could feel the calluses on his warm hands as he grasped her naked flesh. His grip was not brutal, but she felt as if he were branding her, that even if he let her go, she would have the marks of his fingers on her.

He lifted her with effortless strength to one side and released her.

"You lied," she whispered. "You said I'd be safe here."

He smiled bitterly. "But I'm a brute and a bully. You cannot trust the word of such a rogue."

As the door closed behind him, she sank back against

the wall, trembling in every limb. She had never experienced a moment when she had been this helpless. When he had touched her, she had felt totally possessed. Slavery.

Her stomach twisted with panic as she realized that even in Nicholas's house in Constantinople she had never felt that imprisoned. It must not happen again.

But it could happen. Jasmine's dislike might instigate another attack and put her in a position where she would be forced into another confrontation with Ware. He had meant what he'd said. It was possible his anger might lead him to make her one of those women Jasmine said he used for his pleasure. She could not bear it.

Of course she could bear it. She had seen coupling both brutal and gentle in Nicholas's house. It would not be pleasant, but it would not destroy her. The only thing that would destroy her would be to lose what she had already won and to betray Selene. She could not risk being made a toy and kept in this fortress.

No one enters or leaves Dundragon without his permission.

Yet she must leave this place at once. She could not wait, and she must not ask Kadar for help.

But she must make sure all was well before she left. She had tried to carry enough for the journey, but she had not counted on Hassan's attack or the long trek through the desert.

She didn't bother to pick up the gauze blanket Ware had thrown onto the floor. Jasmine had taken away her ragged gown, but she would surely bring a replacement soon. She gathered her strength and haltingly walked across the room toward her basket. She sank down on the bed and carefully opened the lid of the basket.

She gasped with dismay. "No!"

* * *

Kadar was standing and admiring a graceful brass pitcher when Ware walked into the hall. "This is truly a beautiful piece. I was right in making you barter higher at that bazaar." He turned to face Ware. "But, then, I'm always right about everything. It must be a great comfort to you that—" He broke off as he studied Ware's lower body. "But I'd judge you not in the least comfortable at this moment."

Ware strode toward the table and poured wine into a goblet.

"I shouldn't have left you alone with her." Kadar paused. "Did you hurt her?"

"I didn't rape her, if that's what you mean."

"I didn't think you did. You may have prodigious appetites, but if you'd taken her, even you couldn't become this aroused again so quickly." He lifted his wine to his lips. "I was referring to hurting her soul, not her body."

Ware had a sudden memory of those huge amber eyes gazing at him like a wounded doe when he had accused her of seducing Kadar. He forced the picture away. She was no helpless doe. Only a moment later she had turned and stung him. "She made me angry." He glared at Kadar. "You made me angry. Why did you fall into her trap? Don't you know she wants to make use of you?"

"I think she's the one who is trapped." He shook his head. "And the world is not entirely filled with deceit and treachery, Ware."

"It's safer to expect treachery than kindness. Considering the life you've lived, you should have learned that by now."

"It's a very lonely road you've chosen. Someday you'll choose to leave safety behind."

"No." He threw himself into a chair and smiled sardonically. "Why should I choose a different path? I have everything I want. I've a great castle, more gold than Saladin, and the freedom to indulge my every desire." He lifted his goblet. "And I don't have to pretend to be anything but the rogue I am. When I go into battle, I admit it's for gold and not for any higher aim." He added deliberately, "And, when I couple with a woman, it's because I lust and must relieve myself, not because Cupid's dart has pierced my heart."

"You're not a rogue," Kadar said. Then he amended, "Well, not all the time. And when you are, it's because you're in pain. You're like a lion with a thorn in his paw who only growls when he steps on it."

He felt like that wounded lion now, Ware thought. He was weary of Kadar's probing, and his loins were aching and heavy. He wanted nothing more than to go back to that wench upstairs and sink between her thighs. Why hadn't he done it, instead of merely threatening? It would have settled the problem before it became one. "It's Conrad who is the lion." He finished his wine in two swallows. "And he's roaring for me to join him again. A messenger came this morning with an invitation to come to his tent and meet with him. It seems the flush of victory has faded and he wants to make sure Tyre isn't threatened again."

"Will you do it?"

"Perhaps." He shrugged. "Or perhaps I'll offer my sword to Saladin. Of the two, he is the more honorable."

"I thought you no longer cared about honor."

"I care about being paid for my services. Conrad might choose to forget my share of the booty on the grounds I'm a traitor and a renegade. At least Saladin won't be tempted to hand me over to the Temple and let the Grand Master put a convenient and final end to me."

"You believe Conrad would betray you?"

"I wouldn't trust the mercy of the angel Gabriel if the Grand Master applied his influence. You don't know—" He broke off. Of course Kadar didn't know. No one could possibly understand who had not been one of the temple. "I have time to make a decision. Perhaps I'll wait until there's a new player in the game. Richard of England is rumored to be coming to launch a new and glorious Crusade. My price will only go up after Conrad loses a few battles."

"Such power. Ah, to be able to change the course of history to suit oneself." He smiled. "But it's really too bad you don't have the freedom to go beyond these walls without a battalion of soldiers."

Ware carefully kept any hint of expression from his face. He should be accustomed to these jabs by now. They came often enough. "I don't have to stay behind these walls. It's my choice."

"Then why not leave this country? Why be forced to make a choice between Saladin and Conrad? You care nothing for either of them."

He looked down into the depths of the wine in his goblet. "By God, I *won't* let that bastard force me to leave."

Kadar shook his head. "I would have thought the temple would have rid you of the sin of pride."

"Why? There's no more pride on earth than in the temple." He stood up and put his goblet down on the table.

"Except perhaps in Kadar ben Arnaud. Stay away from the Greek woman, Kadar. Lust makes all men vulnerable."

"It's pity I feel. Though I'm a man and I admit to a little lust at the time," Kadar smiled. "She has truly lovely breasts."

Pale and full and crowned with taut, pink nipples.

The memory came back to Ware, and with it a rush of heat to his already aching loins. There was no reason for the intensity of this lust. He had called for a woman to come to his bed last night and had indulged himself thrice before he had fallen asleep. Yet here was need again, sharper and more tormenting than he could remember.

It could not be the woman herself; it must be the anger and defiance she had shown him. The women he had brought to Dundragon to satisfy his needs submitted eagerly to his every wish. It was natural that a challenge might pique his lust.

"Ware." Kadar's tone was warning, his gaze on Ware's face. "She's still not well."

"Then get her well enough to send away from here soon." He smiled recklessly. "It seems she makes that thorn in my paw throb every time I'm near her."

"As soon as I can." He frowned. "There may be difficulties. I'm not sure she will have any place to go. She says her father was killed in the caravan." He shook his head. "I think she was alone."

"Why should she lie?"

"Because she has something to hide. She was at the end of the caravan, where the very poorest are placed. I doubt if she had little more possessions before Hassan's raid than when we found her. A woman without funds, traveling alone..." Kadar paused. "The risk is enormous. Only desperation would lead anyone to take such a chance."

He didn't want to hear about desperation. He had lived with it as an intimate companion and would not risk a feeling of bonding with the woman. "She has to leave here. Find out the problem and then solve it."

Kadar nodded. "I'll try. You must be patient."

Ware didn't feel in the least patient. "Solve it or I'll find my own solution." He strode toward the door. "It's growing dark. I have to go inspect the battlements. Are you coming with me?"

Kadar shook his head. "I wish to consider this matter of the woman. I believe I'll go and see how the falcons have survived my absence."

The guards on the battlement were in place and alert, as Ware had expected. He had taught them that alertness in a hard arena. He watched a boy running about the courtyard lighting the multitude of torches. He was too young, Ware thought with annoyance, probably not more than ten and two. He had told Abdul no one under ten and six was to be recruited from the villages to come to Dundragon. He would send the lad home tomorrow.

He slowly moved to the edge of the ramparts. The sun was down now, and deep-purple twilight lay over the mountains like a dark cloak.

But there was a glimmering in the darkness on the side of the third mountain. A small pinprick of fire. A campfire.

He had known it would be there. It was always there. He came here to the battlements every evening to watch that fire hurl defiantly out of the darkness, telling him he would never be safe behind these strong walls.

"Good evening, Vaden," he said softly to the watcher.

He stood looking at the fire until full darkness fell. Then he strode toward the door leading off the battlements.

"Lord Ware." Jasmine stood in the shadows of the hallway at the bottom of the stairs. It had become her custom to wait for him when he returned from the battlements. Wise Jasmine. Somehow she sensed the bitterness and despair that seared and scarred, and was always ready to provide a balm to soothe the wild tension.

"A woman?" she asked. "To your chamber?"

His chamber was too close to the Greek woman's, and he did not want to be near her tonight. Her tongue had stung and made him think, and her body had aroused him too much. "No, send her to the hall." He moved down the stairs ahead of her. "And wine. Many, many bottles of wine."

"I will send Tasza." Jasmine called after him, "She always pleases you."

He did not demand pleasure. He wanted only relief from the lust aroused by Thea of Dimas.

And to forget that tiny, relentless flame burning on the third mountain.

Thea paused at the bottom of the stone steps, gazing hesitantly at the arched opening leading to the hall. She had heard voices and the sound of a lyre only minutes before, but now there was silence. It was close to midnight; he might have retired to his chamber for the night. Perhaps she would have to wait until morning. Relief poured through her.

The scrape of a chair on stone floor. He was still in there.

Disappointment flooded her as she realized she had no excuse to avoid the confrontation. It was probably for the best; she shouldn't wait. It had already taken her too long to brace herself for this meeting.

She drew a deep breath and strode across the foyer into the hall. She stopped short, her eyes widening in shock.

Ware was sprawled indolently in a high-backed chair before the huge fireplace, a goblet in his hand.

He was naked.

He lifted his goblet to her. "Good evening, Thea of Dimas." His words were a little slurred. "How kind of you to join us."

Naked and drunk.

"Send her away."

Thea's gaze flew to the hearth. His chair half blocked her view of the sheepskin pallet spread before the fire, but she could glimpse a shapely bare leg.

"Now, Tasza, you must not be unwelcoming. It's partially due to her that you're here tonight." He waved a hand. "Come and have a goblet of wine. Tasza will play for you. She's very accomplished on the lyre." He smiled down at the woman. "But it's not her primary skill."

"I don't want to play for her. Send her away."

He frowned. "You're being rude. It does not please me."

"I don't wish to hear her," Thea said quickly. She should not have come. It was clear what was transpiring in this room. The air was heavy with the scent of incense, wine, and musk. Yet she could not leave without accomplishing her purpose. "I came to speak to you."

"I'm not sure I can speak. I seem to be having a slight difficulty. Are you sure you'd not prefer another form of communication?"

"No!" Tasza jumped to her feet. She, too, was without clothes and very beautiful. She was in her middle twenties, with smooth golden skin, and long dark hair half veiling large, voluptuous breasts. "Send her away, my lord."

"You're beginning to annoy me, Tasza." Ware waved a slightly unsteady hand. "If you cannot be courteous, then you'll be absent. Go to your quarters."

"But, my lord—" She stopped, glowered at Thea, and marched from the room.

"You should not have sent her away." Thea moistened her lips. "I didn't come here to pleasure you."

"No? Pity." He lifted the goblet to his lips. "No matter. I'm not sure I could perform at the moment anyway. I've already indulged myself a number of times tonight, and I'm a little drunk."

"More than a little."

"Sometimes it eases me." He drank deep. "Sometimes it doesn't. Sometimes I require"—his gaze went to the door through which Tasza had disappeared—"other means."

She felt a sudden flare of anger. "A woman should not be used for such a purpose. It's cruel and—"

"Did she seem to be suffering?"

"Because she knows no better than to lie down and spread her legs for you is no reason for you to rut with her."

He threw back his head and laughed. "You have a tongue like an asp. It's good that I'm drunk; it mellows the sting."

It mellows the sting.

Her last qualm about being here vanished at his words. If wine mellowed and removed that hard edge, perhaps this would be the best possible time to talk with him. It might be possible for her to wrest a promise from him he would not give if sober. "Are you too drunk to listen and understand?"

His gaze went to the window overlooking the mountains. "I never let myself get that drunk."

"Then I'll stay and talk to you." She strode over to a cushioned stool to one side of the hearth and seated herself.

"How kind of you."

She was now at eye level with his lower body, and she tried to keep herself from staring at him. "Wouldn't you be more comfortable if you garbed yourself?"

"No." He sipped his wine. "Shouldn't you be sleeping? Kadar will be upset if you lose strength."

"I couldn't sleep until I saw you."

"Yet you say you don't wish to couple with me."

She repressed the flare of annoyance. "Women are not only for coupling."

He leaned back and gazed at her from beneath half-closed lids. "Not all women. But you're very suited for the sport." Frowning, he gazed at the thick single braid that lay on her left shoulder. "I don't like to see your hair bound. I want to see it flowing around you as it was this afternoon."

She flushed as she remembered that scene upstairs. "I always wear it this way."

"Take it down."

"It gets in my way."

"If you want me to listen, take it down."

She clenched her teeth in exasperation. Perhaps she should leave him after all. Yet the demand was more sulky than arbitrary. Like that of a little boy who was being denied his way. It would do no harm to let him have his will in this. She untied the cord, loosened her braid, and shook her head to let her hair flow free.

He nodded approvingly. "Very good." His gaze went to her white cotton gown, and she stiffened in alarm.

But he only commented. "Ugly. It swallows you."

She was sure that had been Jasmine's intention, but since it had suited her, she had made no objection. "It's clean and neat."

"You looked better without—"

"I've come to ask a favor," she said quickly to veer him away from that direction.

"I don't grant favors. Ask Kadar."

"I have to ask you. I have no choice. It must be done at once, and I—"

"I'm out of wine." He stood up and moved toward a pitcher on the table across the room. "Go on, I'm listening. Did I tell you that you have a very pleasant voice? Like honey . . ."

She could not take her eyes from him. Strange that such a giant of a man would move with the grace of a lion. If he was a beast, he was a truly magnificent one. His unbound mane tumbled about massive shoulders that bore the scars of battle. His thighs and calves were thick and powerful, stomach and buttocks lean and corded with muscle. A triangle of dark hair thatched his chest, and another circled his manhood.

He glanced up as he poured his wine. "Well, did I?"

It took her a moment to remember what he had asked her. Something about her voice. "No, you compared me to an asp."

"Well, how do I know if it would be bitter to be stung by

an asp? Perhaps it would be honey sweet until the death throes." He set the pitcher down and strolled back to her. "What do you think?"

"I think I wouldn't like to taste the sting to see."

He sat back down. "Neither would I. Sometimes when I'm weary unto death, I think it would be good to go to a final rest." He suddenly smiled recklessly. "But since I doubt if there is rest in hell, I'll not chance it until I'm forced."

She stared at him, shocked. "Surely you believe that you'll be taken to heaven. You're a soldier, and the Pope has promised all Crusaders they will receive forgiveness and divine reward."

"And in return they slaughter the infidel and send plunder to Rome." He stared down into the wine in his goblet. "Do you know, I cannot even remember all the men I've killed in my lifetime. Once when I was drunk, I tried to recall and count them, but there were too many. Somehow I don't think God will be as forgiving as the Pope." He shifted his shoulders as if throwing off a burden and drained his glass. "So I must enjoy myself while I'm still on this earth."

Why did she feel sorry for him? He was a brute and a barbarian who cared nothing for anyone's needs but his own. The weariness and sadness she saw was probably only induced by the wine. Yet she found herself saying gently, "I'm sure you're wrong. God does forgive."

He raised his eyes. "Will he forgive Hassan for killing your father?"

She stiffened and did not answer.

"Kadar thinks you lied. Did you lie, Thea of Dimas?"

She was silent a moment and then said, "Yes."

He shrugged. "It doesn't matter. Everyone lies. Conrad will kiss my cheek tomorrow and stab me to the heart the next day."

"I don't lie." She amended, "Unless I have no choice. And what of Kadar? Does he lie?"

"No. Kadar doesn't lie." He reached up and rubbed his temple. "My head is starting to ache. Usually it doesn't happen until the next day. If you're going to ask me something, you'd better do it now. I grow bad-tempered when I'm hurting."

He was bad-tempered when he wasn't hurting. "Why should I ask? You said you wouldn't grant it."

"Damnation." He glared at her. "Ask it!"

She blurted out, "My worms need leaves."

He stared at her in astonishment and then started to laugh. "Leaves?"

"It's not funny. I had another pouch full of leaves, but I had to leave it with the caravan. I thought I might have enough in the basket, but there are only a few left and—Stop laughing."

"I cannot." He shook his head, his lips still twitching. "Set the poor creatures free and let them find their own leaves."

"I cannot set them free. I *need* them." She leaned forward, her hands clenched tightly together. "They're silkworms. When I settle in Damascus, I'll use them to make silk for my looms. Perhaps I'll even have enough to trade."

"Silk... Is that what you did in Constantinople?"

She nodded. "Wonderful silk. I was an embroiderer for the finest silk house in the city, and I also helped care for the silk beds." She paused. "It's a favor I ask, but I'm willing to pay. As soon as I have my own house, I'll make you anything you like. I have great skill, and my work was much sought after."

"What do you want?"

"Tomorrow I need to go into the foothills and search out a mulberry tree."

"Mulberry? No other tree would do?"

"Not as well. It's what they're accustomed to eating." At least if he was listening, there was a chance of persuading him. "But I understand they do grow in this land. I spoke to a trader, and he said they've spread from China to here. In Constantinople we have the black mulberry, but here they have white, which is even better."

"The tree is white?"

"No, the fruit is white when the tree flowers."

"And what if it isn't flowering?" he said dryly.

"It has tooth-shaped leaves. I'll recognize it." She held her breath. "Will you take me?"

He leaned his head back and closed his eyes. "No."

"You must take me," she said desperately. "I have to have those leaves. You'll be rid of me as soon as I have enough to assure the worms will live until I reach Damascus."

"Go to bed."

"Selene risked a great deal to bring that basket to me—I won't let them be destroyed," she said unsteadily. "You needn't accompany me. Lend me a horse and I'll go by myself."

"No." He opened his eyes. "Go to your chamber."

"Not until you promise me I'll have the leaves."

He started to shake his head and then flinched. "I'll promise anything if you'll stop hammering at me."

"Tomorrow?" she asked eagerly.

"Tomorrow. Get out."

She jumped to her feet and started toward the arched doorway. She had done all she could, but it might all be for naught. He might be too drunk to remember his promise tomorrow, or he could regard a vow made to a woman as not binding.

"And send Tasza back to me."

She stopped in the doorway. "I don't know where she is. You sent her to her quarters."

"I doubt if she went. Tasza can be very determined."

"You've had too much wine. You don't need her. Let the poor woman stay in her own bed."

"I am here." The woman flew past Thea and ran toward Ware. "I knew you would not stay angry with me." She knelt before him and pressed her lips to his inner thigh. "Forgive me. I will make you forget my impudence."

She was fondling him with tongue as well as hands, Thea realized with shock.

And he was responding. Boldly.

His hands clenched tightly on the arms of the chair as he met her gaze over the woman's head. His face was flushed, his lips full and sensual. "Stay," he said thickly. "Watch. I want you here."

The heat mounted to her cheeks. Incense and musk and the smell of burning logs drifted to her. The entire room was charged, throbbing with erotic sights, sounds, and scents. Her chest was so tight, she could scarcely breathe.

He held her gaze. "Stay," he repeated softly.

She turned and ran from the hall and up the stairs. Her

heart was beating painfully hard and her entire body was tingling. Perhaps he was right—perhaps he did belong to Lucifer. Dear heaven, she had never felt like this before. She had actually wanted to stay in that room that breathed of sin and sensuality.

But not to watch.

"Where is that damned basket?"

Thea's eyes flew open to see Ware standing over her bed.

"What?" She clutched the cover to her breast and scrambled to a sitting position. Dawn had not yet broken, and the chamber was in half darkness. "What are you doing here?"

"The basket."

"It's mine," she said fiercely. "You can't have it."

"I don't want the goddamn basket. I want a leaf. I have to have a leaf or I can't find the tree."

She gazed up at him in astonishment. "You're going to look for my tree?"

"I said it, didn't I?" he growled.

"Now?"

"I've no patience for your questions. My head is pounding, my stomach is queasy, and this armor feels as heavy as the drawbridge of this castle. Tell me where that cursed basket is."

"By the window." She hurriedly sat up, wrapped the cover around her, and flew across the room. "But you don't have to have a leaf. I'll go with you."

"Open the basket."

She untied the thong and opened the lid. "There's not much left of the leaves."

He gazed with repulsion at the squirming mass of worms. "God in heaven, they look the way my stomach feels." He leaned against the windowsill. "You get the leaf."

She carefully reached into the basket and retrieved a half leaf. "There's no bigger piece." She spied a small worm on it and gently brushed him back into the basket. "But you won't need this. I'll help you find a tree."

He gingerly took the leaf and turned on his heel. "You'll stay here." The door slammed behind him.

She dropped the blanket and snatched up her gown. She slipped it over her head, then grabbed her sandals. She didn't bother to put them on but carried them as she ran from the chamber. Beneath her bare feet the stone was cool down the staircase and out into the courtyard.

A young soldier was holding the horse's reins while Ware mounted.

"I should go with you." She hopped on one foot as she put on a sandal. "You're not being reasonable. It may take you a long time without me."

He didn't answer.

She put on her other shoe. "What if you come back with the wrong leaves?"

"Then I'll go out and get the right ones."

"And I will help him." Kadar was riding out of the stable and across the courtyard toward them. "But I doubt if that will be necessary. My eyes are as keen as my falcons'. I could recognize the smallest leaf from miles away."

"You're staying here too," Ware said.

Kadar shook his head. "You need me."

"I need no one. I go alone."

Kadar yawned. "It's too early to argue. Take an escort and I'll let you go without me."

Ware's gaze went to the mountains. "I'll risk no men when I can offer them no plunder."

Risk? Thea stared at the two men in bewilderment.

"Then I'll have to go with you," Kadar insisted. "I must protect my belongings."

"I don't belong to you."

Kadar nudged his horse forward. "I hope you carry food in that pack. We cannot eat leaves like the worms."

"You're not going."

Kadar smiled at Thea. "Trust us. We will see that your worms do not starve."

Ware said coldly, "This is not a battle of wills. If you try to go through that gate, I'll knock you to the ground and I won't be gentle about it. You don't go with me."

"Ware, I . . ." Kadar trailed off as he met Ware's gaze. He sighed. "It's very difficult owning a man like you. You will take care?"

Ware nodded and nudged his horse toward the gates.

He was wearing armor. Thea had been vaguely conscious of the chain mail, but it took on new meaning in light of the conversation that had transpired between Ware and Kadar. "Is there danger? He's just going to the foothills."

Kadar was frowning as he watched Ware ride through the gates. "It's very early," he muttered. "He may be safe."

"Are there bandits in these mountains?"

Kadar shook his head. "Not bandits."

Ware disappeared from view and Kadar turned to her. "Stop frowning. The fault is not yours. You didn't know."

She still didn't know, she thought with exasperation. He was making no sense. "I only asked him to fetch me some mulberry leaves, and you act as if I'd asked him to conquer a town."

Kadar smiled. "He would have taken an army if you'd asked him to conquer a town. He could not, in honor, take one to conquer a mulberry tree. He says he has no honor, but you can see that is not true."

"I know nothing about his honor. I know only that you're making too much of a simple task."

"Perhaps you're right." He took her elbow. "At any rate, we cannot help Ware now. We can only wait. Would you like to see my falcons?"

"You raise falcons?" She let him lead her toward the steps. "For hunting?"

"Partly for hunting. Partly to watch them soar. There's no more glorious sight on earth than a falcon in flight." He stopped as they entered the castle. "But first you must break your fast. You're still not well."

"I'm much stronger today, only a little tired."

"Weariness can lead to illness. Garner your strength. You will need it to nurture all your worms. Are you truly a fine embroiderer?"

"The finest in Constantinople." She looked at him in surprise when he burst out laughing. "Well, I am."

"I don't doubt it. I was just delighted by your charming lack of modesty. In truth, I find confidence very admirable. It's like the lovely sheen on a piece of exquisite wood."

"Lord Ware told you of our discussion? I wasn't certain he would remember anything I told him last night."

"He remembers everything." His smile faded. "Which is sometimes a curse."

"Yes." She herself had memories she would rather forget.

"I thought you would understand." Kadar led her toward the great hall. "Now, let us get you fed so that you can admire my beautiful birds."

Chapter Three

"THIS IS ELEANOR." He took the falcon out of her cage. "Is she not handsome? I named her for Eleanor of Aquitaine."

The bird was indeed splendid. "Why?"

"Because she's wily and fierce and has a profound dislike for being held captive. It took me over a year to train her." He chuckled. "Which is better than King Henry did with his Eleanor. He never succeeded in taming her."

"Did your father tell you of Eleanor?"

"My father gave my mother his seed and never looked back. My mother told me he died a great death battling her people." He smiled into the beady eyes of the falcon. "It's a pity he never realized his greatest achievement was producing me."

There was no antagonism in his voice, she realized wonderingly. "You don't hate him?"

"When I was a boy, I hated him. My mother died when

I was five, and life was not easy for me on the streets of Damascus. I was a purloin and shunned by both my peoples." He put Eleanor back in the cage and opened the next enclosure. "But I rose above it."

"How?"

"Knowledge. I stole learning as I did fruit from the bazaars. I learned from the Franks and I learned from my mother's people." He took out another falcon. "To my horror I discovered both were right . . . and wrong about most things. How can you hate when there is no truth that cannot be challenged?" He held out the bird to her. "This is Henry. He's less fierce than Eleanor and does not have her sense of purpose. She never relents once she sights prey. I've discovered that the female can often be more determined when in full flight." He met her gaze. "Haven't you made that discovery also?"

He was no longer referring to his falcons. She said, "But first she must reach full flight," then added, "And there are always those who wish to put her in a cage or use her. Even you, Kadar."

He nodded. "It's the nature of man." He put the falcon back in the cage. "But when their use is fulfilled, I'll set them free."

"And their use is to hunt?"

"Actually, to intercept." He carefully latched the cage. "Saladin and a few Frank commanders use carrier pigeons to carry orders to their troops. Ware decided we should use falcons to make sure the pigeons never reach their destination."

Though Kadar had spoken casually, almost indifferently, Thea shivered. She had a sudden, vivid picture of fierce Eleanor savagely plucking a pigeon out of the sky.

"Life is always a battle. You can't stop it; you can only choose the battleground," he said as if reading her thoughts. "If a pigeon reaches its target, men die. If a falcon stops the pigeon, different men die."

There was no savagery in his voice. Yet she was suddenly seeing a harder, darker side of Kadar. "And you choose Lord Ware's battleground."

"For the time being." He chuckled. "It's my bane for saving his life. Now I find I cannot bear to see him destroyed."

"How did you save his life?"

"I found him wounded and near death. He had fled to the Old Man of the Mountain for safety but didn't reach him in time."

"Old Man of the Mountain?"

"Sheikh Rashid ed-Din Sinan. He is the King of Assassins. It was a clever move on Ware's part. No one ventures into Sinan's domain without invitation."

"Then what were you doing there?"

"Knowledge." He smiled. "One must know the dark paths as well as the bright. But sometimes there's such a thing as learning too much, of delving too deeply. I was becoming lost and was ready to return to Damascus when I found Ware on the path. I nursed him back to health and took him to Sinan's fortress."

"From whom was he running?"

He hesitated and then shrugged. "I reveal nothing that everyone in this land doesn't know when I tell you that he was running from the Knights Templar. What do you know of them?"

"What everyone knows—that the Knights Templar is an

order of warrior monks. They're the finest soldiers in Christendom and the wealthiest. They sell their services both to merchants and to royalty for vast sums. Nicholas paid them once to guard a caravan he was sending to Cairo." Her brow wrinkled in thought as she tried to remember anything else she had heard. "A goodly portion of their fees go to the Pope, but some of their gold is said to be kept in their own storehouses."

"Ah, yes, and you can see why the Pope has such affection for the order." He stroked the falcon's feathers with a gentle forefinger. "And gave them such power that they are feared more than Saladin."

"Why were they pursuing Lord Ware?"

"Unfortunately, they have no fondness for prodigal sons. They wished to wipe him from the face of the earth."

She shook her head. "I don't understand."

"Ware was a Knights Templar, perhaps the greatest warrior in the order. When he was cast out, the Grand Master issued an order that he be killed."

She stared at him, stunned. "He was a *monk*?"

Kadar burst out laughing. "I found it surprising, too, until I came to know him. He has many more sides to his character than you would think."

A vision of Ware sitting in that firelit room while Tasza caressed him with her mouth came back to her. "A monk?" she repeated.

"I'm told sometimes a battle can be as stirring as a woman, and the Knights Templar are a special breed."

"Why did they cast him out?"

His smile faded. "You will have to ask him."

"I don't have to ask." Sensuality breathed in every line

of Ware of Dundragon's body. He would not have been able to bear abstinence. "He is no monk."

"Not now." Kadar tilted his head. "I've told you what danger Ware was fleeing. What are you running from, Thea of Dimas?"

She stiffened at the sudden attack. She had been so absorbed in unraveling the complex personality of Kadar and trying to comprehend the astonishing truth he had told her regarding Lord Ware that she had been caught off guard. "I came here to open my own house of embroidery."

"A laudable ambition. But this land is hard for a woman alone."

"All lands are hard for a woman alone, but I have a skill that's respected here. I'll be able to find a place for myself until I have enough money to open my own house. The Damascenes have been trading embroideries for a long time, and they're truly excellent."

"But not as good as yours?"

She shook her head. "They lack imagination. A true artist designs as well as executes. The Damascenes are still doing the same embroideries they did a century ago."

"How long have you been a craftsman?"

"Since I was a very small child. I can't remember anything else. They first put me to knotting rugs, but my mother convinced him I would be better at embroidery."

"Him?"

Every answer led to another trap. The only safety was in not answering at all. She turned away from the cages and moved toward the window. The grounds of the castle were not all stone walls and fortress, as she had thought. To the north stretched a long green, abounding with grass and trees, that fell off abruptly into a steep cliff. "You can see very far from this tower." Her gaze traveled back to the mountains. "What are those houses to the south?"

"That's the village of Jedha. All of the servants and soldiers here at Dundragon were brought from there. Dundragon was given to Ware as payment for services by a Frank lord who found this land too unsafe for his taste. When he went back to France, he took all his people with him, and Ware had to recruit his officers and soldiers from among the Muslims." He shook his head. "The lords who hired Ware could use the excuse that any tool is justified when fighting Satan, but no one wanted to offend the Knights Templar by actually going over to the renegade's camp. It's a dangerous practice to ally yourself with the Temple's enemies."

"Yet you did it."

"I told you, I had no choice. He belongs to me. Besides, living in the shadows with Ware has taught me as much as I learned from the Old Man of the Mountain."

Shadows. But this day seemed bright and clear and without threat. "He surely should be back before dark."

"Yes. If God wills." He joined her at the window, his gaze fixed on the mountain. "If he's not, I'll go searching for him."

Again that intimation of danger. She didn't understand any of these people. Kadar, whom she had thought kind and gentle, had been taught by murderers. Lord Ware, whom she knew to be brutal and ruthless, had evidently risked much to seek out her mulberry leaves. Nothing was clear or reasonable in this new life into which she had been tossed.

But this disarray was better than the suffocating orderliness in the House of Nicholas. The serenity and concentration that abounded there were necessary to produce fine embroideries, but not the strictures of a cage. Here at Dundragon, she had more freedom, and once she left, the chaos would disappear entirely from her life. She would only have to be patient.

"You can trust us, you know," Kadar said quietly. "We know what it is to be hunted."

She could not trust anyone. She did not have the right when Selene was also at risk.

When she did not answer, Kadar turned away from the window. "It's going to be a long day. Would you like to play a game of chess?"

"I don't know how to play chess."

"You prefer another game?"

She shook her head. "I don't know how to play any games."

"Ah, but games are very important. They stretch the mind and ease the heart."

"I don't need them. I have my work."

He took her elbow and urged her toward the door. "I think you need them more than most people. Come, I will teach you chess."

Ware finally found a grove of mulberry trees after noon of that day. It was not soon enough for him. He was hot, his head was aching and his temper correspondingly raw.

He sliced a huge branch off a tree with one stroke of his sword and watched it fall to the ground. He dismounted, then began plucking the leaves and throwing them into the basket.

Mother of Christ, he felt like a damsel picking flowers on May Day. This was no task for a knight.

How much was enough? Every time he bent down, his helmeted head felt as if it were going to roll off. He finished stripping the branch. He glowered at the contents of the basket; the leaves barely covered the bottom. He cut another branch and then another.

Enough. If that wasn't sufficient, the damn worms could starve to death. He closed the lid and lifted the basket back onto the saddle.

He was being watched.

He froze in the act of fastening the basket, every muscle rigid.

Vaden.

He always knew when it was Vaden. The bond between them had never been broken; it had only become twisted. God, how ironic to die like this. Not in battle, but gathering leaves for a bunch of silkworms.

He leaned his head on the saddle, waiting. Jesus, he was weary of it all. It seemed as if he had been waiting a lifetime for this final moment. He suddenly felt a wild, reckless desire for it to be over.

He whirled on his heel, tore off his helmet, and gazed up at the rocky hillside. "Here I am, Vaden," he shouted. "A clear shot. Aim for the eye. It's surer than trying to find an opening in the armor."

But he had seen one of Vaden's arrows find such an opening. He possessed strength, a steady hand, and a deadly eye. Vaden was the finest bowman Ware had ever known.

He stood waiting, head lifted.

No sound. No whir of an arrow in flight.

But Vaden was *there*. Why didn't he strike?

He slowly put his helmet back on his head. He waited again before he mounted.

It seemed Vaden was not in the mood for killing this day.

But Vaden was not driven by moods, only by cool reason.

Ware waited once again, giving Vaden another chance, before nudging his horse toward the path leading up the mountain to Dundragon.

He could still loose the arrow.

Vaden kept his vision narrowed on the exact spot in Ware's back where the armor joined.

He slowly lowered the bow.

If he'd been going to loose that arrow, he would have done so when Ware had been standing staring up at him in despair.

He could have killed him and it would have been over. He could have returned to the Temple, and the secret would have been safe.

The Grand Master would have said not taking that shot was a betrayal of the Temple. With Ware dead and unable to defend Dundragon, he would have given the order for the stronghold to be razed to the ground and all its inhabitants murdered.

Vaden returned the arrow to the quiver on his saddle. He had never been guided by the Grand Master, and he would not be now. He was the chosen executioner, and he would judge for himself who would have to die and who could live. He didn't know for certain that Ware had revealed to anyone what he had seen in the storehouse. God knew enough blood had been spilled since that night.

He put spurs to his horse and reluctantly veered left to the path leading south. From there he could cut across the valley and be in Acre by tomorrow night. Another message had come from the Grand Master summoning him to a meeting at his encampment outside Acre. He had ignored the first one, but the man's temper was explosive and erratic, so he had best try to soothe it before irreparable damage was done.

He glanced back at the denuded branches on the ground beneath the tree and frowned in puzzlement.

What the devil had Ware been about?

"He's here!" Kadar pushed back his chair, the game forgotten. "I hear the drawbridge." He hurried out of the hall.

Thea stood up and followed him. She found she was experiencing the same relief Kadar was exhibiting. She had been conscious of Kadar's lack of attention for the past two hours, and his worry had been contagious.

Ware was riding through the gates as she came down the steps to the courtyard to stand beside Kadar. The setting sun was behind him, and he was only a massive dark silhouette against a blazing sky as he walked his horse toward them.

Kadar shaded his eyes with his hand as he looked up at Ware. "He didn't follow?"

"He followed. He held his hand." He loosened the basket and dropped it to the courtyard. "Your leaves."

"Why?" Kadar asked.

"How do I know?" He dismounted and turned to Thea. "Are they the right ones?"

She knelt on the stones and opened the lid. She breathed a sigh of relief as she saw the tooth-shaped leaves. "Yes."

"Enough?"

She nodded. "They'll last me at least a month. By that time I should be settled in Damascus and able to find more."

"Long before that time." He turned and moved toward the steps. "I want her out of here, Kadar. I want you both out of here."

"You're always so inhospitable." Kadar followed him toward the steps. "But I forgive you this time. You're clearly exhausted from picking all those heavy mulberry leaves."

Ware took off his helmet and faced Kadar. "I shouldn't have let you stay this long. It's time for you to go."

He looked tired, Thea thought. He still held himself with rigid straightness, but deep lines engraved either side of his mouth and fanned out from his eyes, which held a strange hollowness. It was as if the weariness had passed from his body into his soul.

She said impulsively, "You need a bath and a night's rest." She jumped to her feet, snatched up her basket, and hurried toward him. "I'll go tell Jasmine to have water heated." She turned to Kadar. "Take him to his chamber and get him out of that armor."

"Kadar doesn't need to take me anywhere."

"Nonsense. You look as if you're going to fall down at any minute." She glanced at his neck and shook her head.

"And your muscles are knotted and twisted. I can help with easing that pain."

"I have no pain."

She snorted derisively. "Help him with his armor, Kadar. I have no patience with lies." She moved past him into the castle and encountered Jasmine coming down the steps. "Hot water for Lord Ware."

Jasmine gave her a cool glance. "I gave the command when I saw him ride into the courtyard. You don't have to tell me my duty. I know how to care for my lord. I'll send for Tasza to attend him."

"I will attend him."

"I will send for Tasza," she repeated.

"No." She tried to hold on to her temper. "He's done me a service this day and I'll be the one to ease him." As she met Jasmine's stony expression, her irritation flared. "I've no desire to take Tasza's place in your master's bed. I merely wish to make him comfortable."

Jasmine studied her for a moment, and then the faintest smile touched her lips. "Are you a virgin that you don't know that the best way to make a man comfortable is to rid him of lust?" Then her eyes widened as she read Thea's expression. "Truly? Your manner was so bold, I thought—" She frowned. "Why did you not tell me? I have better things to do than worry about a threat that doesn't exist. Tasza need not be concerned about a woman who has no skills."

Thea stared at her in indignation. "I should not have to tell every passerby on the streets that I've never had a man."

"You should have told *this* passerby . . . if you wished a comfortable stay here." Jasmine proceeded down the stairs. "You may tend my lord. Perhaps you should even couple with him. Once your veil is broken, he will lose interest and Tasza's skills will shine in contrast."

"How many times must I tell you? I don't wish to couple with him."

"My lord's chamber is two doors from your own. I will have Omar bring the water. You will find unguents and salves in the chest in the corridor."

Thea stared after her in helpless exasperation. She felt as if she had tried to stop the flow of a river by standing in its path. Jasmine's sudden reversal in attitude was just as bewildering as everything else at Dundragon.

Well, at least Jasmine would not hinder her today. Heaven knew if she would change her mind again tomorrow. Thea turned and ran up the steps to find the unguents.

Ware was already in the tub when Thea came into his chamber. His eyes were closed and his head was resting on the high back of the tub.

Kadar, sitting cross-legged on the hearth across the room, smiled at her. "Caution. His temper is not good. If you don't please him, he'll probably drown you."

"I've never seen him when his temper was good." She came brusquely forward, set the salves and unguents on the floor, and moved a stool beside the tub. "So I've nothing with which to compare." She tossed a handful of sweet-smelling leaves into the water. "But at least he will have a pleasant scent."

"Go away," Ware said, without opening his eyes. "I have servants aplenty to bathe me."

"You may bathe yourself. That's not why I'm here." She sat down on the stool and poured oil into her palms. "This will hurt at first."

Kadar instantly rose to his feet. "I think I'll go order supper brought up. I detest the sound of screams."

"Coward," Ware said.

"Sage," Kadar corrected as he left the room.

Thea's fingers dug into the bunched muscles of Ware's neck.

"Ouch!" He tried to turn his head to glare at her.

"Stay still." Her fingers dug deeper. "The muscles will ease presently."

"Presently?" He flinched. "You're trying to torture me."

"If I were trying to torture you, I'd leave you with these knots. Now be silent and let me work."

"I'll have bruises tomorrow."

"They won't last. I had bruises when I woke yesterday, and today they're fading."

"Bruises? Where?"

"My shoulders. You were not gentle the night you found me."

He scowled. "I think you mean to make me feel guilt. I saw no bruises."

Heat rushed through her as she remembered that insolent glance. "You weren't looking at my shoulders."

He was silent a long time. "No, I wasn't. I was looking at your— Christ! Do you have a dagger back there? That felt like a knife thrust."

"Good. The pain must come before the easing."

"Are you sure you're not just exacting vengeance?"

"I would not do that." But she had to admit it gave her a certain amount of pleasure to have him helpless in her hands. "I believe in the payment of debts. You did me a great service. I must repay you."

He gasped as another twinge of agony shot through him. "By trying to drive me mad with pain?"

"No, I told you that I would make you a gift. A tunic with embroidery so beautiful that it will stun everyone who sees it."

"Keep your gift. I'm a plain man. I would never wear such a garment."

She thought about it. "Then I'll make you a banner. A warrior should have his own banner. What design should I embroider on it? A falcon?"

"It doesn't matter. Save your efforts. I fight for gold, not glory."

"A banner," she said firmly. "And every knight in Christendom will envy you."

"Then they would be fools," he said with sudden violence. "I'm not a man to be envied."

She paused in midmotion and then resumed kneading. "You are rich. You have a fine castle. Surely there are many who would envy you."

He was silent.

"Well, at any rate, they'll envy you your banner."

His muscles relaxed a trifle. "You're certain you can create something so wondrous?"

"Of course."

He chuckled. "I should not have left you alone with Kadar. He, too, believes he can work miracles."

"Not miracles. I just do splendid work." The muscles of his neck were loosening, so she lessened the pressure. "And one should not be modest about one's work. Someone might believe you less than you are."

"A terrible fate."

"Your neck is feeling better?"

"Yes. You have strong hands." He added deliberately, "Not the hands of a lady who sits at an embroidery loom."

"I knotted the silk in carpets when I was a child. My mother persuaded Nicholas to let her train me in embroidery, but it was almost too late. She had to work three years to straighten the muscles of my hands and fingers."

"Straighten?"

"Children's hands and bones are not fully formed. When they're set to working the carpets for long hours, the muscles become cramped and twisted and the hands crippled for anything but the task."

"Good God. Then why do they set children to do such work?"

"Children's hands are small and the task is delicate," she said matter-of-factly. "Everyone uses children for the carpet making."

"And will you?"

"No, I will not use children at all." She added with satisfaction, "The muscles are almost unknotted. Now it should begin to feel good."

"It does." He was silent a moment. "How did your mother work with your hands?"

"Like this. Every evening she pulled and stretched and kneaded. We were given a rest from the embroidery loom every four hours, and she made me open and close them over and over."

"Why the devil did she let them put you to that task to begin with?" he asked harshly.

"I think you're eased." She started to remove her hands. "I'll tell Omar to bring more hot—"

His hand shot over his shoulder and caught her wrist, his gaze still straight ahead. "Why?"

"Let me go."

He pulled her hand forward until it was in his field of vision. "Small," he murmured. "Clean, well shaped." His thumb rubbed one of the calluses on her forefinger. "But strong. I like your hands, Thea of Dimas." He brought it to his lips and lazily licked the palm. "I would have been very angry if they had been crippled."

She could scarcely breathe. "You would not have known. We would never have met. I'd never have dared to come to Damascus if I'd had only the skills I learned as a child."

He licked her palm again. "Why would your mother be so cruel as to let her child be used so brutally?"

"My mother wasn't cruel." Each time he touched her palm, a strange tingling jolt went up her arm and through her body. "Don't . . . do that."

"The oil on your hands is lemon flavored. I like the taste. Why did she let you be put to that task?"

"She . . . had no choice. She begged Nicholas to—" She was saying too much. Dear heavens, she was feeling too much. She jerked her hand away and jumped to her feet. "Why are you questioning me? That time has nothing to do with now. My mother is dead."

"How did she die?"

"Of the fever. Several women died that winter." She moved hurriedly toward the door. "I will get Omar. . . ."

"Thea."

She stopped with her hand on the door. "I will answer no more questions."

"I . . . thank you."

Her gaze flew back to him. His big body gleamed like

burnished bronze in the water, but it was his expression that held her. Gentleness from the beast?

He quickly lowered his gaze to the water. He said gruffly, "Though I had no need of your services. I was only a little stiff." He scowled. "Well, maybe more than a little."

A smile tugged at her lips. He sounded like a cross little boy.

"And I don't want Omar." He reached for the soap. "Send me Tasza."

Her smile vanished. He was not a little boy. He was a rude, lustful brute who used women only as toys.

"As you wish." The door slammed behind her.

Jasmine was waiting in the hall. Her gaze immediately went to the damp bodice of Thea's gown. "You are wet. Did he put his hands on you?"

"No," she said curtly. "I was leaning against the tub. He didn't touch me." Yet she felt as if he had. Her breasts felt heavy and ripe, and the palm of her hand still tingled. "I told you that was not my intention." She turned and moved down the hall toward her chamber. "He wants Tasza."

"Good. I will go tell her."

Thea closed her door, then moved toward the window and threw open the shutters. The breeze rushed in, cooling her hot cheeks. Why did she respond in this manner to that man? He was rough and had the barbaric sensuality of a wild animal and was everything that was alien to her. She had thought that if ever a man were to draw her, he would be someone kind and gentle, handsome and smooth as a length of Chinese silk. Ware of Dundragon was more like strong, supple leather studded with spikes. It had been a mistake to try to help him.

Yet she could not have done anything else. He had kept his promise and given her what she needed at evidently some risk to himself. She owed him far more than a momentary easing.

"I've brought you another gown."

Thea turned to see Jasmine standing in the open doorway. The woman shut the door, came forward, and draped a blue cotton gown on the back of the chair. "You cannot wear that one every day. You will soil it, as you did in Lord Ware's bath."

"It's almost dry now." That sounded ungracious so she sought to make amends. Quickly glancing at the gown, she commented, "It's a pretty color."

"Lord Ware gave it to Tasza, but it does not become her."

"Tasza?" Thea repeated, startled. "She offered me her gown?"

Jasmine shrugged. "She won't miss it. She has many gowns. When Lord Ware brings a woman to his house from the village, he gives her many presents. When she returns to Jedha, she has a fine dowry with which to make a good marriage."

"But would a man accept a woman who—" She stopped, afraid to offend Jasmine. It was clear the servant had a fondness for Tasza. "In Constantinople men prize women who are untouched."

Jasmine smiled with a touch of bitterness. "It is the same here, but Jedha is a very poor village. We have no fertile land, and before Lord Ware came to Dundragon, we barely managed to eke out a living in these barren hills. He took the young men and gave them fine armor and taught them how to fight. He gave the older men and women a place here as his servants."

"And brought the younger women here to be his lemen," Thea said dryly.

"Well, why not? He never demands a woman who is wed or a girl who has never known a man. Our women come eagerly to Dundragon. He uses them only for a few months before he sends them back with enough gold to assure that they'll have suitors aplenty."

"Is that what will happen to Tasza?"

"No!" Jasmine said quickly. "Tasza is different. She will stay here. She knows how to please him in ways the others cannot. He won't grow tired of her."

"It's true she is very beautiful."

Jasmine proudly lifted her chin. "Yes, and I taught her to play the lyre. She's not very clever, but she has a good heart and is very determined. She will see that he chooses to keep her here and send the others away."

"She does not want the dowry?"

Jasmine abruptly turned away. "Take off your gown and try on this one. Since Tasza is bigger in the hips, it may need an adjustment."

Thea shook her head. "I could not take her gown without her permission."

"You have my permission. It is enough."

Thea shook her head again.

Jasmine stared at her in exasperation. "You're very stubborn. I have the right to give you the gown. Tasza would not even be here if I hadn't brought her to my lord's attention."

"It is still her gown and not yours."

"Tasza would give you the gown if I told her to do so. She's a good, obedient daughter."

Thea's eyes widened in shock. "She's your daughter?"

Jasmine nodded curtly. "Now, try on the gown."

Thea abstractedly stripped off her white gown and slipped the blue one over her head. "And you brought her to Lord Ware's bed?"

"You think I made a whore of my own daughter."

"I didn't say that."

"You don't have to say it," Jasmine said bitterly. "You don't know what it is to be so poor that you can't find even a bit of bread to put on the table. I didn't make Tasza a whore. I didn't even know she had sold herself on the streets of Jedha until it was done. She did it to make sure that we would both survive." She paused. "She had not even reached her twelfth year."

Thea felt sick. "There was nothing you could do?"

"My husband died the year after she was born, and we had no man to help us. There was only one kind of work available for a woman alone in Jedha." She stared defiantly into Thea's eyes. "I also sold myself, but I grew older and men like young, smooth bodies. Tasza decided it was her duty to help me as I had helped her."

"I am sorry," Thea said gently. "I meant no offense."

"I'm not offended. I'm proud of my Tasza. I don't care that the women of the village flinch from us as if we were lepers." She pinched the material of the gown on either side of Thea's waist. "As I thought, it will need to be pinned. Take it off again."

Thea obeyed and handed her the gown. "Does Lord Ware know she is your daughter?"

Jasmine shook her head. "At first I feared he might think my judgment clouded when I called her to his attention. Now it would not matter, but he does not need to know."

"What will you do if Lord Ware does send her back to the village?"

"It will not happen. It cannot happen."

Thea was not as sure as she remembered the offhand manner with which he had spoken to Tasza. "But you said he would give her a fine dowry."

"Are you stupid?" Jasmine asked fiercely. "She's not like those other women. She's a *whore.* Men do not wed whores, no matter how high the dowry. She could only live on it until it was gone and then go back to the streets. She must stay here, where she's safe."

Safe with Ware of Dundragon? The woman was truly grasping at straws, but Thea could hardly blame her. Thea had never thought of her own lot as fortunate, but she had never been hungry, and she had learned a way to earn her bread that wasn't dependent on selling her body. She had never realized how sheltered she had been at the House of Nicholas. "I hope she will be safe wherever she is."

Jasmine took the gown and draped it over her arm. "I will see that she's safe." She moved toward the door. "I will have the gown ready for tomorrow."

"But ask Tasza if I may have it."

Jasmine frowned in disgust. "Very well. Though it's a waste of time. She always does what I tell her."

"I meant it, you know." Ware bit into a wing. "You should leave Dundragon. You've been here too long."

Kadar shook his head. "I've not been here long enough. If I had, your manners would be too polished to try to cast me out so rudely. You clearly still have need of me."

"I don't need anyone." Ware pushed the plate away and leaned back in his chair. "Where's the woman?"

"She declined the honor of our presence. She prefers to eat in her chamber. You must have been particularly surly to our guest. She was only trying to help you."

"I wasn't surly." He thought about it and then added, "For me."

"Which doesn't say a great deal." Kadar reached for his wine. "Did she help you?"

"Yes." By the time she had finished, his muscles had felt so soft and melting, he had thought he would dissolve into the water. But that had changed in the space of a heartbeat after he had taken her hand. By the saints, he had not been soft then. "But Tasza helped me more." It was not true. Tasza had eased his lust, but he had been left curiously unsatisfied. "I want you to take the Greek woman to Damascus day after tomorrow. Find her a place in a fine shop and stay with her until you're sure she's safely established." He took a drink of wine. "And then go your own way. Don't come back here."

"This is a fine wine," Kadar said. "I don't think I could be content with a lesser stock now." He moved to the hearth and curled up in his favorite place before the fire. "I taught Thea to play chess today. She's very clever but has curious gaps in learning. She can cipher and read and write. She speaks Greek, Arabic, and French. Yet she has never learned to play a game, never heard a troubadour tell a tale, never seen anyone dance or danced herself. She knows what is going on in the world, but it's as if she learned it behind the walls of a convent."

Ware's hand tightened on the goblet as he remembered Thea's matter-of-fact words regarding her work on the carpets at the House of Nicholas. "Not unless the good sisters' discipline is crueler than I can imagine."

"And I've told you I think she's running away from something," Kadar said. "If she's as skilled as she claims, she might be considered valuable enough to follow."

"Once she's safe in Damascus, she's no longer my responsibility. I'll cut all ties."

"Some ties cannot be broken. You saved her life."

"I'll cut all ties," he repeated.

"Vaden held his hand," Kadar said softly. "It could mean the danger is over."

Ware knew that Kadar didn't understand. He had tried to warn him without telling him too much but had succeeded only in making Kadar believe the threat less than it was. The danger would never be over, even when Ware was dead. "Go away from Dundragon. Go to Egypt. Go north to China. Just get away from me."

As if he hadn't spoken, Kadar said, "I think we must find out what threatens her before I take her to Damascus. It should take at least a week. I would hate to have you be forced to go rescue her at some later time."

"I would not be forced to—" He broke off as he met Kadar's bland gaze. It was no use, he realized in frustration. Kadar would think and do exactly as he pleased. "You're leaving day after tomorrow." He pushed his chair back and stood up. "I'm going to the battlements."

"And I'll stay here by the fire and drink this fine wine." He leaned back against the stones of the fireplace. "And plan how to convince Thea it's safe to confide in us . . . in the next week."

* * *

No fire burned on the third mountain.

Ware's hands slowly clenched into fists at his sides as he looked out into the darkness.

Something was wrong.

Kadar would have said Vaden's absence was proof that the danger was lessening.

He would have been wrong. The danger never lessened, it only changed.

Where had Vaden gone?

"I'm disappointed in you." Grand Master Gerard de Ridfort frowned. "There has been no opportunity?"

Vaden didn't answer directly. "He keeps himself surrounded by soldiers. Wouldn't you?"

"Every day that he lives the threat grows. He must have already told this Kadar."

"Perhaps."

"And what of the other members of the household?"

Vaden shrugged. "No danger. Ware's officers fear him—they don't love him. He keeps women at the castle for use but never longer than three months. Then they're sent back to their village with a handsome reward. He keeps himself distant from the servants. He keeps himself distant from everyone."

"There *is* danger," he muttered. "Then you have nothing new to report?"

For a fleeting instant Vaden remembered the puzzling branches lying on the ground before he shook his head. "Everything is the same."

The Grand Master's fist crashed down on the table. "It must not remain the same. Do you hear me? He must be killed. It's been two years. It should have been done by now. I chose you because I thought you his match. I didn't know you were a fool."

"A fool?" Vaden said softly.

"A fool and an ill-bred whoreson who—" He broke off as he met Vaden's gaze. He took a step back. "You dare to threaten me?"

"Threaten? Have I uttered threats? I'm merely standing here." Vaden inclined his head in mock obeisance and turned on his heel. "But now I must return to my duty. I'm sure Ware misses me when I'm gone."

"Don't disappoint me again, Vaden," Gerard de Ridfort snarled. "It's been too long."

"Then set someone else to play cat to the mouse."

"You know I cannot. The matter is too delicate to give to anyone else." He paused. "Your father will be very proud of you if you succeed in this task."

"I will succeed in time. My time." Vaden left the tent.

He paused outside to breathe deep of the clean, cool air. He always felt suffocated when in the Grand Master's presence. By all the saints, de Ridfort was a vainglorious fool, full of fanaticism and pride. Did he think Vaden would be swayed by that last remark? He was not doing this for the Temple or for his father. He was doing it because it had to be done. God help them all if Ware's death was left in the hands of the Grand Master.

The Grand Master threw himself into a chair and gazed broodingly at the door through which Vaden had just passed.

Arrogant whoreson. How dare he speak to him with

such a lack of respect? He was the Grand Master. Kings and princes curried Gerard de Ridfort's favor, and this knight with no heritage or name had looked at him with contempt.

After Ware was dead, Vaden would follow.

Vaden's father might question the death, but it would be explained as a necessary thing—that Vaden knew too much and had become careless. . . .

But at the moment Ware of Dundragon was the problem. It was maddeningly irritating that the Grand Master himself could not touch the traitor. Ware was a thorn pricking him, and he would no longer tolerate it.

Dundragon might be too powerful to be overcome at this time, but de Ridfort must do something to show that bastard that he was not out of reach of the temple.

Chapter Four

THE FIRE BURNED BRIGHTLY on the third mountain.

Vaden was back.

Ware's hands closed on the stone wall of the battlement. He should not feel this relief. Vaden was always a threat.

But it was a threat to which he had grown accustomed. Vaden was as much as part of the fabric of his life now as in the past. He had grown almost comfortable with the knowledge that Vaden would be there, watching, waiting.

Until the time he decided to attack.

Well, that time was not now. After three days' absence Vaden had returned to the mountain.

Laughter.

He turned to look down into the courtyard. He had noticed that Thea and Kadar had made a habit of taking a stroll in the courtyard in the cool of the evening. They were now standing talking to the young boy whose task was to light the torches. The boy... He remembered he had intended to send the lad home but had been distracted. He called, "Abdul."

His sergeant broke off his conversation with one of the guards and hurried forward from the other end of the battlement.

Ware gestured to the boy. "He's too young. Send him home."

"Haroun is a good lad. I thought— His father is dead. He needs the money to support his mother."

Ware scowled. "I can't be expected to support the entire village. Am I now to take babies away from their mothers? Send him home."

Abdul nodded and turned away.

"Tell him he can come back in a few years' time."

Abdul nodded again.

"And see that his mother doesn't want until he reaches the proper age."

A broad grin lit Abdul's face. "Yes, my lord."

"And don't do this again. No younger than ten and six."

"Yes, my lord." Abdul hurried back to the soldier on the battlements.

Laughter again.

He glanced down at the courtyard. She was smiling at Haroun, and he was looking at her as if she burned as bright as that torch in his hand.

He might well be right. She exuded a fire and strength he had never seen in another woman. Even in her most vulnerable moments she had shown a courage he would have applauded in any of his soldiers.

She and Kadar were walking with Haroun to light the torches by the front door.

Even her walk was different from that of other women. Her stride was graceful but purposeful, with a touch of almost militant boldness. What life had shaped that boldness?

He frowned as he realized where his thoughts had led him. Let Kadar wonder about her, he would not. He would keep her at the same distance as he did everyone else.

She threw back her head and laughed again. The sound carried full-bodied and rich on the evening air. She never laughed when in his presence. She was always wary and tense, as if she were afraid he'd spring at her. Perhaps she should be wary. He *wanted* to spring on her. He wanted to loosen her braid and cover his naked body with that fair, silky hair. He wanted to cup her breasts in his hands and spread her thighs and go deep within her.

Christ, he was hardening just thinking about it.

So he would not think about it. She was only a woman, like any other. He would call for a woman to sooth his lust and dismiss the Greek from his mind.

"Today I only light the torches, but someday I shall be a great soldier," Haroun boasted. "Just like Lord Ware."

Thea smiled indulgently. The boy was truly irresistible, with those burning dark eyes and endearing smile. "I'm sure you're a very great lighter of torches. There's time for the rest."

His smile vanished and he shook his head. "I must do it right away. I have responsibilities."

"And one of them is lighting the torches," Kadar said.

"Abdul will not be pleased if they're not lit by the time darkness has fallen."

Haroun gave him a stricken glance. "At once, Lord Kadar."

A smile still lingered on Thea's lips as she watched the young boy dash away to the ladder leading to the battlement. She enjoyed the few minutes' chat with Haroun every evening. He was so proud of his place in this grim fortress.

"We should go in," Kadar said. "It grows cool."

"In a moment." Her gaze followed Haroun as he went from torch to torch, leaving a trail of fire in his wake. Children always left brightness where they passed. She murmured, "He reminds me of Selene."

"Who is Selene?"

The question brought her abruptly back to the present. She turned and started up the steps. "You're right, it's growing cool."

"Do you think I'm going to ride off and capture this Selene if you tell me who she is?" Kadar asked as he followed her. "What must I say to prove I wish only what is best for you? Am I not the most charming and kindhearted of men?"

He was both of those things, but he was also the most persistent man she had ever met. During the past three days he had found a way to insinuate at least one subtle inquiry into every conversation. "If you were as kindhearted as you claim, you wouldn't plague me with questions I don't wish to answer."

"But that's only an example of my kindness. If you were as old and experienced as me, you'd realize that you should rely on my judgment in this."

She snorted. "You're perhaps two years older than I am."

"Ah, Thea, I was older than you when I was in the cradle."

She opened her lips to argue with him and then shut them again. In spite of his flippant remarks and smiling face, she still sometimes caught a glimpse of the Kadar she had seen when he had shown her his falcons.

Kadar chuckled. "If I'd *had* a cradle. We were too poor. I slept on the floor of our cottage, wrapped in a blanket. I think that was why I walked so soon. I was afraid the rats would eat me if I didn't run away from them."

She shivered. "That is not funny."

"No, but it's better to laugh at such things than dwell on them." He paused. "Did you worry about the rats when you were a child, Thea?"

"No." Nicholas would have been enraged if there had been any rats near his beautiful silks. She suddenly realized he had done it again—slipped another question into the conversation. She asked in exasperation, "When will you take me to Damascus? I'm well now."

"Soon. There is no hurry."

He might not be in a hurry, but Selene was still in Constantinople. The longer Thea took to establish herself, the longer Selene would have to bear the life at Nicholas's house.

"I wish to leave tomorrow."

"We will see. Would you like to start a game of chess before you go to bed?"

"No." She cast a glance at Haroun, who had just finished lighting the last torch on the battlements. He smiled and waved at her. She felt another pang as she lifted her hand in response. She wanted Selene here now. She wanted to see her smile and know she was well and happy.

No, she was lying to herself. She was also being selfish. Selene was the only person she loved, and she needed someone to love in this alien land.

"You look sad." Kadar urged softly, "Tell me your thoughts."

The man would not stop.

"I will *not* tell you my thoughts." She strode into the castle. "I'm going to bed."

Two nights later she noticed it was not Haroun who was lighting the torches but one of the soldiers.

"He is gone," Kadar answered when she asked about it. "He went back to his village last night. Ware wasn't pleased with him. He was too young."

"But he was so proud. . . ." Anger flared through her. "How old would he have to be to light the torches and run errands?"

"He was too young," Kadar repeated. "This is not a place for children."

No, she thought bitterly, it was a place where women were kept only to couple and serve and men were taught to wage war. "He should not have sent him away."

Kadar shrugged. "He thought it best."

Her gaze lifted to the shadowy figure on the battlements. Ware was always there this time of evening, looking out at the mountains.

Ware had thought it best, and a boy's life had been changed. Ware felt lust, and a woman rushed to his bed.

Ware refused permission, and the gates would not be opened for her.

By the saints, she could do nothing about altering his power over the others, but she would not let him hold her there.

She turned and ran across the courtyard.

"Where are you going?" Kadar called, startled.

She didn't answer as she flew through the hall, then up the steps and finally the long, twisting stairway.

She threw open the door and strode out onto the battlements. She stopped for a moment before approaching him, catching her breath and gathering her arguments.

Sweet Jesus, he looked alone. She could almost touch the wall of terrible isolation that surrounded him.

Well, if he was alone, it was his own doing. A man could expect nothing else if he pushed everyone away from him. She would not feel sorry for him. She had her own worries and he was one of them.

She strode forward until she stood beside him.

"I must talk to you," Thea said.

Ware's gaze never left the mountains. "It's late. Go to your bed."

"It's not late. It's been *five* days. Why are you keeping me here?"

He still didn't look at her. "Kadar says you're not healed."

She snorted. "Even my burn is gone." She moved closer to him. "I cannot linger here any longer. I must start my work."

He didn't answer.

She wanted to shake him. "Why not let me go? You

don't want me here. I've scarcely seen you since you brought me my mulberry leaves."

He glanced at her. "Did you wish me to amuse you?"

She spoke through clenched teeth. "No, I don't wish you to amuse me. You wouldn't know how. All you know is war and coupling."

"War is not amusing, but coupling can be—" He shook his head. "No, that's not amusing either. When the need is upon me, it's too intense to smile about."

He seldom smiled at anything but Kadar's quips. Yet he had smiled that night she had come upon him with Tasza. Did only drunkenness rid him of grimness? No, even that night she had been aware of bitterness surrounding him like a dark cloud.

"If you want amusement, go to Kadar," he said. "Stay away from me."

"I'll *not* stay away from you. Not until you tell Kadar to take me to Damascus."

"He wants you here. He thinks you'll not be safe until he knows everything about you. Tell him what he wants to know and you'll go to Damascus the next day." He met her stare. "As for me, I don't care where you came from or what dangers you face. You don't belong here. You're right, I know only war and coupling. You cannot fight for me, and that only leaves one use." His gaze went to her breasts, and he said without inflection, "I grow hard when I look at you. If you stay here much longer, I'll probably take you to my bed."

The crude boldness shocked her, but no more than her own physical response. Her breasts were swelling beneath his gaze as if he were stroking her. She could feel her nipples hardening, pressing against the soft cotton of her gown. Could he see that betraying response in the bright flare of the torches? she wondered. Probably. His gaze was narrowing, his mouth curving with that same heavy sensuality she had seen in the hall that night.

"Every time I take a woman now, I want it to be you. At first I thought it because I was growing bored with Tasza, but I've tried two others and it's the same." He said thickly, "I want them all to be you. I want you to open your thighs and let me stroke you. I remember how soft your woman's fleece looked. I want to feel it against me as I move in and out of—"

"Stop." Her voice was strangled. "This is not . . . decent."

"Look at yourself. You want it."

"No, I don't." She tried to steady her voice. "I'll not be one of your women. I won't be any man's property. I'm going to have my own embroidery house and be free to live life as I please."

His gaze at last lifted from her breasts to her face. "Then stay away from me." He turned back to the mountains. "And tell Kadar what he wants to know. I've let Kadar have his way in this, but I've little patience. If you stay much longer, I will have *my* way."

"It's none of your concern what life I left behind me. If you don't let me go, I'll find a way of leaving anyway. I'll not let you—What is that glow?"

His gaze never left the third mountain. "Just a campfire."

The answer barely registered as she leaned over the battlement to see better. "No, not there. To the south."

He stiffened. "My God." He turned on his heel and strode toward the door leading off the battlement.

She hurried after him. "What is it?"

"Jedha. The village is burning."

"The village . . ."

The families of all the soldiers who guarded this fortress lived in the village.

He had sent Haroun back to Jedha.

She flew down the steps after him. "I'm going with you."

"No."

"I'm *going.*"

He turned to look at her. "I've no time for this. Do what you wish. God knows, you may be as safe there as here."

"I'll get salves and linens." She ran down the corridor to the scullery. "Jasmine!"

The courtyard was filled with armored soldiers and milling horses when Thea rushed out the door a short time later.

Her gaze searched the courtyard until she found Kadar.

"Kadar!"

He walked his horse up to her.

"May I ride with you?"

He glanced at Ware, who was now mounting his horse across the courtyard. "I think you should stay here. We don't know what we'll encounter at Jedha."

"Don't be foolish. We'll encounter people who are hurt. Jasmine is following with a wagon full of bandages, salves, and food." She held up her arms for him to lift her onto his horse. When he made no motion to help her, she added, "And Lord Ware said I could go."

"He did?" Kadar's expression became thoughtful. "I wonder . . ." He bent down and lifted her onto his horse.

"You are sure?" He galloped across the courtyard and reined in when he reached Ware. "Is this wise?"

"It may not make any difference. I'm leaving a force here, but it may be too small. . . ." He shrugged. "She may be safer outside the gates."

"But if it's a trap?"

"I don't know. I'd have to go anyway. That's my village that's burning." He waved his hand and galloped over the drawbridge with the column of soldiers thundering after him.

"What did he mean?" Thea asked as Kadar followed the soldiers. "A trap?"

"I don't think it's a trap," Kadar said reassuringly. "Ware has made sure his army is stronger than the Knights Templars'. That's why they haven't attacked him yet. They're waiting for an opportunity."

He had mentioned the Knights Templars' pursuit of Ware before, but it seemed impossible they would burn a village to draw him out. After all, they were monks, servants of God. "Fires start all the time. A careless mistake with a cooking flame . . ." He did not seem to be listening. "How far is it?"

"Over the next hill. We'll be there soon."

But would it be soon enough to help the villagers? she wondered desperately, her gaze on the red glare lighting the night sky.

The village was ablaze, every house an inferno.

Thea stared in horror at the flaming chaos before them.

Bodies . . . everywhere.

Men, women . . . Dear God, children . . . little children.

"I have to help them. I have to—" She slipped from the saddle.

"Thea!" Kadar called.

She ignored him and ran toward a little girl lying beside a burning hut. She carefully turned the body over. Blood. Dark eyes staring at the sky. Dead.

"You can't help here." Ware's voice came from beside her. "Wait outside the village with Kadar. If there's anyone alive, I'll have them brought to you."

She dazedly stared up at him, still mounted on his horse. "She's dead."

"It was a clean sword thrust," he said quietly. "She didn't suffer."

"Sword . . ." She glanced at the other bodies. She had noticed only the death and devastation, not the means. An arrow protruded from the back of a man across the path. A woman was crumpled against a wall, clutching a wound in her stomach. She could not believe it. "They murdered them?"

"Wait outside the village."

She shook her head. "Someone may be alive. I have to—"

"I gave my soldiers orders for all bodies to be checked for signs of life. This is their village, their people. They won't make mistakes."

Ignoring him, she stood up and moved to a man lying a few feet away. He was dead also. She moved to another lying next to the well in the center of the square. Dead.

Frozen expressions of fear and horror.

Blood.

A woman swollen with child with an arrow in her back.

The smoke from the burning cottages was now so thick, she could barely see.

Kadar was on his knees beside her. "Ware says you must leave this place."

"I will not," she said fiercely. "Someone must be alive. I have to—" Was that a movement? She leaped to her feet and ran toward the slumped figure on the other side of the well. "Haroun?"

The child opened his eyes. "Mama . . ."

"Shh . . . it's all right."

He shook his head and his lids closed again.

But he was still alive. She turned to Kadar. "Take him out of here."

She found only one other survivor of the massacre. An old man who had hidden beneath a wagon. It didn't seem possible that there could be no one else left alive. Perhaps the soldiers had discovered others. . . . She had to keep searching.

Ware jerked her to her feet. "Will you stay here until you burn to death with the corpses?" He lifted her in his arms and strode down the street.

"Let me go." She started to struggle. "I found two alive. There may be more."

"There are no more." His face was completely without expression. "And if there were, we couldn't reach them. The entire village is engulfed." He set her down on her feet. "Take care of her, Jasmine." He was gone again.

Jasmine. She hadn't seen the wagon arrive. She had seen nothing but death and blood and fire.

"You are weeping," Jasmine said. "Are you hurt?"

She hadn't realized she was weeping. She reached up a hand and touched her wet cheek. There didn't seem to be enough tears in the world for what she had just seen. "No, I'm not hurt."

She turned back to the village.

There was no village, only a solid sheet of flame.

"May Allah be merciful," Jasmine's voice was unsteady. "I was not treated with kindness here, but I would not have had this happen. I grew up in this village."

Thea saw several of the soldiers standing with tears running down their cheeks. This was their home, the place of their birth, the people they had loved in that bonfire. She couldn't stand to look at it any longer. She turned back to the wagon. "Did you look at Haroun?"

"He may not live. He's had a sharp blow on the head. The old man, Malik ben Karrah, has only a few burns."

"Did they find anyone else?"

"One man. Amal, the cobbler. He died before I could look at his wounds."

Two alive out of an entire village. She suppressed the wave of sickness that washed over her. She couldn't help anyone if she was ill. She climbed onto the bed of the wagon. "Then let's get back to Dundragon so that we can care for the boy."

"Are you all right?" Kadar was beside the wagon.

She nodded. "But we have to get Haroun back to the castle."

"Not now. Ware has taken some men and gone on ahead to make sure the road is safe. I'm to wait a quarter hour and then escort you back."

She nodded wearily. She couldn't comprehend what had happened here, but she accepted that it would be foolish to place Haroun in a position of danger. "I'll need water to wash the boy's wound."

* * *

It was a somber, grim Dundragon to which they returned. A pall hovered over the castle and the soldiers who guarded it.

"Take him to my chamber," Thea told the soldiers who lifted Haroun out of the wagon. The boy had not awakened during the journey. Perhaps he would never wake again.

No, she would not think that. She slipped out of the wagon and started up the steps.

"Send word to me when he wakes."

The command had issued from Ware standing a few feet away. He was still in full armor, and his expression was the same impassive mask he had worn at the village. Did nothing move him? Thea wondered.

His hardness suddenly enraged her. "Why? So you can send him back to his village to die again?"

He didn't answer for a moment, and his expression never changed. "Send me word."

She turned on her heel and went into the castle.

Haroun did not wake until near dawn the next day.

"Mama . . ."

Thea's hand tightened around his. She would not lie to him. The pain would just be harder to bear later. "There were only two survivors of the fire. You and an old man . . ." She tried to remember the name Jasmine had mentioned. "Malik ben Karrah."

"Fire?"

He had evidently been struck down before the fires had

been set. "There was a fire." She dabbed at his head with a wet cloth. "Try to go back to sleep."

His lids slowly closed. "Yes." Two tears rolled down his cheeks. "Mama . . ."

He was a child again, no longer the little proud soldier who had streaked about the courtyard carrying his torch like a bright banner. She wanted to gather him close as she had Selene on the morning their mother had died, but he was not her own. He belonged to no one now. She swallowed. "I promise it will be better soon."

She stayed there, holding his hand, until he went back to sleep.

"You should go to your own bed," Jasmine said as she set a fresh bowl of water on the table by the bed. "I'll stay with the boy."

Thea shook her head. With his hand still clasped in her own, she felt that leaving him would be a betrayal. "You sleep. You've not rested either."

Jasmine hesitated and then finally nodded. "One of us must show some sense." She moved brusquely toward the door. "I'll tell Tasza to come to you in a few hours and see if you wish to rest. Tasza is good with children."

But not as good as she is with men, Thea thought dryly, then felt a sudden rush of shame. The girl had become a whore when she was a mere child herself. Who was Thea to condemn her for trying to find security in a world that could orphan children like Haroun in one night of horror? "That won't be necessary. Perhaps she could come to see him in a few days when he's better."

"Today."

Thea wearily shook her head as the door closed behind Jasmine. Why had she bothered to argue? The woman would do as she pleased. She supposed she should be grateful that Jasmine had decided it pleased her to help Thea. Heaven knew she had needed support this night.

"The boy will live?"

Thea stiffened when she saw Ware standing in the doorway. He was no longer in armor, but he might as well have been. His face was as hard as a shield.

"I think so."

He came into the chamber. "Jasmine said he woke and spoke to you. I told you to send for me when he woke."

"Why should I? It seems Jasmine runs to you with every bit of news."

His gaze searched Haroun's face. "I want to speak to the boy."

"No." She moved protectively closer. "He's sleeping again. I won't have him disturbed."

"I have no intention of shaking him awake." He sat down in the chair. "I'll wait."

She did not want him there. His calm indifference grated on her control like salt on a wound. The world had ended for so many tonight and he did not care. "It may be hours."

"I'll wait."

He was master there; she could not banish him. But she could ignore him.

It was not necessary. He did not appear to know she was in the chamber. He stared straight ahead at the wall in front of him.

Haroun opened his eyes three hours later. His gaze immediately fastened on Ware. "My lord?" he whispered.

Ware bent forward. "I need something from you, lad. Are you well enough to help me?"

Haroun nodded and then flinched. "But I cannot fight them . . . yet."

"No, I have soldiers aplenty. I need you to tell me something. I need you to think back to when the village was attacked."

"No!" Thea said.

He didn't look at her. "Can you do that for me, Haroun?"

He nodded and closed his eyes. "They came at sundown. I was at the well drawing water for our evening meal. Mama was standing in the doorway." He stopped. "When they rode into the village, she tried to get to me. They . . . the arrow—"

"Stop this." Thea glared at Ware. "There's no need for this cruelty."

"Be quiet." His gaze never left the boy's face. "I don't need to know about your mother, Haroun. Who were the men who attacked? Were they bandits?"

He shook his head. "I don't . . . think so. They were Franks but not clean shaven like most Franks. Beards . . . a red cross on their mantles." His eyes opened, brimming with moisture. "Is it enough, my lord?"

"It's enough." He rose to his feet. "You've done well. You have the makings of a soldier, lad. Now go back to sleep. We'll talk again when you're better." He strode toward the door and glanced at Thea as he opened it. "Find someone to watch him and come to the Great Hall. I would have words with you."

She wanted words with him, too. She wanted to hurl the same foul words at him she had heard the camel drivers use. She wanted to push him from the battlements.

"I've . . . done well," Haroun said. "Did you hear him?"

"I heard him." She tried to keep the anger from her voice. "Now go back to sleep. When you awake, I'll get you some broth to eat."

"I... did well...." He drifted off to sleep.

Ware was standing at the window, looking out at the mountains when she strode into the hall.

"That was cruel and unnecessary," she burst out. "The boy has just lost his mother. Couldn't you have waited until he healed a little?"

"No. If the attackers were bandits, we would have pursued them."

"So that more people could die?"

He didn't turn around. "Yes, that is war."

"And it means nothing to you, does it? All those men and women and children..."

"Everyone dies."

"Not like that." She moved across the room toward him. "Those children..." She had to stop to steady her voice. "Not the children. It shouldn't have happened."

"No."

"Then why did it?"

"My fault." His voice was almost inaudible.

"What?"

"My fault. I thought it was the ones here at Dundragon who were at risk. That's why I never let anyone but my soldiers stay too long. The villagers were no risk to them...." His fist pounded down on the windowsill. "Dammit, they were no *risk*."

She drew a few steps closer. "I don't understand. Why—" Then she saw his face.

Twisted, tormented with agony. She had never seen such pain.

"They killed them just to let me know they could reach me."

"The Knights Templar? But they're men of God. I can't believe they would do that."

"Believe what you like." He drew a long, harsh breath, and she saw his face become a shield once more. "But I believe it, and I must make sure it doesn't happen again. Never again. I cannot bear—I must protect—" He turned to face her. "And I'll start with you."

She took an involuntary step back at the sudden fierceness in his expression. "Me?"

"They know what goes on at Dundragon. They will know you're here."

"But I have nothing to do with you. I will leave here soon."

"Haroun had nothing to do with me. He was here for only a few days. His mother died . . . the village died." His hands fell on her shoulders. "I'll not stand by and see anyone else die for my sake. I want to know who you are and who they can reach through you."

"I wouldn't tell Kadar." She moistened her lips. "And I won't tell you."

"I'm not Kadar." His grasp tightened on her shoulders. "I'm not gentle or kind. I'm selfish and angry, and I'd just as soon throw you into a dungeon rather than see you die because of me. I *will* know everything about you."

"You're hurting me."

"You should know by now that is what I do. I hurt and kill and—" He broke off and then said haltingly, "You have a warm heart, and I think you must have people you care about. Tell me who they are so that I can protect them."

Selene. But Selene had nothing to do with this. "She's in Constantinople. She's in no danger."

"The Knights Templar are everywhere. They can walk into any palace in Christendom and demand what they like."

"I can't believe—"

"Even if you don't believe, do you wish to take the chance?"

She didn't know what to do. She could take no risk with Selene. Yet wasn't revealing everything to him a greater risk to them both? "You're certain it was the Knights Templar?"

"They wear a cross on their tunics, and when they enter the order, they're commanded to grow their beards." His lips twisted. "I assure you I had no wish for Haroun to tell me I'd murdered his village."

"If I tell you . . ."

"You will tell me."

She suddenly flared. "You won't tell me what to do. I'll decide what is best." She paused. Kadar had said Ware always kept his word. Perhaps she could wrest some safety from this uncertain situation. "You must promise I will be free. You must promise that Selene will be safe and free."

"Who is Selene?"

"You must promise."

"I promise you will be free. Who is Selene?"

"My sister."

"And where is she?"

"Still at the House of Nicholas. It was too dangerous to take her with me, not until I could find a place for us."

"There is no one else?"

"No one I care about."

"Then I'll have her brought here."

Her eyes widened in shock. "What?"

"You heard me." He released her and stepped back. "I can't be worrying about someone so far away. She'll have to come here."

Her heart leaped with hope. To see Selene again...

He turned away. "I'll tell Kadar to go fetch her."

"Wait." She moistened her lips. "He may not want to let her go."

He turned, waiting.

She hesitated and then said in a rush, "Selene is a slave."

He did not change expression. "And you?"

"Yes." She lifted her chin. "No. Not now. I'm a free woman."

"But this Nicholas would disagree with you. You ran away?"

"It was not fair. I worked all my life in the House of Nicholas. My mother died in his service. I deserve to be free."

"But he will want you back?"

"I have great value for him. He would be foolish not to want me back."

"What of your sister?"

"She has skill but she is young. Her value is not as great."

"How young?"

"Ten years."

He frowned. "Will he sell her?"

"You would buy her?"

"It's the safest way to get her away from him. Is it possible?"

"If the price is high enough." Her lips twisted bitterly. "Nicholas is a merchant, and all things have a price."

"The price will be high enough."

She hesitated. "There is something he may use to drive up the price. You should expect it." She paused. "Selene is his daughter."

He went still. "Yes, I'd say that would drive up the price. Is he your father, too?"

"Yes, my mother bore him three children. My brother died when he was born."

"And he still kept you as a slave?"

"It was not unusual for Nicholas to use his slaves for pleasure . . . if they were comely. At least two other women bore him children. But they were boys, and Nicholas took them away and made them servants in his house."

He said slowly, "I don't think I like this Nicholas."

She waved an impatient hand. "You don't have to like or dislike him. You must just realize he'll use her birth to ask a higher price. You must not act too eager or he'll cheat you." She was afraid to believe this was happening. Her dream of bringing Selene to freedom would come true not in a few years but in a matter of months. "You can really do this?"

"Kadar can bargain with anyone over anything. Why not a child?"

Simple words. Why not a child? Why not Selene? Yet they were words that meant everything. "How soon?"

"I'll send him tonight . . . if it's safe."

"This is a miracle," she said unsteadily. "I cannot thank— I *will* repay you. I vow it."

"Miracles are not wrought by men like me. I'm not doing this for you or her. I'm doing it for me." He moved over to the table and poured wine into a goblet. "I'll have no more Jedhas."

"No one could know that such an evil would be committed."

"No?" He drank deep. "I'd wager the Grand Master de Ridfort didn't consider what he ordered evil. He's decreed any means are just if they bring me down."

She stared at him in bewilderment. "Why are they so angry with you? What did you do?" she whispered.

"What did I do?" He poured more wine into his goblet. "They say I stole a wagonload of gold from the Temple storehouse. I'm sure you'll not find that surprising. You called me a thief on our first meeting."

"I didn't know you."

"But now you're impressed with my honesty and gentle demeanor."

"You have no gentleness, but I believe you to be honest. You're too impatient to indulge in deceit."

He smiled crookedly. "So even that attribute is tainted."

"You do have one virtue. You keep your promises." She met his gaze. "And that's the only virtue I care about. You said you'd bring me Selene, and I believe you."

He was silent for a moment, staring into her eyes. Then he turned abruptly away and said harshly, "Go back to the boy."

She started for the door and then stopped. She did not want to leave him alone. Beneath that hard, rough exterior she sensed a pain so great it was almost incomprehensible. "What can— Is there— Can I help you?"

"Help?" He smiled mockingly. "Are you offering me your body as distraction?"

She flushed with annoyance. She should have known better than to try to comfort him. Only fools tried to stroke a wounded animal. "No." She turned on her heel.

"Wait." He was suddenly beside her. "My tongue is clumsy. I did not mean— I strike out when—" He muttered a curse and turned away. "Never mind."

He had been trying to say he was sorry, she realized. She was probably foolish, but she had to try again. "May I help you?"

"I need no help." He moved heavily across the room. "Yes, I do. One thing. Send someone with another bottle of wine."

Chapter Five

THE EMBERS OF the conflagration still glowed dimly in the darkness.

The odor of smoke and death was everywhere as Vaden moved slowly through the ruins.

When he'd seen that malevolent glow, he'd not been able to believe it. He had to come see for himself.

"You madman," he murmured. "Is it worth this?"

The Grand Master thought killing Ware was worth destroying half the world. Vaden's father no doubt agreed with him.

He glanced at the distant castle, its torches burning bright. Dundragon no longer seemed quite so impregnable as it had these two years past.

The net was drawing tighter.

* * *

"How is the boy?" Kadar whispered when Thea opened the door later that evening.

"Better. He ate a bowl of broth an hour ago. He's back asleep again."

"I must speak to you before I go. Can you leave him?"

She nodded, then came out into the hall and quietly closed the door. "I think he's no longer in danger. I just want to be here when he wakes."

"Good. Then you can bid me a fitting good-bye. A few tears, a graceful wave of your hand as I ride through the gates." He took her arm and urged her down the hall. "After all, a man deserves it when he sets out on a journey."

"You deserve more than that. Is it safe for you to set out tonight?"

He nodded. "Ware rode out earlier today, and there's no sign of any danger."

"He did? I didn't think he would stir from the castle today. I left him in the Great Hall with a bottle of wine."

"Wine brings forgetfulness, but Ware doesn't forget what it is his duty to remember," he said as they started down the stairs. "He wouldn't let me ride into danger."

"How do you go to Constantinople?"

"I ride to Acre and then go by ship."

"How long will it take to bring her here?"

"Two or three months. It would be sooner, but it may take me a while to pluck her away from your loving father." He frowned thoughtfully. "I think I will be a wealthy merchant from Cairo who wishes to start his own silk-and-embroidery house. But not too wealthy. I cannot afford any of his most experienced embroiderers. I will choose one of the younger women who will be adequate now and better later. I will ask to tour the House of Nicholas, become struck with the skill of your Selene, and accept no other. Is that not a good plan?"

It was a good plan. "Very clever."

"Because I am clever. But even brilliant men must have knowledge to bring their plans to fruition. I cannot ask for your sister by name. What does she look like? Is she fair like you?"

She shook her head. "She has dark-red hair and green eyes." She frowned. "And she won't like being bought. She'll want to stay at the House of Nicholas where I can find her."

"Do not worry. I can handle one small child."

"When you were ten, were you a child?"

He shook his head.

"Neither is Selene."

He nodded. "I understand. I am not to be overconfident."

"Impossible," Ware said dryly from the door. "You think you can move the world."

"It's not true," Kadar responded. "But sometimes it's possible to persuade others to do it for you." He moved toward Ware. "Like you, my friend. I have high hopes for you."

"Save your hopes for yourself." He opened the door and preceded them down the stairs toward Kadar's horse. "You've hidden the pouch?"

Kadar nodded. "No one will know I'm a wealthy merchant until I reach Constantinople. Until then I'm only a pilgrim returning from the Holy Land." He mounted and smiled down at Ware. "Don't worry, I'm in no danger."

"I'm not worried." He gazed at Kadar a moment and then said gruffly, "Go with God."

"Of course. God will not have it any other way. He has excellent taste in traveling companions." Kadar looked at Thea. "Now you must bid me my proper farewell. Will you lead my horse to the gates as if I were a great knight going to fight a dragon?"

"If you wish," she said, startled. She grasped the reins and moved across the courtyard.

"I do you a service," Kadar said in a low voice.

"A great service."

"I ask a service in return."

She looked over her shoulder at him. His expression was uncharacteristically solemn. "Anything. What service?"

"I leave a possession that must be cared for."

"Your falcons? If you will tell me how to—"

"Not my falcons. The servants know how to care for them." He nodded toward Ware. "He won't let them care for him."

She stiffened. "I've noticed he makes his demands known. You need not worry about Lord Ware."

"I do worry. He's my responsibility." He shook his head. "And this is a bad time for me to leave. He grieves and has need of me."

He grieves.

She had a sudden memory of Ware's agonized expression. Perhaps he did need Kadar but he would allow no one else close enough to comfort him. "I cannot help him. He wouldn't let me."

"You must care for my possession." Kadar's tone was

gentle but firm. "Promise me. So that my mind is free to attend my task."

She gazed at him in exasperation. "The only care he wants is a woman for his bed, and he has no problem asking for that."

"But what he wants is not always what he needs. He's the loneliest man I've ever known. He needs company to ward off that loneliness. He will not accept it readily, but you must battle him until he accepts what is good for him."

She glanced beyond him to Ware, who was standing in the courtyard. She was to do battle with this formidable titan who had known nothing but wars all his life? "I cannot do it."

"You like children. Pretend he is a child like Haroun or Selene whom you must nurture and protect."

Her gaze swung back to Kadar in astonishment.

He burst out laughing. "Ah, your face. But we are all children, Thea."

"Not him," she said flatly.

"You will see." He waved his hand for the guard to lower the drawbridge. "You will care for my possession and I will care for yours. Pact?"

He was going to journey a long distance and bring her Selene. Who knew what dangers he might encounter? "I will try."

"But you're a kind and determined woman, and to try is to succeed. I feel better already."

"I'm not kind. I'm very selfish and I've no desire to do this."

"You try to be selfish because you're afraid of letting anyone too near. To guard themselves is the way of people whose instinct is to nurture and protect." He gave her a brilliant smile and lifted his hand in farewell. The next moment he was galloping over the drawbridge.

"Safe journey," she called.

He waved again as he reached the other side of the moat. He was lost to view as the guards lifted the drawbridge.

She slowly turned and moved across the courtyard. Ware was gone. He had vanished within the castle. Even with his closest friend he would not allow himself sentiment.

And Kadar expected her to soothe and comfort this man? Impossible.

"Go to my chamber and sleep there. Tasza and I will care for the boy." The order came from Jasmine, who had suddenly appeared at her side as she sat next to Haroun's bed. "I think it best I take him to my room tomorrow. He'll be better with me. He's not accustomed to rich surroundings and it will make him uneasy."

Thea was too tired to argue. "We'll talk about it later." She rose to her feet and arched her back to rid it of stiffness. "I don't want him to think I'm abandoning him."

"He will not think that of you," Jasmine said gruffly. "Haroun is not a fool."

From Jasmine that came close to praise, Thea thought wearily. "Wake me if I'm needed."

"You won't be needed. I will have Tasza. Lord Ware doesn't want her tonight." Jasmine's tone was almost indifferent.

"You don't seem upset."

"Lord Ware called the servants into the Great Hall tonight and told us all that our home was here now. We don't have to fear being sent away, and he will keep us safe behind these walls."

I will start with you.

Apparently Ware had moved quickly to see that the other inhabitants of Dundragon were also safe from the Knights Templar. A flicker of uneasiness rippled through her, and then she impatiently dismissed it. For once Ware was demonstrating a kindness and protectiveness that should be applauded, not met with distrust.

"I'm happy for you."

"It feels . . . strange," Jasmine said. "All our lives Tasza and I have had to fight every day to make our way. It will seem odd not to have to worry about tomorrow." She shrugged. "But I'm sure we will become accustomed to it."

"Good night." Thea softly closed the door behind her, then moved through the hall and down the stairs. Everything had changed. It seemed terrible that because of the horrible tragedy at Jedha, Thea was to get what she wanted most in the world and Jasmine and Tasza were to be safe at last. It was as if God had tried to balance the scales in some manner.

She would *not* feel guilty. Surely she couldn't be blamed for wanting Selene to be happy and free. She would not let the massacre at Jedha poison her joy that Selene would be with her soon. She would do all she could for the survivors of Jedha, but she could not make the—

Ware was still in the Great Hall.

She stopped at the bottom of the stairs. He was sitting in the high-backed chair before the fire, his legs sprawled in front of him, gazing into the flames.

He's the loneliest man I've ever known, Kadar had said.

If he was lonely, she could not help it. She was not Kadar, who could amuse and venture where others feared to tread.

She turned toward the door that led to the scullery and servants' quarters.

You will care for my possession and I will care for yours.

But not tonight, when she was so tired she could barely think. Tomorrow would do as well.

He grieves.

By what sorcery had Kadar planted those words in her mind? she thought with exasperation. She would pay no attention to—

"By all the saints," she muttered as she marched into the Great Hall to stand before Ware. "Go to bed."

He slowly lifted his head. "What?"

"You heard me. You look foolish sitting here brooding. Go to your bed and go to sleep."

"Foolish," he repeated, glowering at her.

"Foolish and stubborn and without sense."

"Then leave my presence so that you don't have to look at me."

"Do you think I don't want to do that? Kadar won't let me. He says I must take care of you."

"Oh, my God."

"But I'm too tired to be bothered with this tonight, so go to your bed and let me worry about it tomorrow."

"I'm sorry to inconvenience you," he said silkily. "But I appreciate the tender thought."

"You don't want tenderness, and it *is* an inconvenience. I don't even know how to go about this."

"Then don't go about it. I don't need either your care or your concern."

"That's what I told Kadar. He wouldn't listen."

"He seldom does, one must just ignore him."

"I can't ignore him. He's doing me a great service and must be repaid."

"Then repay him some other way. I'll not have another clucking hen at my heels." He poured more wine into his goblet. "Leave me."

"Are you drunk yet?"

"No." He lifted the goblet. "But soon."

"Good, then maybe you'll fall asleep and I can have the servants take you to your bed." She sat down on the hearth and leaned back against the stones. "I'll wait."

He scowled. "I don't want you to wait. Leave me."

"Drink your wine. These stones are hard."

He crashed the goblet down on the table. "I'll drink when I please."

"I said the wrong thing." She yawned. "I should have realized you'd be contrary. All right, don't drink your wine."

He picked up the goblet and then stopped, frowning as he realized the dilemma. "Christ, now what am I supposed to do?"

"I don't care. Whatever you like."

He smiled sensually. "Then take off your gown and come here."

She was too weary to feel anything but impatience. "Why? The wine will do as well as a woman for your needs now. Besides, that's not what Kadar wanted of me."

His smile vanished. "I'm growing bored hearing what Kadar wanted."

"Then drink your wine and go to sleep."

He muttered an obscenity and then was silent. The only sound in the Great Hall was the crackle of the logs in the fireplace.

"What did he want of you?" Ware growled.

"I'm not sure. He was a little vague," she said drowsily. "I'll have to think about it."

Another silence.

"Go to bed," he said harshly. "You're going to fall asleep any minute and tumble into that fire."

She shook her head.

"I don't need Kadar and I don't need you."

"I know."

"Then leave me."

She shook her head. She wished he would be quiet. Talking was too much effort. "Drink your wine."

"I will not drink my wine."

"Very well." Her lids were so heavy, she could barely keep them open. "Whatever you . . ."

"Christ."

He was picking her up, carrying her.

Climbing the stairs.

No, that was wrong. . . .

"Where are you going?"

"I'm taking you to your bed, where you belong."

"Haroun is in my bed. I'm sleeping in Jasmine's bed."

He stopped at the top of the stairs and then was moving down the corridor. "I'm not carrying you down again. You've been bother enough tonight. You can have my bed. I won't be using it."

Something soft beneath her . . .

He was turning away and striding toward the door.

That was wrong, too.... She couldn't allow him to go.

"No." She struggled to an upright position and swung her legs to the floor. "You shouldn't go back to the hall. Stay here...." She pulled herself up by the bedpost. "I'll go to Jasmine's—"

He whirled on her. "By the saints, why won't you give up?"

She was too weary to argue. She could only shake her head.

His hands clenched into fists at his side as he glared at her. Was he going to strike her? She almost hoped he would. Then she could go to sleep without breaking her vow to Kadar. He was striding toward her, his blue eyes glittering. He *was* going to strike her.

He pushed her down on the bed.

She looked up at him, startled, as he threw himself into the cushioned chair next to the bed. "Go to sleep," he growled. "I'll stay."

"You'll try to sleep?"

"I said I'd stay. I didn't say I'd sleep."

It was victory enough. Kadar couldn't expect more from her tonight. "You might as well." She turned over on her side and closed her eyes. "There's nothing else to do...."

There's nothing else to do.

Ware rested his head on the back of the chair. He could think of any number of things to do at the moment, and none of them concerned sleeping. He hadn't thought he wanted a woman until he saw her lying in his bed.

Now there was no doubt at all what he wanted to do.

So why wasn't he inside her? Why was he sitting there

watching her sleep like one of those foolish gallants in a troubadour's tale? She had angered him, forced him to her will, and he was still not reaching out to take what he wanted.

His gaze slowly traveled over her. She was curled up like an exhausted child, but she was no child. She was old enough to take a man and bear a child. She would have fine sons; she would give them her strength and courage and protect them as she had Haroun.

The thought brought a violent surge of heat to his loins. Christ, what was happening to him? Now he was not only lusting after the woman, but her children. He wanted those sons to be *his,* wanted to see her belly swell with his seed and her breasts grow large with milk.

His hands clenched on the arms of the chair. Not for him. Never for him. If he conceived a child, he would probably never live to see it born.

Yet he suddenly wanted that child with an overwhelming passion. He didn't want to let them banish every trace of him from the earth. Something should live on, someone...

Oh, yes, he thought with self-disgust, get the woman with child and let the Grand Master murder them both as he had the villagers.

Or hold them both hostage to make sure of Ware's death.

Why was he even considering the possibility? He had known this danger for years and had been careful to draw out of the women he used to slake himself. That it mattered so much now was unreasonable.

The destruction of the village must be the source of this sense of urgency. *It could not be the woman.* He admired her courage and endurance, but she was far too independent and bold. Never had a woman defied and ordered him about. Yet if she had not been bold, could she have survived? Gentleness would not have served her on that long trek to Damascus. Meekness would have made her stay in that silken prison in Constantinople.

He could not condemn her for surviving and wishing to live in freedom. He had been driven by that same wish when he'd left Scotland those many years ago.

But he could condemn her for being a constant irritant since he had brought her to Dundragon.

No, in fairness, she had tried to avoid him. It was his own lust that had been at fault. Damnation, was there no way to escape guilt? he thought wearily. Every way he turned, he bore responsibility for some new sin. He should have gone back to the Great Hall and the wine that blurred the guilt and made life a little more bearable.

She murmured something incomprehensible and turned over on her side. She was restless. It was turning cool....

He reached down and carefully drew over her the wool blanket at the bottom of the bed.

A chill rippled through him; the motion had been done without thought, purely instinctive.

He could not let it be the woman.

When Thea opened her eyes, it was after dawn. One moment she was asleep and the next fully awake as if she had been called.

He was still sitting in the chair beside the bed, his head tilted back. He appeared... different in sleep. Not helpless;

even in slumber the tension and wariness were still present. She studied him curiously as she never could when he was awake. She had not noticed before what long black lashes he had. When his eyes were open, one paid heed only to that searing blue. His mouth was well shaped and actually quite beautiful. . . .

"Stop looking at me."

Her gaze flew up to meet that glittering blue glance.

"I meant no—I was half-asleep." Why was she stammering? She had done nothing wrong. She sat up and swung her feet to the floor. "It's dawn. I must go to Haroun. You should go to your bed. You cannot be comfortable there."

He grimaced. "Comfortable? I can't move, and I'm sure this crick in my neck will never go away."

She started to get up. "Then lie down as I told you and all will be—"

"Stay where you are," he snapped.

She froze and then deliberately got to her feet. "I cannot help that you've drunk too deep and have a bad head. I'll not be ordered about."

"Because you're a free woman," he said mockingly. "There is no such thing. A woman is only as free as her husband permits her to be."

"But I have no husband. Nor will I ever." She added harshly, "Do you think I'd risk joining myself to a man? No man, no country, not even the Church gives fairness to women. We are nothing to any of you. My mother told me of a council once held at Nantes where great nobles and churchmen gathered to decide whether women were human or beasts. I'm convinced the only reason they decided we were human was to avoid being put to death for the crime of bestiality."

"You could be right. It would certainly give *me* pause." He went back to the original subject. "You have such a hatred for slavery?"

"There's no use talking to you. You cannot understand."

"Then *make* me understand."

She frowned in puzzlement. "Why are you angry?"

"I'm not angry. I'm just telling you that freedom is not such a prize. Some prisons can be more comfortable and pleasant than the world beyond them. All captivities aren't as cruel as the one you suffered at the House of Nicholas." He paused. "Did he beat you?"

"When I was a child. Later I learned . . ." She shrugged. "What do you wish me to say? I had ample to eat, a clean place to sleep. When I showed promise, Nicholas had me taught languages and numbers so that I could speak knowledgeably with the merchants who came to buy the silk. There was even a walled garden outside the women's quarters where we were permitted to go in the evening after the light failed. My mother said we were more fortunate than many." She folded her arms across her chest. "But as years went by, I began to hate it more and more. I could not *breathe*. I watched Selene bent over her loom from dawn to dusk, and I wanted to pick her up and carry her away to where there was sunlight and the smell of flowers and—" She broke off and drew a shaky breath. "It wasn't fair. No one should be allowed to own another person."

"So it was for Selene you ran away?"

"No, I could have waited until conditions were better, if I had only Selene to consider." She met his gaze. "A prince from Florence came to see Nicholas to buy some bolts of silk for his wife. He had a fondness for fair-haired women and decided he would like to buy me as well."

"Nicholas sold you?"

"Why not? The prince offered a great sum for me. It's true my skill made me valuable, but if my body is worth more . . ." She smiled bitterly. "But Nicholas is a wily trader. The negotiations went on for days. I didn't wait for them to be completed."

"Bastard."

"He never considered himself to be unkind. We were property. Weren't we fed and watered? Disciplined only when we failed in our duty to him? I'm sure he was outraged when I ran away."

"How did you get passage on the caravan?"

"Balzar, the leader of the caravan, came often to the House of Nicholas. For years I'd been working in secret on a silk robe with embroidery fit for an emperor. I offered to trade it to him in exchange for food, water, and a place in the caravan."

He lifted his brows. "A silk robe for sheltering a runaway slave?"

"A robe fit for an emperor," she repeated. "Balzar was very vain. He had to have it. Besides, there was little shelter involved. If I'd been discovered, he would merely have disclaimed knowing who I was."

"You stole the silk for the robe?"

"I don't steal," she flared. "I planted the trees that nurtured those silkworms, and the embroidery was my design and my work. Nicholas's wealth grew tenfold when he started to display my designs. Did I not deserve something? Do you know how hard it was to find the time to do such an intricate design? Every morning I crept out in the garden in half darkness when I could barely see and then later had to rip half the stitches because I'd made mistakes. It took me almost two years to—"

"I wasn't condemning you," he interrupted. "I only asked." He smiled crookedly. "What's a length of silk when all Christendom knows I stole a much greater treasure?"

"Don't be absurd." She was still annoyed with him. "Why do you say things like that? I told you that it was clear you're too blunt to indulge in thievery."

"Indeed? Then how do you account for all the riches you see in the castle?"

"I don't have to account for them. It doesn't interest me." She shrugged. "Perhaps you *are* a thief. Kadar says you ask great fees for protecting caravans and fighting battles. Perhaps that could be considered thievery."

His lips twitched. "Certainly the lords who hire me consider it so."

He had almost smiled, she realized. She had a sudden urge to see if she could make him do it again. "No, I told Kadar the reason you were cast out of the order was your lustfulness. You broke the law of abstinence."

He *did* smile and looked years younger. "It's true I found that restriction a great burden."

She nodded. "I thought as much."

His smile faded. "And what do you know of lust? Kadar tells me you escaped the raping at the caravan."

"I saw coupling at the House of Nicholas. When the merchant was of importance, Nicholas would sometimes invite him to the women's quarters and let him choose one of the women to pleasure him."

"Your mother?"

"Once."

"And you watched it?"

"No, I closed my eyes. She told me it wouldn't hurt her but that I should not watch." She did not want to think back on that night. She had seen nothing, but she had heard the soft laughter of the men, the grunts, the labored breathing, and then later, when her mother had come back to her, the sound of smothered sobs. "She lied. He did hurt her. Perhaps not her body, but he hurt her." Her voice shook with remembered rage. "That is what it is to be a slave. To have no choice, to know that mind and body and skill are not your own. Do not speak to me of a pleasant captivity. There is none."

"Very well. We won't discuss it."

But something unspoken lingered in the room, and again she felt uneasy. She stood up. "I must go to Haroun."

He let her go this time, watching her as she crossed the room. "You say you grew new mulberry trees for Nicholas? How?"

She stopped, puzzled at the change of subject. "Like any other tree. He bought young trees from a trader and planted them in the grove. I tended them and made sure the roots were strong."

"Is that what you plan on doing in Damascus?"

"Yes, or trade for them."

"Another robe for an emperor?"

"You wouldn't scoff if you'd seen it."

He met her gaze. "I'm not scoffing. I believe you."

She felt a rush of glowing warmth. "You do?"

"I believe you can do anything you set out to do."

He meant it, she realized. "I promise that it won't compare with the banner I shall make for you," she said eagerly. "Emperors will envy *you*. You'll be able to pass it on with pride to your sons and they will give it to their sons. It will be—" She broke off as she saw his expression. "What's wrong?"

"Nothing." He moved from the chair and lay down on the bed. "I'm more weary than I thought, and all this talk of sons bores me. I think I'll take a nap. Run along to Haroun."

He had not been bored. It was pain she had seen in his face. What had she said to hurt him? "I didn't mean—" How could she tell the dratted man she was sorry for a hurt he would not admit existed? She would not waste her time.

"Meet me in the courtyard at noon," he said without opening his eyes.

"Why?"

"Because I wish it. Didn't Kadar tell you to bear me company?"

"Yes."

"Then bear me company in the courtyard this noon."

"But I don't—" He had turned over on his side, ignoring her. She opened the door. "If it pleases me."

"I'm sure it will please you to keep your promise."

She sighed with exasperation as she shut the door. She did not want to meet with him again so soon. It was too wearing on the emotions. When Kadar had asked her this service, she had known that it would be difficult, but she had not thought she would feel this vulnerable. It would be easier if she just had to confront surliness and rejection. She couldn't understand his sudden interest in her past when he had told her before that he did not care about the details of her life. Now he was asking too many questions, probing too deeply. It disturbed her. Her instinct was to avoid him until her composure returned.

But she had promised Kadar.

Well, then she would have to make sure Ware had no opportunity to continue that intimacy. He could not ask a multitude of questions if others were present. She would just make certain she was never alone with him.

She had not needed to worry about being alone with Ware, Thea thought dazedly, as she saw the column of mounted soldiers fully armored and filling the courtyard. There was even a wagon being readied for departure at the rear.

"Where have you been?" Ware frowned down at her as he brought his horse closer to the steps. "I told you noon."

"It's only a little after." She was too astonished to take offense at his brusqueness. "Where are you going?"

"I didn't bring you back enough of those damned mulberry leaves," he growled. "You'll need more now that you're staying."

He was right. It would be at least two months before Kadar came back with Selene, and she had only another three-week supply. "You're taking all these men? But you said you wouldn't risk—"

"Things are different now." He bent down and extended his arms. "Come. I want to get back before dark."

"I'm to go also?"

"Why else would I tell you to meet me?"

"You wouldn't take me before."

"I told you, things are different now. I may need you."

Then, of course, she must go. She took a step closer and

he swung her up before him. "But you know what the tree looks like now."

He didn't answer as he waved the column forward.

Riding with him today was different from that night he had brought her to Dundragon. The metal of armor pressing against her back was already hot from the sun, and yet she was oddly comfortable. "Are we bringing the wagon to carry the leaves?"

"Yes."

"We won't need it. A few baskets will be all that's necessary."

"I'm taking no chances."

"But it's a waste of—"

"Are you going to chatter all afternoon?"

"Not if you refuse to listen to good sense. Why should I care if you look foolish before your men?" She abandoned the conversation and leaned back against him. She didn't want to talk anyway. The scent of cypress and palm were drifting to her, and the sun on her face brought its own contentment.

An hour later they drew up on the slope leading to the thatch of mulberry trees. It was too soon, she thought languidly.

Ware dismounted and plucked her from the saddle. His bearing was tense as his gaze raked the grove and then the foothills surrounding them.

"What is it?" she asked. "I saw no one. Is there someone here?"

He didn't answer for an instant, and then she saw him relax. "No, there's no one here." He turned away and barked orders to his soldiers, dividing his forces so that half were to fetch the leaves while the others were to remain on guard. She drifted down the slope and into the grove, gazing with pleasure around her. The trees were strong, nurtured by a kinder sun than in Constantinople. They would give shade and sustenance for many years to—"

She whirled as a branch crashed to the ground. Abdul's sword cleaved through the air and bit into another branch.

"No!" She ran toward him. "Stop it."

He stared at her, startled.

"Stand back." Ware was striding toward her. "He's only getting your leaves." He gestured to the soldiers who were moving with swords drawn on the trees. "For God's sake, that's what you want."

"You must pick the leaves and leave the branches. I won't have the trees destroyed."

"It will take twice as long," Abdul said. "And we have no ladders for climbing."

"Is that how you got my leaves?" Thea asked Ware.

"Did you think I blew on them and they fell to the earth?" Ware asked.

"I suppose it's my fault. I should have told you to be careful of the trees." She turned back to Abdul. "But you cannot cut these branches."

Abdul looked at Ware.

"I'll not have my soldiers take off their armor to climb those trees," Ware said grimly.

"Then I'll pick the leaves myself," Thea said. "It will take a little longer, but I told you we don't need a wagonload of leaves."

"I don't want it to take longer." He stared at her determined expression and then whirled away in exasperation.

"By all the saints. Abdul, have those men climb the lower branches and pick the leaves. But they're not to take off their armor."

Abdul sighed and turned away.

"I'm truly not being unreasonable," Thea said. "These mulberry trees are very important. If you could see what beauty results from the—"

"It's being done," Ware said. "It doesn't matter if it's reasonable or not. I just want this over as quickly as possible." He grimaced. "And I'd wager my men feel the same way. That armor is heavy and not meant to be worn when climbing trees. Besides, there is little dignity in the task. A soldier should not be asked to climb trees and pick leaves."

"It's a worthy task," Thea said. "It should make no difference who does it. A tree gives sustenance—"

A crash behind her.

She whirled angrily, thinking that Abdul had disobeyed Ware's order.

Abdul was sprawled beneath the tree, clutching a leaf to his armored chest. "I slipped," he said apologetically to Ware.

"I see you did," Ware said solemnly.

"It won't happen again, my lord."

Another crash. Another soldier fell to earth. Abdul gloomily amended, "Or maybe it will."

"I hope not," Ware said.

"I should go help." Thea frowned worriedly. "I want no one harmed."

"Stay," Ware murmured. "The branches are too close to the ground to offer more harm than a bruise or two."

She became conscious of some emotion beneath Ware's impassiveness. His gaze was narrowed as he watched the soldiers struggle clumsily on the branches. It was as if he were waiting for something.

Another soldier crashed to earth.

She heard a strangled sound from Ware.

A minute later a fourth man sprawled on the ground.

"They're falling like overripe oranges," Ware gasped.

"It's not fair they should—" She started toward the grove. "I'll tell them to come down."

Ware grabbed her arm. "Don't you dare."

"But I cannot let—"

Ware was laughing. His entire body was shaking with mirth. He had to reach out and grab at his saddle to keep upright.

"You think it funny?" she asked wonderingly.

"Like oranges." Tears were running down his cheeks. "Like oranges . . ."

He was not the only one laughing. She saw to her amazement that the soldiers in the grove were also roaring with laughter.

A fifth armored soldier slipped from a limb, spreading his arms like wings as he tried to catch his balance.

She found her own lips twitching. "I should not—It's my fault that—" She couldn't help it. She started to laugh and couldn't stop. When she could speak, she shook her head. "When I was at Jedha, I didn't think there was any laughter left in the world, and yet today . . . It makes me feel guilty."

"It should not. Laughter is good." He gestured to the men below. "They lost family and friends. Do you think they no longer remember their loss because they found something to laugh about today? Laughter heals." He added almost inaudibly, "I had forgotten. . . ."

She stared at him in fascination. He was a different man from the one she had come to know. The lines of bitterness and cynicism had smoothed from his face, leaving only weariness and a little wistfulness. The softness wouldn't stay; it was already changing. But she had seen it, she had shared his laughter, and she knew she would always remember.

His gaze shifted back to her face, and any hint of softness vanished. "Why do you always stare at me as if I were some odd breed of camel?"

She was immediately on the defensive. "I don't stare—" She stopped as she abruptly realized that antagonism was what he wanted of her. Why should she give him that satisfaction when she was feeling more mellow than combative? "In truth you do remind me of a camel. It is the eyelashes, I think."

He frowned. "Eyelashes?"

"Camels have long eyelashes too. Many women would envy them."

His eyes widened with outrage before his expression became even more forbidding. "Are you saying I have eyelashes like a woman?"

"Woman?" She gazed at him with bland innocence. "I thought we were speaking of camels."

"You know very well—" He broke off and a grudging smile touched his lips. "I begin to feel sorry for Nicholas."

"And you're also as bad-tempered as a camel." She pretended to think. "Though I've never seen you spit at anyone."

"I may start any minute."

"Then I'd better go down and help pick my leaves." She started down the incline. "Your soldiers don't seem to be very good at it." She glanced over her shoulder. "I think you should train them in—" She forgot what she had been going to say when she saw how he was looking at her. Warmth. Amusement. Respect. From Ware such emotions were far more incomprehensible and disconcerting than lust or anger. She hurriedly glanced away and her pace quickened.

An hour later the baskets were filled and loaded in the wagon, and Thea climbed back to Ware.

"We're finished," she said. "Though not with any help from you."

"A knight should never compromise his dignity. My men would never respect me again if they saw me tumbling from a tree."

She made a derogatory noise.

"You don't believe me?"

"I think you have too much pride. But we've prevailed without you. We can leave now."

"Not yet."

"We have more than enough leaves."

"Did you find any young trees suitable for replanting?"

She stared at him, puzzled. "I suppose there were three or four. I paid little attention."

"Get them." He motioned to Abdul, who was standing by the wagon. "Go with her and obey her instructions."

Abdul looked alarmed. "I thought we were done with climbing trees, my lord."

"Digging, not climbing."

A brilliant smile lit Abdul's face. "That is good."

"I don't need any trees," Thea protested. "They would

have to be replanted immediately and would not be of any use for a few years."

"I want the trees."

"There's no place to plant them at the castle."

"The green on the north side overlooking the cliff."

He had clearly thought about this, she realized. "But it would be wasted effort. I'll be gone long before they even take firm root."

"Silk is a profitable business. Perhaps I'll have Jasmine tend the trees and grow silk for the trade." He smiled. "If you'll spare us some of your valuable worms?"

"Of course," she said doubtfully. "And I'll teach Jasmine how to care for them and gather the strands. You really wish this?"

"I really wish it. Perhaps someday I'll grow weary of crunching heads and want a more peaceful occupation. It's not completely beyond possib—" He broke off and went still.

"What is it?"

His head lifted, and his gaze turned to the rocks on the hill.

Danger. The threat vibrated from every muscle in his body. It could not have been clearer if he had spoken the word.

"What's wrong?"

His gaze never left the boulders. "Get the trees."

"You said there was no one here."

"Dammit, there wasn't anyone."

"Is it the same people who set fire to the village?"

"No."

She impulsively reached out and put her hand on his arm. "Then why are you—"

"Don't touch me!" He jerked away as if she had burned him. His eyes blazed down at her. "There's no one there. Go get those trees. Hurry."

She backed away from him, then turned and walked quickly down the hill with Abdul following. Before she reached the grove, five more soldiers joined Abdul. A half-dozen armored men to uproot a few trees? She glanced up the hill.

Ware had moved away from his horse and was standing facing the boulders. Defiance. Boldness. Challenge. He had given her an armed escort, yet he was standing in full view, as if taunting whoever was on that hillside.

Or diverting?

"My lord said to hurry," Abdul reminded her.

She hesitated. Her instinct was to return to Ware, yet if there was danger of attack, wouldn't he have ordered the men back to the castle? Perhaps it was her imagination. Perhaps there was no one on that hillside and Ware's change of attitude was just moodiness. The argument didn't convince her, but if she went to him without the trees, he would only send her to the grove again. The quickest way to resolve the situation was to get the mulberries and ride away from here as soon as possible.

"Then we will hurry," she answered. "Follow me."

Vaden watched the fourth tree being loaded into the wagon.

It was the woman who guided the disposition of the trees. It had been the woman who had forced Ware's soldiers to climb like monkeys. It has been the woman who had laughed with Ware and reached out and touched him.

It did not matter that Ware had flinched away. He had become aware of Vaden by that time, and the motion had been as revealing as what had gone before.

Ware was still standing looking up at him, protecting the woman by offering himself as target. It was a brave move, but Vaden could not make the kill today. If he missed, Ware's soldiers would swarm over the hillside, and Vaden had no desire to die.

Ware mounted his horse, reached down, and lifted the woman. His mailed arm encircled her, covering her chest and part of her belly. He was trying to armor the woman.

But Vaden still had her eyes as target.

Ware was shifting her sidewise on the saddle, burying her face against his chest.

Clever Ware. He had always been brilliant in protecting his flank. The strategy with the woman had been unnecessary. If he couldn't kill Ware today, he wouldn't kill anyone else. Besides, he thought with disgust, he wasn't the Grand Master, who murdered innocents without warning.

But she would have to die. He had no choice.

Ware had allowed her to come too close.

Chapter Six

"I CAN'T BREATHE." Thea struggled to lift her head from Ware's chest. "You're smothering me."

"Be quiet."

"When you stop smashing my nose into your armor."

Ware's arms tightened around her, quelling all movement. "Soon."

She was only hurting herself. She gave up struggling and lay still.

They were several miles from the grove when Ware let her sit up. She drew a deep breath and smoothed the bodice of her gown. "I wonder you didn't make me ride all the way back to Dundragon in that position. It was most uncomfortable."

He didn't answer.

She tried to turn around and look over her shoulder.

"Be still."

His tone was impatient, but there was no tension. The danger was gone. "Who was it?"

"I didn't say anyone was there."

"But there was."

"If my men had been in danger, I would have told them. I wouldn't have risked another Jedha."

She knew he was speaking the truth. She had seen the guilt that tormented him after the massacre. Yet there had been danger today.

"There *was* someone on the hillside."

"Did you see him?"

Him. Singular, not plural. How could one man have caused such a disturbance in Ware? "No."

"Neither did I."

Then he had heard him or sensed him. He had known. She started to argue, but she could see he was closed to her. He had made up his mind and would not yield.

It was not yet sunset when they rode through the gates of Dundragon.

He reined in his horse and lowered her to the ground. "Go to your chamber and rest."

She shook her head. "The trees must be planted at once." She motioned to Abdul. "They're very fragile when they're uprooted. They could die."

He nodded and started to turn away.

"Will they follow us?" she asked abruptly.

He stopped to look at her.

"I want to know," she said fiercely. "You're not being fair. It's my life too. Will they come? Will it be like Jedha?"

"No."

"How can you be sure? Who was it?"

At first she thought he would ignore the question. "Vaden."

He rode his horse toward the stable.

She doubted if she could wrest any more from him than that one word.

But the name was vaguely familiar. Where had she heard it?

On the battlements, the night of the massacre. The tiny campfire on the third mountain.

Vaden...

The last tree was not planted until well after dark.

Would they survive? Thea wondered. The green was open to the sun and winds, and it would require great care to make sure the roots took hold. She rubbed the small of her back as she rose from the ground.

"It is all done?" Abdul held the lantern high, surveying the row of trees.

She nodded. "Thank you, Abdul."

"With these fine trees, you will not need us to go and pluck any more leaves?" he asked hopefully.

She smothered a smile. She did not have the heart to tell him these trees would not be ready for a long time. "We have sufficient."

He breathed a sigh of relief. "There is no dignity in this plucking of leaves."

Ware had expressed the same sentiment. "Yet you didn't object when Lord Ware told you to do it."

"My lord always has a good reason." They started for the castle, the lantern lighting their way. "But I'm glad this plucking is over."

"I was sorry you fell from the tree."

He suddenly grinned. "So was I. It was not funny when it happened, but I found it very amusing with the others. Laughter is good. We needed it."

She was silent a moment. "Did you lose someone in Jedha?"

His smile faded. "My family was already dead, but I had friends who died that night."

"But you don't blame Lord Ware?"

He looked at her in surprise. "Why? He did not do it. These things happen in war. Our village was starving, our young men without hope, when he came to Dundragon. He fed the poor and the helpless and gave the rest of us back our honor."

"So you will continue to serve him?"

He nodded, then made a rueful face. "But I hope that he asks me only to fight his wars, not climb trees."

She chuckled. "I don't think he will do—"

"My mother sent me to get you." Tasza stood in the doorway, gazing coldly at Thea. "She said that it is foolish for you to stay out and risk the night devils bringing you the fever."

Abdul smiled at the girl. "But I was here to protect her from the night devils, Tasza." He bowed to Thea. "I must go have my supper. Good night."

"Good night. Thank you, Abdul." Thea smiled at him. "No more leaves, I promise."

He nodded and strolled down the path that led around the castle to the courtyard.

"You had him helping you dig in the dirt," Tasza said curtly. "You should not have done it. He is a very important man, a leader."

Thea smiled. "He's already told me I have injured his dignity."

"It's not funny." She turned and moved back into the castle. "Don't do it again."

Tasza was bristling with protective outrage, Thea realized. "I didn't mean to insult your friend, Tasza."

"He is not my friend. Whores do not have men as friends." A world of pain layered the sharpness of her tone.

Thea did not know what to say. She couldn't tell Tasza she understood. She knew little of whores or the men who used them and then condemned them. "Abdul seemed to treat you as a friend."

"Because he is kind . . . and he pities me. I've seen it in his face." Her tone was suddenly fierce. "I don't need his pity. I have such skill, I can make men weep with pleasure. Can you say the same?"

"No."

"Of course not. My mother says you're a virgin." She paused. "Are you going to couple with Abdul?"

Thea's eyes widened in shock.

"Are you?" Tasza demanded.

Thea shook her head.

Relief rippled over Tasza's face, but her tone was offhand. "It's just as well. He deserves better than a woman with no skill."

Tasza was jealous. Jealous and hurting and striking out in all directions. What must it be like to have to rely only on your body to find worth in a man's eyes? Thea would not have been able to bear it. She said gently, "You're right, I don't have your skill." She paused. "But you don't have mine."

"Your skills and embroidery mean nothing when a man is in lust."

"But they can bring pleasure for a hundred years, not just for a few moments. And I can earn my bread and be dependent on no man."

Tasza shook her head. "A woman is always dependent on a man. They will allow nothing else."

"Not if we have a skill that they need." She paused. "Men are driven by a desire for gold and power and are more likely to pay heed to what a woman demands if she can offer him one or the other. Silk can become gold. Fine embroidery is valued by all."

Tasza was silent a moment. "You have strange ideas."

"Lord Ware said he's interested in making silk for the trade. He wished Jasmine to learn how to take care of the worms and trees." She added with careful casualness, "I could teach you as well."

"Me? Worms?" She adamantly shook her head.

"I can teach you embroidery, but after you learn the stitches, it will still take years to perfect."

"I didn't say I wished to learn this skill." Tasza paused. "But you may teach my mother. She's no longer young, and I think she would like—" She was silent a moment. "She deserves to be treated as a woman of worth."

"And you do not?"

Tasza glared at her. "You're confusing me. I'll talk no more about this." She turned on her heel. "My mother said to tell you she moved Haroun to her room."

"She didn't have to do that."

"Yes, she did. Give her no argument. She needs to pamper the boy as much as he needs the care. In a few weeks he should be well enough to go to the soldiers' barracks."

She moved toward the door leading to the servants' quarters. "Abdul will make sure he comes to no harm. If he's not distracted digging in the dirt to plant your silly trees."

Thea shook her head as she made her way down the corridor toward the Great Hall. Why had she offered to teach the woman when she had been certain of a rebuff? She was being drawn deeper and deeper into the lives of the people here, and she could not allow it.

But it would do no harm to try to give these women what she had herself. They were both strong and deserved something better than the life fate had doled them. She would not be able to teach them more than the rudiments before she left for Damascus, but perhaps that would be enough. She had taught herself more than she had been taught. Perhaps it would be the same with Tasza and Jasmine.

If Tasza would let herself be taught. She seemed to resent everyone in the world but her mother.

And Abdul.

Well, Thea could not worry about them tonight. She must get something to eat, wash off this dirt, and go to her bed. She would sleep well tonight.

Would Ware sleep well tonight?

She banished the intrusive thought. She had spent enough time wondering if all was well with him. He, too, was insinuating himself into her life. No, that was the wrong word. Not "insinuate," there was no subtlety about Ware. He was like a rock rolling down hill, crushing everything in its path.

Like the boulders on the hillside this afternoon, the boulders that had hidden the threat he refused to discuss.

Let him keep his secrets. Any confidences would draw

her closer to him, and she wanted to be no nearer than she was bound to be by her promise to Kadar. Ware aroused too many unsettling emotions. Perhaps her vow could be kept by seeing that Ware had the means for entry into the silk trade.

No, she thought regretfully, Kadar would not consider that the service he'd required of her. He had told her to keep Ware company. And how was she to do that? she wondered in exasperation. Was she supposed to help him train his troops or join him as he drank his way to oblivion?

Ware was sitting at a table in the Great Hall with a large account book in front of him and a quill in his hand when she went searching for him the next afternoon.

"I've come to play chess with you," Thea announced belligerently.

Ware frowned. "I don't wish to play chess."

"Neither do I," she said crossly. "It seems to me a foolish game with everyone stalking one another. But Kadar said you enjoyed playing, so I must play with you."

"It's a very intelligent game." He paused before adding, "But meant for men of war, not for women. They don't have the bent of mind for such strategy. Kadar should not have attempted to teach you."

"Oh, shouldn't he?" she asked with ominous softness. "Just because I think it a foolish game is no reason to believe I cannot play it."

"I have no time to find out." He scowled down at the book. "Leave me. I have figuring to do, and reconciling these numbers makes me extremely bad-tempered."

"Dundragon has no agent?"

He said with sarcasm, "Most Franks are willing to accept my temporary protection from the Saracens, but not the risk of allying themselves with me against the Templars. Is that not strange?"

"What of a villager?"

"It would take longer to teach one than to do it myself." He dipped his quill in the inkwell. "And I hate—" He broke off and slowly lifted his head. "Kadar usually did this for me."

"He did?" she said cautiously.

"But he's gone now."

She knew where this was leading. "I also hate numbers."

"But Kadar said you learned to do them at the House of Nicholas." He paused. "It doesn't seem unreasonable for you to assume this duty for him."

"For *him*?"

"He was the one who asked service of you."

"I'll play chess with you, but I'll not do these accounts."

He leaned back in his chair. "Perhaps you think they'll be too hard for you? It's true, a woman's mind isn't meant for—"

"I'm not a fool and I won't be played for one. I won't do your work."

He sighed. "It was worth a try. Then go away and leave me to them."

She started to turn away and then stopped. How was she to bear him company if she was not with him? "I will look at them," she said grudgingly.

He instantly swung the book around to face her.

She looked at one page, then turned to another. "By all the saints, this is a hodgepodge. I cannot even read it."

"I was just starting to work on it. Kadar has poor penmanship."

She looked through a few previous entries. "Kadar also cannot add." She glanced up and said, "And I'd wager his penmanship is remarkably like your own."

He gazed at her innocently. "But how can you be sure?" He rose to his feet. "Well, I must go see Abdul."

Like a boy going out to play, he intended to escape and leave her with this numeric nightmare. "I think not." She went around the table and settled herself in his chair. She pointed at another chair a few yards distant. "Sit there."

"I have things to do."

"Yes, you must sit there and explain these hideous blotches that I cannot read. I'll try to straighten the accounts, but you will bear me company." She smiled sweetly. "As I promised Kadar."

He frowned. "I'm to sit here and twiddle my thumbs?"

"Or do the accounts yourself."

He reluctantly sat down. "I don't like to be still."

"One does what one must. Think of something else, as I did when I was a child enduring long hours at my loom." She opened the book to the first page. This task might well last until Kadar returned, she realized crossly.

"What did you think about?"

She looked up in puzzlement and then remembered her words. "Many things. At times I would imagine the designs I would create someday. When I was very little, I dreamed of going to the bazaar. I've never been to one, but my mother told me of a visit there. It sounded a magical place brimming with bright copper plates and fine jewels and strange sweets."

"And thieves and whores and the smell of fish."

"I wouldn't mind." She picked up the quill. "It would be exciting. I shall go see it for myself someday. Perhaps as soon as I reach Damascus. Though I shall be very busy for quite a while."

"You'd be disappointed. It's nothing to see."

His low tone held a thread of violence, and she looked up. His expression was impassive. Perhaps she had been mistaken. "You say that because you've already seen it."

"I say that because it's true."

Again she had an impression of repressed violence. She looked back down at the figures. "Then think of something you find pleasant. What of your homeland?" She tried to remember the name. "This Scotland? Is it a fair land?"

"No, it's a hard, mountainous land. The weather is stormy and wild. The seas are rough and the people rougher." He added bitterly, "And they're all barbarians, like me."

Did he expect her to argue with him? "Then it's no wonder you left it."

"I would have stayed there forever, if given a choice."

"Why?"

"Only another barbarian would understand." He gazed beyond her at the tapestry on the wall, but she didn't think he was seeing it. "All my life we'd been at war with the MacKillians. Douglas MacKillian bested us and took Dunlachan castle. My father was wounded in the battle and we fled to the hills. I wanted to go back and fight, but before he died, he made me promise to leave Scotland."

"I'm surprised you gave such a promise."

"I understood why it was important to him. I was the

last of my line. If I'd been killed, even the memory of our family would have vanished."

"So you came here?"

He shook his head. "I had to flee to England with only my horse and armor. I became a free lance and went from tournament to tournament to win prizes and increase my fame. Then the Grand Master came to England to recruit knights for the Temple. I was very young and dazzled by his words. Everyone knew only the best warriors were allowed to join the order. To be a Knight Templar was to be respected and revered as no other knight on earth."

"But you became a monk. You gave up worldly pleasures."

He smiled. "There were compensations. I was very content those three years I was in the order."

"What compensations?"

He shrugged. "Oh, many things. Fine food—we ate very well to maintain our strength. Clean lodgings. Knowledge. I was an ignorant boy when I became a Templar, and I was given the opportunity to learn."

Her gaze narrowed on his face. "But that is not all."

"No." He paused. "Brotherhood. I had no one, and then I had brothers."

She almost wished she had not asked. She suddenly had a picture of a more vulnerable Ware. A tough, lonely young warrior who had needed the bonds of family and had sacrificed a great deal to get those ties. Now he was more lonely than before. She felt a surge of protectiveness. "Brothers don't seek to kill brothers."

His expression became shuttered. "I beg to disagree. Remember Cain and Abel." He paused. "If you'd set yourself to those numbers and ask fewer questions, we might be out of here before nightfall."

He'd withdrawn into that gruff, harsh shell, and it was clear no more confidences would be forthcoming. It was just as well. She was finding herself entirely too absorbed in the puzzle that was Ware of Dundragon. The more she learned, the more she wanted to delve. "If you'd set yourself to learning to add when you were among your brother monks, I'd not be having this problem. I don't think I believe you when you say you sought knowledge at the Temple."

"Oh, it is true." He smiled bitterly. "But the lessons the Templars taught went beyond mere numbers and scrawled words."

She had heard of mystical secrets and ceremonies conducted by the knights in their Temple. "Numbers are not 'mere' when it concerns gold flowing in all directions." She frowned. "The cost of torches and candles is far too much. I cannot read this entry. What is the second number on—"

"Forgive me, my lord, there is something you should see," Abdul said from the doorway.

"At once." Ware sprang from his chair and moved toward the door.

He thought to escape and leave her to puzzle the accounts out for herself. She would not allow it. She pushed the book aside and stood up. "I'll go also. I feel the need for a walk." She gazed meaningfully at Ware. "It may be a long day... for both of us."

He scowled. "I hate for you to be interrupted. You've just got started."

"My lord, perhaps..." Abdul stopped and then said, "I think the Lady Thea should not see this. It may upset her."

"What is it?" Thea asked, alarmed. "What's happened?"

"If you didn't want her to go, you shouldn't have told her she should stay," Ware muttered as he strode from the chamber.

Thea quickly followed them, almost running to match their stride as they crossed the courtyard. "What's happened, Abdul?"

"A short time ago we saw a knight approaching the castle. He stopped just outside range of our arrows."

Ware stopped in midstride. "Did his mantle bear the sign of the cross?"

Abdul shook his head. "He bore no mark of identification, but he rode a great white horse."

"Christ." Ware started toward the gates at a run. "Is he still there?"

"No, but he left something. I sent Hassan and Iman out to drag it into the courtyard."

"And be trapped?"

"We made sure he was out of view. And, after all, he's only one man, my lord."

"I've seen that man kill eight seasoned soldiers in the space of the time it takes to lower a drawbridge."

The drawbridge was lowering now, and Ware waited as Hassan and Iman crossed the moat. His muscles were braced, as they had been yesterday at the grove, Thea noticed. For the same cause?

"Vaden?" she asked.

He nodded curtly, his gaze on the approaching horsemen. They were dragging something behind them. A body?

She stepped forward as they reached the courtyard.

It was not a body; it was a tree. A young mulberry tree of about seven feet in length.

At least she thought it was a mulberry tree. Every limb had been hacked from its trunk, the roots cruelly severed. It was an act of cold, deliberate destruction.

She shivered as she moved to stand beside Ware. "He killed it," she whispered. "Why would he do that? And why would he bring it here?"

Ware motioned to Abdul. "Get rid of it. I don't want to see it again." He turned and strode back toward the castle.

Thea took one last glance at the butchered tree before running to catch up with him. She suddenly realized Ware's face was pale, his expression grimmer than she had ever seen it. "Why would he do that? It makes no sense."

"You don't venture through those gates," he said harshly. "I don't even want you on the battlements until after dark."

"How could I leave the castle? You permit no one to leave without your consent."

"How do I know what you'll do? You might decide to go after more of your cursed mulberry leaves."

"I told you I had a sufficient—" She stopped as she made the connection. "You believe the tree is a warning."

"I know it's a warning."

She was trying to work it out. "But not against you."

"Vaden has no doubt that I know he's going to kill me."

Not *try* to kill him, but *going to* kill him. He spoke as if his death by Vaden's hand were inevitable. "Then why—" Her eyes widened in shock. "Me?"

"He saw you stop Abdul and the others from hacking off the branches. He knew I'd know what he meant."

She shook her head in disbelief. "He wants to kill me?"

"He *doesn't* want to do it, he feels he must. Vaden is no butcher of innocents."

She could believe that the man who had coldly, methodically dismembered that tree was capable of anything. "You're defending him."

"I'm not defending him; I'm explaining. Vaden is a fair man. He could have killed you yesterday, but he wanted to give warning of his intention."

"But why? I've done nothing to harm him."

"No, you've done nothing. I'm at fault. I was stupid and allowed myself— Christ, you'd think I'd learn. Does the whole world have to die before I—" He turned and moved toward the stable. "Go inside and stay there. I'm going to ride out and see if I can find him."

Fear sliced through her. He had already told Abdul how formidable Vaden was. "You're going alone?"

He nodded grimly. "I won't have my men pay for my stupidity. I doubt if he'll let me find him. He flits around these mountains like a phantom."

"He was on the third mountain. . . ."

"Do you think me a fool? I've tried several times in the last two years. He's always gone before we reach the camp."

Like a phantom, Ware had said. A deadly phantom . . . "He cannot mean it. All this makes no sense."

"He means it." He stopped at the stable door and looked down at her. "I'll leave orders with Abdul that if I don't return, he's to take you from here to a place of safety. You're not to argue, you're just to go. Do you understand?"

"No, I don't understand. I don't understand any of this."

"Go back to the castle." He entered the stable. "I've no time to explain."

She started to follow him and then stopped. He would not be dissuaded, she realized in frustration. He would ride out and try to kill that man who had threatened her life.

It was all madness. He had to be mistaken.

But he was certain enough to risk his life to try to prevent her murder.

She moved slowly toward the castle.

Why weren't women trained to fight their own battles instead of relying on men to do it for them? But it was not her battle. She had nothing to do with Ware of Dundragon. Fate had sent her whirling into his life to be faced with a danger she knew nothing about. It was not fair.

But she was not being fair either. He had saved her and was bringing Selene to her. If he had not bothered to replenish her supply of mulberry leaves, he wouldn't have to venture now from the castle and seek out this madman who wanted to kill her. He was as much a victim of fate as she.

Darkness fell and Ware had still not returned.

She climbed to the falcons' tower and stood looking out over the countryside.

No fire burned on the third mountain.

Did that mean that Vaden had turned hunter?

A chill went through her. Ware might die this night. He might already be dead.

She closed her eyes as a wave of sickness washed over her. It should not mean this much to her. He was almost a stranger, and he had never sought her friendship. In truth, he had rejected her on any number of occasions. He was a rough, arrogant warrior interested only in battle and the gold he received for fighting.

Yet he had somehow touched her. She had wanted to draw closer to him, protect him, help him. By all the saints, she should not have let it happen. Selene and her new life should be the only things of importance to her. She had told Kadar she was selfish, and she should have guarded that selfishness with all her strength.

There was no use looking back in regret, she thought wearily. He had managed to creep under her guard, so she must stop fighting and accept it. She must find a place for him.

If it was not too late.

It was close to midnight when Thea heard the challenge from the guard at the drawbridge.

She flew down the steps and was waiting when Ware rode through the gates.

"What are you doing here?" He dismounted and threw the reins of his horse to a stable boy. "The night is chill. Have you nothing better to do than wander around the courtyard at midnight?"

She was so glad to see him that she felt no anger at his surliness. She said lightly, "I suppose I could have occupied myself by checking those terrible accounts, but there's no Dundragon without you, and I wasn't sure you'd be back. I hate to waste time."

He pulled off his helmet and wearily ran his hand through his hair. "I couldn't find him."

"Well, he didn't find you either." She turned and moved up the steps. "Get out of that armor and come to the Great Hall. I'll have meat and bread ready."

He frowned. "What if I don't want to eat?"

"Do it anyway." She tossed over her shoulder as she entered the castle, "I know it delights you to be contrary, but it will only hurt you to refuse to eat when you must feel hungry. You haven't eaten all day."

"I'm not contrary. I don't like to be ordered about by—"

She didn't wait for him to finish. Instead she strode quickly through the hall and down to the scullery.

She was kneeling, stoking the fire, when he entered the Great Hall. His face was clean, his hair wet, she noticed; he must have refreshed himself at the well after he'd removed his armor. She jerked her head toward the table. "Sit and eat. The meat is cold, but hunger is a fine sauce." She gave the logs a final poke and rose to her feet. "And you are hungry, aren't you?"

"Yes." He sat down and picked up a piece of meat. He scowled. "And I'm not contrary."

"Of course you are." She sat down at the table and poured him a goblet of wine. "And stubborn and rude and most annoying."

He glared at her suspiciously. "You're very cheerful."

"Because I'm glad you're back. I discovered something while you were gone." She made a rueful face. "I find I have a liking for you."

He stopped with the meat halfway to his mouth. "I beg your pardon?"

"I know it's astonishing, since you're most unlikable. It surprised me also. I've decided that I must have the same weakness in my character as Kadar. Or perhaps it's poor judgment. At any rate, liking you will make keeping you company easier. I've not had much experience, but I hear friends make excellent company."

He went still. "I'm not your friend."

"Yes, you are. Or will be."

"I've no desire to be your friend."

"You've no choice. You've saved my life and you're giving me Selene. Those are the acts of a friend."

"Those were the acts of necessity."

He was making this very difficult; but, then, he was a difficult man. In those hours in the tower she had determined that she would not be dissuaded. "You're kinder than you would have it known." She leaned back in her chair. "Finish eating. I'll be silent. All this talk of kindness and friendship must be disturbing to one as churlish as you. I wouldn't like you to have a bellyache."

He finished his meat and reached for an apple. "I'm not churlish." His teeth sank deep into the apple. "You call me your friend and then insult me."

"I tell the truth. I've decided that I must accept your churlishness and try to find qualities in you to admire." She smiled at him. "You cannot dissuade me. I *will* be your friend. Ware of Dundragon."

"You will not—" He suddenly leaned back in his chair and wearily closed his eyes. "Do what you will. I suppose it makes no difference now. It's too late. None of it matters."

She stared at him in surprise. She had not expected surrender. It would not last, and she must take advantage of this unusual vulnerability. "If it doesn't matter, tell me why this Vaden wishes to kill me."

His lids opened, and she was shocked at the hollow

desolation she saw there. "You laughed with me. You touched me."

"What?"

"Vaden knows that you're more than a woman for my bed. He's afraid I might talk to you." His laughter held a hint of desperation. "As I am doing now. I find it amusing that he drove me to the very thing they most want to avoid."

It was not amusing. Thea had never seen such despair.

"You wish to be my friend?" He lifted his goblet to his lips. "You'll change your mind. I'm not allowed to have friends. My friends die."

It took her a moment to recover from the shock brought by his words. "Kadar is your friend. He's not dead."

"Yet. If he doesn't leave me, they'll kill him."

"But why?"

"I told you. They won't take the chance. Vaden has been waiting and watching for over two years. He knows Kadar has been at my side."

"That doesn't mean he'll murder him. Wouldn't he have done it before this?"

"He could afford to bide his time as long as Kadar is with me. He's not like those others who murdered Phillipe. Vaden will kill me before he strikes at anyone else."

"Phillipe?"

"My friend Phillipe of Girodeau. His kinsman Jeffrey was killed by the Templars, but Phillipe helped me anyway when I fled the Temple. For two months we scurried from place to place trying to hide. One night he insisted on going out of the caves to find food, and they captured him. When I found him, he'd been left for dead." His voice hoarsened. "They'd tortured him to make him tell where I was hiding. He was in such pain that he could barely speak to me. He kept saying, 'I didn't tell. They couldn't make me tell. Dear God, why, Ware? Why are they doing this to us?' " He poured himself another goblet of wine. "He died because I let him come too close."

So no one must ever come close again, she thought. She remembered something he had said the night of the massacre. "You didn't let anyone in Jedha come close, and they were killed too."

"I believe the Grand Master was frustrated by my eluding him for such a long time and gave the order for the massacre to show me his power." He smiled bitterly. "He knew the villagers were no danger. I'd been very careful after Phillipe. They died only because I was still alive."

"So much hatred," she whispered. "Why?"

He didn't speak for a moment. "There were tales.... Jeffrey was curious and persuaded me to go down to the caves below the Temple. We saw something there we weren't supposed to see."

"What?"

He shook his head. "I've said enough. I've told you this much only because you deserve to know why you're threatened. If I don't tell you any more, it may save you."

"It didn't save your friend Phillipe."

"No, and it wouldn't save you from the Grand Master, but Vaden is different. If you could convince him you knew nothing..." He shrugged wearily. "I don't know. He might let you go after I'm—"

Dead. He stopped before he could say the word, but his meaning could not have been clearer. The same inevitability had rung clear with one of his remarks before. "Stop that," she said sharply. "You speak as if you're already dead."

"I'd be a fool not to. I have the greatest soldiers in Christendom trying to kill me." His tone became fierce. "But I won't let them take me without exacting my due. A man should leave a mark on the world, and I'll carve mine deep."

She shivered. "With a sword? That's not a mark, it's a scar."

"Then so be it." He smiled recklessly. "It's the only remembrance I'm being allowed to leave behind. Better a scar than nothing at all." He met her gaze and asked mockingly, "And how do you feel now? Do you still wish to be my friend? Do you wish to join Phillipe and those poor souls at Jedha?"

He thought she would say no. Heaven help her, she wanted to say no. She wanted to run away from Dundragon and this man who thought he was doomed. Life and freedom were just opening to her. "I don't want to die."

"I thought not."

"Wait. Hear me out. I don't like it, but you bought my friendship with your deeds, and now I've no choice." She glared at him. "But I won't give up as you're doing. I have too many things to do with my life. I won't be killed and I won't let Selene be killed. So you'd better find a way to save us all. Do you hear me?"

He blinked, and then a slow smile lit his face. "Oh, yes, I hear you."

"And you can stop behaving like a bad-tempered oaf. It appears I'm going to have enough trials to suffer without putting up with—"

"Churlishness?" he finished for her.

She nodded. "Exactly. I'll expect to see you here in the hall tomorrow morning to bear me company while I'm doing your accounts." She rose to her feet. "And now I'm going to my bed. I'd advise you to do the same."

"Go to your bed?"

"No, and I'll not have you saying things intended to make me uncomfortable. I may have to make a place for you in my life, but it will only be on the terms of friendship and respect I choose." She moved toward the door. "You knew very well what I meant."

"Yes, I knew what you meant." She glanced over her shoulder to see him smiling curiously. He said, "But I believe I'll stay here awhile and ponder your tender words of camaraderie."

"There's nothing to ponder. I believe I've made myself clear."

As she left the hall, she heard him murmur, "Oh, but there's much to ponder, Thea."

Chapter Seven

WARE WAS NOT in the Great Hall when Thea arrived there the next morning. However, the account books were stacked neatly on the long table.

Her lips tightening grimly, she went in search of him. The courtyard was filled with mounted men, and she found Ware in the act of mounting his horse. "I told you that I needed your help with the accounts. Where are you going?"

"Nowhere." He looked down at her impassively. "Would I dare to abandon you when you gave me a command?"

"I did not—Well, perhaps I did, but you had already shown yourself entirely too eager to abandon me with the accounts." She relaxed as she noticed he wasn't wearing armor. He would not leave Dundragon without it. "What are you doing?"

"I'm preparing to put my men through their paces. I do it three times a week while I'm in residence at Dundragon. I'll join you in the Great Hall when I'm finished."

She remembered catching glimpses of the training during her first days there. "I'd like to watch."

He shrugged. "Do as you like. Just stay out of the way."

She sat down on the steps and encircled her knees with her arms.

Bowmen were practicing their skills in one part of the courtyard set aside for that purpose. However, for the better part of an hour Ware dedicated himself to the men on horseback, having them wheel on command and then charge across the courtyard with lances lowered. After he was satisfied with their performance, he turned the horsemen over to Abdul. Then he was everywhere, totally in command, instructing, watching, praising, scowling.

"Is he not splendid?" Thea glanced up to see Haroun on the top step. He sat down beside her, his gaze fastened worshipfully on Ware. "He shines like the sun."

Thea did not find the description overaccurate. "I'd say he shimmers more than shines." Like a broadsword in moonlight, lifted and ready to strike. "And should you be out of bed?" She touched the bandage binding his head. "Does it still ache?"

"No," he answered, then gestured impatiently at the soldiers. "I should be out with them. Lord Ware said I am a soldier now, and soldiers don't lie in bed being waited on."

But he was only a boy, Thea thought sadly. So young to be dazzled by the military exercise surrounding him. She said gently, "Perhaps in a few days."

"I'm well now." His words came haltingly. "I mean no

offense. You've been very kind, but it would be good to be busy again."

Of course it would. She and Jasmine had been so concerned with healing him, they had almost forgotten that the best healer, other than time itself, was to be constantly occupied.

"You look in good health." Ware was walking his horse toward the steps, his stern stare fixed on Haroun. "What are you doing sitting with women?"

Haroun flushed and jumped to his feet. "I did not mean— Jasmine said my wound is— I'm sorry, my lord."

"If you're sorry, you'll go to the stable and report to Abdul. He has things to teach you, if you're to be my squire."

"At once, my lord. I did not—" He stopped, his eyes widening. "Your squire?"

"You heard me. I'm weary of having a hodgepodge of soldiers care for my armor and do my bidding. You may be young, but Abdul says you're quick to learn." His gaze bored into the boy's. "Did he tell the truth?"

"I'll be very quick, my lord. You'll see. . . ." He repeated in a whisper, "Your squire. Truly? Just like the squires of the Franks?"

"Better. Just as all my soldiers must be better." He got down from the horse and tossed the boy the reins. "Take my horse to the stable. Abdul will show you how to care for him."

Haroun nodded eagerly and jerked at the reins.

"Easy," Ware said. "He's well trained. You don't have to drag him to the stable."

Thea watched as the boy led the huge horse across the courtyard. Pride and eagerness were in every line of his thin, wiry body, and she was poignantly reminded of that night she had first met him.

"I suppose you disapprove," Ware said. "You cannot pamper the boy forever. He's better off with work to do."

She didn't point out that a few days was not forever. "I agree."

His brows lifted. "You do?"

"When my mother died, I was glad I was forced to work. Why didn't you have a squire before?" Then she realized the reason. A squire worked closely with his master, and Ware had allowed no one close. "Will he be safe?"

"The Grand Master has decreed no one is safe. At least he'll be close enough for me to look after." He strode up the steps. "Come along. You have work to do. You've been lazy enough this day."

"Lazy? I'm not your squire and I do you a service. I will not be called—" She stopped in midsentence as she realized he was smiling. It was a small smile but, amazingly, contained no grimness, only a hint of mischief.

"I jest," he said haltingly. "Have you no humor?"

The pot calling the kettle black, she thought. "You must warn me when you're being humorous. It happens so rarely, I can't be expected to recognize it."

"You laughed with me at the mulberry grove."

But this was different. This was not a response to a farcical situation but came from within. She had caught another glimpse of that younger Ware, and it had disconcerted her. "And evidently condemned myself to death. It's not a result that would encourage a person to—" His smile had vanished and she felt a sudden sense of loss. She impulsively stepped forward and touched his arm.

When he glanced down at her, she repeated his own words. "I jest. Have you no humor?"

The smile came again, warm, almost sweet. She felt as triumphant as if she had created a magnificent tapestry in a single sitting.

"My apologies," he said. "I've been told it comes rarely."

She nodded, and her hand dropped from his arm. "And quite rightly." She preceded him into the castle. "Let's see how much humor you can draw from those account books."

"Why are you rubbing your eyes?" Ware asked.

"I'm about to turn blind trying to decipher this scribbling." She looked up with an accusing frown. "Your fours look like sevens."

"You've been staring at them for six days. You should be accustomed to them by now." He leaned forward and glanced at the number she was indicating. "It's a seven. It seems perfectly clear to me." He frowned. "Well, maybe it's a four."

She glowered at him.

"No, it's definitely a seven," he amended.

"Even you can't read it."

"I'm a knight, not a scholar." He leaned back in his chair. "Which reminds me, I've spent enough time sitting here doing nothing today."

She picked up the quill and carefully clarified the seven. "You don't go until I'm finished with this month's accounts."

"What a demanding woman you are. You're fortunate

I'm a patient man." She didn't rise to the goad, so he pushed a little more. "I've been thinking I've been too indulgent with you."

Her head lifted like a falcon sighting prey. "Indulgent?"

He carefully kept his expression impassive. "What other man would sit in this chair these many days watching you struggle and taking your foul abuse? After all, you are only a woman."

"And you are a dolt who does not even have the sense to speak sweetly to one who does you service. It's no wonder you chose to be a monk, instead of a husband. No woman would suffer your ugly tongue."

"Actually, a number of women have found my tongue very pleasing." He could see she did not understand his hidden meaning. Her manner was so bold that he often forgot she had no carnal knowledge. He decided he had goaded her enough. "But since you have not, I tender my apologies. Perhaps another time."

She studied him. "You're teasing me."

"Is that what I'm doing?" He smiled. "Then I must stop at once and let you return to your work. The sooner you finish, the sooner I can leave this chair."

"I should abandon this... this monstrosity entirely. I may do it yet."

"No, you won't." He had learned that Thea could not leave undone anything she had started. No matter how distasteful she found the task, she worked until she had mastered it. "We both know that's not your nature. So get to it so that we may both be freed."

She sighed and bent her head over the account book. A moment later he realized she had forgotten he was in the room. She would remain in that state until some other annoyance jarred her. He settled back, watching the expressions flit across her face. It was a wonderfully mobile face, brimming with expression, intelligence, and vitality. In the past few days he had made a game of guessing what she was thinking by studying that face.

And God knew that was a change for him, he thought wryly. Expressions had never been what he looked for in a woman. A woman was for coupling, and though he might wish one to enjoy the act, he had not cared if she thought at all.

But he wanted to know what Thea was thinking. Her wit was keen, her temper sharp as a dagger, and he found himself deliberately prodding her to bring it to the forefront. He enjoyed the way her eyes glittered as she went on the attack, the way she said what she thought with no attempt at subterfuge. He liked to watch her hands turning the pages with that strong, graceful movement. He was an active man, and these days of being pinned in one room should have bored him to madness, but the hours had passed . . . pleasantly.

Perhaps too pleasantly.

He immediately dismissed the thought. He found this time pleasant because it was an oasis in the turbulence surrounding him. No doubt he would grow bored if it extended for very much longer. After all, spending a few hours each day with Thea could not endanger her. The harm had already been done at the mulberry grove.

He was making excuses, he realized in disgust, when excuses were not necessary. So he took pleasure from these hours. It was no sin to enjoy a woman's mind instead of her body.

Though he would like to enjoy the body too.

He quickly veered away from that pit. He could not sit here in comfort if he dwelt on what he would like to do to Thea's body. He had tried to subdue his responses as he had in the Order, but it was different now that he was once more accustomed to taking pleasure where he found it. Being forced for hours to sit across a table from a young woman with breasts he remembered as being full and beautifully—

Don't think of them. Think of her face, think of her wit, think of her smile. None of those were forbidden to him and brought their own pleasure.

She looked up suddenly. "You have a most peculiar expression. What are you thinking?"

He feigned a yawn. "That it's too fine a day to be forced into company with a mere woman. Can you not hurry?"

"What are you doing out here?"

Thea looked up to see Ware standing above her. She brushed a strand of hair from her eyes and poured more water at the base of the young tree. "What does it look like I'm doing? I'm trying to keep these trees alive."

He frowned. "You didn't come to the hall this morning."

"Because I was in the stable gathering horse droppings and then out here spreading them underneath the trees." She made a face. "I would almost have rather been working on the account books."

"I thought Jasmine was helping you with the trees."

"She has been a great help, but she has other duties."

"Abdul could have assigned a man to do it."

"I have plenty of time. I'm used to doing such tasks myself." She carried the water bucket to the next tree.

"And I like to be busy. I miss my work." She poured water. "Besides, the accounting is almost all corrected. In a few days I'll be finished."

"You will?" His frown deepened.

"It's taken long enough. Over three weeks. I'm certain you'll be as grateful as I am. You'll no longer have to be glued to that chair answering my questions."

"Very grateful." He was silent, watching her. "Will these trees live?"

"I think they will. If there's not a bad storm to uproot them."

"You like working with the earth."

She nodded. "Growing things makes me feel . . ." She shrugged. "I like to know these trees may be here long after I'm gone. Do you know it's said that some trees live hundreds of years?"

"I never thought about it. I've been too busy staying alive to worry about trees." He ran his fingers over the rough bark. "But I, too, believe that it's important for life to go on. Perhaps there is even life after death."

She remembered what he had said about his father sending him from Scotland to preserve their family line. "But God assures us this is so. Do you doubt that if we are good, we go to heaven?"

"But what is good? The Pope says that it's good to slay, if it's done in the name of the Church." He thoughtfully stroked the trunk. "If that's true, then I must be the most Christian of men, for I slew more than any of my brothers when I was in the order." He moved his shoulders as if throwing off a burden. "Listen to me. I sound like Kadar. He's always questioning even when there are no answers."

"A terrible fault," she murmured sarcastically. "May heaven forbid you stop and think before striking out."

"I haven't struck out at you." He quickly amended, "After our first meeting."

She lifted her brows. "Once is enough."

"The fault was entirely your own. I didn't want to hurt you. You wouldn't listen to me." He waved an impatient hand. "Anyway, that's in the past. Why do you dwell on it?"

"Because I was the one you felled with a blow. I think you'd also dwell on such an act."

"Nonsense. I would forgive and then dismiss it entirely from my mind."

She gazed at him skeptically.

He swore beneath his breath. "You doubt me? It is—" He stopped, then smiled grudgingly. "Well, I would dismiss it . . . *after* I'd exacted appropriate vengeance."

She threw back her head and laughed. "Then you're fortunate my nature is meeker than your own."

He grunted derisively but made no reply. He watched her work for a moment before speaking. "You look very comely with the sunlight on your hair."

She stopped in midmotion and turned to look at him.

He smiled. "Though you smell foully of horse manure." He held up his hand to quell her indignant outburst. "I don't mind. But have it washed off before you sup with me this evening."

"Sup with you?"

"Well, Kadar says you must bear me company. If you're finished with the accounts and object to playing chess with me, I can see no other way for you to keep your promise. Can you?"

She quickly lowered her gaze to the earth so he

wouldn't see the sudden happiness that soared through her. She had not realized until this moment how much she would miss the hours they spent together while poring over those dratted accounts. "No, and, of course, I must keep my word to Kadar."

He nodded solemnly. "Promises are very important." He turned and walked back toward the castle.

HOUSE OF NICHOLAS
CONSTANTINOPLE

"You will find the worker you need here," Nicholas said, puffing with pride. "My women are the most skilled in all the world."

"I can see that by the samples of embroidery you showed me." Kadar carefully kept his tone without expression as his gaze traveled around the huge room.

There was no conversation, no laughter, as women and older children sat hunched over their hoops, shoulders bent, eyes fixed on the pattern in front of them, sewing feverishly. No one there was over her fortieth year, yet they all looked worn and aged. The sparkling cleanliness and brightness of the chamber, with many windows to let in the sunshine, made the theft of youth more horrible, Kadar thought. A truly terrible place.

But not as terrible as the carpet room from which they had just come. He had thought he had become hardened to life in all its forms, but the sight of those small children with their crippled, gnarled fingers had sickened him.

"You're very fortunate. They seem to be accomplishing

a great deal," Kadar said. "How many hours a day do they work?"

"As many hours as the sun shines. Sunrise to sunset. Come along." Nicholas moved down the first aisle. "I must show you Clarissa's work. She has a fine, mature skill even though she's barely ten and four." He cast a sly glance over his shoulder. "And when she's not at her task, she will bring your loins as much pleasure as your purse. Only last week I sank between her thighs and found her—"

"And you'll want a fine price for her." Kadar shook his head. "I told you I wanted someone younger...and cheaper."

Nicholas sighed and moved farther down the row. "Evadne may please you. She is only nine. She has developed little skill as yet, and I may be persuaded to release her."

Kadar's gaze discreetly searched the bent heads. Red hair, Thea had said. Where the devil was she? "How long has she been here?"

"I bought her two years ago. Her fingers were too long for the carpets, so I had her trained on the embroidery hoops." He stopped before a small delicate girl with flaxen hair and haunted eyes. "What do you think?"

He thought Nicholas was a callous bastard. He tilted his head as he appraised the embroidery before the girl. "Not as good as I would like."

"If you don't pay, you can't expect quality."

She was there in the next row. Small, thin, red hair, her gaze fixed on the hoop in front of her. "That one seems to have more skill."

"Selene? It's true she's older, almost eleven." Nicholas moved brusquely toward the child. "But I cannot give you the same price. In three or four years she'll be old enough to give you pleasure . . . as well as children."

No mention yet that she was also his daughter. The whoreson would probably pull in that small fact when the negotiations became more heated. "I have slaves to give me pleasure. I want only her skill."

He stopped in front of the red-haired child's hoop. Her embroidery was exquisite, he thought. Too bad. The price would have been cheaper if he could have argued that point. She had not even glanced up at him. She just sat hunched, ignoring them as her needle went in and out of—

He went still, his gaze on the child's back.

"What is this?" He pushed aside the loose cotton tunic covering Selene's shoulders. Red stripes crisscrossed the girl's narrow back. "Perhaps she has less value than you claim."

Nicholas shrugged. "She has a biting tongue, but that doesn't affect her skill."

Kadar's forefinger traced a white scar. "This one is older." The child did not look up, but he could feel the muscles of her back knot beneath his touch.

"She was caught helping a runaway slave. We needed to know the slave's destination so that she could be recovered."

So Selene had met with punishment when Thea had fled. "And did she tell you?"

Nicholas shook his head. "We could not continue; she would have died. It became a choice of losing two slaves instead of one."

"No, you wouldn't have wanted to do that." No mention that the escaped slave was the girl's sister. He wondered if he could chance cutting the bastard's throat before he left Constantinople. No, he decided regretfully, he would have to deny himself that pleasure. Freeing the child was the important thing. "But these marks do show a temperament that could prove troublesome." His hand dropped away from the child's scarred back. "I suppose you'll have to show me another slave."

He was two aisles away from Selene, listening to Nicholas's praises of another poor child when he glanced back at her.

She was staring at him, bold green eyes glittering with resentment in her thin face.

He smiled at her.

The enmity in her expression didn't change. If anything, her belligerence increased.

Evidently not one to be won over by a sweet smile. He felt a ripple of interest mixed with pleasure. It would be a much more interesting trip back to Dundragon if the child offered him some challenge.

"Lower your eyes."

A squat, heavy woman was standing behind Selene with a slender whip in her hand.

Selene did not lower her eyes.

Nicholas's attention was caught, and he broke off extolling the skills of a dark-haired child. "No unpleasantness, Maya. We have a guest."

"She's wasting time. She must finish this side of the tunic by nightfall," Maya said. "You wished it for the caravan leaving day after tomorrow."

Nicholas's brow furrowed. "True."

Kadar wagered the child would not stop staring at him

while he was in the room even if the whip did fall on her. It was a point of honor to her now.

He turned and moved quickly toward the door. "I'm weary of these discussions. Decisions are so trying. Can we not continue tomorrow?"

Nicholas followed him. "Of course. We will have a goblet of wine and then go visit the baths. It is the most divine of pleasures."

Except beating helpless children. "You're the kindest of hosts." Kadar beamed. "I look forward to it."

The stranger came to the garden that evening.

Selene stiffened as she saw him standing in the arched doorway, his gaze moving casually among the women gathered in groups about the fountain.

He was probably choosing which woman to pleasure him tonight, Selene thought bitterly. Tomorrow after he had relieved his lust, the negotiations for the purchase of a slave would resume.

He was younger than most of the merchants and traders who came there. Young and richly robed, with a beauty as startling as the torch burning on the wall beside him. But comely or not, he was like all the others—greedy for gold and for pleasure.

He was moving leisurely toward the bench where she sat a few yards apart from the other women.

She tensed and then relaxed. He would not choose her for pleasure. Even if he was one who liked children, she was too thin and homely.

He stopped in front of the bench. "You look lonely. Why are you not with the other slaves?"

She did not answer.

He sat down beside her and she caught a whiff of clean soap and fragrant balsam. It was the way Nicholas smelled when he came back from the city baths. "My name is Kadar ben Arnaud, Selene. Do you know why I'm here?"

"To buy a woman to start an embroidery house. We all know that." She added with deliberate rudeness, "But you are too niggardly to pay for any but a beginner."

He did not take offense. "True. You sew very well. Do you like to embroider?"

"No," she said baldly. "You don't have to like something to do it well." She edged away from him on the bench. Why didn't he get up and go away?

"Even if I buy you, I promise I'll not hurt you," he said softly. "You need not fear me."

Panic soared through her. She had thought he had erased her from his list of choices. "I don't fear you." She added fiercely, "But I won't work for you. I'll sit at my hoop and do nothing. Find someone else."

"You prefer it here? Nicholas doesn't seem an overkind master."

"I *must* stay here."

He changed the subject. "Why were you glaring at me this afternoon?"

"You touched me. I don't like to be touched."

"Why not?"

She didn't answer. She wished he would go away.

"That hulking woman is coming toward us. I find her most unpleasant."

He meant Maya, who was edging closer to hear their conversation. "Then you should choose your woman for the night and leave us all in peace."

"Which one should I choose?"

The question startled her. She turned to look at him. "What?"

"It's an indelicate question to ask a child, but I mustn't offend Nicholas by refusing his offer of a bedmate, and I'd prefer a woman who takes pleasure as well as gives it. Is there such a one here?"

What manner of man was he? she wondered in bewilderment. Every one knew a woman's pleasure meant nothing.

"Is there?"

She glanced around the garden before nodding at a small dark woman. "Deirdre. She's not as comely as some of the others, but she is very peculiar. She seems to like it when Nicholas ruts with her."

He smiled. "I thought you'd know. You're one of the ones who watch, aren't you?"

She asked warily, "What do you mean?"

"You stand apart and watch and learn. Poor Selene. I think you have a great hunger for life. Sitting here stitching in this cocoon must drive you mad, so you close everyone out and you think and you watch."

How had he known that?

He answered her unspoken question. "At your age I was a watcher too. I still am when the occasion warrants it." He smiled. "And you do warrant it, Selene."

He was not like the others. He was far more dangerous, for he had eyes to see. She jumped to her feet. "I don't want you watching me. Go away."

"I didn't mean to offend you. In fact, I wished to reassure you." He glanced at Maya. "But now isn't the time.

We will talk later." He wandered toward the women at the fountain.

He said a few words to Deirdre and then took her hand and led her toward the door.

"He says kind words to you, but he only wants to keep you tame until he gets you back to his own country," Maya said behind Selene. "Then he'll set the whip to you."

"He won't choose me to work in his house. You heard what he told Nicholas. He thinks I'd be too much trouble."

"But he finds your embroidery adequate. He will choose you. Tomorrow he and Nicholas will strike a bargain and you'll be gone." Maya smiled maliciously. "You might as well go with him meekly. I know you're waiting for her to come back, but she never will. Thea's probably a whore in the streets by now."

"Be silent."

"How could she free you anyway?"

Selene tried to shut out her words, shut away the pain.

"She was so clever. She thought she was better than the rest of us."

"She was never unkind to you." She met Maya's eyes. "And she was better than you. A dog in the streets is better than you."

Color flared in Maya's heavily jowled cheeks.

Selene knew she should have kept silent. She would pay in the workroom tomorrow. She didn't care. She could stand only so much from Maya.

The gong sounded the signal for bedtime.

A gong to rise, a gong to summon them to meals, a gong to order them to the workroom. Sometimes she heard that gong in her dreams, deafening her, suffocating her.

She passed Maya, who was muttering low threats, and moved reluctantly toward the house of women.

She will never come for you.

Maya's words repeated over and over in her head as she settled down on her pallet.

Thea would come, she thought desperately. Thea loved her. She would never leave her alone.

But Mama had loved them and left them alone. Her arms had been holding Selene and then they had fallen away.

But Thea was different. She was as strong as Mama had been weak. She would not let Selene stay in this place. She would come for her.

She fought back the stinging behind her eyes. She had not cried since Mama died. Tears changed nothing. She had heard Mama weeping in the night sometimes, and it had not helped her. Her life had not got better. She had not lived. Mama . . .

Don't think of Mama. Don't think of Thea. One minute at a time. She could bear life that way. Thea would come for her.

But what if Maya was right and the young merchant chose her and took her far away from Constantinople?

Panic soared through her. Maya was wrong. She would be here when Thea came back for her. God would not be that cruel. Kadar ben Arnaud would choose one of the others.

"I told you," Maya said softly, her eyes drinking in Selene's shock and suffering as if it were a honeyed drink. "You are only a child and a slave. You can do nothing about it. Our master says you must be ready to leave on the morrow."

"You lie." Selene steadied her voice. "It's not true."

"It's true. You sail tomorrow evening. But Nicholas is far from pleased. The young rooster was a much cannier bargainer than he had hoped. They argued all day, but Nicholas could not squeeze more from him." Maya sailed away toward another group of women to spread the word.

Selene sat down on the bench. She was shaking with anger as well as fear. She could not leave. He had no right to tear her from her only hope of freedom.

You can do nothing.

Perhaps Maya was right and she was too young to fight this world of grown-ups who cared about nothing but gold.

Thea, help me.

Thea was not here to help her, and she was not a child. Children were young, and she had lost her youth the night Mama had died.

She must help herself.

"She is gone?" Kadar repeated.

"But I'm sure we will find her," Nicholas said quickly. "She is only a child. Where could she go? No doubt when she gets hungry she will return."

Not even if she was starving, Kadar thought grimly. Christ, he should have gone to her last night after the deal had been struck. But what good would it have done when he would not have been able to talk to her without that muscular mamba hovering nearby? "When did she leave?"

"Some time during the night." He frowned. "She must have climbed the garden wall. None of the guards saw her."

Then she'd had hours to lose herself in the city.

"She has been sheltered under my roof and knows little of the wickedness she will find on the streets. Trust me, she will come running back in a few days." Nicholas paused. "But you understand the bargain was struck. She is now your property. I'm not responsible."

"You're saying you won't return my gold?"

Nicholas did not answer directly. "She's not my responsibility."

Yes, the bastard definitely needed his throat cut. Too bad Kadar had to keep him alive to find out if Selene returned.

"You'll postpone your sailing and stay until you retrieve her?" Nicholas asked.

"I can do nothing else. You made sure she was too costly to leave behind."

"Not that costly," Nicholas said sourly. "Perhaps fate decided to punish you for cheating me of her services."

Not for robbing him of a daughter but of a slave to give service. Kadar had had enough. He turned and strode toward the door. "I'll send a messenger each day to see if she has returned."

He paused outside the gates of the House of Nicholas. Where should he start? He knew nothing about Constantinople. Well, according to Nicholas, neither did Selene. The knowledge brought him a ripple of unease. Cities were all the same, infested with the wolves of the world, all ready to gobble up the innocent and unwary.

He could only hope he reached Selene before the wolves did.

"I was right. Women have no head for chess," Ware said as he looked down at the chessboard. "I find it very satisfying to beat you at the game."

"Is that why you insist we play after we sup each evening?" Thea asked.

"No, I have another reason."

"What reason?"

"Would you like to play another game?"

"What reason?"

He leaned back in his chair and smiled at her.

He wasn't going to tell her. He often had those maddening moments of reticence, but they came less frequently now. "Well, I'll play no more with you." She pushed her chair back and stared into the fire. "And I could win, if it meant enough to me."

"I know you could." When she glanced up, he quickly amended, "At least, part of the time."

She grinned at him. "Most of the time. Your attention wanders on occasion."

"Does it? I must watch that fault. Such conduct could kill a soldier."

"But not here."

"No, not here."

A comfortable silence fell in the firelit room. Who would have guessed she would ever be this comfortable with Ware of Dundragon? she mused. "Isn't it time Kadar returned with Selene?"

"Soon. He may have had trouble persuading Nicholas to relinquish her."

A flicker of anxiety disturbed the peace of the moment. "But he will be able to do it?"

"Kadar can be more manipulative and patient than Saladin himself. If he doesn't wrest victory one way, he'll approach it from another direction. He'll bring her."

"And what if he doesn't?"

"She'll still come to you. I'll go after her myself." He smiled grimly. "But my ways are not as civilized as Kadar's. I may be forced to make orphans of you."

Her eyes widened in alarm. "You jest."

"We've already established I rarely jest." He shrugged. "So we must hope Kadar succeeds."

"It would be too dangerous for you to journey to Constantinople."

"The danger exists every time I leave Dundragon. The threat is no greater in Constantinople than in Damascus. I made you a promise."

"But I would not have you die for it," she said fiercely. "I will find a way to get Selene myself as I first intended."

His gaze fastened intently on her face. "Promises must be kept."

"Don't be foolish. I survived many years in Nicholas's house. Selene can do the same. A few years out of her life is not worth your death. I will not hear more of this— Why are you looking at me like that?"

"I was wondering if you'd weep for me should I fall."

"I do not weep readily." His curious expression didn't change, and it was making her uncomfortable. "And I see no reason why I should weep for a man who would risk himself so foolishly."

"But you have a tender heart and you insist I'm your friend. Would you weep for me, Thea?"

She could not read his expression, but there was a note in his voice that made her hesitate to avoid the question. He was a man who lived constantly with death as his companion. Perhaps the knowledge that he would be mourned meant something to him. She met his gaze. "I would weep for you."

He nodded slowly. "I believe you would."

She could not look away. The room suddenly seemed to be without air. He was trying to tell her something. No, there were no words or thoughts, just . . . what? She didn't know, but she could not bear this intensity. She tried to smile. "But I shall not weep, because Kadar is going to bring me Selene."

"She is ready, my lord." Haroun had appeared in the doorway.

Thea breathed a sigh of relief at the interruption. "What are you doing still awake, Haroun?" she asked him.

Haroun gave her an indignant glance. "I go about my lord's duties." He bowed to Ware. "You said to tell you when she was ready."

She? Thea suddenly tensed as she realized what he must mean. Ware had not called Tasza to his bed of late, but that did not mean he was not coupling with other women in the household. Of course he was using them; he was a man with a lustful appetite. Why did she feel this sense of shock and outrage? She jumped to her feet. "I keep you. You clearly have things to do."

He frowned. "Why are you—" He stopped as he understood. "You think I have a woman waiting in my bed?"

"It is none of my concern." She moved toward the door. "But I'd think you would not use Haroun to arrange such acts."

"My lady," Haroun objected, shocked at what he deemed impertinence.

"It's a squire's duty to make his master comfortable." Ware rose from his chair. "And you're right, it's none of your concern. Still, I believe it will amuse me to have you come with me."

I want you to watch.

The scene that night in this hall came back to her. Ware sitting naked, Tasza crouched at his feet, her lips on his—

A bolt of heat seared through her. "I'll not do it."

"You will." He strode past her. "Because it pleases me. One must always strive to please one's friends. Isn't that true?"

She hesitated, standing watching him. What was he about? He had gone not toward the staircase, as she had expected, but toward the front door.

He opened the door and stepped aside, gesturing for her to precede him.

Haroun took her hand and tugged. He whispered, "You must obey my lord."

Haroun believed everyone on this earth must obey Ware. Still, she was curious. She let him lead her toward the door.

"I please my friend Haroun," she told Ware as she went past him. "Not you."

He chuckled. "I note the distinction."

She started down the steps. "Are you going to tell me where we—" She stopped as she saw a wagon across the courtyard. Four fully armored soldiers were mounted behind it. "What is this?"

But Ware was already striding toward the wagon. Haroun immediately dropped her hand and ran after him. Thea slowly followed them.

As she drew closer, she saw a young woman lying in the bed of the wagon. She was vaguely familiar to Thea, one of the multitude of servants in this vast place.

"I don't want to go, my lord," the woman said, her gaze fixed pleadingly on Ware. "Let me stay."

Ware shook his head. "You will do well in Damascus. All your needs will be met. The babe must be kept safe." He motioned to the driver of the wagon. "Go with God."

Babe.

Thea watched numbly as the wagon slowly rolled toward the gates with the escort following. "She's with child?"

"Four months." Ware was looking after the wagon with an expression she had never seen on his face—a strange mixture of desperation and bitterness. "She had to leave now. Later the journey would have been too hard on her."

Her numbness was gone, leaving raw anger in its wake, an emotion as wild and intense as it was unexplainable. "I'd think you would want to be present when your child was born."

"I would." He turned to look at her. "But the babe is not mine. Fatima is the wife of one of my soldiers."

Another rush of emotion cascaded through her, and she glanced quickly away. "I see."

"No, you don't," he said roughly. "I wouldn't send a woman bearing my child away without my escort. I would be by her side, guarding her and the child from all harm."

She didn't look at him. "She didn't want to go."

"She bears Jusef's child, and a child is a man's only hope of immortality. She must be kept safe. I won't have him cheated."

There was such an intensity of passion in his tone that she was startled. "But will she be safe?"

"I've deliberately sent only an escort of four. Vaden will know that I'd be more careful if they were guarding something of mine."

"He won't harm her?"

He frowned. "Of course he won't hurt her. He's no monster."

"Forgive me," she said with sarcasm. "When you said he wished to murder me, I assumed he was—"

"That's a different matter." He turned and strode toward the castle.

She did not follow him but watched the wagon roll through the gates. Ware was probably returning to the Great Hall. She would go directly to her chamber and avoid any further encounter with him tonight. She had passed through too many emotional peaks and valleys this night. In the space of that few minutes beside the wagon, Ware had changed from the man to whom she had become accustomed to the moody despot she had first met.

But he was not moody, he was a man in pain. She knew now how he covered every emotion with a blanket of thorns. She was trying to ignore it because she did not want to deal with it. Her response had been too strong, too frightening, and she wanted only to hide away.

He was in the Great Hall, as she knew he would be, sitting staring into the fire.

She strode past the arched doorway and started up the staircase.

By all the saints, she couldn't do it.

She sighed and started down the steps again.

"Your face is ugly when you scowl," she said as she entered the room. "It displeases me exceedingly."

"Then go somewhere you don't have to look at it."

She sat down on a stool beside the hearth. "Kadar wouldn't like it."

"Kadar." He turned his head to look at her. "Is that why you're here?"

"Why else would I be—" She met his gaze and shook her head. "It troubles me when you're like this."

"Does it?" He lifted his goblet to his lips. "Would you like to soothe me?"

"I'd like to help you."

"No, you wouldn't. Not in the way I want you to help." He drained the goblet. "But if you don't go away, I may ask it anyway."

She smiled with effort. "That's no great threat. I've refused you before."

"No, you haven't. I haven't fallen that deep into the pit as yet." He gazed at her for a long moment and then shifted his glance away. "Leave me."

She sat unmoving.

His hand tightened with white-knuckled pressure on the goblet. "Leave me," he said through his teeth. "Or, by God, I'll call Abdul and have him carry you from this room."

He meant it. She had never seen him like this. She slowly rose from the stool. "No one need force me. I take no pleasure in your company when you're like this." She started across the chamber. "Good night."

"Wait!"

She glanced over her shoulder to see expression after expression flickering over Ware's face. "What is it?"

"Nothing," he muttered. "Nothing." He lifted his goblet to her and smiled mockingly. "A moment of weakness. Shall we wager whether I succumb the next time?"

"I don't know what you're talking about, and I'm weary of trying to understand you."

"No more than I am. I don't understand myself at all of late." He looked back into the fire. "But I wouldn't wager on either my generosity or strength of will. It would be very unwise."

Thea woke with a start in the darkness.

"Hush." Ware was a massive shadow sitting on the bed beside her. "I'm not going to harm you."

Her heart was beating so hard, she could scarcely speak. "You already have," she said tartly. "Frightening me unto death is harm enough. Light the candle."

"No, there's moonlight. I can see you well enough."

"Well, I can't see you." But she could sense him and the tension that seemed to reach out and enfold her. She was suddenly acutely conscious of scents and textures drifting to her in the darkness. The scent of leather, which always surrounded Ware, the fragrance of lemon, cedar, and mulberry drifting from the trees below on the green, the soft cotton coverlet against her naked body. She swallowed. "Light the candle."

"I don't want you to see me." He reached out and touched her bare shoulder. "Silk," he murmured. "Can you weave cloth this fine?"

Her skin seemed to burn beneath his fingers, yet she didn't want to move. "Finer."

"No," he said thickly. "Not finer."

"Have you had too much wine?"

"No, but I might have had enough." He rubbed gently,

sensuously at the hollow of her shoulder. "Why else am I here?"

"I don't know. Go to your bed. You'll feel better in the morning."

"Not better, but not as mad, perhaps. They say dawn brings a sweet clarity of spirit."

"What do you do here?"

"Madness. I thought I'd told you."

She moistened her lips. "You wish to couple with me?"

"Oh, yes, I've wanted that since the night I brought you to Dundragon. But lust is not madness. I wish something much more dangerous." He paused. "I want to get you with child."

She went rigid with shock.

"That's why I had to be drunk before I came to you." He continued to stroke her shoulder. "I find I have scruples about asking a woman to bear a child who will never know his father. Particularly since the act of conception alone will mark you for death. Wouldn't any man bare his secrets to the mother of his child?"

"I thought you said I was already marked for death."

"Probably. But Vaden might— No, he couldn't, if he knew you were bearing my child." His voice hoarsened. "You see how low I've fallen? I'd risk your life for my own ends."

"Why?"

"Because I *want* this." The air crackled with the intensity of his passion. "I don't want to die and not have something of me live on."

Mother of God, she could not believe she was feeling this wrenching pang of sympathy. "Then have a child by Tasza or one of the others. I'm no mare to be bred at will."

"I want *your* child. I want my son to have your pride and your strength. I'd trust you to care for him and teach him." He was silent a moment and then said jerkily, "It's not such a bad thing I offer you. The danger may be the same whether or not you take me to your bed, and I'll do all I can to protect you. I'd take you to the safest haven I could find as soon as we knew you were with child. Kadar would stay with you and watch over you. You would never want for anything. I'm a very rich man. It would be too dangerous to wed you, but on my death I would see that you had—"

"Be silent." Her voice was shaking as she pushed aside his hand and sat up in bed. "I'm tired of this talk of death from you. I will not have it."

"Very well. I've said what I came for and it appears the answer is no. I expected it would be." He stood up, swaying a little on his feet. "I bid you good night."

His abrupt departure was as startling as everything else that had happened this night. "You're leaving?"

"As you've guessed, I'm more than a little drunk, and I have a tendency toward self-indulgence when I've had too much. I can't stay without taking you, and I can't touch you unless you agree to the child. I couldn't stop myself from spending within you as I do with other women. I've known that from the beginning." He started heavily across the room. "But I should warn you that I'll probably not give up. Vaden used to say that once I got something in my head, I couldn't leave it alone."

"It will do you no good. You'll have to find another woman to give you the immortality you crave."

"I told you, I don't want another woman." He opened the door. His voice had a thread of wonder as he added, "I haven't wanted another woman for a long time. Isn't it strange that no other woman will do?"

The door closed behind him.

She was trembling, Thea realized. It was anger. She was furious with that drunken oaf. Or afraid. It was natural for a woman to be frightened when she was confronted by a man who told her he wanted to use her body. Or bewildered. She had been thrown into a turmoil of shock and confusion at Ware's words.

A child . . .

The thought brought a warm rush of tenderness. She had always loved children.

By all the saints, what was wrong with her? She had no need of a babe. She already had Selene, whom she had practically raised from babyhood. She had her living to make in this world, and it would only be harder if she was with child. It was out of the question, and she was right to be angry with that big idiot of a warrior who thought he could stride into her life and use her body as he saw fit.

Tears were running down her cheeks. Dear God, it was not from anger, she finally realized. Even as she had issued that rejection, she had wanted to pull him close and comfort him, to tell him that he would live forever and had no need of a child. Why did she let him move her like this?

She wiped her damp cheeks with the back of her hand and lay back down. This softness must be banished. Pity was no reason to have a man's child.

What Ware had asked was outrageous and totally out of the question. She would think no more about it, and if he posed the question again to her, she would tell him what she thought of such ruthless selfishness.

She would think no more about it. . . .

Chapter Eight

"MY LORD WISHES to speak with you," Jasmine said. "You must come to the Great Hall at once."

Thea glanced up at her before pouring more water at the base of the tree. "When I'm gone, you must be careful not to give these trees too much water. Too much is worse than not enough."

"Have you told Allah this secret so that he can ration his rain?" Jasmine asked dryly.

"We can do nothing about God, but we can do all we can ourselves."

"My lord wants you."

There was no use putting it off any longer. She had been avoiding Ware all day, but she would have to face him sometime. "I'm coming." She rose to her feet, dusted the earth from her skirt, and started back toward the castle. "I was finished here anyway."

Jasmine fell into step with her. "He set me searching all over the castle for you. You are angry with him?"

"No."

"He is angry with you?"

"I don't know. Perhaps." She changed the subject. "Have you practiced that loop stitch I showed you yesterday?"

Jasmine nodded. "But I'm still very clumsy."

"The skill will come."

"I showed it to Tasza. She did it better than I did."

"You're teaching Tasza to embroider? I thought she had no interest in learning it."

"This is a good thing. Tasza will do as I tell her."

Thea shook her head. "No, Jasmine. She must do it because it is her wish, or it will become slavery for her. I will not have that happen."

Jasmine frowned. "Sometimes she doesn't know what is good for her. I must tell her." She paused. "I think she is afraid."

"Afraid?"

"To fail. Everyone must take pride in something. Tasza may be a whore, but she is a very good whore. Through all the cruelties heaped upon her, she could hold to that. Now she must start at the beginning and it frightens her." Her lips tightened. "But I'll not permit her to stop. I could not save her when she went on the streets, but this is another chance. So do not tell me not to teach her."

How could she remonstrate with Jasmine? She was not even sure she wanted to do so. Both these women had suffered and sacrificed for each other. It was not for her to interfere with a bond of such strength. "If I can help, call on me."

"You can help us by staying. We need your teaching."

She should have known Jasmine would ask that of her. "I cannot stay. As soon as Selene arrives, I must go to Damascus and make a life for us. You can understand how I want the best for her. You feel the same about your Tasza. I'll teach you all I can before I leave."

"It may not be enough."

"Perhaps someday both of you can come and work with me. You are free women. It's best now that you stay with Lord Ware, since I cannot offer you a place. But once I have my own house, I'll send for you."

Jasmine turned and stared directly into her eyes. "You promise me?"

"I promise you."

Jasmine slowly nodded. "Then all will be well."

Thea wished she were as confident. Those first few years were going to be a hard struggle for both her and Selene. "You may have to be patient."

"I have patience." She fixed Thea with a stern glance. "But you must work very hard, you understand?"

Thea smothered a smile and nodded meekly. "Every hour of the day."

"Perhaps not every hour," Jasmine said grimly. "But many hours of the day. And don't wait until you can make a place for us. We'll make a place for ourselves when you open your house. Soon you'll find you won't be able to do without us."

What had she got herself into by that offer? she wondered ruefully. Jasmine and Tasza were both extremely strong-willed. If she wasn't careful, they would be giving her orders in her own house. The thought brought no unease. It would be good to have about her people she knew and trusted when she ventured forth into the world of trade.

They had reached the castle and Jasmine opened the door. "You'll teach me another stitch today?"

Thea nodded. "As soon as I leave Lord Ware. Come to my chamber."

"I'll try to bring Tasza." She started toward the servants' quarters. "It would be easier for her to learn from you than me."

That was all she needed, Thea thought wearily—a difficult confrontation with Ware and then a lesson with a sulky, rebellious Tasza.

She braced herself, then strode quickly down the long corridor toward the Great Hall. She had deliberately kept herself from thinking about Ware or the words he had spoken last night. They brought a twisting pain that filled her with too much confusion and sadness. She must not think now. She must just reiterate her refusal and leave him.

He turned away from the window when he heard her steps. "It took you long enough. Where were you hiding?"

"I wasn't hiding. I was tending the trees."

"All day?"

She brushed the question aside. "What do you wish of me?"

"I told you what I wished." He lifted his hand as she opened her lips to speak. "Don't worry, I'm no longer out of my senses. I've no intention of either coupling with you or getting you with child." He smiled sardonically as he added, "Today. I don't speak for tomorrow. I woke this morning full of guilt and torment, but I can't be sure it will last."

She felt oddly deflated. After bracing herself to resist

him, he had changed again and made resistance unnecessary. "Such conduct was most selfish of you."

"I'm a selfish man. You should know that by now."

A truly selfish man would not be tormented by guilt at taking what he wanted most in the world. By the saints, she was making excuses for him again, she realized with exasperation. "You can be very selfish . . . on occasion."

He waved away her words. "But that's not why I asked Jasmine to find you. I wanted to tell you that I'm going to Acre tomorrow. I'm leaving Abdul here to watch over you, but you're not to leave the castle. Do you understand?"

"Acre?" she asked, startled. "Why?"

"To seek word of Kadar."

"You said that it wasn't unusual for him to take this long."

"It's not unusual."

"Then why are you going?"

"It will do no harm to give Kadar and your sister safe escort back to Dundragon."

"You didn't think Kadar needed an escort when he left here. Why should it be necessary now?"

"Because I wish to go," he snapped. "Stop questioning me. I'd think you'd like to see the last of me for a while."

The last of him. Sudden fear iced through her. Every time he left the castle, there was a possibility it might be his last. "Not when you ride foolishly into danger for no reason."

"I'm taking a small force."

"And will that be enough if you're attacked?"

"Of course it will. Do you think I'd let anything happen to my men?"

"No, you'd probably tell them to leave you and let

yourself be cut down." She tried to steady her voice. "It's stupid for you to go when it's not necessary."

"It is necessary."

"Why? When you said—"

"Dammit, because it will happen again." His eyes were suddenly blazing down at her. "I have to get away from you. Some night I'll drink too much and I'll come to your bed. I want it too much. I want you too much."

"So you would die for lust? You'd die for a child who doesn't exist?" She wanted to shake him. "You said you were back in your senses, but I see no sign of it."

"I'm not going out to die. I'm going to Acre to escort Kadar and your sister to Dundragon."

"And risk your life doing it. You're a stupid, stupid man."

"Not only selfish but stupid." He started for the door. "I'd best go before I become more of a monster than I am already."

He was leaving her. Tomorrow he was leaving Dundragon. "Wait!"

He stopped and looked at her.

"This is madness," she whispered. "Don't go."

"I can do nothing else," he said haltingly. "I've hurt too many people already. I find... I cannot hurt you, too."

She was shaking, she realized, as she watched him leave the room. She was cold and shaking with a knot twisting in the pit of her stomach. She wanted to strike out at him. She wanted to yell and scream.

She wanted to hold and comfort him.

It was the same emotion that had nearly overwhelmed her last night, but now it was stronger, much stronger. She turned and stared out at the mountains. Death could be waiting for him when he rode out tomorrow. The enigma that was Vaden could strike him down. Why would he not listen to her?

She knew why he would not listen. She understood him now, and she wished with her whole heart that she did not. She should not have allowed herself to come this close, but she could not hold at a distance someone she had embraced in friendship. It was not possible.

Any more than it was possible for her to let him ride out of Dundragon tomorrow into danger.

Her hand was trembling on the candlestick as she moved down the dark corridor. Her shadow looked small and fragile in the light cast on the stone walls. Mother of God, what was she doing? She wanted to run back to her own chamber and jump into bed and pull the covers over her head. He might not even be alone. She had purposely waited until the middle of the night, but Ware's lust was great, and he might still be engaged in coupling.

Well, she could not help it if he was. She paused outside his chamber, drew a deep breath, and then threw open the door. "Wake up. I must talk to you."

"I wasn't asleep." Ware sat up in bed and watched her impassively as she came into the chamber and closed the door. "But I have no desire to talk. We've said what we had to say."

There was no woman in his bed, she saw with relief. "You are alone?"

"Obviously."

"Will she be back?"

"Who?" Then he smiled crookedly as he understood. "No, I sent for no woman tonight."

"Why not?"

"Perhaps I've decided to embrace once again a monk's abstinence."

She grunted with derision.

"And it's none of your concern what my reasons were."

"It's my concern if she comes back while I'm here. It's bad enough that I must do this, I refuse to share your bed."

He went still. "Share?"

She glanced away from him as she set the candlestick on the table by the bed. Her chest was constricted and she was finding it hard to breathe. Get it over. It would be better when all was settled. She took off her sandals, then pulled her gown over her head and dropped it onto the floor. "Move over."

He didn't move. "What is this?" he asked hoarsely.

"It would appear evident to anyone who is not a monk, and you are certainly not that." Since he had not made room for her, she went around to the other side of the bed and slipped beneath the cover. "I'll not have your blood on my hands. I have other things to do with my life than sit and brood and wonder if I could have stopped this nonsense. I *will* stop it."

"Get out of my bed."

"Touch me."

Every muscle of his body appeared rigid and locked in place. "I told you that I'd changed my mind."

"And in the next breath that you were leaving to avoid temptation. If you yield to temptation, there will be no reason for you to leave." He still did not move, and she didn't think she could bear the tension much longer.

"*Touch* me."

"I won't have you sacrificing your life for—"

"I'm sacrificing nothing. I won't let anyone deprive me of one thing that I value. Not my life, or my freedom, or anything else. I do this because I choose to do it. You wish my body? Take it. I'm not like my mother. I'll be the same after the coupling is over."

"You may not be the same." He muttered, "I'll probably do my best to make sure that you're not."

"A child?" She shrugged. "I'll leave it in God's hands. I like children, and I'd find a way to protect myself and my babe."

"Not from the Templars."

"They are only men."

"You're wrong, they're not like—" He inhaled sharply as she rolled against him. "Get away," he said through his teeth.

His flesh was hot and burning against her own, but his muscles were still locked and knotted. He had to break. She could not stand this. "Besides, you may not find me so easy to get with child. Nicholas used my mother for three years before she bore me. I'll be here only a few more weeks."

He turned his head and looked at her. He said thickly, "If I touch you now, I may not leave your body until you ride out those gates."

Heat coursed through her, and for a moment she couldn't speak. She moistened her lips. "Don't be foolish. We both know coupling does not take long. I'll be back in my chamber by dawn."

"Will you?" He took her hand and placed it on his chest. "I think not."

The hair on his chest prickled her palm and sent another spasm of heat through her. She could feel his heart drumming fast and hard beneath her touch, and his chest was moving rapidly. She had done this to him. She had stirred him, made his huge body respond. The knowledge brought her a strange sense of power. For the first time she could understand Tasza's pride in her ability to arouse and please.

Tasza. The memory of the girl brought a twisting pang. She didn't want to think of Tasza bringing Ware this pleasure. She reached down and began to stroke his abdomen.

He groaned and his eyes closed. His cheeks were darkly flushed, and his expression was one of unutterable sensual pleasure. So simple. She had not dreamed men could be controlled by a mere touch. In the House of Nicholas it had always been the women who were subjugated.

"I warn you. I cannot hold on." His voice was guttural. "If you leave now, I think I can let you go, but you must—" He broke off with a low cry as her hand closed around him.

Warm and big and weapon hard. She squeezed slowly and watched his face. Pleasure. She squeezed again. His teeth bit into his lower lip as he tried to suppress another groan. She shoved aside the cover to study him.

"What—are you doing?"

She looked up to see that his eyes had opened. "I just wanted to see if it looked any different. Your response was . . . interesting."

"For me also." He looked down at her hand. "But I think you should let me go if you don't want an even more interesting response."

She was reluctant to relinquish that sense of power, but she obediently released him.

"And stop looking at me. It has the same effect as your stroking me." He reached out and outlined her mouth with his forefinger. He murmured, "Christ, you have a lovely mouth."

Her gaze flew to his face as she remembered Tasza's lips kissing his thigh and then moving up to caress . . . Did he mean for her to do that?

He shook his head as he read her thoughts. "Not now. That's not where I want my seed." He reached down and cupped his hand between her thighs. "Here. You'll take me here." He began to rub her slowly, pressing and releasing. "Later we can find other— What's wrong? Why are you shaking?"

Only now did she realize that she was shuddering with every movement of his hand. "I'm not certain. I feel . . ." Empty. Helpless. Hot. Tingling. Was this what she had made him feel? It was as if she were tottering on a precipice. "I think—you should stop."

His gaze was narrowed on her face. "I don't agree. I like to see you like this." His thumb searched and found. He began to press and rotate.

She cried out and arched upward as an unbelievable sensation spasmed through her. "Take down your hair," he muttered as he widened her legs. "I want to see it around you when I come into you."

She gasped as his finger slid within her.

He went deeper. "Take it down."

What was he saying? she wondered dazedly. Her hair?

Another finger entered her, and he began to move in and out while his thumb still pressed and rotated.

She bit her lip to keep from screaming. Her hips lifted

from the bed. With difficulty he slipped another finger within her. "Do it."

She dazedly lifted her hands and loosened her braid. His fingers...

"Run your fingers through it. Bring it over your breasts."

She obeyed, barely aware of what she was doing. She was making little whimpering noises deep in her throat.

"That's right." He took away his hands and moved over her. His lips were curled back from his teeth as if he were in pain as he positioned himself. "I want to feel it against me." He began petting the curls surrounding her womanhood. "I want to feel all of you stroking me while I— No, don't move. I have to get in and I don't want to hurt you."

He *was* in and she felt pinned, unable to move. She lay there, panting, gazing helplessly up at him.

"Stop looking at me," he said roughly. "I can't let you go now. It's not my fault that you're a virgin. You're the one who came to me: It will be over in a minute."

"I didn't ask you to let me go."

"No, you just lie there so tight that I know I'll hurt you if I so much as breathe." He glared down at her. "I told you to leave me. Now all I can do is get it over quickly and then—" His hips plunged forward.

Pain. Invasion. Fullness.

"I told you." He moved again, in, out. The pain was receding, and she was beginning to feel that tingling heat she had known before. "Why do you never listen to me?"

"Be silent," she whispered. There was something here... more than lust... She felt part of something more than his body. It was most strange. "Something's happening. Do you not feel it?"

He went still and looked down at her. A multitude of emotions flickered over his face before it became impassive. "No." He brought her hair between them so that it would touch him with every movement. He began to move slowly, deeply. "This is the only thing I feel. This is all that matters." He reached beneath her and cupped her buttocks, bringing her up to meet each thrust. "Isn't it?"

She gasped as he touched the quick. She reached out blindly and grasped his shoulders. She couldn't breathe. She couldn't think.

Tension.

Thrusting.

Building.

She wanted to scream but she had no voice.

He was the voice.

He was motion and passion and . . . everything.

"It will be over soon," he muttered.

Was that supposed to comfort her? She didn't want it to be over. Yes, she did. She could not bear this tension.

He was moving faster, deeper.

Release.

She lunged upward as the waves of tension shattered.

He was still moving, she realized dimly. Didn't he know the world had just ended? She tried to tell him, but she was too weary and shaken.

He cried out, his arms tightening around her.

Never mind, he had found out for himself.

"You should not have come to my chamber." He stroked her hair. "It was foolish."

How curious that his awkward touch could be both

rough and infinitely gentle, she thought drowsily. "I couldn't stop you any other way." She nestled closer. "You're very large, aren't you? I feel very small lying next to you like this. . . ."

"You still shouldn't have come here. Now it's too late. I may have killed you."

"I feel very much alive." It was an understatement. She had never felt more gloriously, joyously alive in all her life. How odd that a simple animal act could bring boundless happiness. "And if you've killed me, it was with pleasure."

"You shouldn't have come."

He was not about to relinquish the thought, she realized. He would gnaw at it until he devoured all this wonderful contentment. She would not have it. She raised herself on one elbow and looked down at him. "And you'll brood and mutter until you drive me mad. I came because I feel a fondness for you and did not want to see you dead. It was my decision and you are free of guilt." She grimaced. "Though I know that you will not believe me. You seem to prefer being tied down by guilt. Well, I'll not be one of the burdens tethered to you. I've no liking for chains of any sort."

"A child can be a chain."

"True, but it's a bond that I'd welcome just as I welcome my bond with Selene. I've no desire to be alone in this world. The difference between a slave and a free woman is that a free woman has choice. There's no more precious gift on this earth."

"Such passion."

"And I'll not listen to your mockery."

"It's not mockery. I envy you. It's been a long time since I've felt passion for anything."

"Sweet Mary, what is it you've just shown me? You do everything with passion. Now, if you cannot speak cheerfully, be silent." She glimpsed his expression of astonishment before she lay back down and put her head in the hollow of his shoulder.

"I am guilty. You cannot change that by—ouch! You *bit* me."

"I said, be silent."

He was silent and then began stroking her hair again. "Silence doesn't alter truth." He stiffened warily, then relaxed when she made no motion to bury her teeth in him again. "A man must admit his sins and seek to correct them."

"I've not seen any sign that you wish to right this sin with other women."

"I spilled my seed in you. I tried to stop, but I could not—" He buried his face in her hair. His voice was muffled. "And I'll do it again and again. For I will not send you away from my bed."

"Then accept it." She yawned. "As I have."

"You accept it because you don't know what—"

Her patience was at an end. She reached down and grabbed him, tight. "Accept it or I'll—"

"I'll accept it," he said, alarmed.

Her grasp loosened.

He drew a sigh of relief. "You're a woman with neither shyness nor delicacy. A lady should not touch that part of a man without invitation and certainly not with roughness."

"You're a stubborn brute, and delicacy would not have stopped you."

He chuckled. "True enough. You certainly got my attention." He drew her close. "But don't do it again."

She did not answer. She had no intention of consenting to behave in a manner foreign to her nature, but she was in no mood for conflict.

He did not speak for a long time. "We . . . fit."

"I didn't think you would at first."

"No, I mean . . ." He released her and turned on his side away from her. "I don't know what I mean. Nothing, I suppose. Go to sleep."

She wanted him to hold her again. She didn't move for a moment and then rolled closer and slid her arms about his middle, pressing her breasts to his back. That was better, not as good as before, but better.

"What are you doing?"

"I like this, and since you already know I have no delicacy . . ." She rubbed her cheek back and forth along his shoulder blade as if to soften the edge. "But don't roll over. You'll crush me."

"Nothing could crush you." He hesitated, then turned around again and drew her back into his arms. "Now will you go to sleep?"

"Yes." She was already half-asleep as she curled closer to him. "I feel safer now . . . I don't like being alone."

I feel safer now.

But she was not safe. She would never be safe again, and he knew it was his fault. He had taken what she offered with only token resistance, and now she was more at risk than before.

Christ, what else could he have done? He had wanted

her from the beginning. But he had put lust behind him a hundred times in the last weeks. He could have done it one more time. He could have picked her up and carried her to her own chamber and locked the door. She was only a woman, with a woman's strength. He forgot that truth sometimes when she matched him word for word and will for will. Now, sleeping in his arms, she seemed as small and fragile as a child.

But it had been a woman he had taken earlier. She had been full of lust, vigorous passion stronger than any he had known before.

He wanted it again. He could feel himself harden as he remembered the way she had met him thrust for thrust, her cries as he had—

He deliberately blanked out the memory. Not now. Let her rest. She had been a virgin and—

Jesus, he had not treated her as a virgin. She had deserved better than to be glared at and blamed with rough words. What did he know of virgins? It was her fault. She should have stayed away from him.

He was blaming her again, he realized. Blaming her because it was too painful to blame himself for taking what he wanted.

It might not be too late. It could be she was not with child. He could behave with knightly honor and tell her he would stay safely at Dundragon and she need no longer come to his bed.

But it would be a lie, he thought bitterly. It seemed he had no honor at all where she was concerned. Only desire and obsession and the compulsion to seize every moment he could before she was taken away from him. Oh, no, there was no question he would couple with her as frequently as she would let him.

But there must be some way of protecting her. She was his now. She must live, even if he did not. He would find a way to make her safe.

Thea stirred and murmured something beneath her breath. Was she dreaming? He prayed the dreams were good and not the nightmares he endured each night. He drew her possessively closer.

She must live.

Chapter Nine

WARE WAS FROWNING, his brow furrowed in a fierce scowl.

Something had displeased him, Thea realized without concern. On a day this beautiful it would have taken more than a frown to destroy her contentment. She sat back on her heels and watched him as he strode toward her across the green. She enjoyed seeing him move, she thought idly, enjoyed seeing the flex of corded muscle, the grace that came from superb physical fitness and a lifetime of training.

"You left me while I was sleeping," Ware said. "I woke and you weren't there."

"I haven't left your chamber in four days." She smiled up at him as she watered the trunk of the mulberry tree. "The trees needed tending. Isn't it a fine morning?"

"I suppose."

"You suppose? The sky is blue, the sun is shining, and the trees are growing very well in spite of my neglect. Jasmine must have been taking care of them."

"I missed... you. I was worried."

"That wasn't reasonable. What could happen to me here at Dundragon?"

"I was worried. I never said I was reasonable. I don't have to be reasonable."

"How arrogant of you."

"I never said I wasn't arrogant either." He watched her for a moment. "Don't go away again without telling me."

"I won't be with you every minute of the day. Am I to go in search of you to tell you every time I move from room to room?"

"Yes."

She threw back her head and laughed. "You cannot be serious." She stopped as she saw his expression. "Are you?"

"You frightened me."

"For nothing. I'll not be bound by your foolish fancies."

He said nothing for a moment, and then a forced smile touched his lips. "You're right, of course. I'm not accustomed to worrying about others. My response was... exaggerated."

She snorted with derision. "You do nothing but worry about everyone at Dundragon and beyond."

"Not like this." He pulled her to her feet. "And it was not only worry but fear." He whispered, "Do you know what happens to me when I'm frightened?"

"You become surly and unreasonable."

"No." He drew her closer, holding her against him. "I become hard and heavy as a bull."

The evidence of that arousal was pressed against her

and was igniting a response in her. Bull, indeed. She tried to make her tone light to mask her breathlessness. "Then you must have been in terror for the past four days. One wonders what you did when you were in the midst of battle. Surely it must have been most uncomfortable for you when mounted to feel such—" She broke off as his hand pressed against her womanhood and then began rubbing slowly back and forth. "That is . . . not—" She had to stop as a ripple of heat shuddered through her. She tried again. "Stop."

"Why?" His other hand fumbled at the closure of her gown, and the next moment he pushed the bodice off her shoulders and around her waist.

The sun was warm on her naked breasts, the breeze touched her nipples in a teasing caress. She could feel them swell, harden. What had he asked? "We can be seen from the castle."

"I don't care," he muttered. Still, he pushed her a few steps deeper into the grove. "Better?"

"No." The stand of trees was too sparse to hide them. "We could go back to your chamber."

"Too far." He pressed her back against an oak tree and lifted the skirt of her gown. "I wouldn't get farther than the stairs."

She wasn't sure she would either. The feel of his chest against her bare breasts was causing her heart to beat painfully hard. "We . . . could try."

He adjusted his tunic. "Now." He cupped her buttocks in his hands and lifted her.

He plunged deep.

She cried out and clutched at his shoulders. She could feel the hard bark against her back and his hardness within her. Her legs curled around his hips, holding him as he bucked and drove.

"Ware, it's . . ." She trailed off as she felt the tension mount. He was savage and rough, and she would not have him any other way. It had never been this wild before. He was like an animal and made her feel like an animal.

"Come . . . to me," he muttered. His hips lifted and fell with deep force. "I need it. I need you."

His need vibrated between them, so intense she could feel his pain. "It's all right. You don't have to wait. . . ."

"Yes, I do." He reached between them and pressed and rotated. "Come."

She was panting and tears stung her eyes as she tried to give him what he wanted. Her hips moved forward but she could do little but take. So she took and took and took again.

When the climax came, she felt as if she were flying apart. An instant later she felt him flex within her as he uttered a low groan.

His head sank against hers and he stayed there, chest heaving, shuddering as he tried to regain control. "I think . . . it was much easier when I thought only of my own pleasure. This . . . may kill me."

She was too breathless to speak. She could only hold him and wait until strength returned.

He eased her to the ground and lay down beside her. He said nothing for a long time. "You're right. It's a very fine morning."

She chuckled. "I'm happy you finally noticed."

He unbound her braid and loosened her hair. "I was thinking of other things."

"Yes, you were."

He covered his lips with her hair. "I tried not to spend within you," he whispered. "Each time I swear I'll not give you my seed, and then I cannot— Forgive me."

"It's a little late for restraint," she said. "When I came to you, I told you that I was prepared to let God decide the matter. I knew what you wanted of me."

"I've changed my mind. I don't want a child. Not if it means—You must help me. Make me leave your body before it's too late."

He had not changed his mind. He talked no more about a child, but at times, in his sleep, he would reach out and yearningly rub her belly as if she already held the prize he wanted within her. "Let God decide."

He shook his head. "God sometimes seems unconcerned with our troubles. You must help me."

"The decision may already be out of our hands. I may already be with child. We will talk of this again after I have my flux. Now, be silent and let me enjoy the sunshine."

She supposed she should make some attempt to cover herself, but she felt wonderfully languid and didn't want to move. The day was bright, their surroundings beautiful and peaceful, and she felt no shame in what they had just done. It had been as natural and beautiful as the sky overhead.

Perhaps too beautiful. No, she would not worry and take this lovely moment apart. She would accept and enjoy as long as it lasted.

As long as it lasted. Her gaze drifted toward the mountain where the man dwelt who might well put an end to this contentment. "Who is Vaden?"

At first she thought he was not going to answer her.

"You know who he is. He's the man who wants to kill me." He paused. "And you."

"But he didn't kill us when he had the opportunity."

"It was not the time. He has no desire to die himself."

"Vaden of where? Where does he come from?"

He turned on his side to look at her. "Why are you so curious about Vaden?"

Because she sensed a bond between the two men that she could not comprehend. Even though this Vaden was a threat, Ware would not condemn him. "Surely, it's understandable I'd want to know everything I could about a man you say may kill me."

"Only if he could see no other way out," he said quickly.

There it was again. He was defending Vaden. "Was he your friend?"

He gazed out at the mountains. "Closer than friends, he was my brother at the Temple."

"Then why didn't he help you escape?"

"He was away on a mission in Italy."

"Would he have helped you?"

"I don't know. I never knew what Vaden would do. Perhaps. He's always torn between impulse and calculation. He's a complicated man."

Incredibly, there was no derision in his tone. "Loyalty isn't complicated. It's very simple."

"You don't understand."

"No, I don't. I don't understand friends who try to butcher you."

"There are higher loyalties. The Order was everything to Vaden. I used to joke with him about it."

"Did it anger him?"

He shook his head. "But he believed in the Order. He *needed* it."

"Why?"

"I'm not sure. Perhaps because he had no other roots. I think he's illegitimate."

"You don't know?"

"He didn't talk about it." He brushed his lips on her shoulder. "And after he was accepted in the Order, the Grand Master forbade anyone to ask him. He was just Vaden from nowhere."

"Strange."

"Yes, particularly since two of the qualifications for entry into the Order are legitimacy and knighthood. I don't think Vaden was either."

"It makes no sense. Then why was he accepted?"

He shrugged. "I have no idea. He was a great warrior. Perhaps they wanted his sword."

"Weren't you curious? And don't tell me curiosity was forbidden. I wouldn't think you'd cavil at disobeying the order about asking him questions."

"We all had our reasons for being there. It would have been an intrusion to ask him."

She did not understand such reasoning. "If he was your friend, then knowing why he was there might have been a way of helping him."

He shook his head and his expression became shuttered. "To share some secrets is to do irreparable damage."

He was no longer speaking of Vaden but what he had seen in the Temple. "No secret is worth what happened at Jedha."

"The Temple thought it was."

"What do you think?"

He bent his head and blew in her ear. "I think you have divine breasts and the most beautiful hair that I've ever seen. When we were playing chess, I used to watch it shine in the firelight and wonder how it would feel against me. I wanted to wrap it around my body and drown in you."

He was avoiding the question and trying to distract her. "What do you think?" she repeated.

"No." He buried his head in her shoulder. "God, no." His voice was muffled. "Sometimes I feel as if I'm choking on their secrets. When I first discovered what was in the caves, I was racked with guilt and then anger. They were my brothers, my family. Why couldn't they trust me? I would never reveal—" He lifted his head, and she was shocked at the torment in his expression. "I'm no fool. I knew what telling others would mean. Why wouldn't they trust me?"

He may have felt anger, but it was overshadowed by hurt and desolation. He had lost one family and then found another in the Templars. He had given them unbounded loyalty only to be cast out once again. "Because they're blind fools." She drew him close and held him in a fierce embrace. "And you should think no more about them."

He was silent a moment and then he chuckled. "I shall do my utmost, but under the circumstances it's difficult not to give them thought." He sat up and pulled her bodice up over her breasts. "But I assure you that they're never in my mind when I'm in your body. Let's go to my chamber. We will bathe and then banish thought for the rest of the day."

"*Now* you wish to go to your chamber." She slipped her

arms into the sleeves of the gown, then tried to straighten her hair. No need to rebraid it yet; the first thing Ware always did when they were alone was loosen it. It made no difference if she appeared tousled; everyone in the castle must know she was coupling with Ware anyway, since these last days they had seldom left his bed except to bathe and eat. She was not concerned about anyone's reaction except for Jasmine. Tasza no longer needed the security offered by being Ware's leman, but Jasmine was fiercely protective of her daughter and might regard Thea as a threat. Well, she would worry about Jasmine's response later. She was too full of joy and contentment now.

"And I would not need a bath so desperately if you hadn't chosen to wallow with me in the dirt," she told Ware. But he would probably have ordered a bath anyway. She had discovered that Ware was nearly fanatic regarding his personal cleanliness.

It must be the sheepskin drawers.

The words popped into her head. She had almost forgotten Kadar's teasing comment the first night she had arrived at Dundragon. "Sheepskin drawers."

"What?"

"Kadar said the reason you were so devoted to cleanliness was the sheepskin drawers. What did he mean?"

Ware made a face. "In order to encourage chastity all Knights Templar are required to wear two sets of sheepskin drawers and never take them off."

"Not even when they bathe?"

"We were not permitted to bathe either."

She blinked. "Well, that would certainly encourage chastity. No wonder you became close to your brother monks. I cannot imagine anyone else wanting to be within a yard of such stench."

"We became accustomed to it." He frowned. "I don't feel like talking any longer. Will you come?"

"Perhaps I don't wish to go to bed. I have more tending here to do."

"I have more need of tending than your trees." He took her hand and brought it to him. "Don't I?"

She inhaled sharply as she felt the unyielding hardness. Soon it would be inside her again. His lips would be on her breast, and he would be plunging wildly in and out. A ripple of heat seared through her as she realized she was ready for him again. "You're a very lustful man, Ware of Dundragon. Do you never get enough?"

"No," he said thickly. "Not with you. The minute you're out of my sight, I want you again." He stood up and reached down to pull her to her feet. "You will come with me?"

This delirium should end. She had not imagined that the mere act of coupling could bring the kind of fever that could never be satisfied. She wanted to touch him, caress him, even when they were across the room from each other. She found herself watching his expressions, waiting for the moment when he would reach out for her. She had called him lustful, but she herself was as filled with lust.

His big hand was holding hers tightly, possessively, as his thumb stroked her wrist. "Will you come?"

It was happening again, the liquid flowing, the tension, the breathless heat.

She nodded jerkily. "I'll come." She started across the green. She whispered, "Hurry."

* * *

"My lord, I regret to disturb you, but riders approach." Abdul kept his gaze fixed on a point somewhere on the wall above the bed.

Thea's heart leaped in panic as she scrambled upright in bed. Riders. The Templars?

Ware was already out of bed and donning his tunic. "How many riders?"

"Two men." With relief Abdul fixed his gaze on Ware. "We believe there are only two. But it's night and there could be others farther down the road."

"Dress." Ware tossed over his shoulder to Thea, "Hurry." He strode out of the chamber.

Thea wasted no time. Within a few minutes she was dressed and running out into the courtyard.

They were lowering the drawbridge, she saw with relief. Surely they would not do that if it was a foe.

It was Kadar.

Her gaze flew to the small figure on the horse behind him.

Selene. Dressed in a young Arab boy's tunic, robe, and cloak, it was still undeniably, blessedly, Selene.

"Thea!" Selene slipped from the saddle and ran toward her. The turban slipped from her head and her red hair tumbled down her back, reminding Thea of that moment when they had said good-bye at the gates of Constantinople. "I'm here."

"I see you are." She hugged her tightly. Selene. Free. Safe. Here with her at last. "I see . . . you are."

"Stop crying." Selene pulled back and stared at her with

sternness. "I won't have it. Why are you being so foolish? Everything is fine now."

"I know." Thea wiped the tears from her cheeks. "See, I've stopped." She hugged her again and released her. "How are you?"

"Better than me," Kadar said as he dismounted. "Your sister is a very willful creature."

"I'm well," Selene said, ignoring him. "Why should I not be?"

"They didn't find out you'd helped me?"

"Of course not." She looked down at her cloak and dusted off a speck of dirt. "It's like you to fret over nothing. I was not the one in danger's path. But I also worried about you." She gazed at Thea searchingly. "I see I had no need. There's a . . . bloom about you."

"Why were you so long?" Ware asked Kadar. "Did you have problems with Nicholas?"

"No more than I expected," Kadar said. "But then, after the barter was struck, Selene decided she would not be bought and ran away. It took me three weeks to find her in that vast city."

"It was your fault entirely," Selene said. "If you'd told me of Thea's plan, we would have been here long ago."

"I intended telling you after I took you from Nicholas's house. It wasn't safe to do so until then." He added teasingly, "I couldn't be sure that you could keep the secret."

"Am I an idiot that I'd reveal a secret that would bring me my freedom?"

"Not an idiot, but you are a child." Kadar grimaced. "At least I thought you were. I should have heeded Thea's warning." He held up his hand as she opened her lips to speak. "Very well, it wasn't your youth that kept me from telling you, but that dragon that listened in on every word I spoke."

"She was alone on the streets of Constantinople for three weeks?" Thea asked, horrified. "Anything could have happened to her."

"Perhaps you don't know her any more than I did," Kadar said. "When I found her, she was living in the bazaar with a family of bedouins, learning how to make camel bells. In another month's time she would have been ordering them about as she has me during this excruciating journey."

In spite of his mocking tone Thea could discern an odd note of possessive pride in Kadar's voice.

"Don't be foolish," Selene said. "It would have taken me at least six months. The woman was reasonable but the old man was stubborn." She turned back to Thea. "And then after Kadar finally told me it was you who had sent him, I had to send him back to Nicholas to get the silk."

"Silk?" Ware asked.

Selene studied him. "You must be Lord Ware. Kadar told me about you."

"I'm sure he did," Ware said dryly. "What silk?"

"Well, since Kadar clearly had money enough to buy me, I thought he must have some left over. He actually handled the negotiations quite cleverly."

Kadar bowed slightly. "Thank you."

Selene waved an impatient hand. "But he was going to leave without buying silk, Thea. We won't be able to make our own cloth for some time, and Nicholas's is the best-woven silk in the world. I thought if you could embroider the silk and we could sell it, the profits would help us to open our house."

"By the saints," Thea whispered, excitement growing by the minute. She had not thought past rescuing Selene. "How many bolts?"

"Twelve," Kadar said. "She beggared me."

"Since it was my money, I'd say she beggared *me*," Ware corrected.

Thea scarcely heard them. Twelve bolts. She couldn't believe it. "I'll return the money he spent. My embroideries bring a fine price. Far more than the silk itself."

"Kadar arranged to have a wagon bring the other bolts next week, but I brought with me a length of white silk," Selene said. "We cannot start too soon."

"No." Thea could hardly wait to begin. She had not realized how much she had missed her work. "Tomorrow. As soon as the light is good."

Kadar chuckled, his gaze on Selene's intent face. "Now that you've arranged things to suit yourself, may I suggest you retire for the night? I'd wager you're going to be as sore tomorrow as you were this morning."

"I wasn't sore. Well, perhaps a little. He wanted to put me on a mule, Thea."

"As is fitting for women and children," Kadar said. "The latter which you are, the former which you will become."

"I'm sure men put women on mules only so they can look down upon them from their horses." She yawned. "But I am weary. It was a long journey from Acre."

"Come along." Thea slipped her arm about Selene's waist and urged her toward the steps. "You can sleep with me in my chamber tonight. Tomorrow we will find you your own place."

"My own place." Selene looked up at the vast castle,

and for a moment her boldness faltered. "It's very different from Nicholas's house, isn't it?"

Kadar answered from behind them, "As different as the bazaar where I found you. You must promise not to change quite everything to suit yourself. Ware would be most upset."

Selene's moment of uncertainty immediately disappeared. "Thea and I won't be here long enough to make changes worthwhile."

Clever Kadar, Thea thought. He had eased Selene away from that moment of fear without damaging her pride by expressing sympathy. He must have got to know Selene very well on their journey from Constantinople.

Selene stopped suddenly on the top step and turned to face Ware. "I thank you for caring for my sister, Lord Ware."

Thea smiled at the child's solemn formality. It was almost as if Selene were the elder. She had changed since Thea had left her. She seemed freer, bolder. It was clear that surviving life on the streets had given her both more confidence and more knowledge.

Ware did not smile. He nodded with equal gravity.

"And I thank you for sending Kadar to fetch me. We owe you a great debt."

"Then I shall certainly collect," Ware said. "But in the meantime, welcome to Dundragon."

Selene turned and went into the castle.

Thea started to follow her.

"Thea," Ware said.

She stopped at his call. She had been so happy at Selene's arrival, she had not realized this would be the first time she would sleep apart from Ware since they had come together. Would he let her go? She looked at him. His expression was impassive, but she knew he was trying to tell her something.

She moistened her lips. "Everything is different now." Their time of halcyon intimacy was over; it was time to get on with life. She supposed she had known Selene's arrival would signal the end of her stay at Dundragon, but she had not let herself realize it until she put it in words.

He held her gaze for another moment before saying, "Yes, it is. Sleep well, Thea."

"Good night," she muttered, and fled into the castle.

"They're very much alike," Ware said as he watched Thea follow her sister into the castle. Selene had come, a new door had opened, and Thea had eagerly walked through it. Christ, he was hurting. "She's like Thea."

Kadar shook her head. "Selene is like no one on this earth. She's half sage, half imp, and all determination. Trying to keep her under control has been an interesting experience. She has a good heart, but she fights hard to make sure no one sees it. Thea is much softer."

Yet Thea had struggled to give him neither trust nor affection, Ware thought. Even when she had decided she must allow him to come close, she had been defiant. He remembered the night she had come to him and told him he was her friend whether or not it pleased him. "You're wrong. They are alike."

Kadar turned to look at him. "You seem very certain. You've come to know Thea?"

"How could I help it?" Ware said dryly. "You gave me into her charge."

Kadar smiled. "But one never knows how such forays will succeed."

Ware changed the subject. "What news in Acre?"

"Nothing of import. Minor skirmishes between Saladin and the Franks. Has there been trouble here?"

"Yes, Vaden came." He started up the steps. "I don't know how long it will be safe for Thea to remain here. I thought—but everything has changed. We might have to find them a haven."

"Damascus? That's where she wants to go. A city held by Saladin would be safer for her than one held by Christians."

Ware looked over his shoulder at the third mountain. "No, not Damascus."

"Are you hungry? Have you supped?" Thea asked as she led Selene through the hall toward the staircase.

"Yes, I was so excited I wanted to go on, but Kadar insisted we stop at sundown to eat." She frowned. "He's very stubborn."

And Selene was not? Thea smothered a smile as she thought of the battles that must have occurred between them on the journey. "But very kind."

"When he wishes to be," Selene acceded grudgingly. "But he is like Lord Ware. There's a darkness about him."

"You've just met Lord Ware. You cannot know his character."

Selene shrugged. "One would have to be blind not to see the darkness. Kadar's darkness is not as evident, but it may be deeper because it lies hidden." She changed the subject. "Kadar was very careful after we reached Acre. Is there something to fear here?"

"He did not tell you?"

"He said you would tell me." She grimaced. "I think he did not wish me to worry on the journey. As if not knowing of danger would keep me from worrying. Kadar is more clever than most, but he sometimes still thinks like a man."

"A grievous fault," Thea agreed. "You admit he's clever, then?"

"I hid myself very well in the bazaar and he still found me. He stalked me, set a trap, and then he caught me." There was a hint in Selene's voice of the same pride Thea had heard in Kadar's. "Yes, Kadar is clever." She scowled. "Even if he always does wish his own way."

"Well, you need not be bothered with him any longer now that you've reached Dundragon." She started up the stairs. "And we shall be leaving soon."

"Well, actually, he's not bad company when he's not ordering me about," Selene admitted as she followed her. "And he promised to show me his falcons. Are they very beautiful?"

"Yes, though I've never seen them in flight."

"Then how can you judge? I would have made him—"

"I had other things on my mind," Thea interrupted. "And Kadar responds more to requests than orders."

Selene nodded reluctantly. "I've found that also." She went back to her original question. "What danger lies here?"

"Lord Ware has powerful enemies. I will tell you about it tomorrow. You need rest now."

To Thea's surprise Selene did not argue. "I'm dirty and

smell of horse." She yawned. "I'll not be a pleasant bed companion."

"I can bear it." She stopped at the top of the stairs and hugged the girl. "I can bear anything now that you're here and safe. Did I tell you how much I've missed you?"

"Yes." Selene grinned. "Though you seem to have kept yourself very busy."

Heat flooded Thea's cheeks as she recalled how she had been busying herself only an hour ago. Did Selene mean—

"You found us friends in this new land and even mulberry leaves to keep the silkworms alive. Kadar said Lord Ware found a grove of white mulberry trees."

Of course, that was what she meant, Thea realized with relief. The child had an uncanny perception, but she would never think of Thea in any carnal connection. "Yes, we transplanted five young trees on the green at the rear of the castle. Lord Ware is thinking of going into the silk trade. I promised to show him how to use the trees."

"Are they doing well?"

"I think they'll survive."

"Then we'll be able to leave soon. Since you owe him a debt, I can see how you'd feel obliged to stay until you gave him what he needed."

The heat deepened in Thea's cheeks. She had not given him what he needed. She had yielded to him her body, but she had not bestowed on him a child.

Selene nodded with satisfaction. "If the trees are flourishing, you won't have to stay."

"No, I won't have to stay." The thought brought a deep, wrenching pain. She had told Ware everything was different, and he had accepted it. She must do the same. She must forget about him. Selene and she would get on with their plans and their lives. They would be free, doing work they loved. It was what she had always wanted, the goal for which she had worked all her life. She should be soaring with happiness.

"What's wrong?" Selene's gaze was on her face.

"Nothing." She gave her sister another quick hug before she set off down the hall. "It's just that one becomes accustomed to a place, and Lord Ware has treated me with kindness."

"He doesn't look like a kind man—but, then, people are often not what they seem."

Ware looked rough and hard and as dark as Selene had judged him. But he was also generous, protective, and intelligent. "He can be kind."

"You like him."

"We've grown accustomed to each other." She would not evade the question; he deserved better from her. "Yes, I like him very much."

"Perhaps he can visit us in Damascus."

"No, that's not possible." Once she left Dundragon, she must cut the bond that had grown between them. Ware was safe at Dundragon; she would not see him endangered for her sake. The pain within her was growing deeper with each passing moment. She should have realized this would happen. She should have stopped the coupling; perhaps that would have lessened the bond. Too late now. Too late for anything but farewells.

"I've opened the windows and freshened up your chamber." Jasmine was coming down the hall toward them. "You'll be sleeping in your own room tonight?"

"Yes." Thea gestured to Selene. "This is my sister, Selene. Jasmine has been helping me care for the trees."

Jasmine nodded. "It's good she is here. When do you leave for Damascus?"

Jasmine was as eager for her to leave Dundragon as was Selene. "Soon. But there's no hurry. Selene has just arrived from one journey. We're expecting a wagon of silk to arrive from Acre. We must be here to accept it."

Jasmine nodded reluctantly. "But you must not tarry too long." She moved past them toward the staircase.

Selene watched her before turning back to Thea. "She wishes you to go?"

"I've promised her a place once we have our own house. You'll grow to like Jasmine."

As Thea herself had grown to like her. She had developed a fondness for all these strange inhabitants of Dundragon. Jasmine, Abdul, even Tasza. And there was Haroun. . . .

The pain was returning and it must be banished. Her life here was over. She must stop thinking of anything but her hope for the future. She opened the door of her chamber. The shutters were still open, and the room smelled fresh and cool and familiar.

"It is very grand, isn't it?" Selene whispered, her eyes wide as her gaze traveled around the room. "This is all your own?"

"None of this is ours. It's pleasant enough, but we don't belong in castles." She moved brusquely forward to close the window. "We'll find a place far less grand for our own in Damascus." She paused, looking down at the green where she had joined with Ware in passion earlier that day. How long would it be before she could subdue this aching regret?

"What are you going to make of the length of silk I brought you?" Selene asked. "A tunic?"

She was being foolish and weak. She must tie up all these painful, tattered ends and walk away. She firmly closed the shutter and latched it. "No, not a tunic. A banner."

The linens of his bed still breathed of Thea, Ware realized as he lay in the darkness. Soap and lemon and the woman scent that was distinctly her own. He inhaled deeply, letting it flow into him. He would remember that fragrance if he lived a hundred years.

Not that there was a chance of that. He had beaten the odds too long. He would be fortunate to live another year. Every day was a gift.

As she had been a gift, beautiful and loyal, filled with life and vitality.

A gift he had taken and now must return.

No!

He closed his eyes and fought the rejection. He had known this moment would come, but he had not known it would be this difficult. He must smother this impulse to reach out and grab and hold on.

Once more. It would do no harm to have one more time before he sent her away.

Christ in heaven—no harm? When he lay here treasuring her scent on the sheets like a boy with his first woman? Let her go, you fool.

Let her be safe.

Let her live.

* * *

"Let me have that." Kadar took the bucket of water from Thea and opened the door. "You should have one of the servants do this sort of task." His gaze went to the cluster of mulberry trees. "I was surprised when Selene told me that these trees were here."

"You've seen her this morning?"

"I made the mistake of promising her I'd show her my falcons. She was pounding on my door before I had a chance to break my fast."

"She told me she was eager to see them." She started down the path. "But, then, she was eager to see everything. I was going to start embroidering this morning and let Jasmine care for the trees, but I told her to show Selene the castle instead. I can begin on the silk this afternoon." She shot him a glance. "Why are you surprised we planted the trees? The silk trade is very profitable."

"As I saw in Constantinople. But Ware is no merchant."

"Many lords dabble in the trade."

"Ware is no dabbler."

She shrugged. "You must be wrong. He wanted the trees."

"Yes, he wanted the trees," he murmured. "Curious."

"I didn't find it so." They had reached the first tree, and she took the water from him. "It seemed very reasonable."

"Because you're blinded and dazzled by your silk." He grimaced. "I saw thousands of worms devouring the leaves on the mulberry trees in Nicholas's garden. I didn't find it a pretty sight."

"When you see what magic those worms weave . . ."

"I prefer to see the silk and not the process." He watched her water the tree. "You are well?"

"Of course. Do I not look well?"

"Yes, I agree with Selene. You have a certain bloom."

She quickly looked away. "I thank you for caring for my sister. I think you know what it means to me."

"I told you I would care for her." He smiled. "Besides, Ware tells me that you've done what I asked of you."

"What did he say?"

He didn't answer for a moment, and she could feel his gaze on her averted face. "Only that you had grown to know each other." He paused. "What else is there to say?"

It appeared Ware had not told him of their intimacy. He would learn soon enough from the servants, but she found she could not confide in him. "Nothing." She moved on to the next tree. "It was not an easy task you set me."

"Retrieving Selene was not easy either. But we both succeeded in what we set out to do, so all is well. Isn't it?"

She nodded. "And it will be better once we reach Damascus."

"Ah, yes, Damascus. When do you intend leaving?"

"I have a task to complete here that should take no longer than a month. After that, we will leave."

"What task?"

"I promised Lord Ware a banner. I cannot leave until it's completed."

"A month doesn't seem long enough to fashion a banner."

"I'll do it. I can be very determined if I set myself entirely to a task."

"I know that well enough." His expression was thoughtful. "Why Damascus? Wouldn't another place do as well?"

She shook her head. "I considered many towns before I

decided on Damascus. It's a place well-known in the trade, and fine embroideries are treasured there. Our silk house wouldn't do as well in another city. It has to be Damascus."

"I see." He didn't speak until she had moved on to the next tree. "There's a possibility Ware may decide Damascus is not safe."

"I've heard Damascus is a vast city. It should not be difficult for two women to lose themselves in such a place. I'll take the chance."

"But will Ware?"

"I'm a free woman now, with a free will. It's my decision to make."

"Well, there's no sense discussing it at the moment. You still have a banner to create. Tell me, what device will you use? A dragon breathing flames? Or perhaps a bull for obstinacy? Either would be appropriate for our friend Ware."

"He says he doesn't care. When I sit down to draw the design, something will come to me. It always does."

"An idea falls from heaven?" he teased.

She didn't smile in return. "I don't know where it comes from, but it comes. My mother once said she had heard it is so with all artists. I sit down with pen and let the whisper tell me what to draw and then guide my needle."

"Whisper?"

"Not a real whisper. It's inside my head...." She shrugged helplessly as she realized she was making little sense. "Or perhaps my heart. I don't know...it's just there. Whatever it is, it brings beauty. Isn't that what's important?"

"I can't think of anything more important," Kadar said gently. "I'll be interested to see this banner." He bowed.

"But now I must join Ware. We had little chance to talk last night. I will see you at dinner?"

At her nod, he moved down the path toward the castle.

She felt a vague sense of unease as she watched him go. He had posed questions and stirred uncertainty in matters she had thought perfectly obvious. But, then, it was Kadar's way to question everything and everyone, and she had been too filled with new and different emotions to think with any clarity.

None of it mattered anyway. The trees were here and growing strong. Let Ware do what he willed with them. After today she would give them into Jasmine's care and concentrate on Ware's banner.

A strong, beautiful banner, a banner to raise the heart and bring memories of—

Memories of her? Was she so vain that she would use her gift in such a cause? she wondered in self-disgust. Memories came from the soul, not from a piece of silk. She did not need a banner to remember Ware. All her life she would—

Dear God, let those memories dim. Leave the sweetness, let regret fade.

But Ware would know regret. She felt she would have known if life stirred within her. The one gift he wanted, she would not give him.

But she could give of her talent and her labor. She would empty her heart of everything but the whisper and the man himself and give him the most glorious of banners.

* * *

Ware stood gazing out the window when Kadar strode into the Great Hall.

"Did you take Thea to your bed?" Kadar asked without ceremony.

Ware glanced at him before returning his gaze to the courtyard. "Is that what she told you?"

"She told me nothing in words, but her manner... Did you?"

Ware turned to look at him. "What did you expect? You know what I am. You asked her to bear me company."

"I didn't tell her to become your whore."

"She's *not* my whore. I won't have you—" He broke off and shrugged. "It's done. I won't ask her to come back to my bed."

"And what if she's with child?"

"Then I'll find a way to protect her and the babe." He glared at him. "Do you think me so lacking in responsibility that I'd not consider that?"

"And what if she won't permit you to protect her?"

"She will have no choice."

Kadar shook his head. "There is always choice when one has strength." He paused. "You've not told her that she cannot go to Damascus."

"In time."

"If you don't send her, she'll go anyway. She believes that she can lose herself in the city."

"Not from Vaden. She'd need four walls and an army to keep him away from her." He muttered, "And even that may not be enough."

"Four walls and an army," Kadar repeated. "That sounds uncomfortably like a prison. Thea has just escaped from one prison. She would not tolerate another." His gaze narrowed on Ware's face, and then he gave a low whistle. "You mean it."

"She will live."

"That's why you brought the mulberry trees here. You were making a nest for her. A safe, cozy nest, behind stone walls. You were providing her with everything she needed to lure her to stay. That's why you had me bring Selene. It was to be her own little world."

"Why not? She would have been very comfortable here."

"And what if she'd chosen not to stay?"

Ware met his gaze. "She would have been very comfortable here."

"By all the saints." Kadar shook his head in wonder. "I've underestimated you, my friend. I didn't think you capable of such subtle machinations."

"I'll have no more innocent blood on my hands."

"So you seek to protect your entire world." He tilted his head. "Was I to be imprisoned in your castle also?"

Ware didn't answer.

Kadar laughed. "You were going to do it. I cannot believe it."

"I'm no fool. I hoped to persuade you to leave me, and if you would not—" He shrugged. "I've told Abdul that from now on four men are to protect you at all times."

"So you're putting me behind a wall of guards instead of stone."

"Until I can convince you that life would be both safer and more pleasant in some far-off land."

"But not as interesting. I'd miss seeing you attempt to keep Thea imprisoned here at Dundragon."

"I'm sorry to disappoint you, but Thea can't remain at Dundragon. Vaden knows about her, and he may have already told the Grand Master. If something happened to me, he'd know exactly where to find her, and I wouldn't be here to defend the fortress. I have to find a safer place for her."

"She prefers to find her own hiding place and take her own chances." He sighed as he saw Ware's implacable expression. "I fear I'm not convincing you."

"How long before her silk arrives?"

"Wednesday of next week perhaps." He nodded as he understood the relevance of the question. "You're wondering how much time you have to find this haven? You have at least a month." He smiled sardonically. "She wishes to repay your kindness by creating a banner for you. Though she may decide to wrap it around your neck and throttle you with it."

"A month..."

"I'd be curious as to how you intend to find a haven for her in this land when you can find none for yourself."

"I'll have to consider," he said. "But I *will* find it."

"And after you find it, you have only to convince her to use it." He turned away. "All this talk of prisons has made me uneasy. I think I'll go to the tower to see my falcons. Do you know, I'm tempted to set Eleanor free today."

"You've trained her too well. She would only come back to you."

"One never knows. At least I'd have the satisfaction of knowing I'd made the attempt."

"Thea isn't Eleanor," Ware said. "It would be unwise of you to become confused."

"You're warning me?"

"I'm reminding you . . . of Jedha. If Thea was killed, you would bear the guilt. You'll have your own Jedha. I promise you that you'd not like the nightmares that would come after."

Kadar's smile faded. "A persuasive argument. Perhaps I'll wait awhile and see what comes of this search for a haven."

Ware smiled without mirth. "I thought you would. It's all very well to have a tender heart, but you must strike a balance. We can never have everything we wish. A price must always be paid."

"And Thea must pay it?"

Ware turned back to the window. "She won't be the only one."

Chapter Ten

THE SILK WAS BEAUTIFUL, shimmering with a pearllike luminosity on her standing frame.

Thea always loved this moment of anticipation before she began. Soon glowing stitches of color would unfurl on that silken canvas. *Her* stitches, *her* design. She reluctantly turned away from the silk, sat down at the table, and picked up her pen.

But what design?

She closed her eyes and emptied her mind of everything around her. Ware. Think of Ware.

She could hear the sound of birds in the trees below her window, the soft rush of wind.

Or was it the whisper?

Not yet. Soon.

Ware. Ware's banner.

She opened her eyes and began to sketch. It came

slowly at first, and then faster. No doubt. No hesitation. Soon every stroke of the pen came with absolute certainty. The picture in her mind was so clear, she could see every detail.

Strange, it had never been this clear before. . . .

"You must eat," Jasmine said from the doorway.

"Later." Thea drew the gold thread through the silk.

"Now. You've not eaten at all today." Jasmine closed the door. "And only scraps for the last three days. You'll become ill."

"No, I won't."

"And Selene says you don't sleep."

"Of course I sleep." She wished the woman would go away. The gold was dazzling against the creamy silk, and she felt a rush of pleasure. Every stitch brought her that same deep satisfaction and anticipation.

"Not much." Jasmine crossed the room and stood in front of the loom. "I'm not sure I wish to learn this skill if it drives one out of one's senses."

"I'm not out of my senses. I'm working."

Jasmine snorted. "All the hours of the day and night."

"I want to finish the banner so we can go to Damascus."

"You'll not finish it at all if you go blind from working by that dim candlelight."

Even working by candlelight hadn't damaged the quality of the work. Every morning when Thea examined the embroidery, every stitch done the night before was perfect. She bent forward and guided the needle through the silk.

"You're not listening to me," Jasmine said.

"Leave the tray. I'll eat later."

She scarcely heard Jasmine leave the chamber. Another silken stitch, another rush of intense pleasure.

The design was growing, coming alive beneath her needle. . . .

"Thea?" Selene whispered. "Please come to bed."

"Not yet."

Selene sighed and settled down on the floor beside Thea's stool. "I'll be glad when you're finished. I've never seen you like this."

"I want it to be beautiful. It's *got* to be beautiful."

"If Lord Ware were here, he would not permit you to suffer like this for his sake."

Suffer? Thea almost laughed aloud. Working on the banner was as far from suffering as could be imagined. It was like living in a beautiful dream and working to make that dream even more true and shining. "Lord Ware is not here?"

Selene shook her head. "He and Kadar left four days ago."

"Where did they go?"

"I don't know. But Kadar said he'd be back within two weeks' time."

Oh, well, it didn't matter. Nothing mattered but the complexity of the pattern, the tightness of the stitches. No, that was wrong. There was something that did matter. Ware had to be safe. "Did he take Abdul?"

"No. He had a large escort, but Abdul stayed here."

But Ware was protected. Good. Now she could return her concentration to the banner.

Selene studied the embroidered silk on the frame. "It looks as if you're almost finished."

Thea nodded.

"It's beautiful. I don't think you've ever created anything this wonderful."

Thea knew she hadn't, and it was growing stronger and more beautiful with every stitch.

"But it makes me feel uneasy. There's too much... power."

"That's good. A banner should have strength and splendor."

"It's hard to look away from it. It fascinates."

Thea didn't answer.

"The other bolts of silk came last week. I left them in the wagon. There's no use unloading them when we'll need to take them to Damascus. Isn't that right?"

Just a few more stitches and she could start on the scarlet. What had Selene asked? Something about the silk and Damascus. "You were very clever to think of getting the silk."

"You're not listening." Selene sighed as she got to her feet. "I'm moving back in here with you again. It's the only way I'll be sure you get a little sleep."

"Whatever you say."

"And an entire army of turtles are eating the lions in the courtyard."

"I'm sure it will be all right."

Selene shook her head and moved over to the bed. "Nothing will be all right until you finish that banner."

It was done.

Thea wearily straightened her back and stared at the banner. Three weeks and the most intense labor she had ever lavished on any work.

Glorious.

The banner still had to be hemmed, but the design was finished. The scarlet and gold leaped from the silk canvas and held her captive. She could not look away from it.

For an instant she experienced a flash of uneasiness. Selene was right. There *was* power here.

But wasn't all beauty power?

And, of course, she could look away from that splendid scrap of silk.

She stood up and arched her back to rid it of stiffness. She felt strangely hollow, as if she had poured everything within her into the vessel of the banner.

Well, her strength would be replenished after she rested. She carefully took the silk off the frame and folded it. She would hem it after she woke and then give it to Ware.

If he was here. Selene had not mentioned his return. He might still be gone. This chamber had been her entire world for the last few weeks. The castle could have been seized by Saladin and she would not have known it. She would have to ask Selene when she woke . . .

She took off her gown as she moved across the room. Selene was sprawled inelegantly over the entire bed.

"Move over," she whispered, nudging her.

Selene opened sleepy eyes. "Is it finished?"

Thea nodded as she crawled beneath the cover. "All but the hemming."

"I'll do that for you."

"No, I have to do it. I have to do it all." Her lids felt as if they bore weights. "But . . . tomorrow."

Selene threw an arm over her and nestled close. "I'm glad it's over," she murmured.

Yes, it was over.

* * *

"You'll do it at once?" Kadar asked as he watched the drawbridge being lowered.

Ware nodded. "There's no use waiting. The longer she's here, the longer she's in danger. There's no telling when the Grand Master will decide to strike."

"I've no liking for this,"Kadar said. "It's not a good thing."

Didn't Kadar think he knew that? "Then find another solution to keep her alive. God knows I cannot."

"She will hate you."

Ware nodded and spurred his horse across the drawbridge.

Selene was walking toward them across the courtyard, thin, small, but militant as the soldiers in the column behind him. "I'm glad to see you," she said. "Why did you not come earlier?"

"Where is your sister?"

"Sleeping. She's been sleeping for four days. She wakes only to eat and goes back to sleep."

Ware frowned. "She's ill?"

Selene shook her head. "Only weary unto death. She wanted to finish your banner before we left." She turned to Kadar. "Your falcons are doing well. I think they like me better than they do you."

Kadar grinned. "I wouldn't be surprised. They probably feel a kinship for you. You have the same fierceness as Eleanor, while I'm a meek and gentle man."

Selene grunted derisively. "As meek as a striking cobra."

"Cobras can be meek as long as one is careful not to

tread on them." He got off his horse. "And it's unkind of you to compare me to a snake. I regard myself as a lion. Or perhaps a leopard."

"We leave tomorrow," Ware told Selene. "Wake your sister and tell her to prepare for the journey."

Selene's expression lit with eagerness. "Damascus? So soon?"

Ware didn't answer directly. "Tell her to prepare for the journey."

Selene smiled brilliantly, turned, and ran across the courtyard.

Ware turned to Kadar. "Will you go or stay here?"

"You think to exempt me from blame?" Kadar shrugged. "I've always enjoyed journeys. Besides, the blame would still be mine even if I hid myself away from her wrath. You don't intend to tell her where we're going?"

"It would make the journey more difficult for her."

Kadar grimaced. "And for us."

Ware didn't deny it. "She will be happy once she becomes accustomed to—"

"Save your arguments for her . . . and yourself." Kadar moved across the courtyard. "I'll tell Abdul that we leave tomorrow. I suppose we're taking him this time?"

Ware nodded. "We may need a diversionary force."

"Do you think Vaden followed us?"

"I know he did."

"Then he'll follow us again. How do you hope to hide her whereabouts from him?"

"Once she's safe, it won't matter if Vaden knows where she is. She'll be safer there than at Dundragon."

"You once told me Vaden could find his way into any

stronghold, and that was why you kept the torches burning bright."

"Then I must make sure Vaden won't pursue her until he's killed me." He smiled sardonically. "And I'm sure that you'll fly to her rescue like one of your falcons, if that happens."

"If she'll ever trust me again."

"She'll trust you." It was Ware whom Thea would never trust again.

"And you may live longer than any of us. This Vaden can't be as formidable as you've said."

"No? I'd wager he'd rival your Old Man of the Mountain."

"Let's hope you never have an opportunity to compare. The old man was not at all pleased when you trespassed on his domain. I barely managed to pluck you away before he sent an assassin to slit your throat." Kadar sighed. "Little did I know what a problem you'd become to me."

"You can always go back to him. In truth, I believe that would be an excellent idea."

"A covey of assassins surrounding me instead of a wall of soldiers?" Kadar shook his head. "Do you never give up?"

"No." He could not give up trying to save them. No matter what the cost, they had to survive. "Tell Abdul to be ready at dawn."

"Wake up! We're going to Damascus, Thea." Selene jumped on the bed and bounced up and down. "You've slept enough."

Thea drowsily opened her eyes. "Damascus?"

"Lord Ware is back. We're to leave for Damascus tomorrow morning. We must make preparations."

Her gaze went to the folded banner on the table. "We can't go. I haven't finished—"

"You can hem it later and send it to him." Selene's face was luminous with excitement. "Damascus, Thea. It's starting. . . . Our whole life is starting."

Thea wished her head didn't feel as if it were stuffed with cotton. She shook her head to clear it.

"What's wrong? Aren't you excited?"

"Of course I am. I'm still half-asleep." She hugged her sister before slowly sitting up in bed. She felt terribly fragile. The hollowness she had experienced right after she had finished the banner had not vanished entirely. "I don't know why I'm still so groggy."

Selene wrinkled her nose. "Because you didn't sleep for three weeks. It was most strange." She jumped off the bed and pulled Thea to her feet. "But you can't sleep any longer. We have too much to do. What is first?"

"Go ask Jasmine to order me a bath." She tried to think. "And then go make sure the silkworms will have enough leaves for the journey."

Selene nodded and ran from the room.

Perhaps she would have time tonight to hem the banner. No, she must talk to Jasmine and Tasza and make sure they knew how to care for the trees. Oh, well, perhaps Selene was right. She could send Ware the banner once they were settled in Damascus.

But she didn't want to send it. She wanted to see his face when he saw what she had created for him.

But her work had been as much for herself as for him. Once she had started, the banner had possessed her.

As Ware had possessed her. She was suddenly glad for the lingering hollowness. It would make the parting less painful.

She brushed the hair out of her face. She would not think of Ware now. If she did, some of this blessed numbness might disappear. She must just prepare for the journey that would take her away from him.

"Good God, what have you done to yourself?" Ware asked roughly as she came down the steps at dawn the next morning. "You're skin and bones."

"I've lost only a little weight. I've been working."

"That gown is hanging on you, and your wrists..." He trailed off before adding, "I don't want to hear of this foolishness again."

"You will not. After all, I'll be in Damascus and you'll be here. It won't be your concern." She smiled with an effort. "Any more than it is now."

"It's my concern if I say it is. I wouldn't have wanted a banner if I'd known it would have brought you to this."

"I wanted it for you. I *owed* it to you." She found she could not take her gaze from him. He was fully armored, big and boldly masculine, his bright-blue eyes glittering in the glow of the candles. This was the warrior she had seen that first night when she had thought him a brute and a beast. It would have been better if she had not grown to see beyond that facade. It would have made this parting easier.

"Selene said you were sleeping a great deal." He stood looking at her. "Are you... well? I did not—"

"I've had my flux," she interrupted, wanting to get it over. "I am not with child."

"That's good." His face was blank, but she knew him too well now not to sense the pain. "You'll be much safer."

And he was robbed of his chance that part of him would live through his child. The numbness was melting as she looked at him. She wanted to reach out and hold him, comfort him. Dear God, was she always going to feel this aching tenderness for him? She wished desperately that there had been only passion between them. Passion was of the moment, easily dismissed, but tenderness . . .

"What are you thinking?" he asked suddenly.

She swallowed to ease the tightness of her throat. "I was thinking I wish everything to go well for you. You have been very kind to me."

"Have I?" He smiled grimly. "By God, you're easy to please. I took your body, endangered your life, and now I'm going to—" He broke off and turned on his heel. "Come along. Your sister is waiting in the courtyard with Kadar. If it can be called waiting. She was running around, giving orders and arranging everything to suit herself. You'd think she was a woman grown."

Thea followed, grateful that the painful moment was at an end. "She's never been allowed to be anything else." She walked past him down the steps leading to the courtyard. The courtyard was ablaze with the torches carried by the soldiers. Horses milled about uneasily, and Thea glimpsed a wagon half-hidden behind the columns.

Jasmine was standing on the steps and turned as she saw Thea. "I came to bid you farewell. Good journey."

"Thank you." She was tempted to embrace Jasmine, but

she was afraid of offending the woman's dignity. "You'll remember to practice everything I taught you?"

"I told you I would." She paused. "You will not forget us?"

Thea shook her head. "I'll send for you as soon as I can." She hesitated. "I've had little chance to speak to you of late. Lord Ware has— I thought you might resent—"

Jasmine's gesture cut her short. "Don't be foolish. Why should I care if you bed Lord Ware when you offer Tasza a better way to live? You are a woman in this man's world. If you think coupling with him will give you more power, I cannot fault you."

She should have known Jasmine would regard all coupling as a way to gain a goal, Thea thought sadly. Her experience in life would not permit any other conclusion. Well, perhaps she was right. Ware and she both had something to gain. He had come to her because he wished a child. She had gone to his bed because she wanted to make sure he remained in the castle. Surely that was as coolly calculated as any bargain Jasmine or Tasza had ever struck.

Cool? No, there had been nothing cool about their coming together. Their coupling had been hot and stormy, changing every moment, gaining power and strength. Whatever had been their beginning had soon become transformed. But Jasmine would not be able to comprehend that alteration. "I'm glad you understand."

"Of course I understand. Now Lord Ware takes you to Damascus and gifts you with many bolts of silk. It's good for all of us." Jasmine dismissed the subject with a wave of her hand. "Now, you must work hard, but not as hard as you have these last weeks. That was not good. You must not fall ill. We can wait . . . a little while." She turned away. "But not too long."

Thea smiled ruefully as she watched Jasmine enter the castle. She supposed she should be grateful Jasmine had decreed she did not have to work day and night to succeed in their common goal.

"I'm going to ride." Selene rushed up to Thea, grabbed her hand, and pulled her down the rest of the steps. "Kadar wanted me to ride in the wagon, but I told him that it wouldn't do. You must ride too."

Thea shook her head and smiled. "I don't know how, and this is not the time to learn. I'll ride in the wagon."

"No." Ware mounted his horse, then leaned down and held out his arms. "You ride with me."

"Is it necessary?"

"Yes." Then he shook his head. "No." He added haltingly, "but it would please me."

This might be the last time he would ever hold her, she realized suddenly. She took a step forward and held up her arms. He lifted her onto the horse before him.

As he lifted the reins, he spoke in a voice so low, it was almost inaudible even to her. "I thank you. It is most kind of—"

"Be silent." She had to stop to steady her voice. "You're such a fool. It was my wish also."

Tears blurred her vision as they rode through the gates and over the drawbridge. Torches everywhere, fire and flame and light. She remembered her first impression of Dundragon and how she had complained to Ware that such extravagance was wasteful.

"You're shaking." Ware's arms tightened about her. "Are you cold?"

"No. How long will the journey take?"

"Two days, perhaps a little longer. Stop shaking. You needn't be afraid. Nothing will happen to you. I'll keep you safe."

"I'm not afraid." She leaned back against him. It was true. At that moment she did not fear the danger that lay beyond the gates. She felt only sadness and regret and a terrible sense of wrongness. She should not be leaving Dundragon. She should not be leaving him.

She was being stupid. She had no place here. Was she to stay and become his mistress, bear his children, live for his pleasure? She would be as much a slave as she had been in the House of Nicholas.

He did not want or need her. Oh, perhaps in his bed, but any woman would do as well there. He had never said he felt anything but lust for her. When she was gone, he would probably take another woman and be just as content.

By the saints, she would not weep. She determinedly blinked back the tears. This was what she wanted, what they both wanted. It was not as if she were deserting him. He was the one who had arranged the journey and rushed her from Dundragon.

She would not weep.

It was two days later that Thea caught sight of the fortress. The walls seemed high and strong as those of Dundragon, but they surrounded a castle that was completely different. It was like the exotic Arab palaces she had passed on the way from Constantinople.

"What is that place?" Thea asked, her gaze on the fortress. "It's very beautiful."

"El Sunan. It belongs to Kemal ben Jakara," Ware said. "He's a very powerful sheikh and guards this province for Saladin."

"From the Franks?"

He shook his head. "These lands are too isolated to attract the Franks, but there are more bandits in these hills than Kemal can battle and any number of rival sheikhs who eye his power with envy."

"You seem to know a great deal about him."

"We've encountered each other upon occasion."

"But you fought for the Franks."

Ware started down the hill. "All Islam knows that the Templars cast me out. An outcast has no true allegiance. Kemal and I understand each other."

She felt a ripple of uneasiness. "Is it safe to pass so close to his fortress?"

"I told you, Kemal and I understand each other. No harm will come to us."

He kicked his horse into a gallop.

"You're heading straight for the fortress. Are we going to spend the night?"

His answer was barely audible. "Yes, we're going to spend the night."

To her astonishment the gates were thrown open without a challenge, and they rode into the courtyard. The palace was even more beautiful than she had imagined from the hill. Onion-shaped towers crowned the sprawling building, and white marble balconies shone in the strong sunlight.

"Welcome, Lord Ware." An Arab, dressed in flowing

robes and a turban inset with a giant blue stone, was striding across the courtyard toward them. His plump cheeks creased as he smiled broadly. "I see you have brought your treasure."

"Yes." Ware dismounted and helped Thea down from the horse. "This is the lady Thea, Kemal."

Thea gazed with bewilderment at the man Ware had addressed. This must be Kemal ben Jakara, but there was no hint of antagonism in his demeanor. He was a small, plump man, close to his fiftieth year, with snapping black eyes and an eager smile.

Kemal's gaze raked Thea from head to foot. "I can see why you do not wish anything to happen to her. Fair-haired women have great value, and she's very comely. I shall take great pleasure in this task."

Thea stiffened with shock.

"Not too much pleasure. Remember she's not your property," Ware said. "She belongs to me."

"I'm a man of honor. I'll keep my word." Kemal beamed at him. "As long as you keep yours."

"What *is* this?" Thea asked Ware. "What are you talking about?"

A faint frown furrowed Kemal's brow. "She addresses you boldly. You have not taught her well."

Thea's hands slowly clenched. "What *is* this?"

"You'll stay here under Kemal's protection." He turned to Kadar. "Take her and Selene to the House of Women."

Kemal snapped his fingers and a young man ran forward. "This is Domo," he told Thea. "He is chief eunuch, and you'll obey him as you would your master. Go with him."

"House of Women," Selene whispered from atop her horse.

Thea knew the horror her sister felt. She was experiencing the same cold terror as memories of Nicholas's House of Women flooded back to her.

"It will be fine," Kadar said as he lifted Selene to the ground. "It's not like the House of Nicholas. You'll work only when you wish. Your every need will be met. You're likely to go fat with sloth in Kemal's harem."

"Harem," Thea repeated numbly. She could not believe it.

"Go with Kadar," Ware repeated. "I'll come to you and explain after Kemal and I settle the details."

"You're selling me to him," she whispered in disbelief. "It was all a lie. You never intended to take me to Damascus."

"I didn't lie. I never said you were going to Damascus."

"It was a *lie*." Her hands clenched into fists. "You let me believe—"

"Be silent, slave." Kemal was shaking his head in disapproval. "Have you no respect for your master?"

"Slave," Thea whispered.

"No, I'm not selling you to Kemal. It's to keep you safe." He gazed at her pale face for another instant before he whirled on his heel. "For God's sake, *take* her, Kadar."

"You always leave me with the easy tasks," Kadar said wryly. He gestured to the eunuch. "Lead on, Domo."

Thea gazed after Ware as he crossed the courtyard with Kemal. "Slavery."

Selene drew closer to her. "I don't understand, Thea."

Thea understood all too well. Her worst nightmare realized. Betrayal.

She put her arm around Selene's shoulders. "It will be all right. We'll find a way."

Selene whirled on Kadar. "*You* did this."

He flinched. "I admit that I helped. Ware told me to find a different solution to keep you safe. I couldn't do it."

"I was *free*." Selene's eyes blazed at him. "You set me free and then put me back in a cage."

"Please, my master says you must come with me," the young eunuch said gently as he started across the courtyard.

Master. Slave. Thea shuddered, then straightened and braced herself. "We have to go with him, Selene. For now."

Kadar fell into step beside them. "It's not forever, you know."

Thea regarded him coldly. "I know that very well. But only because I will not permit it."

"Ware didn't sell you. He only made a bargain with Kemal. The sheikh is to keep you safe, and in return Ware is to guard his southern border."

"He called me slave."

"Ware had to make sure Kemal knew you weren't free to go, so he told him you were his slave." Kadar went on quickly, "It will be very pleasant here. You'll still have your bolts of silk and do your embroidery, and when it's time for you to leave this place, you'll have a commodity with which to bargain."

"It's time to leave now."

Kadar went on as if she had not spoken. "Ware is even having Abdul fetch some young mulberry trees to be planted in the palace garden."

"How kind." Betrayed. Her fury was building higher by the second. "And why this Arab for a jailer?"

Kadar shrugged. "You wouldn't have been safe with a Frankish lord. Ware couldn't be certain that the Templars wouldn't be able to influence them. Kemal would rather slit your throat than hand you over to the Templars."

"Is that supposed to comfort me?"

"I don't think anything would comfort you at the moment."

"Then you're wiser than you are kind."

"I'm trying to be kind." He paused. "And so is Ware. If we can find any way of releasing you, we will do so. It's just not possible now."

"So we're to remain prisoners until Ware deigns to release us."

"Not prisoners. Guests." When he met her outraged stare, he sighed. "Prisoners."

"Truth, at last."

"I won't stay here," Selene said fiercely.

"You have no choice. Ware has chosen this fortress well. Kemal may not look like a soldier, but he's a very able leader. Even if you got over the walls, his men would catch you before you found your way out of the hills." Kadar added with a coaxing smile, "Why not look upon this as a brief interruption? Stay here, do your embroideries, and be safe."

The eunuch threw open the door and led them into a long gleaming foyer. He said over his shoulder, "You are very favored. My master says you are to have quarters of your own instead of living with the rest of the harem." He opened a fretted door and stepped aside. "Enter."

Thea was assaulted by the spicy scent of incense as she crossed the threshold. Her gaze raked the mosaic-tiled floor, silken couches, arched windows blocked by fretted shutters, tasseled and brocade-draped beds.

"This wing has many beautiful rooms." The eunuch nodded toward a door across the room. "Is it not splendid?"

Thea moved slowly across the floor toward the two windows. She could see blue sky through the beautiful fretting, but when she reached the shutters, she saw they were as sturdy and confining as metal bars. "No prison is splendid."

"Any woman in the harem would be grateful for such fine chambers," Domo chided.

Thea fixed him with an icy stare. "I am *not* grateful."

Kadar stepped between them. "He is not to blame."

"I know who is to blame." Thea turned her back on him and gazed blindly out the window. "Get out. I don't want to look at you anymore. I don't want to see your face or hear your voice."

"Thea . . ." He stopped and said, "I'm still your friend."

"You are not our friend," Selene said. "A friend would not betray us."

"It was not—" Kadar gave up the battle. "Believe me, I'm still your friend. Someday you will see it." He turned to the eunuch. "Come, Domo, it's best we leave them alone. Ware will be here shortly, Thea."

"Why? To make sure I can't escape this prison?"

Kadar sighed. "He knows you can't escape. A warrior always knows how to secure prisoners. He wishes to reassure you."

Thea heard the door shut behind him. No key turned in the lock. They must feel very secure, Thea thought bitterly.

"What are we to do, Thea?" Selene asked.

Uncharacteristic uncertainty trembled in Selene's tone.

Thea must put aside her own frustration and despair and give strength to her. She turned away from the window. "First, we'll make sure Kadar told the truth about the fortifications. Then we'll make our plans." She forced a smile. "There will be some way out. This is a delay, not an end."

Selene looked past Thea to the fretted windows. "This is not fair. We were free. . . ."

"We'll be free again. It may take a long time, but we will never be slaves again."

"Goddammit, I told you that you weren't slaves." Ware stood in the doorway. "Why the devil won't you believe me?"

Thea stiffened as she turned to face him. "Because you lie. Look around you. Do free women live behind bars?"

"If their husbands so decree." He held up his hand to stop the barrage of words he knew would come. "I told you once that no woman is really free. I can't give you freedom, but you'll have every comfort here."

"You didn't give me freedom, I took it. Now you're trying to take it away." She said between gritted teeth, "I won't *have* it."

"Yes, you will. I've made certain—" He broke off and said to someone over his shoulder, "Yes, bring them in." He stepped aside to allow four soldiers to enter carrying the bolts of silk. "Where do you want these? Here?"

Selene jumped to her feet. "No, I'll find a place." She moved toward the door Domo had indicated as leading to other chambers. "Come with me."

Selene's moment of uncertainty was clearly over, Thea thought. She watched her sister lead the soldiers into the adjoining room before she turned back to Ware. "She's only a child. She doesn't understand this. Find her a place in Damascus and set her free."

He shook his head. "It's not safe. Why do you think I had her brought from Constantinople?"

"To make my prison more bearable." It was all clear now. Why hadn't she seen it sooner? "You intended to keep me at Dundragon, didn't you?"

"Yes, until Vaden gave me warning. Then I realized I'd have to find somewhere else to secrete you."

"For how long?"

"Until it's safe."

Rage surged through her in a dizzying tide. "I won't let you do this. I'll make my own decisions and protect myself. You have no right."

"I take the right."

"I'll never forgive you for this. I'll curse you every day of my life."

"I know you will." His face was a shade paler as he smiled mirthlessly. "But perhaps this action will assure that your death will be a long time from now." He turned way. "I'll send Kadar here from time to time to make sure all goes well with you."

"I don't want him here."

"He'll still come. After all, I have to make sure Kemal is keeping to his side of the bargain. My services as a war lord are very valuable." He suddenly turned around and looked at her, searching for words. He finally said hoarsely, "I could do nothing else. I couldn't let you die. I couldn't bear it if—" He broke off and made a helpless gesture with his hand. "I could do nothing else." He whirled and strode out of the room.

He was gone and she was a prisoner. She wanted to run

after him and rave at him, tell him that he could not do this to them.

But he could—he had already done it.

"Now, begone." Selene was ushering the soldiers from the anteroom. "We want nothing more to do with you."

The soldiers fled the chamber as if pursued. Selene must have given them a tongue-lashing. Thea would have smiled at such stalwarts being intimidated by one small girl if she had not been so enraged. "The silk is unharmed?"

Selene nodded. "Should I unpack our boxes?"

It would be good for Selene to be busy. "Yes." Thea moved back to the window. Ware had mounted his horse and was looking down at Kemal. They were speaking, probably discussing her and Selene's imprisonment, Thea thought bitterly. Then Kemal stepped back and Ware lifted his hand and moved toward the open gates.

Thea's fingers gripped the keyhole openings in the fretting. He was leaving. He was riding through the gates.

A wave of despair and desolation rocked her. She knew now she had not believed it would happen, that he would really desert them in this alien place.

"Thea?" Selene was standing beside her. "Don't worry. I was frightened at first, but we're together and that makes it better. Everything will be all right."

She should be the one comforting Selene, she realized dimly. She took her sister in her arms. "We'll see that it is."

After a moment Selene stepped back and disengaged herself. "I've put our clothing in the chest across the room." She nodded at the bundle of folded silk on the table by the door. "I found the banner in your box. What shall I do with it?"

The banner. Ware's banner. "Burn it."

Selene gazed at her in astonishment. "I will not. I can see why you wouldn't give it to him, but you labored too long and hard to create it. I'll not see your work wasted."

"Then do with it what you will. I never want to see it again." She turned back to the window. The gates were closing. They were alone. "But I'd rather you burn—"

"I bid you welcome to my home." The door had been thrown open, and Kemal ben Jakara stood beaming at them. He swept into the room and closed the door behind him. "I have thought about it, and I believe your boldness was caused by your surprise at my friend Ware's decision to leave you in my care." He added magnanimously, "I forgive you."

"Oh, do you?" Thea asked softly. She wanted to slap his plump, dimpled cheeks.

"But you must realize that I will not tolerate such rebellion in my household. Lord Ware has won certain privileges for you already, but I'm a peaceful man and I will have peace. You will be allowed the freedom of the women's quarters and the garden as long as you cause me no disturbance." He frowned "Though this business of hundreds of worms crawling about doesn't please me. I may seek to renegotiate that portion of my bargain with Lord Ware." His face cleared. "But I've no complaint about your sewing. Such tasks are proper women's work. Now, have I not been generous?"

She wondered what he would do if she pulled his bejeweled silk turban down over his eyes and kicked him in the stomach. She opened her lips to speak, then thought better of the scathing words she had been about to utter. It would do no good to antagonize their jailer. If she was to escape from this place, the little freedom he was offering might be of advantage.

Kemal's smile widened. "I can see you're speechless at my kindness. Now, that is how a proper slave should behave." He started to turn away. "It is good we've come to an understanding. Lord Ware will be—What is this?" His gaze had fallen on the gleaming silk bundle on the table.

He reached out and shook out the cloth. "A banner? Let me see if your work has val—" He broke off, his eyes widening as he stared at the red-and-gold design. "By Allah's sword," he murmured. One plump finger reached out and reverently traced the design. "Magnificent. You did this for your master?"

Master. She felt another surge of rage. "Yes."

"Perhaps I will permit you to do one for me. In truth, I have never seen such a fine banner."

"Then take it." She felt Selene's startled gaze on her face. "Lord Ware doesn't want it."

"Any warrior would want such a banner."

"Would he have left it with me if he'd wanted it?"

Kemal doubtfully shook his head. "You're sure he would not mind?"

"He told me before we left Dundragon that he wished I hadn't made it. Leave it with me and I'll finish hemming it."

"Today? I'll want it tomorrow." He looked eagerly at the design. "It will bring me great good fortune. I can feel it."

"You'll have the banner tomorrow morning."

He gave her a brilliant toothy smile as he handed her the banner. "I can see now why Lord Ware bargained to keep you safe. Such willingness and skill are rare qualities in a woman. You can be taught the rest." He moved toward the door. "I'll send a servant to get the banner tomorrow."

"Pompous rooster," Selene muttered as the door closed behind him.

Thea nodded. "But the rooster rules this fortress. It will do no harm for him to think us less than we are until we're ready to escape from this place." She sat down on the cushions. "Bring me thread and needle, Selene. I wish this banner out of my sight."

Chapter Eleven

"I BELIEVE YOU'VE MADE a more bitter enemy than the Grand Master this day," Kadar said as he glanced over his shoulder at the gates of El Sunan. "You won't change your mind?"

"I cannot change my mind." Ware's tone was fierce with leashed frustration. "How many times must I tell you? You wouldn't have helped me if you hadn't realized there was no other way out." He kept his gaze straight ahead. No use looking back. Don't think about her face when she realized she had been betrayed. It was done. "Unless you can offer a solution, be silent."

"I've been thinking about that. You could take her far away from this land."

"I'll not leave here."

"Don't you think it's time to forget pride and remember good sense?"

"Pride?" He gave him a weary glance. "My God, do you still think I'd care if anyone thought they'd chased me away?"

Kadar studied him and then slowly shook his head. "No, I do believe you may have changed. I wonder why?"

"Jedha. Isn't that enough?"

Kadar seemed about to argue but held his peace. "So why not leave the Holy Land?"

"It would do no good. The Templars are everywhere."

"But not in such numbers. The world is wide. You might be able to find a pocket of land where you'd be safe."

"And would Thea be content to hide herself away? You know she would not. She has a dream. She'd fly away to the nearest city to set up her silk house. Sooner or later Vaden would find her."

Kadar gave a low whistle. "Then it's Thea who keeps you here."

"It's my fault she's in danger. She's my responsibility."

"A responsibility that may cause you to be slaughtered like those poor souls at Jedha. Protecting Kemal's borders isn't going to be an easy task." Kadar again glanced over his shoulder at the gates. "One wonders which one of you is the real prisoner."

"Ask Thea. She has no doubt."

"I fear her judgment is clouded at the moment."

Clouded by anger and bitterness and hatred, Ware thought. She had looked at him with the same horror and distrust as the night he had found her in the desert. No, it was not the same; it was far worse. "Then you'll have to make your own decisions. She's not likely to change her mind." Christ, he had to get away from Kadar. He would keep talking, and each word was like a blow from a mailed fist. He spurred ahead and left Kadar and El Sunan far behind.

Ware kept a brutal pace for the rest of the journey, and Dundragon came into view near dawn of the next day.

Ware reined in his horse and called over his shoulder, "Kadar."

Kadar rode forward. "You've decided I'm worthy of conversation? You've been very rude, you know. I should ignore you completely and—"

"If I don't return in three days' time, tell everyone to leave Dundragon and scatter to the four winds. Then go to El Sunan and take Thea and Selene away."

"Return? Where are you going?"

Ware's gaze lifted to the third mountain.

Kadar instantly shook his head. "From what you've told me, it will do no good to offer yourself as sacrifice."

"I'm no martyr. I've no intention of letting Vaden kill me. I only need to talk to him."

"Because he'll know you took Thea to El Sunan? You don't think Kemal could protect her?"

"Not if Vaden decides he wants her dead. Kemal could keep her safe from everyone else, but not from Vaden." He turned his horse. "Protect my people at Dundragon."

"And who will protect you?" Kadar called after him. "He's been stalking you for years, and now you wish to skewer yourself on a spit for the serving."

Ware didn't answer.

"You need me. I won't have you killing yourself when your life is mine."

"The best way to make sure he slays me is if I don't go to him alone," Ware said. "Three days."

He could hear Kadar cursing with frustration as he rode toward the third mountain.

Vaden was watching him.

Ware stared into the flames of the campfire.

He was there in the darkness behind him. Ware had heard nothing, but he could *feel* him.

The white flag he'd speared into the ground glimmered in the darkness to the right of the campfire. The Grand Master would disregard any truce gesture and strike him down. Who knows? Vaden might do the same. He must have grown as tired of this game as Ware. No, no one on earth could be that weary.

"Are you coming or not?" His gaze never left the flames. "I don't remember you being this timid, Vaden."

Silence. Then an amused chuckle and the sound of footsteps behind him. "You were never subtle in your challenges, Ware. Did you think a charge of cowardice would bring me running?"

"It did."

"I was planning on joining you anyway. I was merely waiting to see if you were desperate enough to set a trap for me."

"Under a flag of truce?"

"Desperation can change a man. I've pushed you hard." Vaden sat down across the fire from him. He took off his helmet and ran his hand through his tawny hair. "And, after Jedha, you've reason to wonder if there's any honor left in the world."

"You had nothing to do with Jedha."

"How do you know?" Vaden's dark eyes narrowed.

"How can you be sure? Perhaps I was growing weary of cat and mouse and wished to stir you to action."

"You wouldn't do it. You're not capable of such an act."

"Ah, but you're wrong. You're judging me by your own standards. You could never have committed that depravity, but I'm fully capable of any sin. It's merely a matter of choice with me."

"Foolishness. Sin is always a question of choice. You wouldn't have destroyed Jedha."

"Have it your own way." He held out his hands to the fire. "But, then, you always did. You could always see only one path. Right was right. Wrong was wrong. There were no shades in between. At times I envied you that blindness."

And Ware had envied Vaden's cleverness, the coolness, the ability to hold himself aloof even in the heat of battle. It was strange that their differences had not prevented them from becoming friends. His own hot-headedness and eagerness had been balanced by Vaden's control and cynicism. He had never felt he entirely knew Vaden, but he'd sensed that whatever lay beyond that icy, beautiful exterior was no threat to him. Sadness rushed through him as he thought of that time that would never return. "There were no shades of right and wrong about the massacre at Jedha." He paused. "Or about the killing of Philippe. There might have been some reason to kill Jeffrey. He had trespassed, but not Philippe."

"The Grand Master said he knew too much."

"He knew *nothing*. Even if I'd confided in him, he would never have told anyone."

"They couldn't be sure. He was a weak man."

"A poor excuse. I'm not weak, but you'll kill me for the

same reason." He added with sudden harshness, "For God's sake, you *know* me. I would keep my vow."

"Perhaps. But you always had a soft heart. If you were given the choice of another Jedha or telling what you saw in the Temple, which would you choose?"

"That wouldn't happen."

"Which would you choose?"

He met Vaden's eyes across the fire. "Life, goddamn you. I'd choose life."

"I thought as much."

"And so would you."

Vaden shook his head. "A tiny village or the end of our world as we know it? You know what chaos could ensue. I assure you that I wouldn't choose your Jedha."

"I don't care what you say. You couldn't do it. You're not like them."

"No, I'm not like them. I'm worse. They wish to kill you in the name of God. I'll do the deed to protect myself and my place in life." His smile faded. "I hope you believe me when I say that it's not by my will. When I found out it was you who had fled the Temple, I wanted to throttle you. Why in heaven couldn't you keep your curiosity in check? If I'd been there, I'd have put a sword through you before I'd have let you go down to those caves."

"You know Jeffrey. He wanted to see what was secreted down there. If I hadn't gone with him, he would have gone alone."

"Christ." Vaden shook his head. "I should have guessed. Will you never learn you can't protect the entire world? You should have let Jeffrey run his own risks."

"He was my friend," Ware said simply. "My brother."

"And so was I. So much for friendship. In our own way we'll both be the death of you."

"I'm not dead yet." He lowered his gaze to the fire. "I don't want to talk about the Temple. That's not why I came here."

"The woman? Did you really think Kemal could protect her from me?"

"No, that's why I'm here." He said haltingly, "I want to ask you to let her live. She's not a threat. She knows nothing."

Vaden was silent.

Ware's voice was suddenly hoarse with intensity. "As Christ is my witness, I didn't tell her. Let her live."

"You care about her."

Vaden could read him too well for Ware to make a total denial. "A woman should not die because a man has a . . . fondness for her. It's not right."

"But you might care enough about her to lie. Would you lie for her, Ware?"

"No." It was the answer he should make, but he suddenly knew it was the wrong one. "Yes, I would lie. What are a few lies when it means she would live?" He raised his gaze to Vaden's face. "But I'm not lying. You always said I had no guile, that you could read me without effort. Am I lying to you now?"

Vaden studied him before slowly shaking his head. "Not unless you've changed more than I thought possible." He shrugged. "Grand Master de Ridfort would say the risk is too great."

Ware tensed. "You told him about her?"

Vaden shook his head. The relief that poured through Ware didn't last long.

"Not yet," Vaden said. "It wasn't necessary. Why should I trouble them when they're occupied with trying to recapture Acre?" He shrugged. "Not that it will do any good. De Ridfort is a fool to think we can triumph over Saladin's vast army."

Ware didn't give a damn about Acre. "It's still not necessary to tell him. She's not involved in this."

"She's involved with you, and that guarantees she's as immersed as the rest of us. You should have been more careful."

Vaden's tone was genuinely regretful, Ware realized with a leap of hope. "Then the guilt is mine. Leave her alone."

Vaden shook his head. "You know that's not possible."

"I *don't* know it." Ware tried to temper the anger in his voice. "Very well, then, at least promise me you'll do nothing right away. Think about it. There's no risk while she's imprisoned at El Sunan."

"True." Vaden was silent, thinking. "If she remains at El Sunan."

"She'll remain there. Kemal will make sure of that. I struck a bargain to guard his southern border."

Vaden lifted a mocking brow. "A bargain with the heathen infidel?"

"If it brings me what I need. It shouldn't surprise you. Am I not regarded as a heathen myself?"

"It doesn't surprise me. It was bound to happen. As I said, desperation changes a man. We left you few doors to open." He paused. "But I find it interesting you didn't open this one until the woman came."

"You place undue importance on her. She's only another responsibility." He could see he was not convincing him. He went back to firmer ground. "She'll stay at El Sunan. You can keep watch on her."

Vaden didn't answer.

"You need do nothing now."

Vaden's expression was unreadable. What the devil was he thinking?

Ware tried again. "I told her nothing. You said you believed me."

Finally Vaden nodded. "I do believe you. Very well, I'll hold my hand as long as I believe she's no danger." He grimaced. "God knows, I've no desire to kill a woman."

Ware felt nearly light-headed with relief. Thea was safe.

Vaden's eyes were narrowed on Ware's face. "She means too much to you. You shouldn't let me see your weakness. I might be tempted to use your temptress as bait."

"Not you. You wouldn't have the stomach for it." He grinned. "In spite of what you say, you're an honorable man."

"What is honor? We both know it's defined by most men to suit their own needs." His flippant smile faded. "Except by you. When I first met you, I thought you were no different from the rest. Only a rough, bawdy soldier out to win riches for himself. I almost wish you were that man. It would be easier for me."

"I *was* a rough, bawdy soldier. The rules of the Order were never easy for me."

"Yet you would never have broken your vows. You were like an eager child reaching out and clasping all of us to your bosom. We were all your brothers." He smiled sardonically. "I found it most disconcerting to be included in that affection. I kept pushing you away, but you kept coming back. I finally decided it was easier to become your friend than to go on with the battle."

Ware suddenly smiled slyly. "Do you know what I thought of you when we first met? I thought you were the lover of some powerful monk or priest, perhaps even a cardinal."

Vaden's eyes widened. "You thought me a sodomite?"

"It was possible. I could think of no other reason for the Templars to break their rules to allow you entrance. It would have been a safe place for a jealous lover to send you, because everyone knows the Templars aren't corrupted in that way." He tilted his head in appraisal. "And you were certainly comely enough to attract anyone's attention."

"Thank you." Vaden did not sound grateful. "I am *not* a sodomite."

Ware's lips twitched. He had evidently touched a sensitive spot. "It was only a first impression."

"And a stupid judgment." He added dryly, "But it puts an entirely new light on your persistence in welcoming me into your circle. Perhaps I was in error regarding your brotherly love for me."

As usual, Vaden had turned the tables. He was never at a disadvantage for long. It was one of the qualities Ware had found most appealing in him. "No, you were not in error. I could not have loved a brother more." He could have bitten his tongue. Christ, next he would be sniveling like a babe. "But, then, I was only a boy and had little discernment. I no longer intrude where I'm not wanted."

"I didn't say it was an intrusion." Before he could reply, Vaden was rising to his feet. "And now I bid you good-bye. Don't come to me in truce again. I won't honor it."

Ware looked back at the flames. "Yes, you will."

"You're still laboring under the false assumption that I'm an honorable man. It may be the death of you. I fully intend to kill you, Ware."

"And probably will someday." He reached out and poked at the wood with the stick. "But you're having a good deal of trouble bestirring yourself to do it. In all this time you must have had opportunities. I know I gave you at least one."

"I had my reasons for holding my hand."

"And you're a patient man." He lifted his gaze to Vaden's face. "But not that patient. I often wonder what you think about when you sit at your campfire at night."

Vaden smiled mockingly. "You shouldn't flatter yourself that you're my only concern. It's true you've been designated my primary duty, but the Grand Master makes use of my sword when he needs it. For instance, I go to battle at Acre tomorrow."

"And when you return to your duty here?"

"I meditate. I read the scrolls of scholars." He paused. "I wait."

"Not a life you'd choose. I'd think you'd want to hurry and complete the task. Could it be you're having doubts?"

"I never have doubts once I've set upon a course. You should remember that about me, Ware. Have you ever seen me waver?"

"I've never seen it. That doesn't mean you've never done it."

Vaden's smile vanished. "I cannot waver in this. Don't make the mistake of thinking I'm softening because I choose not to complete my mission until I see fit. I warn you, the woman will live only as long as I perceive her as no danger."

"And you won't live for a day after I hear you've killed her."

"Ah, Ware, and you say she means nothing to you but responsibility?" Vaden shook his head. "Perhaps I was wrong. It may be the woman, not I, who will be the death of you."

He moved out of the firelight and faded into the shadows.

Silence. Only the crackle of the wood on the fire sounded in the night air.

Loneliness.

By the saints, he was mad. He should be filled with hatred and thoughts of revenge. Vaden was his enemy and that time of friendship was gone. When would he learn to give up those memories and realize Vaden meant what he said?

Tonight. From now on he would regard Vaden as any other enemy. To do anything else would endanger Dundragon and Thea. He must close away this sense of loss and behave with sanity.

The entire world was a barren place. To accept that Vaden was his enemy did not make the loneliness more desolate.

It only seemed to make it weigh heavier, much heavier.

Kadar visited El Sunan four times in the six months following Thea's and Selene's imprisonment. On the first two visits she refused to see him; on the third she saw him only long enough to order him to replenish her store of silken thread. On the fourth visit he decided it was time he was a little more aggressive and received a sharp set-down for his trouble.

"How is she?" Ware asked as Kadar rode into Dundragon's gates on his return from that visit.

"In splendid health. In very bad temper."

"Is Kemal treating them well?"

"Exceptionally well. Kemal is cosseting our Thea as if she were an empress." He dismounted. "He wants nothing to happen to those magical fingers."

Ware frowned. "What are you talking about?"

"He's convinced himself that she's a sorceress."

"You're jesting."

Kadar's lips were twitching, but he answered solemnly. "No, it's true. He thinks she has the power to embroider spells into her cloth. He says he has proof of it."

"I can scarce wait until you tell me what proof," Ware said caustically.

Kadar took off his gauntlets and started across the courtyard. "Your banner. Thea gave him the banner she made for you. Kemal said every time he takes it into battle, he's victorious. He's had six skirmishes with bandits since you left her at El Sunan. No matter what the odds, he's vanquished the foe."

"Superstitious fool." He frowned. "She gave him *my* banner?"

"Surely you didn't expect her to send it to you with her fond regards?"

"No." He knew his outraged response was out of proportion. He didn't care about a banner he'd never even seen. But he did care that she had seen fit to slap him in the face in this manner. She could not have told him any more clearly that any feeling she had had for him was gone. Goddammit, he would not accept it. "It was *mine*."

"And now it's Kemal's."

"I want it back."

"Back? You've never had it."

He was not prepared to be reasonable. "She made it for me."

"Are you willing to give up Thea's haven and fight Kemal for its return? I assure you, he won't give up his talisman without a battle."

Of course Ware was not prepared to make such a sacrifice. "But I want it back."

"Wait until he's lost a few battles to prove this 'magic' false. Then I'll approach him with gifts and sweet words and you'll have your banner."

"Did you see it?"

Kadar shook his head. "He uses it only when he rides into battle. At other times he keeps it in a special trunk with his armor." He shook his head as he understood the direction in which Ware was going. "And I won't steal it. I may be a magnificent thief, but I won't risk my extremely handsome head when waiting will bring you what you want. We both know Kemal's streak of good fortune cannot last."

Ware knew Kadar was right. Kemal had been trained to protect a fortress against siege but did not have a warrior's mind. The reason Ware had been able to strike a bargain with him so easily was that Kemal's defeats were becoming too frequent and the sheikh was afraid of reproof from Saladin.

But he wanted the banner *now*. It belonged to him, just as she belonged—

Christ, what was he thinking? He could not have Thea, so he would take the banner and put her at risk again? This fragment of silk was not Thea and would bring only bitter memories.

No, the memories would be sweet. Thea lying next to him at night. Thea in the firelight, her brow furrowed as she looked down at the chessboard. Thea watering the mulberry tree with the sunlight on her hair.

"Ware?"

He turned to meet Kadar's quizzical stare. Stop thinking like a lover. Maudlin sentiment would not keep her alive. "Forget the banner. I have no need of it."

"You are sure?"

"I'm sure." A thought occurred to him. "No, wait. Don't forget about it. When Kemal starts losing battles, he'll be too vain to blame himself. He'll fault the banner. We may have to move if he also blames Thea. Increase your visits to once every month and keep watch on the situation."

"These visits are not easy for me. I felt more welcome with the Old Man of the Mountain and his assassins." He sighed. "I suppose I'll have to call on all my reserves of charm and intelligence to get Thea and Selene to accept me again. It's a great strain."

Ware smiled sardonically. "While I have only to journey forth and do battle along Kemal's border."

"I'm glad you realize the two problems don't compare in scope." Kadar's brow wrinkled in thought. Then a brilliant smile suddenly lit his face. "I know. I'll take them a present."

* * *

"I wish you to make me another banner," Kemal announced.

Thea looked up from the tunic she was embroidering. "Indeed?"

Kemal frowned as he entered the chamber and closed the door. "Why do you bother with embroidering all those tunics and robes? It's banners you should be sewing."

"Only warriors need banners."

"I am a warrior."

"But you're not my master."

"That is true." He smiled coaxingly. "But Lord Ware is my great good friend. He would tell you to make me another banner."

She drew the gold thread through the silk. "I will think about it."

He was not pleased. "You are very proud for a slave."

"I gave you one banner. Aren't you pleased with it?" She knew the answer. She had heard the whispers from the eunuchs and women of the harem. At first she could not believe anyone could be so foolish as to believe such nonsense. Her second thought was to use that foolishness to her own advantage. "It's a very fine banner."

"Very fine. I want another."

"It takes a long time and much effort to create a banner of such power." She smiled. "I hear it's brought you good fortune. It doesn't surprise me."

"I want to give one to Saladin as a gift."

"So that he will look on you with favor? A very clever move." She pretended to think about it. "But Lord Ware might not like my making a banner to give good fortune to Saladin. After all, Lord Ware is a knight of Christendom."

"He is a renegade."

"But his roots are with the Frankish lords." She sighed. "No, I fear there is too much risk."

"He values you. He will not slay you."

"I cannot be sure. What would you do to a slave who betrayed you?"

His gaze slid away from her own. He knew she must be aware of his treatment of the women of the harem. Only yesterday he had ordered a young girl whipped senseless because she had displeased him. "I would not tell him."

"My banners speak boldly." She paused. "But if I felt safe, I might be persuaded to make you such a gift."

Eagerness lit his face. "I tell you, he will not know."

"Perhaps if he also does not know where I am . . ." She took a tiny stitch. "If you could free me, send me away from here—"

"I'm a man of honor. I would not betray my bargain."

"Not even to sit at Saladin's right hand?"

He was silent a moment. "Lord Ware has protected my border well these last months."

"But do you need him? I hear you've won many battles yourself."

"I'm a man of honor," he repeated.

"Saladin is your liege." She raised her gaze to his face. "Is it honorable not to share your success with him?"

Good—Kemal was frowning uncertainly. Did she have him?

"Saladin has success enough without my help. These Franks are nothing before him." He bit his lip. "Perhaps if he needed my help, it would not be dishonorable to—But he does not." He glared at her. "And you are a wicked woman to so tempt me."

She smiled at him. "I merely searched for a way to give you what you wished of me. Think on it." She looked back down at the tunic. "But not too long. A banner is not created overnight. Lord Ware may decide to return and take me away from you."

"We struck a bargain. He won't return." She heard his retreating footsteps. "We are both honorable men."

The door slammed behind him.

"You made him angry." Selene came out of the adjoining chamber. "Do you truly think he'll do it?"

"You heard?"

Selene nodded. "It's true what the women say. He really believes it." She grinned as she plopped down beside Thea on the pillows. "Why did you never tell me you could create magical banners?"

"You may laugh, but his foolishness may be our way out of this fortress." She frowned. "He's very stubborn. It may take some time to persuade him."

"And what if he begins losing battles?"

"I'll tell him the magic lasts only for so many battles and that a new banner will have to be created." She made a face. "And hope he believes me."

Selene looked at her in surprise. "You've been thinking about this."

Thea nodded. "Since the moment I heard the rumors from the harem." Soon after arriving in El Sunan, she had found that escape from the fortress would be difficult if not impossible. The guards were loyal, the walls were high, and what would they do once they had escaped? She would take the risk herself, but fleeing through the hills was too grave a danger for Selene. No, it would be infinitely better to use Kemal to arrange their release. However, she must not mention to Selene that she feared for her, that would immediately bring about rebellion. "We may have to be patient, but if Kemal can be persuaded to release us, we'll be able to take all our work with us."

Selene picked up the shawl she was embroidering. "Then we'll be patient. I don't want to leave one inch of silk for that pompous buffoon."

"Smile at me," Kadar commanded Thea as he swept into the chamber a week later. "I come bringing precious gifts."

"I don't want your gifts." Thea fixed him with a cold stare. "I want you to leave."

"I swear on my hope of paradise that you'll want these gifts." He stepped to one side with a flamboyant gesture. "Am I ever wrong?"

"You were wrong when you brought us to this—Jasmine?" Thea rushed forward but stopped before she reached the woman. Was this another trick? "What are you doing here?"

"It seems very obvious." Jasmine slipped her mantle from her hair. "You were not in Damascus, so Tasza and I had to come here."

"I do not like this place." Tasza followed her and disdainfully glanced around the room. "I would rather have stayed at Dundragon."

"Hush," Jasmine said. "You can see no farther than the tip of your nose."

"I can see that this place is no better than a harem. At least I get paid for giving my body."

"It's not a harem," Kadar said. "I give you my word you will be held in all honor."

Jasmine glared at Tasza. "Did I not tell you?"

"What is this about, Kadar?" Thea asked.

"I thought you would like to have Jasmine by your side. Are you not glad to see her?"

Thea *was* glad to see her. She had not realized how much she had missed Jasmine. "Not enough to have her made a prisoner for my sake."

"She's not a prisoner. She can leave whenever she wishes. All she has to do is ask, and I'll return her to Dundragon."

"But I won't ask," Jasmine told Thea. "We have much to learn from you, and we cannot learn with you here, and us at Dundragon." She turned to Tasza. "Now, tell her that you are happy to be here and will work hard."

"I'm not happy to be here." She added grudgingly, "But I will work hard. What else can I do in this place?"

"You see, Thea, everything is going to be splendid." Kadar beamed. "You will have pleasant company and help to do your embroideries. You may thank me now."

She looked at him in astonishment. Did he really think she would forget his part in their betrayal?

"No?" He must have read her thoughts in her expression. "But now you know I wish you only goodwill. If you'd forgive me, it would please me." He made a face. "And make my visits far more pleasant."

"I don't forgive you."

"You could pretend. That would be nearly as good,"

he coaxed. "And maybe someday pretense could become reality."

She stared at Kadar as the persuasive golden strands he wove so well wound themselves around her. But she would not soften. He could have fought Ware instead of aligning himself with him.

Yet she knew Ware would not have been dissuaded no matter how strongly Kadar had disagreed. And Kadar had believed that Ware was doing what was right to keep them safe. A little of her resentment was melting, but she would not let him triumph this easily. "Perhaps I could pretend." She smiled with malice. "If you can convince Selene you meant only the best for us."

He groaned. "You would make me face that termagant without your protection? I was hoping you'd intercede for me."

"Why should I? You're the one who is suing for pardon. You'll find her in the garden. I send her out each afternoon to relax and play, but she spends her time tending the trees." She had no doubt Kadar's charm would eventually triumph, but Selene would make him suffer first. It would do the rascal good. She turned to Jasmine. "Come, I will show you where you'll sleep. There's a room facing the garden that's very pleasant. Did I tell you how glad I am to see you?"

More than glad. She had two more allies in this scented prison, and her sense of helplessness was rapidly dispersing. She had only to wait and work and be patient and she would gain her freedom. In the meantime, she could control this world to which Ware had exiled her. She had learned long ago that one had only to supply what the enemy desired to be in a position of power. She had something Kemal wanted, and she could dangle it before the sheikh while undermining Ware in every possible way. She wouldn't let Ware succeed in keeping her there against her will.

She would be the one to hold power at El Sunan.

Chapter Twelve

EIGHTEEN MONTHS LATER
JUNE 10, 1191
EL SUNAN

KADAR GAZED UP at the branches of the mulberry trees with a sigh. "It seems a pity to have such pretty trees beset by pests. I've no admiration for your worms, Thea."

"They aren't pests. Everything feeds on something else. You don't scorn the fine silk tunic I gave you." She grimaced. "As I remember, you nagged at me unceasingly until I gave you what you wanted."

"It was for our mutual good. I like fine garments."

"And why is that good for me?"

"You could see me in them. I'm sure not one man in a thousand could show your work to such advantage." He paused. "Except Ware. He'd look quite splendid in one of your tunics."

It was a blatant lie, Thea thought. Kadar knew as well as she did that one never noticed what Ware wore; only the man himself. And it was the third time since he had arrived last night that he had mentioned Ware. It was clear he was leading up to something, but she had no intention of helping him. He knew she would not speak of Ware. She changed the subject. "It will be time to gather the cocoons soon."

"I'm grateful the trees at Dundragon aren't being put to such use. They flowered quite prettily this year. Of course, Ware has little opportunity to appreciate their beauty. He hasn't returned to Dundragon for over a month. The border has exploded at rumors that King Richard will be arriving shortly to help Philip of France in this new siege of Acre. The rival sheikhs are edging closer because they know there's a possibility Saladin may summon Kemal to help defend Acre." Kadar smiled. "A man unbeatable in battle could be a boon to a city in such dire straits. Kemal's fame as a warrior has spread even to Jerusalem."

"Indeed?"

"You know it has. I'd wager you're aware of every message that goes between Kemal and Saladin."

She gazed at him innocently. "But how could that be? I'm only a humble slave here."

"A most peculiar slave. Kemal permits you the freedom of the entire fortress. He's even given you and Selene fine horses to ride when he believes women should never leave the harem."

"We must have exercise if we're to keep in good health. How can sick women perform their work?"

"And horses afford a much better chance at escape."

"Kemal doesn't worry about my escaping. He thinks me content."

"Then he's more fool than I believed. Oh, well, I suppose I shouldn't be surprised at that indulgence when he gives you everything else you wish."

Except one thing. Kemal had proved very stubborn, but if the situation at Acre was as desperate as she had heard, she might be close to gaining that prize. "Wasn't giving me what I wish part of the agreement Ware made with Kemal?"

"Not to this extent." He paused. "You play a dangerous game when you let him think the banner is responsible for his success. It's incredible that his luck has held this long. One defeat and Kemal will turn against you. They burn witches, you know."

"I'll face that threat when I must." She turned to face him. "It's none of your concern, Kadar."

"Unfortunately, it is my concern. I helped to bring you here." He shook his head. "You've been very clever. I've watched with great admiration as you manipulated Kemal to this point. Kemal has grown colder and more distant toward Ware with each passing month. Tell me, do you intend to ask Kemal for his head?"

"No."

"My head?"

"Don't be foolish."

"I take that as no. What a relief."

"I wish no blood shed. You know my purpose. I've made no effort to hide it."

He nodded. "And I've told Ware. He believes Kemal will remain true to his word."

"Then you have nothing to worry about."

"But he's not been back to El Sunan and seen you with our friend the sheikh. You play on Kemal as you would the strings of a lyre. It's an astonishing sight."

"Did Ware truly think I'd sit and meekly embroider and wait for him to release me?"

"No, he probably didn't think at all. He just wanted to see you safe. That's why he brought you here to—"

"Remain a prisoner for two long years," she finished. "I don't wish to speak of him."

"You're a hard woman. You've forgiven me. Why not him?"

Because she had let Ware come too close, she had permitted herself to trust him, and he had betrayed her.

"He wears himself to a mere shell fighting in your service." His voice turned coaxing. "There's no woman in Islam or Christendom who has a knight so devoted to her well-being."

"Then let him find another woman to imprison."

"Admit it. He had good reason."

"I do not admit it. No reason is good enough. I don't care if Vaden or the Grand Master de Ridfort were knocking on the front gates, he had no right."

"Well, de Ridfort won't be knocking on any gates but those barring him from heaven. He was killed at the first siege of Acre two years ago."

She stopped and turned to stare at him in astonishment. "Why did you not tell me?"

"Because Ware says it makes little difference. The Grand Master de Ridfort was mad, and his death may prevent another incident like Jedha, but it doesn't lessen the danger to Ware . . . or to you. The death decree would have been passed on to the next Grand Master. Ware said it will go on forever."

Forever. Ware was condemned forever to—Why had her first thought been of Ware when she had banished him from her concern? She must think only of her own problems. "Ware may do as he wishes, but I will not stay here forever."

"If Ware can find a way, he will—"

"*I* will find a way." She drew a shaking breath and tried to temper her voice. "I've told you, I won't speak of Ware. If you continue to insist, you'll have to go away."

He sighed. "Very well, tell me more about these wriggling monstrosities on the trees. How long before your silk is ready to be harvested?"

"Not long. A week or two after the cocoon is formed we'll be ready to reel the silk." Her serene smile held a hint of challenge as she strolled down the path. "Providing we're still here."

Kadar rode direct from El Sunan to Ware's encampment in the hills above the southern border.

"You look as worn as ancient leather," Kadar said as he dismounted and handed his reins to Haroun. "When did you sleep last?"

"I don't know. Two nights perhaps." Ware led the way toward his tent. "Have you eaten?"

Kadar nodded. "Before I left El Sunan." He sat down on the heap of blankets inside the door of the tent. "And when did you last eat? You're thinner."

"I eat." He sat down and handed the water skin to Kadar. "How is Thea?"

"She glows, her eyes are bright, there's a flush on her cheeks. Purpose makes her thrive." He drank deep before leaning back on one arm. "And I come back to you and see you dwindling away to a mere shadow."

"I'm not a shadow. I've lost a few pounds because there's been no time to stop to eat. We've been hit hard this week."

"Kemal is eagerly awaiting an invitation to join the fray at Acre. He's brimming with pride." Kadar paused. "And Thea is brimming with plots. She's taken advantage of every win Kemal has made."

"So you've told me."

"But I detected a certain excitement in her this time. I believe she may be closing in for the kill."

"And what do you wish me to do about it?"

"Whatever you have to do. She won't believe her situation grows in danger." He paused. "You could go to El Sunan yourself."

"She wouldn't see me."

"But Kemal would. You could reinforce your position with him."

"Good God, I've fought myself to exhaustion keeping his border safe," he said harshly. "What else does he want from me?"

"Absence is your enemy and Thea's friend. It's easier to betray a man if the memory of his face has blurred."

Ware was silent.

"Go to El Sunan before it's too late. There's some mischief in the air between Kemal and Thea. I think she's promised him something."

Ware's head lifted swiftly. "What?"

Kadar shrugged. "I'm not sure." Then he shook his head as he saw Ware's expression. "Not to bed him. With a harem of thirty-two wives such a promise would not bring much excitement." He added, "Except to you. I'm glad to see something can bestir you."

"What else could she give him? He already has the banner. *My* banner, dammit."

"I've told you all I know. I'm no seer. Go find out for yourself."

"I'm needed here. I can't chase after every phantom you think—"

"My lord, a messenger from Dundragon." Haroun stood in the doorway of the tent, his eyes glittering with excitement. "He's ridden hard. Shall I bring him to you?"

Ware got to his feet. "No, I'll come." He left the tent.

Kadar took another drink of water. It was difficult convincing a man of something he didn't want to know. It was clear Ware would rather face swords and battleaxes than confront Thea again. He could not blame him. Thea's tongue could be sharper than a scythe, and Ware was vulnerable to—

Ware rushed back inside his tent. Donning his armor, he spoke to Kadar. "I've told Haroun to saddle my horse and a fresh one for you. I'll leave Abdul in charge here. We go to El Sunan."

Kadar didn't move. "I said *you* should go. I've ridden enough for one day."

"I may need you."

"Then wait until tomorrow."

"I can't wait." He put on his helmet. "I've just had word from Acre. King Richard has landed and joined the siege. Acre will probably fall."

"And Saladin may call on Kemal and his other sheikhs for support," Kadar murmured as he rose to his feet.

"Exactly."

* * *

There were no signs of military activity when Ware and Kadar rode through the gates of El Sunan, but Kemal's greeting was distinctly cool.

"Why are you here? Why are you not protecting me from those traitorous interlopers?" he demanded as he strode toward them. "Must I do everything myself?" Kemal had always been pompous, but it appeared his arrogance had grown to the outer bounds of tolerance.

"I don't think you've had anything to complain about in the service I've given you." Ware met his gaze with an icy stare. "Or am I wrong?"

Kemal's glance sidled away. "No, you've done everything you've promised. It's just—" He broke off as a thought occurred to him. "You haven't come to take her away?"

"It crossed my mind. Kadar says Thea's not behaving as a proper slave should. I would not have her become a bother to you."

"She is no bother." Kemal defiantly stuck out his chin. "You cannot take her. We struck a bargain."

"I've had word that Saladin may be summoning you to Acre. Who will protect my property?"

"Falsehoods. Saladin knows Acre has no chance of withstanding Richard this time. He would not waste me on such a task." He smiled with satisfaction. "Tomorrow I ride out to meet with him and discuss the defense of Jerusalem."

"And I still have no protection for my property."

"I'll be back within a fortnight. Your property is safe. Kadar must have told you what care I've taken with the woman."

"He has told me. Now I'll see for myself." He dismounted and started toward the women's quarters. "I'll join you shortly. I trust you'll offer me food under your roof?"

"'Of course, you are not my enemy. But why must you see her? I don't wish her to become disturbed. She becomes easily upset."

"Disturbed?" Ware glanced at him over his shoulder in astonishment. Kemal's expression was uneasy, almost fearful.

"I told you," Kadar murmured.

Good God, Thea must have truly cast a spell over the sheikh to have him quake at the mere possibility of disturbing her. He said sarcastically, "I'll try not to upset her."

"You'll not upset me." Thea was walking toward him.

At Thea's voice Ware stopped walking and watched as she approached him. She was garbed in an exquisitely embroidered silk gown the color of the twilight sky. She did not look older, only bolder, more confident. And beautiful—my God, how beautiful.

She *glows*, Kadar had said.

She did glow, but not with a soft sheen. She reminded him of a sword heated white-hot over a campfire. Her gaze meeting his was just as sharp and full of challenge as the last time they had met. What else could he expect?

"You don't upset me. I would not permit it." She stopped directly before him. "But I don't want you here."

Christ, he wished he hadn't been forced to come here. "I'll leave soon."

"I want you to go now."

She was not as composed as she had first appeared. He could see the pulse pounding rapidly in her throat. He had touched that hollow with his lips, felt the life pounding through her.

She tore her gaze away from his face and looked at Kemal. "It would please me to have him leave."

Kemal frowned uneasily. "I cannot— He is your master. Perhaps you could go to your quarters so that you don't have to see him. He will leave in the morning."

"See that he does." She whirled on her heel and walked away from them.

"I told you that you would upset her." Kemal stared at him reproachfully. "She has no liking for you."

"Since when have you cared if a slave liked or disliked you?"

"You must know she is different. One must treat her with consideration." He smiled slyly. "It didn't take me long to see why you wanted to make sure this treasure was not stolen from you. You were wise to come to me."

"Yes, I had to be sure the man who held her was honorable." He paused before deliberately adding, "Did I choose well, Kemal?"

Kemal flushed. "Do you doubt my honor? I've kept faith even though I found I had no need of you. I could have banished my enemies myself."

"You needed me. I've heard you've had great success, but even Saladin cannot triumph without help. Why else would he call on you?"

Kemal's irritation disappeared. "Yes, he does need me. Only I can bring him victory during this dark time." He turned on his heel. "I have no time for you. I must prepare for my journey."

Ware watched him cross the courtyard. Merciful God, the pompous cock actually believed his own words, and

Ware hadn't a doubt Thea had been the one to reinforce that belief. A surge of rage and frustration tore through him.

"I'd say Kemal's loyalty is beginning to waver," Kadar said. "What are you going to do?"

"Wait. Watch. What would you have me do?" He started across the courtyard toward the women's quarters. "I have no safe place to take her."

"You're going to give her warning?"

"I may strangle her."

"Oh, you mustn't do that." Kadar's mocking words followed him. "It might 'upset' the gentle damsel."

Thea's fingers clenched the window fretting as she watched Ware cross the courtyard. He would be here soon, in this room with her. She had known he would pay no attention to her rejection. He always did what he wanted to do.

He looked the same and yet different. He cast the same long shadow on the stones, but there appeared to be less bulk. He was leaner and harder than she had ever seen him, his cheeks hollowed, the bones higher, sharper. But his mouth was the same, with that full, sensuous underlip, and his eyes were the icy blue she remembered glittering beneath straight black brows.

Dear God, she was staring at him with a kind of hunger, she realized with shock. Not desire, but a deep need, as if she were starved for the sight of him. It made no sense when she only wanted him gone.

"You're shaking," Selene said from behind her. "Are you afraid of him?"

"No, of course not." She tore her gaze away. "We're safe

here. Kemal won't let him harm us." She forced a smile. "But he'll probably be unpleasant. Why don't you go to the garden? I'll call you when he's gone."

"I'll stay if you like."

She shook her head. Ware would only send Selene away, and she could not bear any added conflict. "Go on. I can deal with him."

"If you can stop shaking," Selene said dryly. "No man would ever make me fear him enough to tremble at his coming."

She wished it was fear. She hadn't expected her body to respond in this mindless fashion. Bitterness should have prevented such a betrayal. "I'm only surprised. I'll be fine."

Selene gave her a doubtful glance before slowly leaving the room.

She took a deep breath, and then another. She could hear Ware's quick, heavy steps in the hall. She must not let him see that she was not in control.

"What madness have you been about?" Ware said roughly from behind her.

She turned away from the window to face him. He looked as out of place as a huge, ravenous wolf in this gleaming chamber. He slammed the door and came toward her. "Kemal is preening like a peacock. He thinks he can move the world."

She was grateful for the harshness of the attack. It banished that insidious weakness as nothing else would have done. "Why blame me?"

"You know why. He thinks that blasted banner has magical powers."

"And what if he does? He came to that belief himself."

"And you never fostered it."

"Should I have turned my back and walked away when opportunity came knocking?"

"You're damn right you should have." He reached out and grasped her shoulders. "If he believes you bring good fortune, he'll also blame you when his luck turns. Don't you know that?"

"Let me go."

"Listen to me. Tell him any magic the banner might bring is gone."

She gazed at him defiantly.

"He worships Saladin. If he humiliates himself before his master, he'll come back and cut your throat."

"He won't humiliate himself. There will be no battle. He goes only to meet with Saladin on this journey."

"And what if Saladin changes his mind and takes him to Acre?"

"I'll face that possibility when it occurs."

"You will *not*. As soon as I find a place, you'll leave El Sunan."

"And have you take me to still another prison?" Her eyes blazed up at him. "I'll not leave here until I go as a free woman. You have no power here. Kemal won't let you take me away."

"Do you want to die?" He shook her. "Do you want Selene to die?"

"I only want you to leave us alone. I'll take care of Selene." She jerked away from him and defiantly lifted her chin. "Go on. Tell Kemal that you're going to take me away. It may be the prod that will bring me what I want."

She thought for an instant that he would reach out for her again, but he turned away with a muttered curse and strode toward the door. He was leaving.

Her relief was short-lived. At the door he whirled to face her. "Kadar said he thinks you're dangling some prize before Kemal. What the hell did you promise him?"

She could refuse to tell him. But why should she waste the effort? she thought impatiently. She wanted him gone from here and he could do nothing to stop her. She smiled at him. "A banner for Saladin. But only on my terms."

He stared at her in disbelief. "Christ."

The next moment he had slammed the door behind him.

The anger was draining out of her, and she felt as bruised as if she had fallen down a mountain. She would not permit him to do this to her. She had spent the last two years blocking him from her thoughts and memory, and the first time she saw him again, it was as if he had never left.

"Is he gone?" Selene came into the room. "He didn't hurt you?"

"No, but he was angry. He may try to take us from El Sunan."

"What are we going to do?"

"I'll talk to Kemal when he returns from the journey. He should be puffed up by Saladin's praise and ready to be plucked." She frowned. "And it would do no harm to make a few preparations. Tomorrow we'll start packing our embroideries, and next week I'll send Jasmine and Tasza back to Dundragon."

"They won't go."

"They have to go. It wouldn't be fair to drag them with us when we're not certain what we'll face. We'll have to convince them that we intend to send for them as soon as we're settled." Though heaven knows when that would be, she thought wearily. Another beginning. Sweet Mary, beginnings were hard.

She turned back to the window. Neither Ware nor Kadar were in sight. They had probably gone to sup with Kemal. Tomorrow they would leave El Sunan.

And she must be gone before Ware returned again.

Ware and Kadar rode out of the gates at dawn the next morning.

"You're very grim," Kadar said as they rode up the hill. "You've spoken scarcely a word since you visited our lovely Thea last night."

"There wasn't anything to say."

"And Kemal was most distant also. I felt my glowing presence wasted on the two of you."

Ware glanced back at the fortress. The courtyard had been filled with Kemal's soldiers when they had left, and the gates were still closed. "He's full of dreams of glory. Thea has promised him a banner for Saladin."

"My God."

"My response precisely."

"Is it not enough she plays her game with Kemal?"

"Evidently not."

Kadar started to laugh. "What a clever puss."

"A puss who may be skinned by Kemal at any time. We have to find another place for her."

"It will be difficult. With Richard on the attack, I doubt if you can find another Saracen who would take in a Christian woman. They're far more likely to offer her head to Saladin on a silver tray. And you've already decided she cannot go to the Franks. What is left?"

"God knows." His frustration was building more by the moment. "Why does she have to be so stubborn? Doesn't she know she's better off where she is?"

"She does not like prisons." Kadar glanced at him. "You would do the same."

"I'm a man."

"She would not regard that as a valid argument."

"Because she's a willful, obstinate woman who was put on this earth to plague—"

Drums.

He glanced over his shoulder to see two columns of six soldiers marching through the gates, pounding rhythmically on huge conical-shaped drums. Kemal was clearly exiting his fortress with all pomp.

Ware reined in as he reached the crest of the hill. "I'm surprised Kemal doesn't have fan bearers waving palm leaves before— Jesus!"

"What's wrong?" Kadar's gaze followed his to Kemal's plump, ornately armored figure riding through the gates. "He does look a trifle ridiculous. How do you suppose he manages to wield a sword bearing all that weight?"

"Not Kemal," Ware whispered. "The *banner*."

"That's right, you haven't seen it before." Kadar tilted his head appraisingly as his glance shifted to the flag bearer. "It's magnificent, isn't it?"

"No." It was a nightmare.

"You must not be unfair because you envy Kemal. Thea did fine work. I've never seen a more splendid banner."

Splendid was not the word for it. The scarlet-and-gold pattern came alive as the first strong beam of sunlight struck it. The muscles of Ware's stomach clenched as he saw those fierce gold eyes.

"The birds in the four corners are phoenixes rising from the flames, the symbol of rebirth," Kadar explained. "You can't see it from here, but there are also tiny butterflies hovering over the flames. Thea says butterflies are the symbol of joy."

"She told you about the banner?" Ware asked hoarsely.

"I asked her about it after I saw Kemal riding out of El Sunan one day."

"Why didn't you tell me, dammit?"

"And have you tell me to steal it? I thought it best not to mention it."

"What—" He swallowed to ease the tightness of his dry throat. "What did she say about the lions?"

"Nothing. She was even very grudging when she told me about the phoenix." Kadar gazed at the two standing lions facing forward, backs arched, each with a paw extended in the center of the banner. "Their attitude is very royal, isn't it?"

"Yes."

"It's an unusual position. Do you suppose they're supposed to be marching?"

"No." The column was closer now, and the throbbing of the beating drums resounded in every vein of Ware's body. A breath of wind caught the banner, and the lions appeared to move. "They're sitting."

"I don't think—"

"They're sitting." He jerked his gaze away. "It's a throne." He wanted to rage and howl. He wanted to ride down the hill and grab the banner from the flag bearer. He wanted to flee until he reached the ends of the earth. "It's a lion throne."

"I don't think so. I've never seen a throne like—" He

broke off as Ware wheeled his horse and put it to a gallop. "Ware!"

The wind struck sharply at Ware's cheeks as his horse's stride lengthened to a run.

Escape.

Forbidden.

Don't look at it.

Thea. My God, Thea.

He didn't rein in until he reached a brook running through a small grove many miles from El Sunan. He got down from his horse, staggered into the trees, and threw up.

He sank down on the ground and leaned back against the trunk of a tree with eyes closed.

It did no good. He could still see the lions.

"I suppose there's a reason for this."

Kadar's voice.

He opened his eyes to see Kadar sitting on his horse a few yards away.

Ware got up and lurched the few feet to the brook. He rinsed out his mouth before splashing water on his face.

Kadar dismounted. "My dear Ware, if this is envy, you really must get it under control. Such extremes are bad for you."

Ware ignored the gibe. "We have to get that banner from Kemal."

"Because you want it yourself?"

"I don't want it. I'd be happy never to see it again." He moistened his dry lips, trying to close out those blazing golden eyes, the flowing mane. "But we can't let Kemal keep it."

"Why not?"

"It's not safe. Vaden may see it. It's a miracle he hasn't seen it already."

"On the contrary. Kemal has taken the banner only on little skirmishes within his own province. It would have been pure chance for Vaden to have seen it."

Kadar was right. He wasn't thinking clearly. Jesus, he was surprised he could think at all. "He'll see it if Kemal goes into battle with Saladin. All the Knights Templar will see it."

"And what difference will that make?"

"It's the lion throne." Kadar didn't understand. Why should he? Ware had made sure he knew nothing about the throne. Even now, when he realized he had to tell him, the words were sticking in his throat. Yet he had to have Kadar's help to get the banner, and he couldn't expect him to follow blindly.

"The minute Vaden or any of the high officers of the Temple see the banner, they'll find out who created it and send someone to kill Thea."

"For stitching a banner?"

"For knowing what I saw in the caves below the Temple of Solomon."

Kadar shook his head. "You told her nothing."

"But she knew," he whispered. "Christ, she *knew*. How in heaven or hell did she know about the lion throne?"

"And what is this lion throne?"

"It's why Jeffrey and I went down into the caves. We'd heard tales of the throne that had been brought from Canaan. We wanted to see it." He closed his eyes, seeing it again, reliving that moment. "It was in a small hidden room in the depths of the cave. The lion throne."

"And because you saw this . . . this throne, the Templars want to kill you. Why?"

He would say no more. He had told Kadar too much already. "Because it was the lion throne."

"I grow weary of your secrets, Ware."

"We have to get the banner back."

"I think you imagine the lions in the banner form a throne. I didn't see it."

"Anyone who ever saw the real throne will see it. Vaden knew about the throne. He believed me when I said she knew nothing. He won't believe me now. He'll consider her as much a danger as he does me. No—a greater danger, because she put the throne on a banner for all the world to see." He murmured, "Pray God he doesn't see it before we can manage to take the banner from Kemal."

"We? You expect my help?"

Ware met his gaze. "I ask for your help. I have no right to expect it."

Kadar smiled. "And you tell me no more than bits and pieces about this throne of mystery. I'm tempted to withhold my help until I learn all your secrets." He sighed. "But then you would be so beset by guilt that you'd become unbearably tedious. I'll get your banner for you, my friend."

Relief rushed through Ware. "Not yet. Not until we find a way to get Thea away from El Sunan."

"Make up your mind. You said it was urgent we get the banner."

"I'll stay and set up camp here to stand guard over El Sunan. I want you to go to Saladin's camp and watch Kemal. If he merely meets with Saladin and then returns home, we may have time to make plans."

"But if I hear he's going to do battle against the Franks

with banner flying, I'm to come back here to tell you."

Kadar nodded. "I approve. I was afraid you were going to forget reason and be ruled by your emotions."

He couldn't afford to give in to the fear tearing at him. He must not make any mistakes. Danger was closing in all around them, and one misjudgment might mean Thea's death. "Don't let Kemal know you're in Saladin's camp."

"Am I a fool?" Kadar mounted his horse. "No one sees me if I don't wish to be seen." He looked down at Ware. "It's truly the same lion throne in Thea's banner?"

Ware nodded. "I swear it. Though God knows how she knew."

"I have a suggestion." Kadar's eyes were twinkling. "Perhaps you talk in your sleep."

Ware shook his head.

"Or maybe you murmured it with the sweet words you gave to her."

"I gave her no sweet words."

"Never? No wonder she finds it hard to forgive your sins." He turned his horse. "If you won't admit to a loose tongue, then it must be chance. Fate does not seem to favor you, my friend." He lifted his hand in farewell. "It's just as well you have such a stalwart, brilliant comrade to balance the scale."

"Yes, it is," Ware said simply.

Kadar glanced over his shoulder, disconcerted. "At last you realize my worth."

"I've always realized it. I could have no truer or more valiant friend on this earth. Go with God, Kadar."

Kadar, for once, appeared at a loss for words. His pace as he spurred through the grove back toward the road resembled flight. His discomposure didn't last long. "You forgot about 'brilliant'," he called back over his shoulder. "True, stalwart, valiant, *and* brilliant."

"Brilliant." Moisture stung Ware's eyes as he watched Kadar until he was out of sight. After all these years of striving to distance himself, he had deliberately drawn Kadar down into the quagmire surrounding him. Once the Templars knew about the banner, no one who had made contact with it would be allowed to live.

Scarlet lions with slanted golden eyes.

Power and majesty.

Death and rebirth.

Dear God, how had she *known*?

Chapter Thirteen

TWO MONTHS LATER
AUGUST 20, 1191
ACRE

"THE FOOL IS GOING to do it." Vaden watched with disbelief as the soldiers drove the long line of Muslim captives outside the gates of the city. "For God's sake, stop him."

"It is disrespectful to speak so of His Majesty." Robert de Sable, Grand Master of the Knights Templar, gazed straight ahead. "Saladin has shown ill faith in the surrender negotiations. King Richard believes he must be taught a lesson."

"It's not ill faith. Saladin seeks to strike a fair bargain to protect his people. Richard need only have a little more patience."

"His Majesty wishes to push on toward Jerusalem to liberate the holy city from that infidel."

"That 'infidel' treated his captives with utmost honor when he captured Jerusalem four years ago. He could have followed the example of butchery set by the Crusaders during the Second Crusade, but he did not."

Robert de Sable turned to look at him. "I find it curious you would defend him when captured Templars are never ransomed but executed immediately on his orders."

"A compliment. He doesn't want his men to face us in battle again." Vaden's hands clenched on the stones of the battlement. "There are women and children among those captives. Speak to Richard. He thinks well of you, or he would never have persuaded the Order to accept you as Grand Master."

"He thinks well of me because I'm not foolish enough to interfere when I know it will do no good. He wishes to teach Saladin a lesson."

"The devil he does. He doesn't want to bother with caring for captives on the way to Jerusalem." He could tell by de Sable's expression that his protests were to no avail. Why was he even trying?

Because it was senseless. There should be some reason in this world. Men should not take life on a whim or because they could.

But they did and called it glory.

"I think it best you leave here. I will not risk you offending His Majesty." Robert de Sable added, "The Marshalls tell me you're a great warrior, but I've noticed a certain arrogance in your demeanor."

Vaden flung out a hand at the soldiers below and spit out, "Perhaps you'd rather I go out and join the other soldiers. I have a strong right arm. I can sever a head from a man's shoulders with one blow."

"I don't appreciate such levity." The Grand Master fixed him with a cool stare. "You have another mission which you've been neglecting since Grand Master de Ridfort's death. Now that I'm Grand Master, that will not be tolerated. After this is over, you will return to Dundragon at once. We must bring an end to this threat."

Bring an end to Ware but not to the horror going on below.

"Or perhaps your dedication to the task is wavering?"

"I know it must be done. I will finish it."

"Then leave Acre to Richard." His gaze shifted away from Vaden to the hill above Acre. "Ah, I see Saladin has heard rumors and sent some of his people to witness."

"The moment Saladin hears of this, no Christian hostage or captive will be safe."

"Saladin will be too fearful of Richard to act."

Did de Sable actually believe that madness?

"What a magnificent banner," the Grand Master murmured. "Richard would find those lions most appropriate for himself. They call him the lion-hearted, you know. I must tell him. . . ."

De Sable was mumbling about banners when that royal idiot was going to ignite all of Islam with this blood spill?

"He may decide to take it for his own when he returns to France," de Sable said. "Is that Saladin's banner?"

Vaden cast an impatient glance at the group of Saracens gathered on the hill. He recognized only Tariq Jallal and Kemal ben Jakara. "I've not heard Saladin has lions on—"

My God, Ware, have you gone mad too?

"Well, is it Saladin's banner?" the Grand Master asked with impatience.

"No. But I see Kemal ben Jakara, Sheikh of El Sunan. I suppose the banner belongs to him." Robert de Sable clearly didn't recognize the lion throne in the design.

When he had taken power he had only been told of the throne; he would not be able to see it until Jerusalem was liberated. Christ, but any of the Grand Marshals would instantly see the danger. And they knew of the agreement between Kemal and Ware.

"El Sunan." Robert de Sable smiled slyly. "I'll tell Richard. He may want to pay a call on the sheikh on his way to Jerusalem. A captured fortress has no need of banners."

"El Sunan isn't on the way to Jerusalem." He gazed at the flag with anger and frustration. The woman held captive by Kemal ben Jakara had to be responsible. My God, why had Ware permitted her to flaunt her knowledge to the world?

Ware had told her of the lion throne. He had lied to Vaden. It should not be a shock. All the world lied, and with far less reason.

It was a shock. He felt betrayed.

Foolishness. Ware had told him he would lie to keep the woman alive.

And then he had let Kemal come there waving a banner that would be her death warrant.

"Such a banner is worth a detour." Robert de Sable's glance returned to the Saracen captives, and his voice harshened. "I believe they're ready to begin. I want no protest from you. You will stand here and watch, and if you show any emotion at all, it will be approval. Do you understand?"

Vaden watched as a soldier decapitated the first captive with one slice of his sword. Was the captive one Vaden himself had delivered to Richard? The cry of approval that went up as the blood spurted reminded him of the howl of a hungry animal. He said impassively, "Oh, yes, Grand Master, I understand perfectly."

A rider, coming fast.

Ware shaded his eyes with the edge of his hand.

Kadar.

A chill rained through Ware as he moved out of the trees and waited for Kadar to reach him. Kadar's pace was as forbidding as the grimness of his face.

Kadar reined in before him. "Get them out of El Sunan. Now. Today."

Ware's heart leaped. "How bad? What happened? Someone saw the banner?"

"Saladin sent Kemal to Acre to bear witness and report back to him. It's likely both he and the banner were seen." He slipped from the saddle and led his horse toward the brook. "Even if that were not so, it doesn't matter now. Kemal will kill her anyway. Have there been any horsemen before me today?"

"No."

"There probably will be. As I left Saladin's camp, I saw messengers streaming out, bound for every province of the land." He knelt and splashed water on his face. "I doubt there will be a Christian captive left alive by the end of the week." He lifted his head. "King Richard ordered twenty-seven hundred Muslim captives put to the sword. They were driven from the city to a field outside the gates and butchered like cattle."

"God."

"I saw no sign of any deity at Acre that day," Kadar said.

"Though I may be mistaken. After all, Richard says he's God's instrument in the battle to win back the Holy Land."

"Almost three thousand lives..." It was beyond comprehension. "Why?"

"You'll have to ask Richard. I could see no valid reason." He stood up. "But I could see the danger to Thea and Selene."

And so could Ware. Kadar was right—Kemal might not even wait to get back to El Sunan to have Thea executed. No personal reward for himself would count against avenging the atrocity that had just been committed. Ware's arrangement with Kemal was known to Saladin, and Kemal must erase any taint of dealing with the Franks. Even now an assassin might be on his way to El Sunan.

"How long do you think we have?"

"A few hours. I didn't stop to eat or sleep, but we can't count on Kemal to pamper himself on this journey. It's known he bargained with a Christian, and he'll have to prove he's a true believer or become an outcast among his people."

"We'll have to be well gone from El Sunan by nightfall, then." Ware moved quickly toward his horse and began to saddle it. "Wipe down your horse and clean yourself. We don't want anyone at El Sunan to suspect you had reason to ride hard."

"You have a plan?"

"Yes, we're going to ride into El Sunan and claim my property."

"Hardly very clever."

"We don't have time for clever. We have to be gone from El Sunan before they hear about the massacre." He tightened the cinch. "Kemal's soldiers are accustomed to seeing you, and my arrangement with Kemal is common knowledge. We'll tell them that Kemal and I have come to a parting of the ways and I'm releasing him from his guardianship."

"And hope that they'll let you take her."

"Yes."

"And that Thea and Selene will come without argument." Kadar shook his head. "Impossible."

"What's impossible is leaving them there and doing nothing." Ware put on his armor. "Kemal took his most trusted officers with him. Those in charge will be uneasy about making any decisions. Two men riding alone into El Sunan will not put them on guard as an army would."

"True. I'm feeling better already about riding into an enemy fortress." He ran his fingers through his damp hair and began to dust off his tunic. "It should be no trouble at all plucking them from El Sunan."

"Do you know any of the officers who may be there?"

"Kemal left Hallam ben Lallak, one of his captains, in charge. I've diced with him a few times. I'll work my powers of persuasion while you get Selene and Thea." He snapped his fingers. "What of Jasmine and her daughter?"

"They're no longer at El Sunan. I saw a wagon pass by here four days ago with them in it."

Kadar began to wipe down his horse. "It seems Thea has been busily making her own plans."

And they would not include riding off with him, Ware knew. Worse, he didn't have time to argue with her. There was no telling when Kemal's messenger would arrive, and seconds might count. What a shambles. Even if he managed to get Selene and Thea away from El Sunan, where would he take them? The entire countryside would be in flames after Richard's action. If the Templars had seen the banner, not only Kemal but the Templars would be on their heels.

He would have to consider possibilities on the way to El Sunan. The only thing of importance now was getting Thea away from the fortress.

The lion banner waved in the wind in taunting challenge.

Vaden put spurs to his horse to keep Kemal's escort in sight as they thundered toward El Sunan. It had not been easy to strike a balance between speed and caution when he wanted only to ride with reckless speed. God, he was sick of caution . . . and of waiting.

I will finish it.

If he got the chance. The Grand Marshals had seen the banner, and Vaden had watched them gather their forces after the massacre. The Templars would employ a little diplomatic maneuvering to explain to Richard why the most skilled fighting force in his army was not marching to Jerusalem in his wake, and then the Templars would ride to Dundragon. And when they didn't find Ware there, they would seek him out elsewhere. Nothing would stop them now.

Damn the woman. Damn that cursed banner. Ware was *his* prey. He would not have de Sable interfering.

I will finish it.

As those captives at Acre had been finished.

Well, why not? Innocent blood was always spilled in war, and when had he ever worried about anyone but himself? Ware was no innocent. He had made a mistake, and such mistakes were not permitted in this world; they were paid for in blood. Vaden had known this moment would come since the day he had been told why Ware had fled the Temple. He could wait no longer.

It had to be finished.

Thea's gaze flew to the door as it burst open.

Ware!

She stared at him in stunned disbelief as he strode into the chamber and slammed the door. "What do you do here?"

"Get your cloak. Where is Selene?"

She put her embroidery aside and stood up. "Why are you here?"

"We're leaving." He glanced around the room. "Dammit, where's your sister?"

"I go nowhere with you." Her hands clenched with anger as she understood. He was taking advantage of Kemal's absence to reclaim her and destroy all her plans. "Never again."

"You *will* go." In four strides he was there before her, glaring down at her. "We have no time for your protests. You'll come with me, or I'll knock you senseless and carry you out of here."

He meant it, she realized with fury. He would strike her down as he had that first night in the desert. "I see you've armored yourself to face an unarmed woman."

"You've never been unarmed. I've armored myself to keep us alive."

"Leave here and you'll stay alive."

"But you won't. Where's Selene?"

"We're not going with you." She took a step back. Should she turn and run toward the door leading to the hall or to the garden? The garden. Dusk would soon fall, and there were more places to hide there. "I'll call Domo, and he'll tell the guards that Kemal's property has to be protected."

"But everyone here knows you're my property, including Domo."

"And Kemal has shown them I'm to be treated with respect, my every command obeyed."

"Except as pertaining to your freedom. Don't fight me, you're going." He glanced at the window behind her. "By all that's holy, stop arguing, it's getting dark."

She backed toward the door.

His gaze swung to her and his hoarse voice rang with desperate sincerity. "Don't do this to me. I don't want to hurt you. I'm trying to keep you alive. Kemal is on his way back here to slaughter you."

She froze in place. "Why should I believe you? You've lied to me before."

"I don't lie now. Look at me, listen to me." He held her gaze. "If we're not out of this place soon, we'll all be dead."

She moistened her lips. "The banner?"

He shook his head. "Richard butchered twenty-seven hundred Muslim captives at Acre."

She stared at him in shock. "No," she whispered.

"You know Kemal. What do you think he will do?"

She knew what he would do. She felt a surge of wild frustration and anger. Freedom had been so close. "How much time do we have?"

He gazed at her warily. "You believe me?"

"You don't lie well. If I hadn't trusted you, I'd never have let you trick me when you brought me here."

He flinched. "I had no choice. I had to—" He broke off and returned to the matter at hand. "We've no time for talk. Kemal could be arriving here within the hour."

"Selene!" Thea called as she strode toward the door. "Get your cloak and the bag we packed. We're leaving."

"Now?" Selene came to the door. Her eyes widened as she saw Ware. "What's happening? Why would we—"

"No time," Thea said. "Hurry. Danger."

"The banner." Selene sighed. "I knew it would bring us grief. I'll be right back." She vanished from the doorway.

Thea opened the carved wardrobe box at the end of the bed and drew out her cloak. "Is Kadar here?"

Ware nodded. "Trying to soothe an uneasy captain."

"He'll have no problem. It's good you left the falsehoods to him. Kadar can talk anyone into anything. He even persuaded me to forgive him." She put on her cloak. "Since he's busy, you'll have to get our wagon from the stables."

"Wagon? We'll take the horses Kadar said Kemal gave you, but no wagon."

"We've packed all our goods and a basket of silkworm eggs in a wagon." She quickly folded the tapestry she had been embroidering. "We have to take it with us."

"No," he said flatly.

"You don't know exactly when Kemal will arrive, and it will take only a few minutes longer to harness the wagon."

"It may be a few minutes too long."

"Your threatening to strike me down wasted more time than it would take you to harness the wagon. You should behave sensibly and assume I have the intelligence to realize danger when I see it. We'll take the risk. To leave our work would be to lose these two years." She added fiercely, "And you've taken too much from me already. Now, go get the wagon. We'll meet you in the courtyard."

For an instant she didn't think he'd obey her. She drew a sigh of relief as he turned with a muttered curse and strode out of the chamber.

Selene hurried out of the chamber with their packing box. "What's happened?"

"Kemal is on his way here to avenge a massacre at Acre." She moved toward the door. "No one here knows yet of the massacre. Kadar is trying to convince the captain that Lord Ware is only reclaiming his property."

"Where are we going?"

"We'll worry about that when we're away from here."

"We're taking the wagon, aren't we?"

"Of course." She stuffed the tapestry into the bag. "We must display meekness and sadness as we leave."

"Meekness? Then they will certainly suspect something is amiss."

Selene was probably right. Thea had made her presence felt here, and any change of demeanor would be wrong.

Domo was standing uneasily by the horses in the courtyard when Selene and Thea left the women's quarters. "I do not know . . . You are my responsibility. Lord Kadar says that Lord Ware and my master have decided to dissolve their bargain, but perhaps Lord Ware should wait until my master returns."

Thea shrugged. "Your master has been very kind to me. It would please me to stay and say good-bye, but my master says I must go. It's not for us to question." Was that too meek? She could see by Domo's surprised expression that it probably was. "But perhaps you could intercede for me. Speak to Lord Ware."

Domo's eyes widened in alarm. "I could not. It is not my place."

Thea sighed. "Then I suppose I must go with him. You are right. It's not our place to question."

"I did not say—" He stopped as he saw Ware driving the wagon across the courtyard with two horses tied behind. "Or perhaps I did."

Kadar broke away from the young captain and came toward them. "Domo, help the women into the wagon. We must leave while there's still a little light."

Selene frowned. "I don't wish to ride in the wag—" She stopped as Thea pinched her arm. Kadar was right—the sight of women riding on horseback through the gates would jar their captors, and that was to be avoided. "Oh, very well."

Domo said, "Perhaps you should wait until morning."

"Lord Ware is impatient."

After a moment's hesitation Domo lifted first Thea and then Selene onto the bed of the wagon. "May Allah bless you."

Domo would be grateful, she knew, to have back the peaceful life he had known before Thea had disturbed his existence. He had been annoying at times but never unkind. She hoped her escape would not cause Kemal's wrath to fall on him. "May heaven protect you also, Domo."

The wagon started with a lurch, then rumbled toward the front gates.

How many times had she stood at her window and

looked out at those tall gates, seething with frustration and bitterness?

The soldiers rushed forward, the gates swung open, and they rode through.

A wild surge of joy soared through Thea.

Kadar rode up to the wagon and said in a low tone, "We can't look as if we're in too much of a hurry, so we'll go at a moderate pace until we're out of sight."

"I want to ride," Selene said.

"We're all aware of that. Later." He spurred on ahead of the wagon. "I'll go ahead to spy out the road over the hill."

What awaited them over that hill? Thea tensed as she remembered how fragile was the freedom she had welcomed so joyously.

"This wagon is too heavily loaded." Ware's voice was as tense as Ware felt. "We're going to have to move fast. Is it worth your life?"

No, but it represented two long years of her life. Disappointment washed through her. "Can we hide the wagon somewhere and come back for it?"

"There's a grove several miles up the road. We can hide it there." Ware paused. "But I won't promise we'll come back for it. It may prove too dangerous."

Not for her. She would find a way to retrieve her precious silks. "Then we'll hide the trunks and wagon and loose the horses to return to El Sunan."

"I didn't think you'd be this sensible," he said slowly.

"I'm not stupid. I can see that we must move quickly. I won't risk our lives."

Kadar was waving from the top of the hill.

No riders in sight.

* * *

They had just finished hiding the trunks and wagon deep in the grove and brushing all signs of their passing away with branches when Kadar heard the hoofbeats.

He lifted his head like one of his falcons scenting wind. "He's coming."

Ware went still. Then, as he heard them too, he exploded into motion. "Take the horses and watch out for the women, Kadar." He ran toward the road.

Thea was right behind him.

Dozens of torches moved in a molten stream from the north. The horsemen would be there within a few minutes.

"What will we do?" Thea whispered.

He drew her back into the screen of trees. "Pray that Kemal won't decide to water the horses at the brook. He may not. It's only a short distance to El Sunan."

"And if he does?"

"Circle around the south end of the grove and hope we're not seen."

She watched with horror as the fiery torches bore down on them. It would be her fault if they were captured, she thought, stricken. It had been at her insistence that they'd stopped to hide the wagon instead of abandoning it. Their lives might be forfeit because she had wanted to ensure Selene's and her own future well-being.

The flames came nearer.

The hooves beat louder on the rocky ground.

The riders were close enough now so that she could see the cloud of dust surrounding them.

The banner.

The golden eyes of the lions shimmered with a strange

luminosity in the torchlight. Thea shivered, as if those eyes could pierce the shrubbery and see them where they hid.

Idiocy. She was being as foolish as Kemal. This was a banner made of silk and thread and the fruit of her labor. It was fear that made her imagine anything else.

Her glance moved to Kemal riding behind the banner. His expression was grimmer than she had ever seen it.

The riders were only a few yards away now.

She held her breath.

Kemal hesitated, glanced at the grove, made a half motion as if to rein in.

No, please. Go on.

The flag bearer had drawn even with the trees behind which Ware and Thea were hiding.

Shimmering golden eyes.

Don't stop, she prayed.

Kemal shook his head and his spurs dug into his horse.

The riders swept past them in a roar of thunder and a cloud of dust.

Thea sank back against the tree, limp with relief.

Another chance. They had been given another chance.

"Come along." Ware took her arm and drew her away from the road. "It's only a reprieve. The moment Kemal reaches El Sunan and finds we're gone, he'll wait only to change horses before he sets out again. We have to make use of that time."

"And where do we go from here?" Kadar was striding toward them. "Dundragon?"

"Where's Selene?" Thea demanded.

"I told her to stay and tend the horses. I wasn't sure what I'd find here." He asked Ware again, "Dundragon?"

Ware shook his head. "I won't lead Kemal or the Templars to Dundragon. Neither would hesitate to wipe it from the earth now. After Jedha, I promised my people safety."

"The Templars have been too cautious to strike at Dundragon before," Thea said.

"But that was before Kemal took the banner to Acre. They won't wait for an easy strike now."

Thea frowned in puzzlement. "What matter does the banner make to the Templars?"

Ware's eyes narrowed on her face. "You don't know?"

"Would I ask if I knew?"

"I never know what you'll do or how you come to know things you should not. It is not—" Ware broke off and wearily shook his head. "All I know is that we cannot return to Dundragon. We'll lead Kemal in another direction away from it."

"What direction?" Kadar asked. "With the entire country lusting for blood, you will be safe from the Templars *and* Kemal nowhere."

"One place may be safe from both of them." Ware met his gaze. "With you as guide. It was before."

"Before?" Then Kadar gave a low whistle as comprehension dawned. "You would certainly be safe from them there. That doesn't mean you would survive. You were within a hair of being removed from this earth before. He won't take kindly to your trespassing again."

"We have no other choice. We need a haven until I can think of some other solution." He paused. "Unless you refuse to take us."

"It's not a place I'd choose. I don't wish to be drawn back

into that web." He shrugged. "But I never refuse fate when she comes knocking. I deem it extremely discourteous."

"What are you talking about?" Thea asked impatiently.

Kadar said, "It seems we're going to visit the Old Man of the Mountain."

Chapter Fourteen

THEY TRAVELED ALL THAT NIGHT and through the next day, stopping only to rest and water the horses. Ware reined in at a clearing on a hillside at sunset. "We'll set up camp here for the night."

"Is that wise?" Selene asked. "You need not stop because of Thea and me. We can go on."

"You stalwart women may be able to go on, but I'm far too weary." Kadar got down from his horse and spoke to Ware. "I saw a brook a quarter mile down the hill. You can make camp while I go water the horses and stake them."

Ware nodded as he dismounted, then he lifted Thea from the saddle.

"I'll go with you." Selene took her horse's reins and followed Kadar down the trail.

How could Selene retain that much strength after the past two days? Thea wondered tiredly.

She turned to Ware and echoed Selene's question. "Is it wise to stop?"

"It's wiser than killing the horses and ourselves. Kemal has to rest and eat too. We'll leave early in the morning."

"We've not seen any sign of Kemal. Are you sure he's following us?"

"Oh, he's following us. He must remove the blemish on his honor before he faces Saladin again." He turned away. "Sit down. I'll have fire and food ready soon."

She sank down onto the ground. She would not argue with him. Every muscle in her body felt bruised, and she could barely keep from collapsing. Sitting at an embroidery hoop was no training for this kind of physical punishment.

She felt better later, after she had eaten a little, but she was still dazed with weariness.

Selene was in little better condition, she noticed. The energy or proud pretense that had kept Selene going ebbed swiftly after she sat down before the fire. She was the first to lie down between her blankets and was asleep moments later.

Kadar smiled. "It's good she is asleep. She would probably insist on taking her turn at guard duty." He stood up and stretched. "I will go first," he told Ware. "You'll relieve me at midnight."

Ware nodded.

Thea watched as Kadar moved up the trail to a higher point that would allow him a view of the entire valley below. "He's been very quiet on this journey. That's unusual for Kadar."

"Yes." His lips thinned. "If there had been any other

way, I'd never have asked him to return to the Old Man. It's too dangerous for him."

"More dangerous than for us? He told me he lived with the assassins."

"But he broke away from Sinan, and he told me once that he'd rather be stung by a scorpion than be drawn back into that circle." He added, "I can't blame him. Better a scorpion than an asp."

"Is that what Sinan reminds you of? A serpent?"

He shrugged. "In his deadliness, perhaps. But one can kill a snake. I've often wondered if—" He shrugged. "Pay no attention to me. I was ill when I stayed at Maysef, Sinan's fortress. The fever made me imagine strange things."

"And when should we arrive at this serpent's mountain?"

"We'll arrive at the Nosairi foothills by tomorrow evening," Ware said. "I'm surprised you gave me no argument about going to Maysef."

"Of course I gave you no argument. You wouldn't take us into a serpent's pit if there was anything else to do. I don't see why you persist in thinking me lacking in reason."

"You're a woman. I'm not accustomed to women who think at all."

Thea bristled with irritation. "Perhaps you were too busy taking their bodies to notice if they did or not."

"That could be true." He paused. "But my mother was not like you. She sang sweet songs and laughed and always bowed her head to my father's will. I saw no signs of thinking in her."

"I'm not like your mother. Nor would I want to be."

"I didn't say I wanted you to be like her. I merely told

you that I wasn't used to women who think." He thought for a while. "I believe if you did not think, I'd miss it in you."

"Astonishing."

"But I wouldn't miss that stinging tongue," he said with an edge to his voice. "I'm not your enemy. You've no cause to cut me."

He was wrong. She had every cause to keep him at a distance. "I treat you like an enemy because you've behaved like an enemy. You've taken two years of my life."

"And given two years of service to keep you safe."

"You expect me to be grateful?"

"No," he said wearily. "I knew when I took you to El Sunan that you wouldn't forgive me."

"Very wise. I will not." She looked down into the fire. "And when we're free of danger from Kemal, we will part. I'll not let you put me in another prison."

"Kemal is the smallest danger you're facing. The Templars will never stop hunting you now." He broke out with sudden violence, "Christ in heaven, nobody but Vaden knew you were a danger. Why did you have to tell them?"

"I don't know what you're talking about. I told no one anything. How could I?"

"The banner. The lion throne. How did you know?"

She stared at him in bewilderment. "Know what?"

He studied her expression. "My God, you don't know," he said wonderingly. "I thought Kadar might be right, that I'd somehow told you without being aware of it. But you don't know about the lion throne."

"Of course I do. I created the pattern and stitched the banner."

"And you realized it was a throne?"

"Don't be ridiculous. Nothing could be clearer."

"It wasn't clear to Kadar. Was it clear to Selene?"

She frowned. "I don't know. We didn't discuss it. I suppose she knew it was a throne."

"Ask her. I'll wager she didn't."

"What difference does it make?"

"I don't know." He shuddered. "But it does make a difference. You could see it and they couldn't. Maybe it was my fault. Maybe it was something I did."

To her amazement she saw that his face was pale in the firelight. "You're talking nonsense. I stitched a lion throne and it's your fault?"

"It wasn't any throne, it was *the* throne." He paused. "It was the throne I saw in the caves below the Temple. It was *her* throne."

"Her?"

He opened his lips to speak and then shook his head. "You know too much already. I cannot—"

She felt a sudden burst of rage. "Oh, no, you won't do that to me. You say that these Templars are now going to hunt me down and kill me no matter what I do. You've wrapped me in silence and treated me as if I had no mind of my own. You're going to answer all my questions. I *will* know the reason why this is happening to me."

"It's best that I—"

"This is my life. You've stolen two years of it. I'll not let you steal my right to make decisions for myself ever again."

He gazed at her a moment longer before shifting his gaze back to the fire. "Ask your questions."

"Whose throne was it that you saw?"

"Asherah."

"And who was Asherah?"

"She was a goddess worshipped by the Israelites in Canaan many centuries ago."

She nodded. "Before they realized there was only one true God."

"No."

She went still. "What do you mean? After Moses came down from the mountain with the Ten Commandments, they worshipped only one God."

"No."

She whispered, "You're saying the holy books lie?"

"I'm saying that the holy books were written by men, and perhaps they didn't wish to admit to falling from the true path."

"It could not be."

He smiled bitterly. "You see how it shocks and horrifies you? Our religion is based on the holy books, and you cannot conceive that they're not perfect. You're afraid that if one lie exists, the entire fabric could be rotten."

"Blasphemy. There is only one God."

"Did I say anything else? All I'm saying is that the Goddess Asherah was worshipped in Canaan even though it was forbidden. God was known as Yahweh and the goddess Asherah was His wife. They called her the Lion Lady, and she sat on the lion throne and was known as the Goddess of Fertility."

She shook her head. "I will not believe it."

"It happened. The Canaanites would not give up their goddess. Finally, in an attempt to sweep her from the earth, the holy men destroyed every idol and religious relic pertaining to Asherah." He paused. "Except the lion throne. They brought the throne to the Temple of Solomon and hid it deep in the caves together with a tablet forbidding that it ever again see the light of day."

"Why did they not destroy it?"

"Superstition. They'd been guided by the goddess for centuries and, according to the Canaanites, she was the wife of the one true God. The lion throne was the symbol and seat of her power. What if there was some truth in the myth and they offended her by destroying it?"

"I cannot believe the Templars were equally superstitious."

"No. By the time they uncovered the throne and tablet, thousands of men had fought and died in the Crusades to prove to the infidels there was only one true God. They desperately wanted to destroy the throne. But they couldn't do it."

"Of course they could do it."

"Perhaps they were afraid to. For another reason. There was something in the tablet that confused and terrified them. Something that could have been taken in one of two ways."

"What are you talking about?" she whispered.

"There was a phrasing.... There was some doubt that Asherah was a separate goddess."

She looked at him in bewilderment. "What?"

"It appeared there was a possibility that Yahweh and Asherah were not man and wife... but one. One god... or goddess."

She stared at him, stunned. He could not mean it.

"They couldn't take the chance of destroying a truly holy relic. The throne had to be kept inviolate, but no one could ever know it existed."

"Everyone knows God is male."

"Of course they do. But the tablet— Perhaps it only meant that Asherah was the part of God that gave fertility. Surely God must have many sides to His vast power."

"And one side is a woman?"

"I did not say that."

"Because you're afraid to say it. Just as they're afraid to say it." She shivered. "I'm afraid to say it also." God must remain the deity she had known since childhood. Everything else in the world could change, but God must remain the same. "I will not believe it."

"Then don't believe it, but realize that the Templars will do anything to make sure that no one else will believe it either. The Pope and Church rule the world. Nothing about the doctrine they decree must be questioned."

"I do not question. How can anyone question the true faith?"

"Listen to me: the Templars fear you *will* question it. You created a banner that is a taunt and a challenge to them." He paused. "And you gave it to the infidel."

"Nonsense. My banner had nothing to do with gods or goddesses. It was your banner."

"If it was mine, why did you give it to Kemal?"

"You know why. I would have given it to Satan himself to get it out of my sight."

"And that's who the Temple will think you gave it to. They'll believe I told you of the throne and you crafted a banner to give support to the infidel." He shook his head. "And it won't help that Kemal claims the banner miraculously helped him to win every battle since you gifted him with it."

Her eyes widened. "But the banner had nothing to

do with it. It was mere coincidence that he began to win battles."

"Was it? Tell that to Kemal, tell the Grand Master of the Knights Templar."

"I tell you, there is no magic connected with the banner. It was only chance that led me to create—" A sudden memory swept over her of those days of possession when she had worked unceasingly creating the banner. She said shakily, "I'm no witch. I can weave no spells. I only wished to create a banner that would be yours. I focused my thoughts on you, and the pattern came. . . . It was there."

Ware met her gaze.

"It was *not* magic." Her hands clenched into fists. "I will not accept that it was anything but chance that the pattern was similar to your lion throne."

"I won't argue with you. I have no way of knowing what is truth or not." He rubbed his temple. "Perhaps it is only chance. Everything has been blurred since the night I saw the throne."

"It's not blurred for me. All you've told me is foolishness, and if the Templars believe it to be true, they're more than fools, they're madmen." She scooted down under her blankets and turned her back on him. She must stop shaking. There was no reason to be upset. Nothing had changed since Ware had spoken the unspeakable. God would not strike her down for merely listening to such blasphemy. Yet she felt as if everything had changed and that the firm ground beneath her feet had been swept away.

"Don't be afraid."

"I'm not afraid."

"Then you're braver than I was." Ware's hand fell on her shoulder. "I know how you feel. After I saw the throne,

I had no time to do anything but run and hide. It was only after I was wounded and Kadar was caring for me that I began to think. I felt like a child in the dark."

"Don't touch me."

"It is only in comfort," he said haltingly. "I believe you need comfort."

"I need nothing from you." She should move away from his hand, but, dear God, she did need comfort. She wanted to roll over into his arms and let him hold her and shut out all the uncertainties.

He took his hand away. "Very well."

She was suddenly cold and alone. She wanted him to touch her again.

"But listen to me. If you believe in God, you must believe that there is a pattern to His creation. Perhaps the pattern is not stitched in exactly the manner you thought it to be, but the pattern exists. We must hold to that truth." He paused. "And I don't believe God will punish you for looking differently at the pattern of life. God is good, it's man who is evil."

"Everything is exactly the same. I'm not looking at it differently."

"You will." She heard rustling sounds as he lay down between his blankets. "You'll try to keep it out, but it will creep in under the barriers. Let it come. Make terms with it. God gave us minds. Surely He meant us to use them." He was silent a moment before he said, "You've done nothing wrong. If any sin has been done, it's been by me. I'm the one who will be punished."

"Not if your enemies have their way."

"They won't have their way," he said. "Go to sleep. We must be on our way tomorrow at dawn."

Sleep? She had doubts that she would sleep this night. Her mind was a terrifying whirl of visions of lion thrones, banners, and forbidden goddesses. Even the alien idea that God could have womanly aspects was as frightening as the rest. As a slave she had always thought of God as if He were the ultimate master who could be kind or cruel, a God who gave man His favor and woman only His tolerance. She had fought to free herself from the bondage of other masters, but her mother had taught her she must accept and revere the God of the holy books without question. It did not matter that God let Church and man decree that slavery was acceptable. God was God.

She must block all these wicked thoughts out of her mind. In spite of Ware's advice, she would not let any of his words affect her.

Her efforts were to no avail. The last image in her mind before she fell into a restless slumber was of golden eyes shimmering from a silken banner. . . .

"There it is. Maysef lies a few miles straight up this trail." Kadar reined in and looked up at the mountain. "You are sure, Ware?"

"I'm sure. We have no choice." He glanced over his shoulder. "I saw puffs of dust on the horizon behind us when we stopped the last time."

Thea felt a rush of fear. "Why didn't you tell us?"

"So that you could worry too? It would not have been sensible."

No, Ware would never share a burden if he could bear it alone. "I would like to have known."

He shrugged. "Now you do." He glanced at Kadar. "You go first. They know you."

"Let us hope the Old Man doesn't have new acolytes who aren't familiar with me." Kadar nudged his horse past them on the trail. "Oh, well, follow me."

"Do you think Kemal will stop here?" Thea asked, looking over her shoulder. Was that haze in the distance the dust clouds about which Ware had spoken?

"It depends how much he values his head above his honor," Ware said. "I'd judge he'll come after us . . . until he runs into the first of the Old Man's followers. Then he may be discouraged."

Thea shifted her gaze to Selene, who was following Kadar up the trail. "I won't have her put in danger. Could we leave her hidden here in the foothills?"

"Would she stay behind?" Ware shook his head. "Not unless we tied her to a tree, and then she'd be helpless if Kemal found her. She's safer on the mountain with us."

The mountain did not appear to possess any aspect of safety to Thea; it was dark and shadowy and full of menace. She shifted her shoulders uneasily. Imagination. It was only a mountain like any other.

But assassins did not lurk behind trees and rocks on any other mountain.

"Shouldn't we go faster?"

"Not until it becomes necessary. The horses are tired and we may need a sudden burst of speed."

"Won't Kemal's horses be tired also?"

"Perhaps. If he didn't bring extra horses to switch."

She had not thought of that possibility and did not wish to dwell on it. "Why won't this Sinan welcome Kemal? Is he not a follower of Saladin?"

"He hates Saladin."

"Well, then won't he welcome the Templars if they come after us?"

"He hates the Franks also."

"Then where does his allegiance lie?"

"With his own sect, the assassins. He rules an independent state here in the mountains. For the most part he's content to watch and wait for Saladin and the Franks to kill one another." He paused. "If they do not offend him."

"And if they do?"

"At one time Saladin sought to destroy the assassins. He came here and laid siege to Maysef. Sinan was not in residence, and it should have been no trouble to capture him when he journeyed back to defend his fortress. For some reason they found it impossible to intercept him. Then Saladin became troubled by hideous nightmares every night. He was afraid to go to sleep. He became worn and haggard, jumping at shadows. One night he woke in his tent and found on his bed some hotcakes that only the assassins were known to bake, a poisoned dagger, and a paper with threatening verse written on it. Saladin was convinced that the Old Man of the Mountain himself had been in his tent. His nerve broke, and he sent a message to Sinan asking to be forgiven for his sins and begging self-conduct out of the mountains. He promised to leave the assassins forever undisturbed." Ware smiled sardonically. "Sinan graciously pardoned him."

Thea found the tale darkly fascinating. "How did the assassin get into Saladin's tent? He must have been surrounded by his army."

"Ask Kadar. Infiltration is part of the training of all Sinan's followers."

Her gaze went to Kadar. "Would he answer me if I asked him?"

"Probably not. He doesn't talk about his time with Sinan."

Kadar's words came back to her. *One must learn to walk the dark paths. But sometimes it's possible to learn too much, delve too deep.*

She suddenly realized she didn't want to know about those dark paths. If she did, she wasn't sure she would ever view Kadar in the same way. She went back to the original subject. "Do you suppose the guards were bribed to be blind when the assassin slipped into Saladin's tent?"

Ware shook his head. "Sinan has been known to use bribery and deception to position his players, but those close to Saladin are too loyal to be swayed. No, Sinan used other means."

Nightmares and terror. Thea shivered. "How can a man's dreams be controlled? It must have been pure chance." The sentence sounded familiar, and she recalled she had used the same words in regard to the creation of her banner. She quickly veered away from the memory. "You don't believe in the magical power of this man, do you?"

Ware didn't answer directly. "I believe he's a brilliant man with a monstrous self-love and no soul. Put those qualities together, and there are roots planted for a morbid blossoming. Over the years he's become accustomed to being worshipped and feared more than any man in this land. Death in battle has become commonplace, but a man who can steal life when it's least expected holds the ultimate power."

"Will he hide us?"

"If Kadar discovers him in the right mood. He finds Kadar interesting and is prone to be lenient toward him."

"And if he's not in the right mood?"

"Then we'll run as if Satan were after us." He added grimly, "As indeed he will be." He glanced over his shoulder and stiffened. "They're coming."

Thea turned and then inhaled sharply.

Armored riders. Coming fast.

Her gaze was drawn to the man in the forefront of the riders.

Over Kemal's head the lions on the banner shimmered strong and vivid in the fading light.

"Come on." Ware grabbed her reins and spurred his own horse to a gallop up the steep, rocky incline.

Pounding, driving speed.

The wind tore at her hair and stung her cheeks.

The horses labored, their breathing heavy, nostrils flared as they struggled up the trail.

Hoofbeats behind them.

Her heart leaped with fear as she glanced over her shoulder.

How had Kemal gained on them so quickly? Extra horses, Ware had said.

Ware was muttering curses as he urged the horses.

They could go no faster, and the hoofbeats behind them were louder.

Shouting.

Kemal's shrill voice. "Acre. Avenge Allah. Avenge Acre."

Dear God, he sounded right behind them.

A small flat plateau ahead. They would be able to go faster.

But so could Kemal.

His riders streamed around them, surrounding them.

Kemal raced toward her, sword drawn. His eyes glittered wildly. "Witch. Daughter of demons."

Ware wheeled and rode in front of her. "Take care of her, Kadar."

"No!" Thea cried.

He paid no attention. He was riding directly at Kemal, fighting his way through the multitude of soldiers that had closed in around him. "Me, Kemal. Where is your courage? Honorable soldiers don't fight women."

A mace struck him in the shoulder, jarring him in the saddle. He was not deterred. "And they do not hide behind their men. Come and meet me."

"Did your King Richard face the men he butchered at Acre? You deserve no more honorable death than a dog." Kemal gestured to the soldiers. "Cut him down. I want his head for Saladin."

Kemal's men swarmed around Ware.

Kadar grabbed Thea's reins as she tried to ride into the fray. "No. Stay. You can do nothing."

"Stay? They're *killing* him." Ware was warding off most of the blows with his shield, but not all. How long could he withstand such punishment? she wondered in agony. "Do something Kadar. Or let me do something."

"Not yet." Kadar's head was tilted, listening. "I hear— It may be . . ." Excitement lit his face. "If he can hold them at bay . . ."

Ware was holding them. His sword downed men to the right, to the left, as he wheeled and struck again and again.

Thea jerked fiercely at the reins Kadar was holding. "Let me go to him."

"Listen," Kadar insisted.

"I hear it, too," Selene said. "A drumming."

Kemal's head was lifted, his face turned to the rocks bordering the plateau.

"What is it?" Selene asked.

"They're called death drums. There's a superstition that anyone who hears them will never live to fight another battle."

The throbbing of the drums echoed over the hills, ghostly, menacing.

Thea scarcely heard them. Ware was down.

He had been toppled from his horse at last. A man on foot was doubly vulnerable. They would cut him to pieces.

The drums throbbed louder.

And Kemal's soldiers were frozen in place, their gaze on the ring of rocks that formed a ledge around the plateau.

A white-robed figure appeared on the ledge. Another was suddenly standing a few yards from the first. The assassins flowed in a circle, silent, watching white ghouls at a death feast.

The drums became louder, faster.

"Yes," Kadar murmured. "Let them hear it."

Kemal's soldiers were fleeing, streaming down the mountainside in a panic.

Thea could not believe it. Ware was safe.

"Come back here, cowards," Kemal shouted. "There's nothing to fear. I have the banner."

Thank God they were not listening. Thea jerked her horse's reins from Kadar's grasp and rode toward Ware. His helmet had been knocked off in the fall, and he was on his knees, struggling to get up.

"I have the banner," Kemal screamed again. His face was flushed, his eyes popping with anger. His gaze flicked to the ledge, and a ripple of fear crossed his face as he realized he was alone. His frustration exploded as he wheeled on Ware. "Vile dog!"

His sword crashed down toward Ware's unprotected head.

"Ware!" Thea's scream was without voice, the horror too great for sound.

Ware managed to deflect the point with his shield but took the broad side of the sword on his temple.

Kemal was gone, riding over Ware and down the mountain after his men.

Ware lay crumpled on the ground, white and still. His temple was bleeding and looked . . . dented.

Thea was off her horse and beside him. "Ware." She sank to her knees and gathered him to her breast. "You will not die. Do you hear me? I will not have it."

Ware's lids opened. "Listen . . . Kadar." Ware's voice was a mere whisper. "Take—her away—from this land. Too much danger—here."

"He will take me nowhere." Her arms tightened fiercely around him. "If you want me away from danger, you must live and take me yourself."

His gaze shifted back to her face. "Stubborn—woman . . ." His eyes closed and he slumped.

Dead?

No, she could see a faint movement of his chest beneath the armor. He lived, and she would find a way to fan that spark of life to flame. She glanced up at Kadar and demanded, "What do you know of healing?"

"I know he is very bad and that there is nothing either of us can do." He held up his hand as she opened her lips to protest. "It is true. With a head wound you can only wait and tend and hope he will wake. With severe blows sometimes the sleep becomes death."

"Don't tell me that I can do nothing. I won't let him die."

"Can you turn back the clock and prevent Kemal from striking the blow? That's the only way you can help. The rest is not in our hands."

She closed her eyes as sickness swept over her. She must not give in to this weakness born of despair. She could not help Ware unless she remained strong. Her eyes flicked open. "Can we move him?"

Kadar shook his head.

"Then we will set up camp here."

"They're gone." Selene's wondering gaze was fixed on the ledge where the robed figures had stood. "Where did they go?"

"Back to the fortress. They accomplished what they came for."

Not in time, Thea thought. Not before Ware was struck down. "I'll tend him, and you must make sure we're not disturbed until he's well."

"A small task," Kadar said with irony. "I must contend only with the Old Man of the Mountain, on whose land we're trespassing, and Kemal, who is sure he cannot be defeated as long as he carries your banner."

"Then take the banner away from him," she said. "But first help me remove Ware's armor."

Selene stepped forward. "I'll help you." She knelt beside Ware. "Together we can do it." She fixed Kadar with a stern look. "Go about your business and let us tend to ours."

"Yes, my lady." He bowed mockingly. "Should I have a favor to carry into battle?"

"If you're clever, you won't have to do battle," Selene said. "So be clever. This Sinan must bear you some affection if he took the trouble to scare off Kemal. Go see if he will help us escape Kemal. And don't come riding back here dripping blood and begging us to help you. It's enough to have one sick man to tend."

"I shall earnestly try to spare you that bother." He moved toward his horse. "Your temperament is clearly unsuited for such tasks."

"Yes, it is."

Thea could not bear listening to them any longer. "*Help* me with him," she said. "He could die while you stand here talking, Kadar. Does he mean so little to you?"

"He belongs to me. One always cares about one's possessions." Kadar mounted his horse. "Naturally, I will do everything I can to preserve his life. Don't leave this place until I return, and keep a good watch. Since I'm going to all this effort, I'd hate to have my efforts wasted." He turned and trotted up the mountain.

Flippancy in Kadar at this tragic moment was incomprehensible to Thea. "I don't understand him."

"He's afraid," Selene said quietly. "I think he's seen too much death. He armors himself against feeling deeply for anyone because he fears he will lose them. Don't worry, he will find a way to help."

All the help in the world would do no good if Ware slipped away from her. But he would not slip away; she would not permit it.

* * *

Ware did not wake that night.

Thea sat beside him, moistening his lips and head with water. She and Selene had taken off his armor, and without that protection he looked frighteningly vulnerable. He was no longer a warrior but a man open to all harm.

Selene came to her at dawn and knelt, gazing at Ware's pale face. "He is no better."

"He might be." Thea could hear the desperation in her own voice. "Perhaps the sleep is healing him."

"Perhaps," Selene said without confidence.

"He will wake soon."

"And what if he doesn't?" Selene asked gently. "You must accept the possibility that he may die."

"I will not accept it."

"Because he gave his life for you?"

"He didn't give his life. He's not going to die."

Selene was silent a moment, studying her. "I was a fool," she said harshly. "All this time I believed you when you said you hated him. You love this man."

"Yes." How simple to confess it now when she had not been able even to contemplate the idea before.

"Then why did you lie to me?"

"I didn't lie to you. I didn't know— I was afraid to love him." She ran her hand wearily through her hair. "And he had no right to do what he did. I was angry and hurt." She was still angry and hurt, but at this moment that meant nothing in light of the fact that Ware might die. She repeated, "I didn't know."

"You should have chosen another man to love." Selene's hands clenched with anger. "You should have known Lord Ware would bring you pain."

"I didn't want it to happen. It just . . . came."

"And now look at you. When he dies, you will grieve, and I'll be able to do nothing about it."

"He's not going to die," Thea repeated. "Go away. I won't have you here thinking bad thoughts."

"Thoughts don't kill. Let me help you."

She couldn't take the chance. She had the feeling Ware was teetering on the brink, and even a breath would cause him to fall. "I'll take care of him myself."

Selene shook her head as she rose to her feet. "It's worse than the time you made the banner. You wouldn't let me help then either, but at least you didn't think I'd bring death by being in the same chamber." She shrugged and strode away. "I'll go back and stand watch. Call me if you decide I can help."

She had hurt Selene, Thea realized wearily. She would have to make amends later. She supposed her sister was right. This desperation and obsessive determination were similar to what she had felt when she had been embroidering the banner. But the terror, the sickening fear, had not been present then.

The banner.

Asherah.

Had Ware been struck down by God for questioning the holy teachings?

She would not believe it. If he died, it would be because he had given his life for her. Whatever trespass he had committed, surely such a sacrifice would not be demanded of him.

* * *

Kadar could feel the thrust of power as soon as he entered the gates. It was as strong and compelling as the throb of the ghost drums.

Time had not weakened the Old Man.

Sinan waited for him on the steps of his castle, a fierce smile of satisfaction curving his lips. "You came back to me. I knew you would."

"I came to ask for sanctuary. I will not stay."

"Sanctuary for those weak fools below? They would have been slaughtered if I hadn't sent the drums."

"But you did send the drums."

"For you, not for them."

"Then, for me, send help to keep Kemal from attacking them again."

"But you are here. I have no need to keep them alive now." He smiled coldly. "And I will make sure you soon forget them. You already feel far, far away from them, don't you, Kadar?"

Kadar could feel the whirlpool of power draw him deeper as Sinan exerted his will.

He had forgotten how hard it was to resist that will. It took a moment before he was able to break free. "I will not forget them." He paused. "And if they die, I will remember them always. Memories can be much stronger than a living presence. They tend to grow until they are in every corner of your mind and heart." He could see Sinan did not like that idea and followed it quickly. "So why not send someone to watch over the weak ones and make sure Kemal doesn't make them into memories?"

Sinan stared at him with no expression. "You were always troublesome, Kadar."

"But you don't permit anyone to trouble you."

"Nor shall I. I almost had you before. Ah, how I wanted you to stay. You were without equal. The strongest always feels the pull the most and fights it hardest." He turned and started up the stone steps. "But I have you back now. We'll see how much you wish to save these Franks."

Three days passed and still Ware did not wake.

Thea dropped water on his tongue, but she could get no food down. How could he heal if he had no nourishment? she wondered desperately. He seemed to be growing thinner and weaker before her eyes.

"I'm done with asking you to sleep, but you must eat."

Selene was beside her, holding a wooden bowl filled with stew. The stew Ware had refused to swallow. She shook her head.

"You'll eat it or I'll knock you down, straddle you, and force it down your throat." Selene's expression was grim. "I'm out of patience. You persist in killing yourself for a dying man, and that idiot Kadar is probably lying dead somewhere on this stupid mountain. I'll not have it." She thrust the bowl into Thea's hands. "Eat it and I'll bother you no longer."

It was easier to obey than argue with her. Thea quickly finished the food and gave the bowl back to Selene.

"Good." Selene turned away and said over her shoulder, "If this is what love for a man brings to a woman, I'll make sure I never allow myself to feel it. You're more a slave than you ever were at the House of Nicholas."

It was true, Thea thought dully. She was chained to Ware in ways she had never thought possible. She felt so close to him, it was as if she were a part of every breath he drew. At times she thought if that breath stopped, she would also die.

Terror iced through her. He must not die. She had done everything possible to keep him alive.

But everything she had done had not been enough. God was going to take him.

"No," she whispered. She closed her eyes. "Give him back to me." Why was she praying? God had not listened when she had prayed for her dying mother. She wasn't sure God ever listened to women's pleas. He probably regarded females as unimportant, as man did. Yet if Asherah was part of God, then there was a slim chance God might understand a woman's desperation. She had to try. "Listen to me. This man has a good heart. He wants to live. He deserves to live. I won't ask for any other help to save us. Just let him live, and I'll do the rest."

Silence.

What had she expected? A crash of thunder to signal a miracle?

Her hand tightened on Ware's.

Live.

No stirring, no sign of waking.

She blinked back the tears stinging her eyes. It was stupid to feel disappointed. She had never been one to believe in miracles anyway. She had been right. God didn't listen to women.

An hour later she spooned a little stew from the bowl beside her and put it on his tongue.

He swallowed it.

She stiffened, afraid to believe it.

She placed another spoonful on his tongue and held her breath.

He swallowed that bite also.

The tears she had refused to shed overflowed and ran down her cheeks.

Not with a crash of thunder but with an act so small, it was almost imperceptible in the pattern of life.

A miracle.

Chapter Fifteen

WARE OPENED HIS EYES just before dawn.

"Safe?" he whispered. "Are—you—safe?"

"Quite safe." She tried to steady her voice. In another moment she would be weeping, she realized with panic. She instinctively sought a way to prevent that indignity. "Through no help from you. First, you rush forward and try to get yourself killed, and then you delay us by remaining out of your senses for days."

"Should have—left without me."

"Yes, we should have." She patted his head with a damp cloth. "But Kadar was too fond of you to abandon you."

"Kadar." He tried to turn his head and then flinched. "Where is—"

"Don't move. Do you wish to do yourself more injury? Close your eyes and go back to sleep. Everything is fine."

His lids closed. "I seem to be able—to do nothing else. Sweet Jesus, my head . . . hurts."

"Perhaps that will teach you not to blunder forward and place yourself needlessly in harm's way."

"Ungrateful . . . woman. I did not blunder . . ."

He was asleep. But he would wake. She knew he would wake.

She knelt there, drinking in his face as if she had not stared at it these many days. The faintest flush colored his cheeks, and his breathing was light and even.

She lay down beside him, not touching but close enough to be aware if he stirred.

She was deeply asleep in less than a moment.

"Where is Kadar?" Ware asked.

She fought her way out of the webs of sleep and lifted herself on one elbow to look down at him.

His voice was stronger and his eyes bright and alert. A surge of joy brought her fully awake. "You're better. I'll go get you something to eat."

"I have it here." Selene was beside them, handing her a bowl. "I thought you two would never wake." She studied Ware. "I believe you may live, after all."

"Your enthusiasm heartens me," Ware said.

"You betrayed us. I'm not like Thea. I don't forgive easily." She turned on her heel and strode away from them.

"Then she's very like you." Ware grimaced. "No one forgives less freely than you."

"You're right. I'll never forgive you for taking me to El Sunan. Open your mouth."

"I can feed myself."

"Open your mouth."

He reluctantly obeyed her. "I feel like a babe."

She scooped another spoonful into his mouth. "Then eat and grow strong. Do you think I like doing this?" She did not mind. She would not have minded anything now that he had come back to her.

"Where is Kadar?"

She could no longer evade the question. "He went to seek help from Sinan."

"How long ago?"

"Four days."

He muttered a curse and tried to sit up. She pushed him down. "What do you intend to do? Go riding after him when you can scarcely move? If he had been murdered by the assassins, would they not have been here in this camp by now? There's been no sign of anyone since you were felled."

"Kemal?"

She shook her head. "No one."

He looked down at the bits of meat in the bowl of stew. "How have you lived?"

"Selene set traps for small game and kept watch." She spooned the last bite into his mouth and sat back on her heels. "Are you dizzy?"

He shook his head. "And my head aches only a trifle. I could ride right now."

"In two days we will see."

He glared at her. "Now."

She glared back at him. "Kadar said we should wait here for him, and I'll not have my work ruined after all the bother I've taken with you. Try to get up, and I'll tie your legs to this tree we're under. Now, go back to sleep."

"You couldn't do it. I'm not so weak a woman could best me."

"You're so weak, a caterpillar could best you." She could see he was not convinced, and fear rushed through her. "We'll strike a compromise. Tomorrow, if you're better, we'll see if you can sit a horse."

"Of course I can sit a horse. I've ridden fifty miles with a wound through my stomach."

"Then you were very foolish. Someone should have stopped you. Tomorrow."

He stared at her in rage and frustration. "Kadar may need me."

"One more day won't matter to him, and it may mean a great deal to you. You aren't going to face murderers when you have no more strength than this. Go to sleep." She rose to her feet. "You might as well do as I say, for you'll have no horse. I'm going to take all of them down to the brook and groom them." She grimaced. "And myself. I've not left your side since you were wounded, and I badly need a wash. I must smell as you did when you wore your sheepskin drawers."

His anger disappeared. "You stayed by my side for four days?"

"You were most uncooperative. You would not wake." She started toward the tree where the horses were tied. "But that was not your fault. The blame will lie with you if you do something stupid now."

"Four days?"

She did not answer. She could feel his intent gaze on her as she gathered the reins and started down the incline. She kept her back very straight and did not look at him. She had never experienced such melting tenderness. She wanted to run to him and gather him close and tell him everything would be all right, that she would do whatever he wished. Even in their moments of passion she had not felt like this, and it frightened her. Much better to keep him at bay with harsh words than let herself flow into him and lose herself.

"I'll help you." Selene was beside her, grabbing her horse's reins. "Why did you not ask?"

"I've already allowed you to do too much." She paused. "And without thanks."

Selene did not look at her. "When have thanks been necessary between us? And you did not allow me to help much."

And denying her that service had hurt her, Thea thought. "It is not— He was hurt and I was afraid. You didn't understand."

"No, I didn't. I still don't." Selene's words came haltingly. "I've been thinking about it, and I see no reason why you should let yourself love Lord Ware. We would be much happier off by ourselves."

"It's not a question of letting myself."

"Fate? Magic? You never believed in it before. Have you lost your senses?"

Perhaps she had lost her senses. She had certainly changed. "Lord Ware has a good heart. He saved my life."

"So? You don't have to give it to him. Reward him in some other way."

Such a simple solution. "It's not a reward. You don't understand."

"You keep saying that. I do understand." Thea could almost see Selene withdrawing into herself. "Well, go ahead.

Love him. Go to him. I don't need you. We're all alone, anyway. We just like to pretend we aren't."

"You're not alone." Thea lovingly touched her arm and flinched as Selene stiffened. "I'll always be here when you need me."

"It won't be the same."

"Don't be stupid." She lost patience. "Nothing is ever the same, but that doesn't mean it's not good. You're my sister and my friend, and I'll neither forget nor stop loving you. You're the one who is pushing me away." She grabbed Selene's shoulders and shook her. "I won't have it. We need each other and I won't lose you."

Selene stared into her face for a moment before saying gruffly, "Perhaps you haven't quite lost your senses. You may yet get over this madness." She shrugged off Thea's grasp. "I suppose I'll wait and see." She reached into the pocket of her gown and handed Thea a bar of soap. "I'll tend the horses. You bathe and wash your hair."

"We'll both tend the horses first," Thea said with firmness. "We do things together."

"Only some things." Selene grimaced. "For I will have nothing to do with this strange malady that's overtaken you."

Ware was still awake when she returned to the camp two hours later.

"Why?" he asked.

"You're supposed to be asleep."

"It appears I've done nothing but sleep for the past few days. Why did you not leave my side?"

She tied the horses to the tree. "You needed my care."

"To that extent?" His eyes were fixed on her face. "That you could not leave me for even a moment?"

"It's one of my faults that I can do nothing halfway." She shrugged. "But now that you're on your way to health, I can take time to help Selene." She added, "If you'll be sensible and not make more work for me by trying to do too much too soon."

"I find it strange that you'd work so hard to save a man you hate." He paused. "You did say you had not forgiven me?"

"And it's true. What you did was unforgivable." She ran her hands through her damp hair to aid it in drying. "But you saved my life. I couldn't let you die."

"Why won't you look at me?"

"You're not overpleasant to look upon. You have four days' growth on your cheeks."

His hand involuntarily lifted to his rough cheek. "That's not the reason."

"That's all the reason you'll get from me."

He was silent a moment, watching her. He said in a low voice, "Could you not leave your hair down? I've not seen it unbound for a long time."

Since the night Selene had come to Dundragon. It seemed a century ago. She had a sudden vivid memory of writhing under him, making soft, frantic cries. His hands in her tresses holding her still as his hips drove forward, again and again, filling her, stretching her until she could—

She quickly drew her hair over her shoulder and began to braid it.

He said wearily, "I shouldn't have mentioned it." He

closed his eyes. "I should have known you'd not give me that pleasure. It seemed a little thing. . . ."

It was not a little thing. The memory had brought to life that part of her she had buried for the last two years. She would not be able to look at him now without remembering pleasure.

And wanting it again.

Not now. Not until she could come to terms with this loving. Everything was happening too fast. She already felt too weak and needy; taking him into her body would only make it worse.

He was asleep again. Dear God, his big body looked helpless lying there. No, not completely helpless. She could already see the faint signs of returning strength. Soon he would be himself again, strong, stubborn, willful, carving his way through life, sure that only his path was best. She would have to be wary every moment if she was to hold her own.

But that moment was not now. She slowly crossed the clearing and lay down close to him, savoring his nearness. If he woke, she could use his weakness as excuse.

She cuddled closer, and a warm sweetness flowed through her. This was good. She did not have to worry about either yielding or holding herself aloof. She could lie here and know that, for this moment, it was safe to let herself love him.

She woke in the middle of the night to see him staring down at her with wonder.

"Thea?"

She was too vulnerable, too full of love. She should

move away from him. She should close her eyes so that he could not see.

She did not want to close her eyes. She wanted to keep on looking at him forever.

"Why are you afraid?" he whispered. "I've been feeling your fear since I came back to my senses."

She was afraid she loved him too much, afraid she would give him everything and have nothing left for herself. She said shakily, "You're still out of your senses, if you think I fear you. I don't—"

"Stop." His finger gently touched her eyelash. "There's something here, something I can almost see, if you'd only stop blistering me with words."

She did not want him to see. Not yet. She must be more sure of herself before she let him be sure of her.

She shut her eyes. "You won't hear me blister you with words if you don't talk and disturb my sleep." She could feel his gaze on her face for another moment before he settled down beside her. "Why did you lie with me?"

"To keep you warm. You must not get a chill. I'll leave if you like."

"No, stay." Then he repeated in a low tone, "Stay, Thea."

Ware straightened in the saddle. "Hand me my helmet."

Thea shook her head. "It's too heavy. I won't have that metal pressing on the wound."

"You'd rather have my head split open by one of Sinan's men. Hand me my helmet."

Thea ignored him. "Get our horses, Selene."

Ware shook his head. "You'll stay here and wait until I return."

"We go to Maysef." Selene returned with the horses from the trees, and Thea swung into the saddle. "I'll not change my mind, so you might as well be silent and save your strength. You may need it to protect us."

She rode ahead of him up the trail.

She heard his muttered expletive behind her.

"I won't be this weak forever," he called grimly. "Enjoy it while you may."

She was not enjoying his helplessness, but she was taking advantage of it. He looked strong and warriorlike sitting in that saddle, but she couldn't believe he was as well as he appeared. She would not let him go alone to that fortress where unknown dangers lurked. "If you admit to weakness, you should have the sense to take care of yourself. Since I see no sign of it, I'll have to do it myself." She glanced back over her shoulder to make sure Selene was out of hearing. "I believe we'll be just as safe at Maysef as we were waiting for Kemal, but I want a promise from you." She paused. "If there's a choice to be made, I want you to save Selene."

"Instead of you?" He shook his head. "I'll not make that promise."

"You must. Selene has nothing to do with this. We've swept her along, taken away all her choices." She moistened her lips. "We have to keep her safe. Can't you see that it's not fair?"

"I don't care if it's fair or not. Dammit, I cannot make that promise." He met her gaze. "You know I cannot."

Darkness and fire. Torches burning, lighting the unknown. Closeness, bonding, two together.

Shaken, she forced herself to glance away from him. "It's not fair," she whispered.

"What about this has ever been fair?" He smiled bitterly. "I'll try to keep you both alive, but don't expect me to let you die and another live." He spurred ahead of her. "It will not happen."

"Ah, I see you've obeyed my orders with your usual precision."

Thea's glance flew up the trail. "Kadar!"

He clucked reprovingly as he rode toward them. "Did I not tell you to stay until I came for you? And look at you, riding to beard Sinan in his den." His gaze shifted to Ware. "I'm glad to see you recovered. I suppose this is your doing. You wished to relieve yourself of your obligation to me, so you rush to pluck me from Sinan's stranglehold. Well, it won't be that easy. I fear you must remain my possession a little longer."

"I believe I can tolerate that state," Ware said gruffly. "You are well?"

"I'm wonderfully fed, splendidly clothed, but spiritually barren. Sinan is all brain and no soul, which has a certain numbing affect." He looked beyond them to Selene. "But I was most tactful with him. I didn't wish to come back dripping blood and inconveniencing you."

"Very wise," she said impassively.

"But it took all my powers of persuasion to get him to extend an invitation to you. He didn't think you'd prove amusing." He turned his horse. "Though he's found terrifying Kemal's soldiers these last few days a very gratifying experience. Perhaps he thought he'd wrest the same pleasure from intimidating you."

"Kemal?" Thea asked, cutting through the chaff to the kernel of importance. "What of Kemal?"

"He's camped in the foothills, trying to incite his soldiers to follow him back up the mountain to gut you. It's been most difficult when every night one of the poor fellows is found with his throat sliced from ear to ear."

"Your suggestion?" Ware asked.

"Well, I judged poison to be too subtle and inconvenient for the situation." He glanced at Thea. "But frightening Kemal away from here would have been much easier if he didn't have such confidence in his beloved banner. He may yet convince his followers to come after us."

"Only a suggestion?" Selene asked suddenly.

Kadar met her gaze with limpid innocence. "You malign me." He changed the subject. "On no account must anyone tell Sinan of Kemal's belief in the banner, and when you meet him, lower your head and don't speak until he speaks. He will probably ignore you. He views women as one step above animals of the field, and I won't have my negotiations jeopardized."

"I won't lower my head, but I've no desire to speak to him," Selene said. "And most men consider women as animals that exist only for their use."

"Oh, I believe you'll find Sinan does not resemble anyone you've encountered to date," Kadar murmured.

Something was different about Kadar, Thea realized suddenly. On the surface he was the same, but underneath there was something . . . hollow. No, not hollow . . . dark. Oh, she wasn't certain.

But she could see Selene sensed something also. Her sister's eyes were narrowed on Kadar with apprehension.

Apprehension? Nonsense. This was Kadar, their friend. There could be nothing to fear.

Nothing to fear. Thea repeated the words over and over as they entered the grim fortress of Maysef and rode past Sinan's guards. The Old Man's white-robed followers gazed at them without expression as they stopped before the austere castle that loomed grim and gray in the late-afternoon sunlight.

The interior of the castle was equally austere, and the halls felt cold on this warm day. Imagination, she told herself as they entered the high arched hall and moved toward the robed man seated in a high-backed chair at the far end of the huge chamber.

Power.

Thea had to keep herself from taking a step backward as she drew closer to Sinan.

She had expected evil, but not this sense of cold, unfathomed power. They called him Old Man of the Mountain, but his face, though lined, appeared oddly ageless, and his dark eyes shimmered with a zeal that seemed an entity in itself. She was relieved that his glance rested on her for only an instant before shifting to Ware.

"You are here again." Sinan's tone was flat. "Kadar tells me you're a great warrior, but I have grave doubts. Every time you come to my mountains, you are wounded. If one of my followers was so clumsy, he would be discarded."

"It's not clumsy to be overcome by superior numbers."

"It's clumsy to rush forward into a situation where you're surrounded, as I'm told you did. You should have let the woman die."

"As I told you, he thought to use her to barter later," Kadar said quickly.

"Yes, you told me. But, then, you lie well. Almost as well as I do. You do many things well, Kadar." His faint smile was as chilling as that impression of boundless power.

Kadar did not seem to feel the chill. "I've been well taught."

"But many men have neither the talent nor the fortitude. They fear the darkness, you embrace it." Sinan's indifferent glance moved to Ware. "This one has no love for the darkness. He has lived in the shadows, but the darkness would strangle him. I don't know why you bother with him."

"He has great strength. Strength is like a beacon that draws me." Kadar shrugged. "But we have discussed this before and we do not agree. I brought them to you, and you can see they're not as weak as you thought. Now, what is your decision?"

"I did not say I would make an immediate decision." He smiled again at Kadar. "I don't wish it to end as yet. Perhaps I can persuade you to stay here with me permanently. After all, I cannot live forever."

"I'm not sure of that," Kadar said.

Sinan's smile broadened. "Well, they say I must die sometime. You could stay and see." He tilted his head as if thinking. "Perhaps I'll slaughter these weak ones and then you'll have no reason to leave."

Thea tensed and took a step closer to Ware.

"It's a game," Ware murmured. "Don't be afraid."

If it was a game, it was a frighteningly macabre one. She had no doubt Sinan would not hesitate to kill them all if the whim took him.

Ware took a step forward. "If you think me weak, bring forth your champion and let me do battle with him."

"And kill in that childish way of the Franks? Full of pomp and bravado?" Sinan's tone was scornful. "We are masters of death here. We do not play at it."

"Then let me fight your way."

"No." Kadar stepped forward. "This is a waste of time, Sinan. You don't wish to see such an uneven battle."

"On the contrary, it might be amusing. I've grown a little bored of late."

Kadar met his gaze and said softly, "I will take two tonight."

Sinan's attention was immediately diverted. "Indeed?"

There was a strong bond between them, Thea realized incredulously. It seemed impossible that the chilling evil of the Old Man could be connected in any way to Kadar, a youth under his twentieth year, glowingly handsome and sparkling with life. Yet she could almost see the twisted cord binding them together.

"Two?" Sinan repeated. "You challenge yourself as a man should do. That will be interesting. Then we will wait before testing this Lord Ware. Give them quarters and food, Kadar." He rose to his feet. "Except the red-haired child. I will use her tonight."

"No!" Thea lunged toward Sinan, but Kadar stepped swiftly between them.

"She means no disrespect. She is concerned for her safety if you become ill."

Sinan frowned. "Ill?"

"The child was raped by Kemal and his soldiers at El Sunan and shows signs of having the whore's disease."

Sinan's cold, speculative glance moved over Selene.

"Pity. There is so much life in the young ones. I would have enjoyed her."

"But not the aftermath," Kadar said. "I've heard it's a lingering illness that ends in madness and death."

"And not one I'd choose." Sinan smiled meaningfully at Kadar. "As I believe you know." He moved toward the door. "But I've often thought if one wanted to kill without suspicion, and immediacy was not important, sending such a diseased woman to an enemy would bring great satisfaction. Perhaps we will have use for the child later."

Thea whirled fiercely on Kadar as soon as the door closed behind Sinan. "He will *not* use her."

He held up his hand to halt the angry outburst. "No, he won't. Sinan is always thinking of new ways to kill. This is just another. Besides, his assassins are all men. He would not trust a woman."

"How comforting," Selene said. "But he clearly trusts you."

"Of course—he looks at me and sees himself as a young man. He once told me he wished he had a son like me, that I was a reflection of him. He doesn't realize almost all mirrors are distorted."

Astonished, Ware said, "He thinks of you as a son?"

"He flatters himself. I'm much more clever than Sinan will ever be." He moved across the chamber. "Come along. I'll take you to your quarters. I'll keep Selene with me in my chamber in case Sinan changes his mind. It's best Thea stay with you for her protection, Ware."

"I had every intention of staying with him," Thea said. "He needs me. He's far from well yet. He was practically stumbling on his feet when he issued that foolish challenge."

"It was not foolish. A man cannot be called weak."

"Even when he is." Thea turned to Kadar. "How long do you think we must stay here?"

He shrugged. "Until Sinan becomes bored and wants to put an end to the situation. I hope to persuade him that the most felicitous conclusion would be to crush Kemal and get him off his doorstep."

"Is there a way we can increase his boredom?" Ware asked.

"Not without risk." He smiled. "And I'm a cowardly soul. I prefer to gain our objective without danger. Let me work at it for a few days and see if I can mold events to our advantage." He stopped before a brass-bound oak door. "You won't be guarded. Sinan knows we have no place to go but Kemal's arms. You'll find life here very simple. Meals will be brought to you in the morning and evening. On no account should Selene or Thea be permitted to wander alone about the fortress. I doubt if Sinan will issue orders protecting their safety."

"Since we're mere beasts of the field," Selene said.

Kadar smiled. "On second thought, you may be safe, since you're a diseased beast of the field. But I don't believe we'll chance it." He took her elbow and urged her toward another door down the hall. "I'll call for hot water and clean garments for all of you. I'll bid you good night now. I'll not see you again this evening. We'll meet in the morning and talk then."

"Why won't you see us this evening?" Ware asked. "It's barely sunset."

"I must sleep now. I have a few things to do later." He shut the door before any other questions could be asked.

Thea hesitated, staring at the closed door. "I don't like this."

"Kadar will not harm her."

At first, she did not understand, and then she gazed at him in amazement. "You think I worry about Selene's virtue?"

"It occurred to me. She is older now."

"Kadar is still Kadar. Because she has begun to have breasts does not necessarily turn a man mad." She entered the chamber. "No, I worry about Kadar. He's too secretive."

"He will not betray us."

"I know he won't. I just don't want him—" She broke off in helpless frustration. She could not express the uneasiness she had felt when she had watched Kadar and Sinan together. But it was no use worrying now when she could do nothing about it. "You should rest." She glanced around the chamber and found it as austere as the rest of the castle. A simple table, a bed, two stools, and a washstand were the only furniture in the room. She spied a bellpull on the far wall and moved toward it. "There are not enough covers on the bed. It grows chill at night. I'll call for more." She shivered. "This entire castle is overcool."

"Perhaps Sinan doesn't feel the chill," Ware said. He moved toward the window and gazed out at the mountains. "It wouldn't surprise me."

It would not surprise her either, Thea thought. She forced herself to dismiss the Old Man from her thoughts. "You'll take the bed. I'll curl up on a blanket on the floor."

Ware shook his head. "I let no woman sleep on the floor."

"You've been ill. You must have a good night's sleep."

"I'm not ill now."

She sighed in exasperation as she realized the obstinate man would not be dissuaded. "Very well, we will take turns. I'll sleep half the night in the bed and then you'll wake me. Come, I'll help you with your armor."

Chapter Sixteen

KADAR ROSE FROM HIS PALLET, cast a quick look at Selene sleeping on the bed before moving silently toward the door in the darkness.

"Where are you going?" Selene asked, wide-awake. "It must be the middle of the night."

Kadar shook his head ruefully as he stopped and turned to face her. She had been watching him all evening; he should have known she was only pretending to slumber. "Go back to sleep. I'll return soon."

She raised herself on one elbow. "If they don't catch you."

He raised his brows. "I beg pardon? Sinan gives me free run of the fortress."

She sat up in bed, her cotton robe a white blur in the darkness. "I don't want you to go."

"You'll be quite safe. If you're disturbed, run down the hall to Thea and Ware."

"You think I fear for myself?" she asked fiercely. "I'm not such a coward."

"I must go." He started to turn away.

"Not two," she said. "One is dangerous, two would be folly."

He went still. Then he turned back to her, waiting.

"It's not Sinan's assassins who kill one of Kemal's men each night. It's you."

"Is it?"

"It's part of the game you play with Sinan. You keep him interested and retain his respect in the only way you can. You creep into Kemal's camp and kill one man a night. But today, to distract Sinan from Lord Ware, you had to promise him a bonus. Two instead of one." She said desperately, "You cannot do it."

"I have great talent. Ask Sinan."

"He would not talk to a beast of the field." She swung her feet to the floor. "You know they'll be expecting you. Don't go."

"Perhaps you're wrong. It could be I'm only going for a walk in the courtyard. Thea and Ware seem to have no suspicions."

"Thea can think only of Lord Ware, and he is still not well." She was suddenly there before him, her hands grasping his arms. "Find another way."

Her face appeared pinched and pale in the moonlight, but her eyes glittered with their usual indomitable spirit. He had always found it fascinating to watch the emotions flickering behind the outward boldness of those huge green eyes. "There is no other way." He gently extricated himself from her grasp. "We need Sinan."

"It's not only Sinan. You *want* to go."

"I would be mad to want to put my head in Kemal's hands."

"But you do." Her gaze searched his expression. "I can see it. You're . . . excited."

"Am I?" He smiled. "Then it would be useless to persuade me not to go, wouldn't it?"

"Oh, *go* away. Let them kill you. See if I care." She whirled and stomped back to the bed. "I'll think no more about you."

"Excellent idea." He left the chamber and moved quickly down the hall. He knew she would not sleep. She would lie there and worry . . . and curse him for making her worry.

Then he closed all thought of Selene from his awareness with the discipline and focus he had been taught. She was right, he was excited. At these times excitement always made his blood pump through his veins with exhilarating speed. He allowed himself that excitement because it made his mind sharp and his responses swift. But no other emotion must be present; he must wrap himself in the concentration of the act to come.

Nothing must intrude as he walked the dark path.

Footsteps echoed on the stone outside the door.

Instantly awake, Thea lifted her head from the pillow.

The footsteps passed and faded in the distance.

"It was probably only a guard." Ware turned away from the window, a dark silhouette framed by the moonlight.

She sat up in bed. "Kadar said we wouldn't be guarded."

"That doesn't mean Sinan doesn't have other treasures he wishes to keep safe. The Old Man is paid very well for his services."

She didn't wish to dwell on those deadly services. She glanced at the window; the sliver of moon was now high in the sky. "You let me sleep. Why didn't you wake me?"

"I wasn't tired. I had to think." He lit the candle on the table. "We have to decide what we're to do after we leave here."

"Dear God, we haven't even escaped from Kemal yet."

"We have to have a plan. After Kemal there will be the Knights Templar. We cannot run forever."

"So you must rob yourself of sleep now."

"We must come to an agreement." He paused, as if bracing himself. "You must leave this land. I'm going to tell Kadar he's to take you and Selene to a safe port and take passage."

"To where?"

He scowled. "You won't like it."

"Where?"

"Scotland."

She stared at him in amazement. "That barbarian land?"

"It's safer than anywhere else. The highlands are wild and barren, and the Knights Templar hold no power there."

"And what would I do in this barren place?"

"Live," he said fiercely.

"And who would buy my silks?"

"I don't care." He frowned. "Well, I do care, but I'd rather see you alive than prosper in your trade."

"Why that chill Scotland? Why not send me to the wilds of China? At least it's civilized, and that's where the silk trade began."

"I have no familiarity with that place."

"What difference does that make?"

He didn't answer at once. He finally said jerkily, "When I think of you, I'd like to imagine you in the land of my birth. It would be . . . pleasant."

She felt a melting deep inside. She forced herself to say brusquely, "That is very selfish of you."

"I know." His gaze shifted to the flame of the candle. "But if you go to Scotland, I can tell Kadar where it's safe and where there is danger. I'd like you to buy my father's lands, but that might be too dangerous. You must have no connection with me."

"Then you don't intend to go with us?" she asked, though she knew the answer.

He shook his head. "Perhaps I'll go to Rome. Vaden lived there for a time, and he told me it's a vast city. A man could lose himself in such a place." His lips curled. "And the Templars would not expect to have me crouch on the Pope's doorstep."

"And you'll live in civilized comfort while we shiver in your highlands." She shook her head. "I think not."

"You *will* go." His gaze flew to her face. "For God's sake, can't you see? What does it take to make you accept that the danger is real?"

"I know the danger. I just don't agree with your plan."

"You can't go to Damascus."

"Nor to Rome?"

"No."

"Because it's too dangerous?"

He didn't answer.

"Dangerous for me but not for you? You see, it's a faulty plan."

"It's not a faulty plan, and you'll go to Scotland if I have to stuff you in a trunk and send you there in the cargo hold."

"Oh, I have every intention of going to your Scotland." She paused deliberately. "As long as you go with me."

He went still. "You know I cannot go."

"I know I won't go without you. Make a choice."

"They'll never stop searching for me. I can't stay with you."

"Because you fear they'll scoop me up too, if they find you. Well, I believe we're more clever than they are. I think we can lose ourselves and live a fine, full life."

"I hope you can. Kadar will make sure you have funds and the opportunity to—"

"Together." She stood up and moved toward him. "We go together or not at all." Mother of God, his expression was tormented. Why wouldn't the stubborn man see reason? "For I will not live without you."

He smiled bitterly. "After you assured me you'd never forgive me, I didn't expect this kindness. It is very noble of you to—"

"I'm not noble and I won't forgive your betrayal." She paused. "Be sure that I'll make you pay for it in any number of ways in the years to come. Every time I wish something you find unreasonable, I'll remind you of it." She stepped forward and laid her head on his chest. She could feel the beat of his heart through the cloth of his tunic. How strange that all her fears were vanishing as she battled

Ware's. She whispered, "And the first thing I wish is that you wed me."

His muscles went rigid. "Wed? You know I cannot wed you."

"I'm tired of your 'cannots.' You cannot go to Scotland, you cannot wed me." She rubbed against him. It was like rubbing against the unyielding trunk of a tree, she thought ruefully. "It seems you will do both. For I'll have it no other way."

"Why?" he said harshly. "Has your life so little value to you that you wish to join it with mine?"

"It has great value and grows richer every day. It's truly amazing, when you're always seeking to make it more difficult."

"Stop touching me." His voice was hoarse.

"It's necessary that I touch you. Your mind is not working properly, but your body is always ready." She brushed her lips along his collarbone. "And I wish to be with child by the time we board this ship for Scotland."

"No!"

She leaned back and looked into his face. "I will wed you and have your child. This I swear. It will do you no good to fight me. I'll have my way in this."

His voice shook. "I will not be the death of you."

"No, you will be the life of me." She cupped his face in her hands and stared straight into his eyes. "I love you and I think you have love for me. Don't try to tell me it's guilt or duty; it is love."

"If I tell you I don't love you, will you leave me?"

"No, for you would be lying. Wouldn't you?"

"Yes." His voice broke as he buried his face in her hair. "God help you."

His arms were crushing the breath out of her, but she didn't complain. "God did help me. I prayed and He answered. He kept you alive. I'll ask nothing else from Him."

She could feel something warm and wet on her temple. "I will," he said. "I'll ask Him to do what I cannot do. I'll ask Him to send you away from me."

"He won't listen. He obviously prefers me. I was the one He chose to make a banner for Him."

He gazed wonderingly down at her. "You're jesting. You're not afraid any longer?"

"I cannot believe in this magic banner, but the God who answered my prayer listened to a woman. I did not believe that possible. I didn't think He paid any attention to a woman's needs." Her eyes glowed luminously. "This is a thing of wonder. If Asherah is the part of Him that gave you back to me, then there's nothing to fear."

"Except Sinan and Kemal and Vaden *and* the Knights Templar."

"We can do nothing about them now." She smiled. "But we can do something about the babe I'm to have."

He shook his head. "I risked your life before. I will not do it again."

She took a step back, pulled her robe over her head, and dropped it onto the floor. "You keep repeating the mistake of thinking that you're the one who chooses the risks I take. It's my right alone." She moved naked to the bed and lay down. "Just as it's your choice to be foolish and stand there all night when we could give and take pleasure."

"Cover yourself," he said hoarsely.

She didn't move. "You cover me."

His muscles were knotted with a terrible tension. He

moved slowly, heavily, toward her as if drawn by a magnet. "I cannot do it. Why do you wish this child so much?"

"Life. With such a stubborn man I must do everything possible to keep you with me. You wanted a child because you were sure you couldn't have life. I want one because I believe you'll do everything possible to stay alive to protect your child." He was beside the bed now and she reached out and took his hand. "It wasn't only that the risk was great, I think you believed you didn't deserve life. Too many people had died because you found the lion throne." She lifted his hand to her cheek. "You *do* deserve to live. God could have taken you, and He did not. Doesn't that prove something to you?"

His hand was shaking. "I cannot— Cover yourself."

She moved over on the bed. "Lie with me. I'll not do more than hold your hand if that's your will."

"My will?" He laughed desperately. "I seem to have no will."

She tugged at his hand. "Lie with me."

He was on the bed but lying apart from her. "I cannot go with you to Scotland. Your danger would increase tenfold if I—"

"And your child will have no father to protect him if you do not come." She lifted his hand to her lips and kissed the palm. "Shh, don't think of Scotland. Is this not pleasant?"

"No. Yes." He did not look at her. "If one likes excruciating pain. I've heard some take pleasure in it."

She kissed his palm again. "They must be very peculiar folk. I promise you there will be no pain for you in my body."

A great sigh racked his body. "You're a cruel, cruel woman."

"Because I must have my way in this? It's taken us too long and the path has been too painful." She whispered, "I love you and I will love no other. I don't wish to spend my life alone. We must give ourselves a chance. Do you think this is easy for me? My body craves you, not a babe. It's been a long time since you—"

He gave an explosive sound and was suddenly over her, parting her thighs. "Too long," he muttered as he tore off his tunic and threw it aside. "I cannot stand—"

He plunged deep.

She gasped and reached out and grasped his shoulders.

Fullness.

The sensation lasted only an instant, replaced by heat and need as he thrust wildly, deeply. "Take . . . ," he muttered. He lifted her buttocks to meet each savage thrust. It wasn't enough. It was as if he were starved and could not get deep enough, move fast enough, hard enough. He lifted her legs and put them over his shoulders, leaving her open and vulnerable. "Look—at us."

She dazedly looked down at their joining and another surge of dark excitement rippled through her. It seemed impossible she could take him, and yet she was. Over and over. Deeper, deeper.

She bit her lower lip to suppress a groan as the tension built to unbearable heights.

His hands were on her, smoothing her, plucking at her.

Her back arched as a spasm shook her.

She was panting, her nails digging into his shoulders.

"Ware, it's—"

"Yes." His lips were drawn back from his teeth in a

contorted grin. "Too—long. It—hurts. I can't be—" He gave a low groan as he plunged to the hilt.

He collapsed on top of her as his release tore through him. His heart was beating so hard, she could nearly hear its thunder.

"I didn't want—" He gasped. "You see what—I am? I cannot even be gentle. I nearly tore you apart."

She couldn't answer until she got her breath. "I seem to be in one piece." She brushed her lips along his cheek. "But this position is not—natural to me. Not that I minded it when we—"

"I didn't mean to hurt you. I didn't think—" He was moving off her, his arms enfolding her. "I had to have more of you."

"You didn't hurt me. I don't remember complaining." Not that she had been able to think at all during those wild moments. "You gave me exactly what I wanted."

"Too much." His palm rubbed her belly. "If you're not with child tonight, it will be a miracle."

"No, if I'm *with* child tonight, it will be a miracle. A child is always a miracle." She smiled. "You did very well. However, I believe we will do it again soon. It's very convenient that we have little else to do while we wait for Kadar to smooth the way for us. I find I've missed this very much."

He chuckled. "It will be my pleasure. I'm relieved it's not just my seed you wish."

"A babe would not be necessary so soon if you weren't such a stubborn man. I must tie you to me in every way I can, or you'll start having qualms about doing what must be done."

"Wedding you and getting you with child?"

"And living with me for many, many years."

"Years . . . ," he repeated wistfully. "You seem so certain. I cannot believe. I can only hope."

"At least you hope. I was beginning to think you'd remain lost in gloom forever. I was growing very weary of it." She said with emphasis, "But I believe. That is enough."

"It appears it will have to be." He kissed her on the tip of the nose. "For you have me too muddled and bedazzled to put two thoughts together."

"Do I?" Her arms tightened around him. "Good. For that was my purpose. When you think, I have only trouble with you."

His expression clouded. "I should think. I should not let you—"

"Hush." She followed the command with a quick, hard kiss. "You see? Nothing but disturbance. We deserve this and I'll not permit you to spoil it." She pushed him back on the bed and rolled on top of him. "Though after El Sunan you must prove to me that you deserve me."

"I don't deserve you. And I cannot prove what isn't true."

She could feel tears sting her eyes. She swallowed hard. "I'll endeavor to keep you firmly of that belief. You're a proud, arrogant man, and it's taken me much too long to convince you of my worth."

"You didn't convince me, I always knew it. You are sunlight and strength and joy." He added simply, "And that's why I will love you to my last breath."

Dear God, it was dangerous to love a man this much. This was what she had feared, that love would leave her vulnerable. She could not be flippant or raise any barriers against him when he moved her like this.

His index finger traced her jawbone. "I would like to give you a gift. Women like gifts, don't they?"

"I suppose everyone likes gifts."

"What can I give you?"

He might already have given her the gift she had demanded of him. But she would not speak of the babe until they were safely away from this land.

"Only one thing," she whispered.

"What?"

"Smile. You are too grim. You must smile more." She smiled herself, but she knew it to be a poor, tremulous one. "A husband should look happy, or everyone will think you've taken a terrible shrew for a wife."

It was close to dawn when Kadar returned to the chamber.

Selene watched him move like a shadow toward his pallet. She would not feel this overwhelming relief. He had been foolish not to heed her plea.

"Say it," Kadar said as he lay down. "Or you will surely burst."

"Two?"

"Two."

"Then you don't deserve to be alive."

"The deserving don't always get their just rewards." He rolled over and pulled up his cover. "If you're finished, I'd like to go to sleep."

"I'm finished." She lay there a minute longer. "Kemal's men would have butchered us if given the opportunity. They almost killed Lord Ware."

"Yes."

"Then you should feel no guilt."

"I feel no guilt."

"I think you do."

"You're wrong. Once the decision to kill is made, I feel nothing. I've been well trained."

She was suddenly aware of an aura of remote hardness surrounding him that frightened her. "By that foul Old Man. You're not like him."

"He thinks I am." He paused. "I don't really want to argue with you anymore tonight. Do you suppose you could restrain yourself and go back to sleep?"

His voice was heavy with unutterable weariness, and for some reason that exhaustion only made her angrier. "You won't sleep."

"Of course I will."

The certainty in his tone increased her uneasiness. She sat up and lit the candle on the table next to the bed.

He turned his face to look at her. "Blow out the candle."

The flame was reflected in his dark eyes, but they mirrored no warmth. Cold. Cold and yet as burning as the eyes of the Old Man of the Mountain.

She stared at him as stunned as if she had been pierced with a sword. Panic tore through her.

No, by the Saints, she would not permit this.

She threw aside the cover, ran across the room, and dropped to her knees beside him. "You must not do this again. It's bad for you."

"I assure you, it was far worse for Kemal's men."

"I don't care about them." She took his hands in her own. How strange that they were warm when he seemed so remote and cold. "I don't like to see you like this. Do you hear me?"

"I could hardly help it." He paused. "Aren't you afraid to touch my hands? There's blood on them, you know. Only figuratively speaking. I was careful to wash when I reached the courtyard."

He was trying to jar her, push her away, so that he could retain that hard, hollow core. Her hands tightened on his. "Stop trying to make me afraid of you. I'm not going to let you go."

"Why not?"

"Because you're—" She stopped. There might be only one way to reach him, but it was the most difficult for her. She said haltingly, "I need you the way you were."

"Need?" He arched a brow. "You?"

"Stop mocking me. Thea's going away from me. I need someone to be there."

"So you choose my unworthy self."

"I won't be alone. It . . . hurts."

"Does it?" He gazed up at her face. "Poor Selene. It must hurt very much to bring you to me."

"You're the only one I can go to. You know me. You've always known me." She paused. "And I know you."

He shook his head.

"I *do*. I've always known what you are. I don't care."

He studied her for a long time before saying slowly, "I believe you. Extraordinary."

"So you must come back to me. I won't be alone again." Her eyes met his, demanding, fierce, compelling, before she threw herself down beside him and buried her face in the hollow of his shoulder. "I won't have you leave me and become like that man."

He stiffened in surprise. "Get up and go to your bed, child."

"So that you won't rape me as the Old Man would?"

"Don't be stupid. I would never—" He broke off and chuckled. "Very clever. Strike where you know there is no armor."

She didn't feel clever, she felt desperate and afraid, but the darkness around him was lessening a little. "It's hard for me to lie here. I don't like to touch people."

"It makes you uneasy to lower your guard."

Were the muscles of his body loosening? He seemed less stiff and resisting. "See, I told you that you knew me. You don't touch people either." She amended, "Except when you rut with the women at Dundragon, and that doesn't count."

"You knew about that?"

She ignored the question. "All men rut, but lust is different from affection. Affection makes one hurt when people go away. My mother went away, and now Thea is going too."

"Thea would never leave you."

"But she'll never belong to me in the same way again. You'll probably go away too, but I won't have you go like this. There's no reason why you can't stay with me now." She paused. "Is there?"

She held her breath, waiting.

He did not reply.

She tried to keep the panic from her voice. "Answer me."

His hand hovered over her hair like the delicate brush of the wings of a butterfly, scarcely a touch at all.

"You're not going to give up, are you?"

"No."

"You'd really be much better off without me, you know."

She was almost limp with relief. He was *hers*.

He sat up and gathered her in his arms. "And I'd be much better off with a few hours' rest." He stood up and carried her to the bed. He covered her with the blanket with great care and stood looking down at her. "Will you go to sleep now?"

"Of course. Do you think I'd lie awake and dwell on this nonsense if there was no need?"

He chuckled. "Not you, Selene." His smile faded. "What would you have done if I hadn't decided—"

"Anything," she answered simply. "My first thought was to hit you on the head, sling you over your horse, and ride out of here."

He said solemnly, "How fortunate for me that you didn't have to resort to such measures."

"I thought so too." She closed her eyes. "And I don't want to worry anymore about your going to Kemal's camp. Think of something else."

"Yes, my lady."

She yawned. "And we must find a way to retrieve those boxes of embroidery from the grove."

"Anything else?"

"Yes." She said haltingly, "It seems fitting that you hold my hand until I go to sleep . . . if you don't mind. Only for tonight, you understand."

"I don't mind." He sat down on the bed. "I agree. It's entirely fitting."

His hand enfolded hers. Comfort. Warmth. Safety. She could feel him hovering over her, extending his protection like the dark wings of a falcon.

A falcon. She fought off slumber long enough to murmur, "Eleanor and Henry. We'll have to get your falcons. . . ."

Dawn poured through the narrow window, painting a strip of brilliant light on the coverlet.

Kadar shifted a few inches on the bed to block it from Selene's face. The child was sleeping deeply, trustingly, her hand holding his even in slumber, refusing to let him go.

So much fire and determination. He had never dreamed anyone would ever care enough to venture into the darkness to pull him into the light. He felt bewildered and awkward and filled with a strange sense of wonder.

And a stranger sense of grace.

"Selene informs me that my way of ridding ourselves of Kemal is without merit," Kadar said when Ware opened the door to his knock. "It seems we will have to decide on a new plan of action." His gaze went beyond Ware to Thea, who was clutching the blankets to her breasts. "Good afternoon, Thea. You look very . . . rested."

Heat flushed her cheeks. "Where is Selene?"

"Still sleeping. She had a troubled night." He entered the chamber. "Put on your tunic, Ware. We must talk, and it's clear Thea is not comfortable with your nakedness."

Ware bent down, retrieved the garment from the floor, and pulled it over his head. "What plan?"

Kadar dropped down into the chair and stretched his legs out before him. "I hoped you would have an idea. After all, you're the warrior. Whatever it is, it must be soon. Sinan may lose patience, since I've chosen not to amuse him any longer. He's most unpredictable when he doesn't get what he wants."

"How much time do we have?"

"I can stave him off a few days, perhaps."

"Will you be safe long enough for me to bring Abdul and my troops here from the border?"

Kadar tilted his head, considering. "Three days there, three days back. It's possible."

"Don't tell me it's possible. I have to know."

"I can do it." His lips curved ruefully. "Though Selene may not be pleased with my methods. You will leave at once?"

"As soon as darkness falls."

"No," Thea said. "I won't have it. How will you get past Kemal?"

"With extreme care," Kadar answered. "One rider might be able to do it if there is a distraction." He shrugged. "And I'll provide the distraction. It should not be difficult. Kemal's men should be very nervous right now." He snapped his fingers. "The death drums. They terrified them before. I'll take a few of Sinan's men and—"

"It's too dangerous." Neither of them were listening to her, she realized. She wrapped the coverlet around herself and stood up. "Even if you get past Kemal, what of the Templars? The whole countryside may be a battleground by now."

"If it is, we'll be helpless without an army." Ware went to the washstand and splashed water onto his face. "It's our only hope."

"You're too weak. You were lying almost dead a few days ago."

He smiled. "Have I not proved my vigor?"

"Stop crowing like a rooster and listen to me. A ride like that could kill you."

"It was my head, not my body that was hurt. My endurance is not harmed." He crossed to stand before her. "Now, stop arguing and think. I'm a warrior. I can do this. My men will follow only me into battle, so I'm the only one who can do it. You know it."

She did not want him to be right, but she could not deny it. "I don't want—" She stopped and then said fiercely, "You will come back to me. And it won't be with your stupid head crunched or a sword through your belly. Do you hear?"

"I hear you." He tenderly brushed her cheek with his hand. "Did you ever hear such sweet words of parting, Kadar?"

"I've said all the sweet words you'll hear from me until you return." She had to steady her voice. "And this is the last time I'll be put aside. Next time you go into battle, I go with you."

"When we reach Scotland," he promised. He brushed her cheek with his lips. "I'll do the embroidering and you can wage war. You see, I'm jesting, and you're the one who isn't smiling."

"This is not funny." She gazed at him, outraged as she saw the eagerness in his expression. "You *like* this. You want to go."

"What can I say? I am what I am. I'm tired of being helpless and glad to have something to do that may help us." He turned away. "Come, Kadar, we must make sure my horse has rested enough to be able to make the journey."

"You can switch horses when you reach the camp." Kadar gave Thea a wary glance as he stood and followed Ware.

Ware had already forgotten her. No, not forgotten, but put her aside, she realized. Last night the power had been hers, but now he was in control.

And would she have really wanted it any other way? She wanted a strong man, not one who could be ruled by her.

Well, perhaps a man *sometimes* ruled by her. It would not hurt to take turns.

She just wished his turn had not come in a fashion that would put him in danger and make her feel this helpless.

But she was not helpless, and she would not accept that niggardly farewell. She dropped the cover and moved toward the washstand. She would dress and go to the stables and garner every bit of his company she could before he left Maysef.

"If I don't return, you'll take Thea and Selene to Damascus and arrange passage to Scotland. I look to you to protect her." Ware tightened the cinch. "Pay no attention if she protests. She'll be safer there."

"It's difficult not to pay attention when Thea protests." He watched Ware strap a water skin and packet of rations to the saddle. "I was surprised she had agreed to go with you. Selene was right, Thea must be truly enslaved by your charms."

Ware winced. "Don't mention enslavement. I fear I'll suffer the rest of my life for El Sunan." He stepped away from the horse. "How will you distract Kemal?"

"The camp will still be awake, so I cannot rely on action. I'll have to depend on fear." He smiled. "Fear can be a terrible weapon. Sinan uses it almost as frequently as poison."

Ware fixed him with a probing stare. "We heard footsteps last night. I told Thea it was probably a guard, but I know your step well. You went to Kemal's camp."

"Did I?"

"I want your promise you'll not go again while I'm gone. The risk is too great."

"The risk grew less with every visit."

"You cannot kill all of them."

He shrugged. "I won't give you my promise. I'll do what is necessary to protect us while you're gone." He grimaced. "Even if I break my vow to Selene."

It was the second time he had mentioned Selene. "What does Selene have to do with this? She's only a child."

Kadar chuckled. "Ah, but she's a child who owns me. And I know my duty far better than you in such a situation."

"She saved your life?"

"No, something far more valuable." Kadar's gaze went beyond Ware's shoulder. "Here is Thea to bid you goodbye. I'll leave you alone. I must go make arrangements for our 'distraction.' "

Ware turned and watched Thea striding toward him, bold, fair, purposeful. "I would have gone back to say farewell."

"She's not one to wait."

No, she wasn't. She would always grasp the moment and make it her own. As she had made him her own, thank God. Last night still seemed a miracle to him. He forced himself to look away from her and returned to the odd comment Kadar had made regarding Selene. "But what could be more valuable than the saving of a life?"

Kadar smiled over his shoulder. "Why, a soul, my friend. What else?"

Chapter Seventeen

IT WAS NEARLY MIDNIGHT when Kadar rode into the courtyard.

Thea's gaze desperately searched his face, but the shadows made it impossible to read. "He got through?"

She went limp with relief when Kadar nodded.

He lifted a brow. "Did you expect anything else?"

"You're sure he's safely away?"

"I assure you, they didn't even realize he'd slipped past them. They were too terrified by the drums." He got down from his horse. "It was most enjoyable to see Kemal dashing about trying to pour some backbone into them."

"You have a strange idea of enjoyment."

"That's been brought to my attention. Let me escort you back to your chamber. You should not be here. I told you it wasn't safe for you to wander freely in this fortress."

He took her arm and strolled with her toward the steps. "Truly, Kemal will not harm Ware."

"I notice you don't mention Vaden."

"There's been no sign of Vaden. Perhaps he died at Acre."

Thea couldn't believe Vaden was no longer a threat. He had been too long a part of Ware's life. "I don't think so."

"Well, don't worry about something you can do nothing about. Ware will have to confront Vaden at some time."

And by creating the banner she had made sure that time would come sooner, Thea thought. It made no difference that the design's resemblance to the lion throne had been unintentional; the effect was the same. "It's my fault."

"Nonsense. You know that's ridiculous. The Knights Templar had marked Ware for death long before you came."

"But the banner will serve to remind them of the urgency of killing him," she said bitterly. "You cannot deny that truth."

"No, the banner has certainly stirred a hornet's nest."

"And will continue to do so as long as it exists." Kemal had almost killed Ware and would not now be camped in the foothills waiting to pounce if his courage hadn't been bolstered by his belief in the banner. "It must be destroyed."

Kadar shook his head. "Not unless you burn it in full view of Kemal *and* the Knights Templar. If it disappears, they'd merely think you'd secreted it away. It would become legend and therefore infinitely more valuable."

She had not thought about that possibility, she realized

in exasperation. "There must be some solution. After we leave this land, we won't need to fear Kemal. Maybe if I sent the banner to the Knights Templar for them to destroy, it would ease their pursuit."

"Before you make any more plans to destroy it, may I remind you that you no longer have possession of the banner?"

"Then I must get it back. I'll not have Ware put in more danger by a banner I created."

"Am I to assume that I'm to be involved in this retrieval?" He shook his head. "Did you think I'd not considered stealing the banner and pricking the bubble of Kemal's courage? The banner is kept in a chest in Kemal's tent, and the tent is very well guarded. You'll have to wait for Ware to return with his army."

"Ware will *not* go to battle Kemal while he still has the banner." The words tumbled unbidden and without thought from her lips.

"Ah, I see." Kadar smiled. "You believe the banner does have power."

"I didn't say that. Of course it doesn't. I should know. I made it. It's just that—" She stopped as she realized the words were coming jerkily. She steadied her voice. "Maybe Kemal will fight fiercer if he has the banner. I'll not take the chance."

"And I'll not take the chance of losing my head or leaving you and Selene unprotected for the sake of a scrap of silk. We'll wait for Ware."

"I didn't ask you to go after it. The banner is my responsibility. I may need your help, but I'm the one who will go to Kemal."

Kadar muttered an exclamation. "And then Ware will cut my throat, instead of leaving it to Kemal. What do you intend to do? Just walk in and ask him for it?"

"You need not be sarcastic." She paused before saying with effort, "If Kemal must die, I'll do it."

"Easily said, not easily done. Taking a life diminishes the taker."

She gave him a cool glance. "You've killed and you do not appear diminished."

"Because I'm extraordinary?" He raised a brow. "But then how do you know what heights I'd reached before I was diminished?"

She ignored his mockery. "I won't kill unless it becomes necessary, but I won't let Kemal face Ware again."

"Ware could squash him without effort. If he hadn't been weakened and off guard, Kemal would never have got near him." Kadar studied her expression. "It's not Kemal but the banner you fear, isn't it?"

"I told you the banner has no power." They had reached her chamber and she quickly opened the door. "Will you know when Ware approaches?"

He nodded. "Sinan knows when a camel sneezes as far away as Damascus."

"And you'll go to Kemal's camp to help Ware. I'll go with you. Just before Ware attacks should be a good opportunity to go to Kemal's tent. When the sentry sounds the alert, the guards at his tent will be distracted by the uproar."

"And Kemal will be awake and reaching for his sword... and the banner," Kadar said. "It's not a good plan. Let Ware defeat Kemal, and the banner will be easy to pluck from—"

"Let me know when you hear of Ware's approach," Thea interrupted. She had made her decision. "I'll be waiting."

"I have no doubt." Kadar sighed as he turned away. "I'll go tell Selene all is well. Will you sup with us?"

Thea nodded impatiently. She did not want to be alone. "I'll join you after I refresh myself." She entered the chamber and closed the door.

The chamber echoed with emptiness. Ware was gone.

She sank back against the door, fighting off an overwhelming sense of panic. Ware would return. God would surely not have brought them through all these trials if He had meant to tear them apart. The God who had saved Ware would not let him die now. It would make no sense.

Keep busy. She moved quickly to the washbasin and poured water from the pitcher into the bowl. Keep busy doing what? She had no embroidery, and Kadar would confine her more here than she'd been at El Sunan. She would find something. She would probably spend much of her time watching Kadar and have Selene watch him also. She knew he would not tell her when Ware was coming. Like all men, he'd choose protectiveness over fairness. He didn't understand why she couldn't let Ware fight this battle for her.

Dear God, she wished she could. The thought of going to Kemal's tent for the banner sent a chill through her.

But the thought of Kemal retaining control of the banner when he faced Ware again terrified her more. The terror might be without reason, but she could not hold it at bay. This love was too new and fragile; she could not take any risks with it.

Golden eyes searing her with their power.

She swiftly blocked the vision as she bent over the washbowl and dipped her hands into the water. She was mad enough to risk her life to retrieve the banner; she would not addle her mind by dwelling on it.

Golden eyes . . .

"Kadar's gone. He just left." Selene stood in the doorway of Thea's chamber, a pale shadow in the darkness. "I think Ware must be coming. A messenger came to the door a short time ago."

Only five days had passed since Ware had left, but Thea had known the message would come soon. She jumped from the bed. "Your clothes?"

"I brought them." She sat on the bed and watched disapprovingly as Thea hurriedly dressed in Selene's boyish garb, donned the cloak, and tucked her hair under the turban. "I should be the one to go. You'll bungle it and Kemal will kill you. You're not good at things like this."

Who was good? Thea wondered desperately. Who could creep into a tent and steal from a man who wanted to kill you? Kadar, perhaps, but he had already told her that not waiting for Ware would be foolish. "I'll be careful."

"Let me go with you."

"We've already talked about this. You have to stay. Sinan will know when I leave the fortress. As long as one of us stays here, he'll know that we'll return. We don't want him to interfere when the battle starts." She moved toward the door. "Lock yourself in your room until I come back."

"Wait." Selene held out a glittering object. "You should have this."

A dagger. Slender, shimmering, strangely beautiful in its deadliness.

"Where did you get that?"

"Kadar. He left it on the bedside table. That's why I know Lord Ware has come. He wouldn't go into battle without leaving me a way to defend myself in case he didn't return." She said fiercely, "And he knows I would use it. Will you?"

Thea stared at the dagger with repulsion. Then she drew a deep breath, snatched the weapon, and thrust it into her waistband. "Yes."

She whirled and ran from the room.

Moments later she was riding through the gates and down the mountain. She could see the pinpoints of Kemal's campfires in the foothills below. Dear God, what if Ware reached Kemal before she did? She spurred her horse to a gallop.

She reined in a good distance from the camp, slipped from the saddle, and tied her horse to a tree.

She tilted her head, listening. Surely she would hear the hoofbeats of Ware's approaching army. Nothing. She still had time.

She ran down the hill, her gaze fixed on the large tent at the south of the camp. It was lit within, but she could see no movement. Did Kemal sleep with a lantern burning to protect him? It wouldn't surprise her, since his men were being killed one by one under his nose. She stopped to catch her breath as she drew near the clearing.

Two guards in front of the tent. Two in the rear.

But the side facing her was unguarded. Her hand tightened on the hilt of the dagger. She prayed that she had to use it only to slit an opening in the tent.

She dropped to the ground and started crawling slowly out of the underbrush toward the tent.

Golden eyes, waiting . . .

Only a few feet more.

She froze. One of the guards had spoken.

No threat. They were laughing, talking casually.

She started crawling again.

She reached the tent and drew a deep breath. Her heart was beating so hard, it was shaking her entire body.

No, she realized in panic. It was the vibration shaking her. She couldn't hear the hoofbeats yet, but she could feel them. Ware was coming.

But he was not there yet. Just a few minutes more.

She sliced through the fabric of the tent.

Don't let them hear it.

Please.

She carefully drew back the torn flap and looked inside. The lantern hanging in the center of the tent provided little light; most of the tent was in shadows.

Kemal was lying on cushions facing her only a few yards away.

Shock made her go rigid. Was he awake?

He didn't move or call out. He must be asleep.

Her glance flicked around the tent. There it was.

The carved chest bound elaborately in brass. She had seen Kemal take the banner out of that chest many times.

She braced herself and slowly wriggled through the opening. She lay beside Kemal.

The vibration was heavier, shaking the pillows on which Kemal lay.

He would wake, she thought in agony.

He was moving. He suddenly rolled on top of her!

The impact made her drop the dagger. She struggled desperately, fighting against his weight, finally squirming out from under him. On her feet, she reached for the dagger and glared down at him.

Kemal was dead.

Rigid with shock, she stared into the sightless eyes.

A ripple of blood was seeping from the wound in his chest. Blood everywhere. On him, on her.

She could feel the sticky dampness on her face and hands.

She shuddered, unable to look away from those dead eyes.

Kadar?

A shout outside the tent broke the spell. Ware had been sighted. If she was found here when they came to summon Kemal, she would be butchered. She ran to the carved chest and threw open the lid.

No banner.

It had to be here. She knelt and rummaged desperately beneath the armor. The banner was gone.

Another shout.

Kadar must have taken it. There was no other explanation.

The clash of sword on sword.

She could not stay here. She dashed toward the slit she had made in the tent wall.

"Aiii!"

She glanced over her shoulder. One of Kemal's guards stood in the doorway of the tent.

She stopped, frozen.

She expected him to rush her, sword drawn.

He stood staring at her with the same horror as she stared at him.

She suddenly realized how terrifying she must look covered in Kemal's blood.

"Assassin," he screamed. He turned and ran from the tent. "Devil murderer!"

He thought she was one of Sinan's followers. Kadar had clearly done his work of terror well if the guard preferred to face Ware's soldiers than to face her.

But that didn't mean the next soldier who came into the tent would be as cowardly. She dived through the slit in the wall of the tent and wriggled outside.

A horseman thundered toward her.

She rolled to one side and barely escaped the horse's hooves.

By the saints, if she wasn't killed by Kemal's men, she would be lucky not to be killed by Ware's soldiers.

The encampment was a melee of fighting men. Moonlight shimmered on drawn swords.

"For God's sake, put that dagger away."

Ware!

He leaned down and gathered her up on his horse. "Are you hurt?"

Ware. Strong and blessedly safe.

"You're covered in blood. Answer me."

"I'm not hurt."

He rode his horse to the edge of the encampment. "I'm going to kill Kadar." He tore the turban from her head and her hair tumbled free. "Don't put it back on. Being a woman may be your only protection. Hide behind that rock and don't let anyone see you with a weapon in your hand."

He wheeled his horse and went back into the fray.

Her hands clenched at her sides as she watched the battle. It was terrible to be forced to stand on the sidelines and feel so helpless. A woman should be taught the same skills as warriors.

However, Ware did not seem to need her help. Kemal's followers were outnumbered and outfought. It was only a short time later that Kemal's men capitulated.

Ware rode toward her. "Will you never obey me? Would it have hurt you to hide?"

"Kemal is dead."

"You're sure?"

She nodded. "I saw him. And the banner is gone. I think Kadar did it. Where is he?"

He gestured. "I caught sight of him on the other side of the camp as I rode in."

She started in the direction he'd indicated. "I have to go ask him if—"

"Oh, no." He scooped her up and set her before him. "I won't have you running around in an armed camp. We'll let him find us."

"But I need to know—" She stopped and leaned back against him. No urgency existed now, and it was good to be held like this. "I'll ask him later."

"And I have questions to ask of you," he said grimly. "What are you doing here?"

"I came for the banner."

"My God."

"And I'll hear no harsh words from you. You didn't ask

my permission when you risked your life. I did what I thought necessary. Now, finish what you have to do here and take me back to Maysef. I didn't like leaving Selene alone in that place." She lowered her voice. "And I would be alone with you so that I can express my affection without the witness of an entire army."

"Affection? I've seen no signs of affection." Nevertheless, his arms tightened around her as he rode back into the center of the confusion. The next few minutes he devoted to giving orders regarding the securing of prisoners and receiving reports on the wounded.

"You look as if you've been fighting hand to hand, Thea," Kadar said as he rode toward them. "May I say you don't look at all well bathed in blood?" Then he added, "I suppose I should have known you'd follow me."

"If you knew it, why didn't you stop her?" Ware asked grimly.

"One can only do so much." Kadar changed the subject. "What do we do with the prisoners?"

"Take their horses and set them free," Ware said. "With Kemal dead they'll give us no trouble."

"Kemal is dead?"

Thea could see no sign of anything but surprise in Kadar's expression. But, then, Kadar was expert at disguising his emotions. "And the banner is gone," she said. "I thought you had killed him."

Kadar shook his head. "Perhaps one of his men grew impatient with his stubbornness in remaining here and decided to save his life and take Kemal's." He smiled teasingly. "Or it could be that your banner grew weary of being used by such an unpleasant man and worked its magic on him."

She met his gaze. "Or it could be that you don't wish to

get into Selene's bad graces if she finds out you broke your word to her."

"Yes, that's a possibility also." He gazed at her innocently. "We shall never know, shall we? Unless we discover the banner in one of the prisoner's possession." He turned to Ware. "I feel obligated to clear my name of this crime by conducting the search myself."

And so be in a position to make sure the banner is conveniently discovered, Thea thought.

"It doesn't matter who killed Kemal," Ware said impatiently. "We have to go back to Maysef and get Selene. We need to leave this place by dawn tomorrow. I barely avoided one of Saladin's troops on the way here. Every minute we waste makes the journey more dangerous."

"If Sinan decides he wishes us to go," Kadar said. "He may be quite peevish that we've robbed him of his amusement at watching us kill each other."

Dear heaven, she was weary of facing a new danger every time she turned around. "Will you be able to convince him?"

He shrugged. "Perhaps Sinan can be persuaded that our leaving will be to his advantage, but it may require a bargain Selene has forbidden me." He changed the subject. "Don't take your soldiers to Maysef. Sinan would make sure they never entered any gates but those of hell."

"I had every intention of leaving them camped here," Ware said. "We may need rescue."

"Pray that we don't require rescue. I assure you the soldiers would be no help." Kadar turned his horse. "I'll go ahead and talk to Sinan. Give me a few hours alone with him."

* * *

Sinan stood waiting on the steps as Kadar rode into the courtyard. Kadar was reminded of the night he had first come to the fortress.

He rode up to the steps and stopped before Sinan.

"You know why I'm here. We've removed Kemal from our path. Is it your will that we leave?"

"It is not my will. You know what I wish of you."

"I cannot walk your path."

"You're wrong, no one can walk it better. You just will not." Sinan said harshly, "These foreigners have swayed you with their soft words. I will not have it."

"When have I ever been swayed by a will other than my own?" He paused. "Even yours, Sinan. Is that not why you wish me to stay?"

"You will stay."

"Only in death."

A flicker of expression crossed Sinan's face. "You will yield before I have to kill you. You embrace life with too much pleasure."

"But the first lesson you teach is that death is never to be feared. Not our own and not the ones we cause. You say I'm a reflection of you. When you look into your mirror, do you see a fear of death?"

Sinan's gaze held his. "You mean this," he said slowly.

"I mean it." He smiled. "But death should never be wasted. Particularly of one you value. So why not make me pay a price of passage and let us go?"

"A price of passage," Sinan repeated slowly.

Kadar was careful to keep any hint of fear from his thoughts or expression. Sinan fed on fear, and Kadar had seen many instances of the Old Man's uncanny perception.

"Get down. We will talk about it." Sinan turned on his heel and started up the steps. He glanced back over his shoulder, and his smile breathed of malice. "On consideration, there may be a price only you can pay."

The courtyard was deserted except for the usual white-robed guards.

"I don't like this," Thea said uneasily. She had felt sure Kadar would meet them when they rode through the gates. He had known they would be anxious regarding his interview with Sinan. She got down from her horse and moved toward the watering trough. Anxious or not, she must wash the blood from her face and hands before Selene saw her. "Where could he be?"

"In the stable." Kadar smiled as he strolled toward them across the courtyard. "I was helping Selene saddle her horse. I decided we should not wait until dawn to ride out of this hospitable place. It's always more pleasant to travel in the cool of the evening."

"Your talk did not go well?" Ware asked.

"If it hadn't gone well, we would not be alive at this happy moment. I just wish to be gone from here before Sinan decides to ask more of me."

"What did he ask?"

"Enough." Kadar changed the subject. "But I fared better in our bargain than I thought possible. How fortunate that you have such a brilliant negotiator in me. We not only have our freedom, but a ship and a crew to sail it."

"What?"

"I see you understand the importance of such a coup. No one who is not mad would try to seize a ship belonging to the Old Man of the Mountain. Sinan is sending a message to Hafir, to Ali Balkir, the captain of the *Dark Star*, requesting that he place himself at your disposal. He will take us to Scotland and then return to report to Sinan."

"Report what?" Thea asked.

"Where he left us." He held up his hand as Ware started to protest. "Don't worry, no torture would ever make Sinan's followers reveal something he didn't want them to tell."

"But Sinan would know."

"You fear he'll tell the Knights Templar?" He shook his head. "Why should he? He hates them. He wants to know only where he can put his hand on me if I fail in the task to which he set me."

"And what task—"

"It's better you do not know." Kadar's tone became flippant. "I should think you'd have learned by now how dangerous other people's secrets can be."

"You do this for us," Ware said. "That makes it my secret."

"It's no use questioning him," Selene said as she led Kadar's and her own horse out of the stable. "He's probably promised Sinan some foul or impossible deed, but he won't tell." She added grimly, "Right now."

But Selene's chances of extracting that information from Kadar were better than anyone else's, Thea thought.

"May we leave now and discuss my concerns later?" Kadar swung into the saddle. "We need to be gone from here. Your army should be out of the foothills by evening if we don't wish to make Sinan impatient."

"A ship," Ware murmured. "An entire ship." His brow was furrowed in thought as he rode after Kadar through the gates. "It could be . . ."

"What is it? What are you thinking?" Thea asked.

"Dundragon." Excitement illuminated his face. "I was worried about my people there. I planned on sending Abdul and the army back with orders to distribute money and find a place for them. But now I don't have to do that. I can take them to Scotland with me, can't I?"

She should have known, Thea thought, her throat tightening with emotion. Ware would never abandon any burden he had willingly assumed. He would protect his world even if he had to take it with him. "Yes, you can bring them." She swallowed and tried to steady her voice. "Providing they wish to come. You can't just whisk them on board the ship. Abdul will have to give each person a choice."

Ware frowned. "It wouldn't be safe to tell them where we go."

"No, so they must make the choice blindly. They may decide to stay here, where all is familiar." She could see he was about to rebel. "I know you wish only to keep them safe, but I'll have no one in this new land who obeys blindly. Only slaves act without free will. They will choose. Do you understand?"

She didn't think he was going to agree, but then he nodded jerkily.

She breathed a sigh of relief.

They had almost reached the camp when he murmured,

"But I'll tell Abdul to make sure they know what a wondrous, free life they'll lead if they go with me."

"How can you promise—" She shook her head and gave up the battle. He was impossible.

An utterly impossible, stubborn, gloriously splendid man.

Chapter Eighteen

WHEN THEY REACHED THE CAMP, Ware moved with speed to divide his army. He sent one division under Abdul's command back to Dundragon, and he took the other under his command. They broke camp and galloped away from Sinan's mountain as the first weak streaks of dawn streamed through the clouds.

"I leave you here," Kadar announced when they were safely out of the Nosarai mountains.

"What?" Ware asked, startled. "You're not going with us to Scotland?"

"Of course I'm going. It's clear you cannot do without me." Kadar put spurs to his horse and said over his shoulder, "I'll join you in eight days' time at Hafir. Don't sail without me."

"But where are you going?" Thea asked.

"I have a task to complete."

"No," Selene shouted after him. "Come back. I won't have it."

Kadar waved. "Eight days."

Ware grabbed Selene's reins as she tried to ride after him. "You can't follow him."

"He's going about that evil man's business," Selene said. "And he does it for us. I'll not let—"

"You can't stop him. Do you think I wouldn't try? He'll only slip away later," Ware said. "Kadar always keeps his promises. He said he'd come back to us."

"He shouldn't do it." Selene's voice was agonized, her gaze on Kadar's rapidly vanishing figure. "You don't understand. It . . . damages him."

"In eight days he'll be with us," Thea said, trying to comfort when there was no comfort to be had. She was as terrified as Selene. "He'll come to Hafir."

If he was still alive.

"What is it?" Thea edged her horse closer to Ware. It was the third time in the past hour he had reined in and looked back over his shoulder. "What's wrong?"

"Nothing."

"Don't tell me nothing. I won't have it."

"Vaden."

She inhaled sharply. "Did you see him?"

He shook his head. "But I *feel* him."

"You set a man to watch our rear. He's not reported any riders."

"He would see an army, he wouldn't see Vaden."

"Then he may not be there. You cannot know."

"I know. He's been watching me so long, sometimes I feel as if he's a part of me."

She moistened her lips. "And what if he is following us? He'd be mad to attack. One man against so large a force. He's never taken a chance before."

"We've never been this close to escaping before. He must know by now that we're heading for Hafir. By tomorrow we'll be under Sinan's jurisdiction again, and even Vaden would have trouble getting to us there." He put spurs to his horse. "I don't think he'll wait. Let's get out of these woods before dark."

Dark was already falling, and in the dimness trees loomed on either side of the path, shadowy ghost figures hovering over them.

Like the shadow that was Vaden.

Thea muttered an imprecation and followed Ware. "Come along, Selene. Hurry."

"What's wrong?" Selene asked as she came abreast of her.

What could she say? A threat that could not be seen, only felt? Yet Thea could not discount the danger when she remembered how Ware had sensed Vaden that day at the mulberry grove. Oh, she didn't know. Perhaps in some mystical way the two men were joined. "I'm not sure. Ware doesn't like these woods."

"I don't either, but it's less rough than those mountain trails." Selene stood in her stirrups and peered ahead. "I think the forest ends a little after we cross that stream. It's difficult to tell with all these shadows, but I don't see any more trees."

Ware was already slowly crossing the shallow stream, his gaze searching the shadows on either bank.

He reached the other side of the stream and waved at them to cross.

They were almost at the other bank when fire arched out of the heavens toward them.

"Christ!"

Thea barely heard Ware's exclamation as she saw the burning arrow speeding toward her.

No, not toward her. The burning arrow struck the water in back of her.

The ribbon of water exploded into a wall of flame!

"Dammit, get out of the stream, Thea." Ware's voice.

Selene was directly in front of her. Couldn't he see she couldn't move until Selene reached the other bank?

She could hear the soldiers shouting, horses neighing in terror on the bank behind her. She glanced back to see that they were cut off by the wall of flame licking down the stream. As she watched, the fire leaped up onto the bank, catching bushes, moss, and piles of dry leaves ablaze.

"Thea." Selene had reached the other bank. Sparks had ignited the trees there. Soon Selene would be surrounded by an inferno.

"Don't wait." Thea desperately nudged her horse forward, but he was rearing, struggling, terrified by the combination of water and flames licking at his hindquarters. "Go ahead. Get out of the trees."

Selene did not move.

"Go!" Ware's hand came down hard on the rump of Selene's horse and set him tearing through the blazing trees toward the clearing. Then he was riding back into the blazing stream.

"No, you have to go too. The fire is—"

"Be silent," he said harshly. "Do you think I'll lose you

now?" He grabbed her horse's reins and with sheer might jerked the beast's head down. He wheeled his horse and started across the stream. "Hold tight and kick him—hard."

She obeyed and then clung desperately as Ware half dragged, half pulled the horse through the water.

Fire.

All around them.

Devouring trees and bushes like a hungry monster.

So fast. How could it spread so fast?

Curls of black smoke before them and behind them.

Searing their lungs, stinging their eyes.

She could only pray that Selene had made it through the woods in time.

They reached the shallows and the horses struggled up the bank.

She realized with despair that she could no longer see the clearing through the dense smoke.

"Take a deep breath and hold it." Ware's hand tightened on her horse's reins. "We're going through."

The acrid breath she drew hurt her lungs, but she had no time to think of pain.

Smoke.

Black as the deepest reaches of hell.

Heat.

She closed her eyes as tears streamed down her cheeks from her stinging eyes.

She couldn't hold her breath any longer. It rushed out and she was forced to inhale. She was immediately punished by a fit of coughing.

She couldn't breathe. Panic rushed through her as she began to gasp.

Ware was coughing too.

Dear God, they were going to die in this blackness.

"Thea!"

Selene. Thea opened her eyes and could see nothing. But she had heard Selene's voice just ahead. She must not be caught in this hideous trap. "Don't come back. Don't—" She broke off as she began coughing again.

"It's all—right," Ware gasped. "We're—through."

How could he say that? The smoke . . .

No, it was lighter, a thick gray fog instead of a black wall.

The sky, she could see the sky. Cool, twilight purple and glittering icy stars. "Thank God."

The horses sensed salvation too. They streaked toward the edge of the forest.

They reined in as they reached the plain, and Ware slipped from his horse. He was still coughing as he lifted Thea down and reached for his water skin. "Drink." He handed it to her. "Slowly."

She was coughing so hard, she couldn't swallow. She finally managed a small drink. Gentle balm on her tight, dry throat. She handed him back the water skin, and he carefully sipped the water. His face was so smoke blackened, he looked like a Nubian, she noticed wearily. She probably looked the same. "But where's Selene? I heard her just ahead."

"We'll find her." He drew his sword. "He doesn't want Selene."

She stared at him.

"It was Vaden's arrow. Water doesn't catch fire by itself. He poured oil on the stream."

The arrow. She had not thought beyond surviving the

fire, but now the threat of Vaden returned. "He wanted to kill us with the fire?"

"Don't be foolish. I merely wanted to separate you from the others. I knew Ware would manage to get you through the blaze."

She whirled at the unfamiliar male voice.

A man in armor was strolling out of the forest, sword drawn. Selene was walking before him, fingers clenched.

"Vaden," Ware murmured.

Vaden's face was as soot blackened as Ware's, and he looked like a devil from the hell they had just come through. But his sword was from this world and poised only inches from Selene's back.

Thea took a step forward and said fiercely, "Let her go."

"He jerked me from the saddle just as I reached the plain." Selene glared at Vaden over her shoulder. "I wasn't expecting him."

"Even so, I had trouble subduing her," Vaden said. "In the smoke I had no idea she was the child. I thought she was your lady, Ware."

"Get away from her," Thea said. "If you want a hostage, take me."

"Unfortunately, I *will* have to take you. You've given me no choice." He added regretfully to Ware, "You should never have described the throne to her. I was hoping to find some way to spare her."

"I didn't, dammit. The design on the banner was just coincidence."

Vaden lifted a brow in disbelief.

"I tell you, I didn't lie to you."

Vaden shrugged. "It doesn't matter anymore. It's gone on too long. It has to be finished."

"Or you'll kill Selene?" Thea asked. "She's only a child."

"He won't do it," Ware said.

"No? I watched many children being killed at Acre only a short time ago. No one saw me flinch."

"You witnessed the massacre?"

His lips curled. "Oh, yes, from the best vantage point by the side of the Grand Master."

Terror tore through Thea as she thought of the callousness it would take to watch the killing of twenty-seven hundred souls.

"Good," Ware said.

Thea turned to stare at him in astonishment. His expression as he looked at Vaden was filled with eagerness and some other emotion she could not define.

"I assure you there was little good at Acre that day." Vaden gestured to the sword in Ware's hand. "I'll give you a chance. Come forward and do battle."

Ware didn't move. He said softly, "It was like Jedha, wasn't it? All those helpless and innocent dying."

"The helpless and innocent always die, only the strong survive. We both know that. Come forward and do battle." He smiled. "Who knows? You may kill me and live."

Ware still didn't move, his gaze searching Vaden's face. He slowly shook his head. "Battle would be too easy for you. The blood runs hot and makes it hard to reason. That's what you want, isn't it?"

"The time for thinking is over." Vaden's hand tightened on his sword.

"Yes, but realization has just begun." Ware threw away his sword.

"What are you doing?" Vaden said harshly.

Ware walked toward him, unarmed.

What in heaven was he about? Thea thought desperately.

"Step away from him, Selene," Ware said.

"I will not. What foolishness is—" Selene broke off as Vaden swept her aside with one swing of his arm. Then he took an eager step forward.

"You wish to kill yourself? Then come ahead, Ware."

"No, I wish to save myself. Life has never been sweeter."

"Then pick up your sword, goddammit."

Ware took off his helmet and dropped it onto the ground. "You see, I'm making it easy for you, Vaden. Just as I did once before."

"There were reasons why I didn't take your life then. They don't exist now."

"I think they do." He fell to his knees before Vaden and jerked his mail down to bare his throat. "Strike now. One clean blow should do it."

"Stand up and get your sword," Vaden said between his teeth.

"Were they forced to kneel at Acre?"

"Stand up."

"I told you that you couldn't do it."

"I *can* do it."

"Then one clean blow."

Vaden raised his sword.

"No!" Thea started toward them.

"Stop, Thea." Ware's gaze held Vaden's. "This isn't your concern. You couldn't reach me before his sword anyway."

"*You're* my concern." But he was right, she realized in despair, and her interference might hasten the blow. "I'll kill you myself if you hurt him, Vaden."

Ware ignored her. "Strike, Vaden."

Vaden's blackened features were twisted. Thea had never seen a wilder or deadlier visage. His hand tightened on the hilt of the sword.

The blade sliced through the air.

It passed by Ware's head by no more than an inch.

"Goddamn you." Vaden hurled the sword to the side. "May you burn in hell."

"If I do, I won't be sent there by your hand."

"Don't be too sure. A momentary weakness."

"A realization." Ware rose to his feet. "It comes to all of us."

"Because I'm choking on blood after Acre?"

"Because you realize I'm your friend and you love me," he said simply.

Vaden stared at him. "Christ, what a fool you are."

"I was a fool," Ware said. "I always thought you were a threat. I didn't understand that you were there protecting me."

"Protecting you?" Vaden repeated, stunned. "You're truly a madman."

"No, you always stood between me and the rest. Even if you didn't realize it. Think about it."

"I won't think about it. It's not true."

"Then pick up the sword and kill me."

Vaden glared at him. "This softness won't last. I'll come after you again."

"I'll welcome you," Ware said. "As friend to friend."

The sound that came from Vaden's throat was the frustrated growl of a tiger robbed of its prey. He turned on his heel and strode back toward the forest.

For the first time in the encounter Thea drew a deep breath.

Vaden rode a white stallion out of the woods a moment later. "Hand me my sword."

Ware reached down and handed him the weapon hilt first. He stood looking up at him, the blade of the sword between them.

Thea stiffened as she saw Vaden's hand open and close yearningly on the hilt.

"A fool like you doesn't deserve to live," he said. "Fortune blessed you today, Ware."

"A good friend is always a blessing."

Vaden shook his head incredulously. He put spurs to his horse and started to ride away. He had gone only a short distance when he reined in, wheeled his horse, and galloped back. Before they knew what he was doing, he had gathered the reins of Ware's horse, then Thea's.

"What are you doing?" Ware called, startled.

"You can't expect fortune to give you all its bounty. You made me very angry. It will be pleasant to think of the two of you walking the rest of the way to Hafir." He smiled maliciously. "I'd walk very fast, if I were you. A troop of Knights Templar cannot be more than a day's ride behind you on the trail."

He was gone in a flurry of dust.

Thea watched him tear across the plain in bemusement.

"I was stupid," Selene said in self-disgust. "It's all my fault. I made you lose the horses."

"It could have been worse." Thea suddenly realized what an understatement that was and began to chuckle. "Oh, yes, it could have been much worse." She turned to Ware. "Do we start to walk or wait until the fire dies out?"

"What?" His tone was absent. "Oh, we wait. I don't want to risk being caught in the open. The fires on the other bank were minor. He torched only this side of the stream. It should burn out before dawn, and the men should be able to cross."

She frowned. "He shouldn't have killed those trees."

"Better the trees than us," Selene said. "The fire is drawing closer. I'll go get my horse before the flames do." She moved toward the edge of trees and then stopped. "No, it's your horse now, Thea. I shouldn't be allowed to keep it when I made you lose yours."

Selene had to be feeling exceedingly guilty to sacrifice her horse. "I'm sure that Ware can persuade one of his men to lend me a mount."

Selene's expression brightened. "Oh, good." She still hesitated before saying haltingly, "I would appreciate it if you would say nothing to Kadar about my stupidity."

"You were surprised. It wasn't—"

"It was *stupid*."

It was clear Selene was not accepting words of comfort. "Ware and I won't mention it to him."

Selene muttered as she strode away, "Not that I should care if he thinks me foolish when he's idiot enough to wander away into Lord knows what danger."

Thea turned to see that Vaden was almost out of sight. "You were so certain he wouldn't kill you?" she asked Ware.

"No."

She whirled to face him. "Then why did you run the risk?"

"I wasn't sure I could best him in battle. If he'd killed me, he would have been committed to his course and been forced to kill you too."

"So you put your head under his sword." Her hands

clenched. "I may kill you myself. Vaden was right, you are a fool."

"It was the only way to save us all."

She shivered as she remembered how close that sword had fallen. "Was he really protecting you all these years?"

"I think so." He whispered, his gaze on Vaden, "God, I hope so."

"You risked too much for hope."

He finally turned to face her and smiled. "How can you say that? When it was you who taught me to hope again."

Five days after Thea, Ware, and Selene reached Hafir, the wagons from Dundragon came.

Wagon after wagon, filled with furniture and goods and people, poured into the valley. Behind the wagons walked a stream of more men, women, and children.

Ware gave a low whistle. "We may need another ship."

"What did you expect?" Thea asked. "You see, choice is best. There's little for them here but one kind of slavery or another. They know you will guard and care for them even in a foreign land." As she knew he would care and guard her. "I wonder if—" She broke off when she saw Jasmine walking behind the second wagon. "There she is." She had thought Jasmine would come, but there was always a chance she would stay behind. She ran toward the woman. "Jasmine. I'm so glad you decided to come with us. I was afraid I'd have to send for you later."

"Where else would I be?" Jasmine asked. "But I would rather go to Damascus than on this ship to nowhere. I've never been on the water and I hear it's a fearsome experience."

"Neither have I sailed. But Selene did all the way from Constantinople, and she says it can be quite pleasant when the weather is fine." She looked searchingly beyond Jasmine. "Where's Tasza? Didn't she come?"

"Of course she came. She's lolling behind talking to Abdul. She cannot see or hear anything but him when he's within a mile of her." Jasmine looked down at the ship in the harbor. "Abdul said it belongs to the Old Man of the Mountain. Some of our people are afraid that death clings to it."

"It's safer for us than a ship flying under any other flag." She added gravely, "But I cannot promise safety. I cannot even tell you where we're going until we set sail."

"But we'll still have our house of silk?"

"I'm not sure what the conditions will be for the making of silk." Her lips tightened. "But if we cannot make it, we'll get it from somewhere and I'll still have my house. I'll persuade Ware to settle near the sea. Where there are ships, there can be trade. No one need know where the embroideries come from, and if they're fine enough, people will be too glad to get them to ask questions. We'll find a way."

"Good," Jasmine said. "Now I must go pluck Tasza from Abdul. He has more important things to do than listen to her chatter."

"So we're to settle near the sea," Ware murmured from behind Thea. His hands fell on her shoulders, affectionately kneading them.

"It will be good for you also. It's safer to have a way of escape if we're attacked," Thea said. "You're taking me to this land of mists and mountains. I should be the one to say where we live in it."

He chuckled. "And what we are to do once we get there."

"I'm telling you what *I'm* to do. You may do as you wish as long as the danger is not too great." She leaned back against him. "You must take great care of yourself so that you can protect our son and daughter."

"Daughter? Before, it was only a son."

"I decided I must have a daughter to learn my skills. So you must stay home enough to get me with child at least twice. A son would probably be like you, running about the countryside and making war."

"A hideous prospect."

Warmth rushed through her as she thought of a son with Ware's eyes and great heart. "Not so hideous." She qualified, "If he doesn't have your obstinacy."

His lips brushed her ear. "I believe I can promise to be at your side any time you require me. In fact, you'll have to sweep me out of your presence when I'm not wanted."

She would want him every minute of every day. She wanted to linger there even now when she should be overseeing the unpacking of the wagons. She sighed and stepped out of his arms. "I have to find Selene and have her help me. She needs to keep busy. She's been watching the road for Kadar since we set up camp."

"So have I," Ware said. "Perhaps she's right—maybe I was wrong to let him go."

And was now suffering his usual burden of guilt. "You weren't wrong. What you said was true. Kadar would have found a way to go anyway." She added to comfort herself as well as him, "It's only been five days. He said he would return in eight."

Ware nodded. "He'll keep his word."

* * *

Kadar did not arrive in the next three days.

Nor on the day after.

Selene did not eat or sleep. She did nothing but watch for Kadar and care for his falcons, which Abdul had brought from Dundragon. Thea had tried to keep her busy, but the ship was quickly loaded and ready to depart. Now they could only sit and wait.

At sunset on the tenth day Thea climbed the hill to Ware, who was sitting, watching the road. His face was almost as strained as Selene's, she thought wearily. Her own expression was probably equally drawn. She sat down beside him. "What will we do if he doesn't come?"

"I'll wait another two days and then you'll set sail. I'll go in search of him and we'll join you in Scotland."

She had no intention of setting sail without him, but she would not argue now. "You don't even know where he went."

"Sinan knows."

She closed her eyes. Dear God, she didn't want him to go back to that devil's stronghold. "Is there no other—"

"He's coming!"

Thea's lids flicked open to see Selene running down the hill toward the road. She jumped to her feet.

A rider was on the horizon, a dark silhouette against the setting sun.

"Selene, come back. It may not be—"

"It's Kadar." Selene's shout rang with joy. "Do you think I don't know him?" She had reached the road and was running toward the rider. "It's Kadar!"

Her voice was so certain, Thea's heart leaped with hope. She ran after Ware, who was already striding down the hill.

"Ah, you come to greet me," the rider called. "A fitting welcome for one who has striven ceaselessly on your behalf."

It *was* Kadar.

Selene had already reached him and grabbed the reins. "You're late. You broke your promise. You said eight days."

"I had a few problems discharging my task." He got down from his horse. "And I knew you would wait. It's not often people are gifted with such a splendid individual in their midst. You would have been most depleted by—" He broke off. "Tears, Selene?"

She angrily brushed them from her cheeks. "I always cry when I'm angry. You should have kept your word. You should never have gone."

"But you told me to go." He reached out and touched the child's wet cheeks with exquisite gentleness. "What a beautiful treasure tears can be. I thank you for the gift."

"Are you mad? I didn't tell you to go," Selene said. "I would never have told you to do the bidding of that Old Man. I want to *slap* you."

"But Sinan didn't set me this task. You did." He turned and glanced back the way he had come. "You said you wanted your boxes of embroidered silks. It was not easy. I had to find horses and someone to drive the wagon, and then we had to dodge both Richard's and Saladin's forces on the way here. At one point we had to backtrack and go around—"

"You went after our embroideries?" Thea interrupted, stunned. "You have them?"

"Ali should be in sight any moment— Ah, there he is."

Kadar gestured at the wagon silhouetted against the horizon. "I could not bear the slowness of the wagon, so I hastened ahead to—"

"We thought you went on Sinan's task," Ware said gruffly.

Kadar was genuinely surprised. "Why? I said nothing about Sinan."

"You said nothing about anything," Selene said. "You just left."

"More tears. Your anger must be truly great." He smiled coaxingly. "Will it lessen if I promise I'll tell you when I go to pay Sinan's price?"

"No, it will never lessen. You're stupid and without kindness or—" Her voice broke and she stalked away from them.

Kadar sighed. "I thought I was doing a good deed. It's going to be difficult being owned by such a one." He hurried after her. "Think of your beautiful embroidery I saved from the weather and the ants. Does that not deserve praise instead of harshness?"

She did not answer.

"And consider the risk I ran to bring it to you. Let me tell you of the travail I suffered, the nights I did not sleep. . . ."

Thea could no longer hear Kadar's words, but she could see his lips move and the persuasive smile she knew so well. She hoped Selene would forgive him. She was as irritated as her sister, but his intentions had been good and his gift beyond price.

Evidently, Selene had the same thought. She was tilting her head as if listening, her pace slowing.

She stopped and turned to Kadar. A luminous smile lit her face.

His head went back and his laughter rang out.

"Why are you frowning?" Ware asked as he slipped his arm through Thea's. "Kadar is safe and you have your embroideries."

"But what about next time?" she whispered. "Kadar will never truly be safe. Sinan will always be like a huge spider spinning his web to draw him back."

"He's a match for Sinan. Kadar has survived for nineteen years, and he gains more weapons as time goes on."

"But Sinan has weapons we don't even know about."

Ware suddenly chuckled. "Do you know what you've said? My love, none of us are safe. I've been trying to convince you that both you and I will be forever in mortal danger, and you worry about Kadar."

"That's different."

"Because God saved me once and you're convinced he'll not allow His handiwork to be ruined?"

"Not as long as I'm with you and here to remind Him."

He brushed her temple with his lips. "Then I'll most certainly have to keep you safe just to preserve my own life. How clever of you to so obligate me."

"But women are far more clever than men. Do we thunder about and try to kill one another? No, we try to build, not tear down. That's why the more I consider it, the more relieved I am that Asherah is an aspect of God. She must be the part that furnishes not only fertility, but wisdom as well."

"Next, you'll claim she's the part that created heaven and earth," he said dryly.

"I'll have to think about that." Her gaze went back to

Kadar on the path ahead. "Does he have the banner, Ware?"

"We may never know. This journey took overlong. If he did take it, he may have tarried to find a courier to send it to the Knights Templar."

"I hope he did." A sudden thought occurred to her. "He would not have used the banner to bargain with Sinan?"

He shook his head. "Remember? He cautioned us not to let Sinan know about Kemal's belief in the banner."

She didn't believe he would have gone to the Old Man either, but she was glad to have her intuition reinforced. "He said Sinan knew everything that goes on in this land."

"Why are you worried?" He glanced away from her. "You said the banner has no power."

She was making him uneasy for no reason. They must forget about this war-ravaged land and lion thrones and banners that seemed to have a life of their own. "Perhaps he will tell us someday." She took his arm. "Come, we must see to the safe storing of the embroideries in the hold."

"And then tell everyone to board the ship." His pace quickened with eagerness. "We'll leave on the midnight tide."

Epilogue

TWO YEARS LATER
SEPTEMBER 7, 1193
MONTDHU, SCOTLAND

SELENE WAS WAITING on the cliff overlooking the harbor.

Kadar had seen her as soon as he had sailed into the harbor, and she had not moved as his ship neared the shore. She stood with hands clenched at her sides, the blustery wind blowing her brown gown against her slim body. She looked as if she were ready to battle the world, Kadar thought. He waved his hand as he moved toward the gangplank.

She didn't return the salute. She was already running down the cliff path toward the dock.

He met her before she reached the bottom of the path. So full of glorious life and more glorious spirit. He wanted to reach out and touch the shining red hair tumbling about her shoulders. He did not. "You should have worn your cloak."

"Is that all you have to say to me? You've been gone four months."

He smiled slyly. "Have you been waiting for me on that cliff all this time? I wonder you didn't turn into a statue."

"Conceited ox. If I waited for you, it was only to hear what success you'd had with our embroideries."

"Great success. The merchants of Spain were dazzled by your skill. I came back with a chest full of gold."

"I think you should take me with you next time."

"Oh, you do?"

"Yes." She started up the hill. "Someone besides you should be trained in the trading of our silks. You take too many chances. What if you were killed? Then what would we do?"

"Beat your head on the ground and mourn forever?"

"Don't joke." She suddenly whirled on him, her eyes glittering. "Take me with you."

It had been too long since he had looked into those wonderful eyes. He found the barriers weakening that he always lifted against her. "To protect the trade?"

"Take me with you. You *need* me."

"Ah, yes, I do." He permitted himself to touch her cheek. Exquisite pleasure surged through him in a golden tide. "But not to protect the trade."

"No," she whispered.

He had known this would soon come, but he still found he was not prepared for it. "You are too young."

"I'm ten and five. Many women have wed and borne children before they reach that age."

"I know."

"And you wouldn't have to rut with strangers. I would be willing to— Why are you laughing? I *would* do it."

"I don't doubt you." He had almost been swayed this time. She was fully mature in so many ways and only had these rare flashes of childhood. "I appreciate the sacrifice."

"I don't think it would be sacrifice." She moistened her lips. "I've found that I—do not mind—being touched by you."

"Because I offer you no threat?"

"No, you do offer me threat," she whispered. "More than anyone. You make me feel—"

"What?"

She shook her head and then said defiantly, "Why should I tell you? You will only laugh and tell me that I'm too young."

"There is that possibility."

"Then I'll not waste breath on you." She started up the hill again. "And there are others who don't think me too young to wed."

"Indeed?"

"Lord Kenneth of Craighdhu is paying me court. He comes here to visit at least every fortnight."

"And do you find him a pleasing suitor?"

"Why not? He's young and comely and says I'm sweet as honey."

"He must not be a good judge of character. I think you should send him away next time."

She cast him a shrewd glance. "Ah, I thought you would not like it."

He had masked his displeasure, but she knew him too well. "I don't like it," he said softly. "I like it so little that, if I see him near you, I may be forced to vent my dislike in a way you've told me I should not."

She thought about it for a moment and decided to

retreat. "Well, I don't like him anyway. He talks only of horses and my hair. You'd think there were no other red-haired women in Scotland."

No woman like you, my love. No woman in the world like Selene. "Be tolerant with him. Red is a most peculiar color."

"Be tolerant with him, but not in a way you reserve for yourself." She frowned. "You're most unfair."

"You'll learn that's the nature of men with women."

Her brow cleared and she smiled. "Oh, yes, I'm learning more all the time. You called me a watcher, and it's you I watch now, Kadar. I watch and I learn." She deliberately reached out and took his hand. "You will not go on many more journeys without me. On this I give you my word."

Healing, brightness in darkness, a flame that has no end. Selene.

Let her go. Not yet. Let the promise be fulfilled.

Ah, but it was such a glorious, tempting promise. His grasp tightened around her hand, and it was a moment before he could force himself to release it. "But I fear if I took you with me, there is a grave problem that could never be resolved."

"What problem?" she asked, puzzled.

He smiled. "Why, my dear lady, which one of us would captain the ship?"

"Ware, I've decided you must get me another ship," Thea announced as she came up the hill toward him. "I must have a constant supply of silk, and heaven knows if I can get my worms to survive and multiply in this climate."

"You seem to have no trouble."

She glanced down at her swollen belly. "But I'm not a silkworm."

"I've noticed that." He smiled as he reached out a hand and helped her to level ground beside him. "You're much more demanding. I should have seen it coming when Kadar arrived yesterday. You had barely finished greeting him before you started quizzing him about the availability of silk in Spain. I've already supplied you with one ship to use in the trade. Why is it not enough?"

"I must have the silk when I need it. Are my embroiderers to sit twiddling their thumbs while I wait for Kadar to get back from a trading journey? It's not reasonable."

"It's not reasonable for me to have to spend my gold on another ship when I need it for craftsmen to build my fortress." He glanced at the multitude of busy workers a few yards away. "It's more important that we have strong walls to protect us than you have silk."

Thea glanced at the high stone outer walls that had just been completed. The work on the castle itself had been started, but it was going slowly. Ware demanded perfection: every window must be cut in such a way as to repel arrows, the battlements must be unscalable. "Silk brings more gold, and it will take years for you to finish here. We're very comfortable in our cottages." She paused. "Need you be so careful? It seems a different world here. It's as if we're the only people on earth."

Ware drew her close. "You like my highlands?"

He had never asked her that question before. It had been a hard two years, a time of building cottages and planting crops, of teaching embroidery skills, of settling disputes and dealing with arguments and births and deaths. Did she like this Scotland?

It was a land of mists and purple shadows, of chill, blustery winds and seas that shimmered like green-gray silk under summer skies—a hard land.

A land of challenge that bred strong men like Ware.

"It's not a land you 'like,' " she said slowly. "That is too weak a word. But it's a place that becomes part of you. I belong here now." She went back to the original argument. "But we've seen no sign of threat. If we're careful, must we live in a fortress?"

"Yes." His lips thinned. "I will take no chances."

She sighed and leaned against him. It was the answer she had expected. Ware had lived too long as a hunted man ever to feel safe. "Well, could you not delay—"

"A rider comes, my lord." Haroun's eyes were bright with excitement as he ran toward them. "From the south."

Ware tensed, and she put a soothing hand on his arm. "It could be Lord Kenneth from Craighdhu. You know he's been riding here to see Selene."

He was not listening; he was striding up the hill to a higher vantage point.

She followed him. "I tell you, it need not be danger."

His muscles were locked, his eyes on the approaching rider.

It was not Lord Kenneth. The armor of the man coming toward them shone brightly in the sunlight, and he rode a white horse. She had seen that horse only once before, but she would never forget it.

"My God," Ware muttered.

"Vaden." Fear tore through her. "Alone?"

"So it appears."

A little of her terror ebbed. Even if Vaden had changed his mind and come after Ware, this was Ware's place and hers, their land, their people. One man alone could not prevail against their numbers.

But Vaden was a great warrior who possessed a strange hold over Ware. Who knew what would happen if Vaden challenged him to a battle, one on one? Ware had said he wasn't certain he could best him.

Vaden stopped his horse and sat looking up at Ware.

He was drawing his sword!

He hurled the weapon with such a force that its point pierced the ground and the sword stood vibrating back and forth.

He nudged his horse and continued up the hill.

"What does it mean?" she whispered.

"I'm not sure," Ware said. "But I think it's a white flag."

Dear God, Ware's expression was full of eagerness. Vaden had many other weapons, and yet Ware was placing his trust in him. "Let me call Abdul."

He didn't take his gaze from Vaden. "No."

She took a protective step closer to him and watched Vaden come toward them.

Vaden reined in a few yards distant from where they stood and took off his helmet. "No wonder you chose to come to the Holy Land, Ware. The land of your birth is not a welcoming place."

She stared at Vaden, stunned. At their first encounter he had been covered with black soot, and she had been conscious only of danger and devilish ferocity. This man had the bright manly beauty of Apollo. Tawny hair framed a face whose perfection held one spellbound, and she could see his eyes were a glittering sapphire-blue. She impatiently shook off her amazement. What difference did it make that he did not look like a gargoyle? He was still a threat. "And we do not welcome you either. What are you doing here?"

Vaden's gaze turned to Thea. "Ah, the lady Thea. Greetings. I've been looking forward to meeting you in less unhappy circumstances." His gaze shifted to her belly. "Your child, Ware?"

"Yes." He paused. "And my wife. You should not have come, Vaden. I cannot let you leave to tell others where we are."

"How do you know they don't know already?"

"Do they?"

"I could tell you that they do. It would save my life. You look for an excuse not to kill me."

Thea felt a rush of despair as she realized how well Vaden knew Ware. Knowledge was a greater weapon in his hands than the sword in the ground. "Stop toying with us. How did you find out where we'd gone?"

"The Old Man of the Mountain."

Ware shook his head. "He would never have told a Knights Templar. He'd have killed you before you set foot in the fortress."

"He almost did. Several times. It was a long, laborious process. I stalked him as I stalked you, Ware." He smiled. "Finally it began to amuse him, and he allowed me into his rather gruesome presence. But it was almost another year before I could persuade him to give me the information I wanted. He cared nothing about you, but I had to give him my promise I'd leave your friend Kadar untouched."

The story was incredible, but Thea could almost visualize the Old Man and Vaden together. Darkness and light, but both possessing a core as hard and cold as iron. "Why couldn't you leave us alone?"

He turned to her. "It occurred to me. In truth, I almost turned my back on you forever. But I found it impossible, dear lady."

"Why?" Ware asked.

Vaden smiled sardonically. "Ware, Ware, will you never learn? Look at you. You wish me to tell you that I've changed and that we can be friends forever. I will never change and nothing lasts forever."

"Then why did you come after us?"

Vaden's smile faded. "I didn't change. To my infinite disgust I merely learned that there are some prices I'm not willing to pay to keep the world as it is. I'd rather risk everything than stand by and watch another massacre like the one I witnessed at Acre."

"Your Jedha?" Ware murmured.

"Perhaps. Though it galls me to admit you might be right." He shrugged. "So that's why you're a dead man, Ware."

"No!" Thea stepped forward, her hands clenched.

"Wait," Ware said.

"I believe she was going to attack me." Vaden smiled faintly. "I can almost see why you've given two years of your life in service to her."

"I'll give her all the years of my life." Ware's eyes were narrowed on Vaden's face. "If I'm permitted."

"Such devotion. I was sure you wouldn't wish to live without her, so she is dead also."

Ware tensed. "How?"

"After all these years I found you defenseless at last and executed my duty to the Temple. You both died just outside the gates of Dundragon. Your friend Kadar was also killed defending you. Your bodies were dragged into the fortress for burial by your loyal followers."

Thea was beginning to understand the incomprehensible. "You told the Knights Templar you killed us?"

"I drove your horses before me so that the trail would reflect pursuit." He shrugged. "Actually, you made it very easy for me to cover your departure. Dundragon was deserted when I burned it to the ground. It was still in flames when our brothers of the Temple arrived from El Sunan."

"El Sunan?" Thea repeated. "But you said that the Knights Templar were only a day's ride behind us."

"A small untruth." He smiled with sly satisfaction. "I was very irritated with Ware that day and thought it would do no harm to worry him a bit. I didn't want them to interfere with my dealing with you, so I sent a message to Robert de Sable telling him I'd heard rumors that Kemal had returned to El Sunan and was swearing that he would burn the banner. De Sable decided it would do no harm to delay his attack on Dundragon, if it meant getting the banner for Richard."

"You went to a great deal of trouble," Ware said.

"Don't endow me with virtues I don't possess. Everything I did was to protect myself as well as you. Robert de Sable isn't a madman like de Ridfort, but he wouldn't hesitate to order my death, if he found I'd risked the world knowing about the lion throne."

"But you ran the risk."

"Very well, I ran it. Satisfied?"

A broad smile lit Ware's face. "Yes."

Vaden ruefully shook his head. "You're truly impossible."

"But why are you here?" Thea asked. "You said you'd decided not to follow us."

"I did." His lips tightened grimly. "But I had to bring you something." He reached into his saddlebag and tossed the bundle of silk he drew out of it to Thea. "Good riddance."

She shook it out and stiffened in shock. "The banner," she whispered. Her gaze flew to his face. "Kadar did send it to the Templars, and you took it from them?"

"Kadar?" He shook his head. "I don't know what you're talking about. I stole it from Kemal the night Ware attacked."

"You killed him?" Thea asked.

He shrugged. "I had to have the banner. Several knights of the Temple recognized the lion throne at Acre. I was planning on taking it back to de Sable."

"You followed Kemal from Acre?" Ware asked.

Vaden nodded. "He had the banner, and after the massacre I knew he would lead me to you."

"But why didn't you take the banner back to the Grand Master as you planned?" Thea asked. "Why bring it to me?"

"Why not?" He shook his head. "At first de Sable wanted it only for Richard, but then the Marshals told him what the design meant. The Knights Templar took El Sunan, and they came back with stories of a magic banner that brought victories to those fighting beneath it. Foolishness, of course, but I thought it best not to give Richard or the Templars any more reason to shed blood, so I told de Sable the banner had disappeared, perhaps destroyed." He looked at Ware. "You did know Richard failed to take Jerusalem?"

"No, we hear very little news of the outside world here."

Vaden glanced at the stark isolation of the land around them. "It doesn't surprise me. Richard signed a treaty with Saladin and abandoned the Crusade but was taken for ransom by Duke Leopold of Austria on his way back to England." He added grimly, "May he rot there." He put on his helmet. "Now I bid you farewell." He inclined his head mockingly. "If you'll permit me to leave without slicing off my head, my lady?"

"Wait." Ware took a step forward. "At least stay the night."

Vaden shook his head. "I've done what I came for. If I stayed, I'd have to put up with seeing a great warrior curled on his hearth like a tame pussycat."

"You're afraid," Ware said softly. "It's possible you might find that hearth both welcoming and desirable."

"You'll never know." Vaden turned his horse and started down the hill.

"Don't go back," Ware called. "What is there for you there?"

"Nothing. I won't go back to the Order."

"Then stay here. It won't be such a tame life. The highlands have more strife than any place on earth."

Vaden smiled. "You have too good an influence on me. I find it most disconcerting."

"Vaden," Thea called, "if you won't stay, why did you come all this way? Why didn't you just burn the banner if you didn't want them to have it?"

"I couldn't." He reined in his horse where he had buried his sword and reached down to pluck it from the ground. "I had to bring it."

"Why?"

He frowned with annoyance. "What difference does it make?"

It was clear he didn't want to talk about it, yet she felt compelled to keep probing. "It seems strange that you would undertake such a long journey when it was not—"

"Dammit." The glance he threw over his shoulder glittered with intense frustration and an odd sheepishness. "I brought it because I could do nothing else. It *wanted* to be here." He put spurs to his horse and galloped down the hill.

Her hands clenched in the folds of the banner as she watched him streak away from them as if the devil were after him.

"Good riddance," Vaden had said as he'd tossed the banner to her.

"Imagination?" Ware asked softly, his gaze still on Vaden.

"Is he a man who is overly imaginative?"

"No."

She had not thought he was, and yet his words could have only one meaning.

To her amazement the knowledge brought no fear. The silk of the banner felt comfortingly familiar in her hands, and she was experiencing a sense of overwhelming *rightness*.

Ware's gaze was searching her expression. "You've accepted it."

"That the banner has power?" She shook her head. "How can such a thing be when I was the one who created it? I am neither saint nor sorceress. I don't even know how it came into being. I wondered at one time if my love for you was so great, our souls so close, that I read your thoughts."

"And you decided?"

"That I will never know." Her brow wrinkled in thought. "But perhaps, if there is power here, it's some sort of sign that God is not only for men, that he doesn't approve of the slavery man has decreed for women. Do you suppose that could be?"

"Anything *can* be." He smiled. "And it doesn't surprise me that you would think so." He sobered. "What will you do with it?"

"What do you want to do with it? I created it for you."

"I told Vaden the truth—this has always been a strife-filled land. Do you wish me to fight under your banner?"

"No," she whispered.

"I didn't think so." He touched her cheek with his hand. "I don't wish it either. It would be too dangerous if it was ever seen. Besides, I fear I have too much self-love. I dislike the thought of relying on a banner to fight my battles." He looked down at the banner. "Then you'll have to choose what we're to do with it. I suppose you could burn it."

It wanted to be here.

"No, I won't destroy it." She tucked the banner beneath her arm. "Since you leave the decision to me, I choose to find a safe hiding place and leave it there."

"A hiding place..." Ware mused. "They put the lion throne in a safe hiding place and I found it. Hiding places don't always remain safe."

She felt a ripple of disquiet. "Then we must make sure that we find a better place than your Knights Templar." By the saints, how foolish they were to worry about this. They would never be entirely safe, but Vaden had made sure they all had freedom and opportunity in this new land. Joy suddenly soared through her.

"We have better things to do than brood about a banner." She kissed Ware lovingly on the cheek before taking his arm and turning away from Vaden's now distant figure. "That's all in the past. Now, about finishing your castle. Since we know we're more secure than we thought, cannot it wait another winter so that I may have my ship?"

About the Author

IRIS JOHANSEN has more than twenty-seven million copies of her books in print and is the *New York Times* bestselling author of *Stalemate, Killer Dreams, On the Run, Countdown, Blind Alley, Firestorm, Fatal Tide, Dead Aim,* and more. She lives near Atlanta, Georgia.

Available now from Bantam Dell . . .

The never-before-published sequel

The Treasure

Read on for a sneak peak

of THE TREASURE . . .

THE TREASURE

MAY 3, 1196

FORTRESS OF MAYSEF

NOSAIRI MOUNTAINS

SYRIA

HIS POWER WAS WANING, fading like that blood-red sun setting behind the mountains.

Jabbar Al Nasim's fists clenched with fury as he gazed out at the sun sinking on the horizon. It should not be. It made no sense that he should be so afflicted. Weakness was for those other fools, not for him.

Yet he had always known it would come. It had even come for Sinan, the Old Man of the Mountain. But he had always been stronger than the old man in both mind and spirit. Sinan had bent before the yoke, but Nasim had prepared for it.

Kadar.

"You sent for me, master?"

He turned to see Ali Balkir striding along the battlements toward him. The man's voice was soft, hesitant, and he could see the fear in his face. Nasim felt a jolt of fierce pleasure as he realized the captain had not detected any loss of power. Well, why should he? Nasim had always been master here, in spite of what outsiders thought. Sinan might have been the King of Assassins, feared by kings and warriors alike, but Nasim had been the one who had guided his footsteps. Everyone here at the fortress knew and groveled at his feet.

And they'd continue to grovel. He would not let this monstrous thing happen to him.

Balkir took a hurried step back as he saw Nasim's expression. "Perhaps I was mistaken. I beg your forgiveness for intrud—"

"No, stay. I have a task for you."

Balkir drew a relieved breath. "Another attack on the Frankish ships? Gladly. I brought you much gold from my last journey. I will bring you even more this—"

"Be silent. I wish you to return to Scotland where you left Kadar Ben Arnaud and the foreigners. You are to tell him nothing of what has transpired here. Do not mention me. Tell him only that Sinan is claiming his price. Bring him to me."

Balkir's eyes widened. "Sinan? But Sinan is—"

"Do you question me?"

"No, never." Balkir moistened his lips. "But what if he refuses?"

Balkir was terrified, Nasim realized, and not of failing him. Nasim had forgotten that Balkir was at the fortress at the time Kadar underwent his training; Balkir knew how adept Kadar was in all the dark arts. More adept than any man Nasim had ever known, and Kadar was only a boy of ten and four when he came to the mountain. How proud Sinan had been of him. What plans he had made for the two of them. He had never realized Nasim had plans of his own for Kadar.

All wasted when Kadar had left the dark path and rejected Sinan to live with the foreigners. What a fool the Old Man had been to let him go.

But it was not too late. What Sinan had lost, Nasim could reclaim.

If Kadar did not die as the others had died.

Well, if he died, he died. Kadar was only a man; it was the power that was important.

"He won't refuse," Nasim said. "He gave Sinan his word in exchange for the lives of the foreigners."

"What if he does?"

"You *are* questioning me," Nasim said with dangerous softness.

Balkir turned pale. "No, master. Of course he won't refuse. Not if you say he won't. I only—"

"Be gone." Nasim waved his hand. "Set sail at once."

Balkir nodded jerkily and backed away from him. "I will bring him. Whether or not he wishes to come I will force—"

The words cut off abruptly as Nasim turned his back on him. The man was only trying to gain respect in his eyes. He would have no more chance against Kadar if he tried to use force than he would against Nasim, and he probably knew it.

But he wouldn't have to use force. Kadar would come. Not only because of his promise but because he would know what would result if he didn't. Sinan had spared the lives of Lord Ware, his woman, Thea, and the child Selene and given them all a new life in Scotland. Nasim had permitted the foolishness because he had wanted to keep Kadar safe until it was time to use him.

But no one would be more aware than Kadar that the safety Sinan had given could always be taken away.

Kadar had shown a baffling softness toward his friend Lord Ware and a stranger bond with the child Selene. Such emotions were common on the bright path, but Nasim had taught Kadar better. It seemed fitting that he be caught in his master's noose because he'd ignored his teachings.

The fortress gate was opening and Balkir rode through it. He kicked his horse into a dead run down the mountain. He would be in Hafir in a few days and set sail as soon as he could stock his ship, the *Dark Star*.

Nasim turned back to the setting sun. It had descended almost below the horizon now, darkness was closing in. But it would return tomorrow, blasting all before it with its power.

And so would Nasim.

His gaze shifted north toward the sea. Kadar was across that sea in that cold land of Scotland, playing at being one of them, the fools, the bright ones. But it would be just a matter of months before he would be here. Nasim had waited five years. He could wait a little longer. Yet an odd eagerness was beginning to replace his rage and desperation. He wanted him here *now.*

He felt the power rising within him and he closed his eyes and sent the call forth.

"Kadar."

AUGUST 4, 1196
MONTDHU, SCOTLAND

"SHE'S BEING VERY FOOLISH." Thea frowned as she watched Selene across the great hall. "I don't like this, Ware."

"Neither does Kadar," Ware said cheerfully as he took a sip of his wine. "I'm rather enjoying it. It's interesting to see our cool Kadar disconcerted."

"Will it also be interesting if Kadar decides to slaughter that poor man at whom she's smiling?" Thea asked tartly. "Or Lord Kenneth, who she partnered in the last country dance?"

"Yes." He smiled teasingly at her. "It's been far too peaceful here for the last few years. I could use a little diversion."

"Blood and war are not diversions except to warriors like you." Her frown deepened. "And I thought you very happy here at Montdhu. You did not complain."

He lifted her hand and kissed the palm. "How would I dare with such a termagant of a wife."

"Don't tease. Have you been unhappy?"

"Only when you robbed me of craftsmen for my castle so that you could have them build a ship for your silk trade."

"I needed that ship. What good is it to produce fine silks if you can't sell them? It wasn't sensible to—" She shook her head. "You know I was right, and you have your castle now. It's as fine and strong as you could want. Everyone at the feast tonight has told you they have never seen a more secure fortress."

His smile faded. "And we might well have need of our fortress soon."

She frowned. "Have you heard news from the Holy Land?"

He shook his head. "But we walk a fine line, Thea. We've been lucky to have these years to prepare."

Ware was still looking over his shoulder, Thea thought sadly. Well, who could blame him? They had fled the wrath of the Knights Templar to come to this land, and if the Knights found out that Ware was not dead, as they thought, they would be unrelenting in their persecution. Ware and Thea had almost been captured before their journey started. It had been Kadar who had bargained with Sinan, the head of the assassins, to lend them a ship to take them to Scotland. But that was the past, and Thea would not have Ware moody tonight when he had so much to celebrate.

"We're not lucky, we're intelligent. And the Knights Templar are foolish beyond belief if they think you would betray them. It makes me angry every time I think of it. Now drink your wine and enjoy this evening. We've made a new life and everything is fine."

He lifted his cup. "Then why are you letting the fact that your sister is smiling prettily at Lord Douglas upset you?"

"Because Kadar hasn't taken his eyes off her all evening." Her gaze returned to her sister. Selene's pale-gold silk gown made her dark red hair glow with hidden fires, and her green eyes shone with vitality—and recklessness. The little devil knew exactly what she was doing, Thea thought crossly. Selene was impulsive at times, but this was not such an occasion. Her every action tonight was meant to provoke Kadar. "And I didn't invite the entire countryside to see your splendid new castle so that she could expose them to mayhem."

"Tell her. Selene loves you. She won't want you unhappy."

"I will." She rose to her feet and strode down the hall toward the great hearth, before which Selene was holding court. Ware was right: Selene might be willful, but she had a tender heart. She would never intentionally hurt anyone she loved. All Thea had to do was confront her sister, express her distress, and the problem would be solved.

Maybe.

"Don't stop her, Thea."

She glanced over her shoulder to see Kadar behind her.

He had been leaning against the far pillar only seconds ago, but she was accustomed to the swift silence of his movements.

"Stop her?" She smiled. "I don't know what you mean."

"And don't lie to me either." Kadar's lips tightened. "I'm a little too bad-tempered tonight to deal in pretense." He took her arm and led her toward the nearest corner of the hall. "And you've never done it well. You're burdened with a pure and honest soul."

"And I suppose you're the devil himself."

He smiled. "Only a disciple."

"Nonsense."

"Well, perhaps only half devil. I've never been able to convince you of my sinful character. You never wanted to see that side of me."

"You're kind and generous and our very dear friend."

"Oh, yes, which proves what good judgment you have."

"And arrogant, stubborn, and with no sense of humility."

He inclined his head. "But I've the virtue of patience, my lady, which should outweigh all my other vices."

"Stop mocking." She turned to face him. "You're angry with Selene."

"Am I?"

"You know you are. You've been watching her all evening."

"And you've been watching me." One side of his lips lifted in a half smile. "I was wondering whether you'd decide to attack me or Selene."

"I have no intention of attacking anyone." She stared directly into his eyes. "Do you?"

"Not at the moment. I've just told you how patient I am."

Relief surged through her. "She doesn't mean anything. She's just amusing herself."

"She means something." He glanced back toward the hearth. "She means to torment and hurt me and drive me to the edge." His tone was without expression. "She does it very well, doesn't she?"

"It's your fault. Why don't you offer for her? You know Ware and I have wanted the two of you to wed for this past year. Selene is ten and seven. It's past time she had a husband."

"I'm flattered you'd consider a humble bastard like myself worthy of her."

"You are not flattered. You know your own worth."

"Of course, but the world would say it was a poor match. Selene is a lady of a fine house now."

"Only because you helped us escape from the Holy Land and start again. Selene was a slave in the House of Nicholas and only a child when you bought her freedom as a favor to me. She was destined to spend her life embroidering his splendid silks and being given to his customers for their pleasure. You saved her, Kadar. Do you think she would ever look at another man if you let her come close to you?"

"Don't interfere, Thea."

"I *will* interfere. You know better. She's worshipped you since she was a child of eleven."

"Worship? She's never worshipped me. She knows me

too well." He smiled. "You may not believe in my devilish qualities, but she does. She's always known what I am. Just as I've always known what she is."

"She's a hardworking, honest, loving woman who needs a husband."

"She's more than that. She's extraordinary, the light in my darkness. And she's still not ready for me."

"Ready? Most women her age have children already."

"Most women haven't suffered as she suffered. It scarred her. I can wait until she heals."

"But can she?" Thea glanced toward the hearth again. Oh, God, Selene was no longer there.

"It's all right. She and Lord Douglas just left the hall and went out into the courtyard."

How had he known that? Sometimes it seemed Kadar had eyes in the back of his head.

"Kadar, don't—"

He bowed. "If you'll excuse me, I'll go and bring her back."

"Kadar, I *won't* have violence this night."

"Don't worry, I won't shed blood on the fine new rushes you put down on the floor." He moved toward the courtyard. "But the stones of the courtyard wash up quite nicely."

"Kadar!"

"Don't follow me, Thea." His voice was soft but inflexible. "Stay out of it. This is what she wants, what she's tried to goad me to all evening. Don't you realize that?"

Where was Kadar? Selene wondered impatiently. She had been out here a good five minutes and he still hadn't appeared. She didn't know how long she could keep Lord Douglas from taking her back to the hall. He was a boring, stodgy young man and had been shocked when she'd suggested going out to the courtyard. "It's a fine night. I do feel much better now that I've had a breath of air."

Lord Douglas looked uneasy. "Then perhaps we should go back inside. Lord Ware would not like us being out here alone. It's not fitting."

"In a moment." Where *was* he? She had felt his gaze on her all evening. He would have seen—

"The Saracen was watching us," Lord Douglas said. "I'm sure he will tell Lord Ware."

"Saracen?" Her gaze flew to his face. "What Saracen?"

"Kadar Ben Arnaud. Isn't he a Saracen? That's what they call him."

"Who are 'they'?"

He shrugged. "Everyone."

"Kadar's mother was Armenian, his father a Frank."

He nodded. "A Saracen."

She should be amused that he had put Kadar, who could never be labeled, in a tight little niche. She was not amused. She fiercely resented the faint patronizing note in his voice. "Why not call him a Frank like his father? Why a Saracen?"

"He just seems . . . He's not like us."

No more than a panther was like a sheep or a glittering diamond like a moss-covered rock, she thought furiously. "Kadar belongs here. My sister and her husband regard him as a brother."

"Surely not." He looked faintly shocked. "Though I'm sure he's good at what he does. These Saracens are supposed to be fine seamen, and he does your silk trading, doesn't he?"

She wanted to slap him. "Kadar does more than captain our ship. He's a part of Montdhu. We're proud and fortunate to have him here."

"I didn't mean to make you—"

She lost track of what he was saying.

Kadar was coming.

She had known he would follow her, but Selene still smothered a leap of excitement as she caught sight of him in the doorway. He was moving slowly, deliberately, almost leisurely down the stairs. This was not good. That wasn't the response she wanted from him. She took a step closer to Lord Douglas and swayed. "I believe I still feel a little faint."

He instinctively put a hand on her shoulder to steady her. "Perhaps I should call the lady Thea."

"No, just stay—"

"Good evening, Lord Douglas." Kadar was coming toward them. "I believe it's a little cool out here for Selene. Why don't you go fetch her cloak?"

"We were just going in," Lord Douglas said quickly. "Lady Selene felt a little faint and we—"

"Faint?" Kadar's brows lifted as he paused beside them. "She appears quite robust to me."

He's not like us, Douglas had said.

No, he wasn't like any of these men who had come to honor Ware tonight. He was like no one Selene had ever met. Now, standing next to heavyset, red-faced Lord Douglas, the differences were glaringly apparent. Kadar's dark eyes dominated a bronze, comely face that could reflect both humor and intelligence. He was tall, his powerful body deceptively lean, with a grace and confidence the other man lacked. But the differences were not only on the surface. Kadar was as deep and unfathomable as the night sky, and it was no wonder these simple fools could not understand how exceptional he was.

"She was ill," Lord Douglas repeated.

"But I'm sure she feels better now." Kadar paused. "So you may remove your hand from her shoulder."

Selene felt a surge of fierce satisfaction. This was better. Kadar's tone was soft, but so was the growl of a tiger before it pounced.

Evidently Lord Douglas didn't miss the threat. He snatched his hand away as if burned. "She was afraid she would—"

"Selene is afraid of nothing." He smiled at Selene. "Though she should be."